"Even though this is a continuation of the *Desolation Point* plot, [*Tumbledown*] is an entirely different sort of thriller with elements of a police procedural. Other thriller authors (yes, I'm looking at you Patterson and Grisham) could take lessons from Hunter when it comes to writing these babies. Twists and turns and forgotten or unconventional weaponry along with pluck and spirit keep me breathless and reading way past my bedtime."—*Out In Print*

By the Author

Snowbound

Desolation Point

Tumbledown

No Good Reason

No Good Reason

by

Cari Hunter

2015

Credits
Editor: Cindy Cresap
Production Design: Susan Ramundo
Cover Design By Sheri (graphicartist2020@hotmail.com)

Acknowledgments

Thanks and a packet of chocolate HobNobs to Rad and Sandy at BSB for giving this one the green light, pointing me in the right direction, and saying yes to more books featuring this lovely cast. To Cindy for her editing prowess and for whacking some of my more arcane Brit-speak on the head. To Sheri for finding the right rocks and the right light to go with them. To my Work-Wife, Kelly, for keeping me laughing, sharing my love of biscuits, and directing all my daft research questions on to her long-suffering husband, Col. (Thanks, Col!) To everyone who's read my books, sent feedback, written reviews, and become friends. And to Cat—as ever—for her patience and skill as a beta, but mainly for being daft enough to marry me.

Dedication

In Memory of

Fiona Bone & Nicola Hughes
(12601)   (14846)

"Born Brave"

PROLOGUE

She hurt. She hurt when she opened her eyes, and she still hurt when she closed them. Her tongue felt thick, too big for her mouth, and sticky against the cloth bound across it. She shouldn't be able to feel the cold grit beneath her bare thighs, the dampness of the air, the raging thirst; she had never been able to feel them before. She had never been able to move before, either, to touch her fingers to the slick stone or to raise her hands and feel what they were tied with: some kind of plastic-coated rope, knotted tightly enough to bite into her skin. The muscles in her arms were leaden and slow to obey, her fingers fumbling as she pulled the cloth away from her lips. She tore at the rope with her teeth, snarling and weeping with frustration when it refused to slacken. A slither of sound made her freeze, breath held, heart racing, but nothing followed, no footsteps, no grunt of effort as if something heavy were being lifted. He never seemed to be gone for long, but then how could she gauge the time through the darkness and the drugs?

She jumped as a droplet of water splashed against her shoulder. "Fuck..."

She was unsure whether she had drifted to sleep, unsure what she had been trying to do beforehand. Her hands twitched as if to prompt her, and with a shock of remembrance, she began to work at the rope again. Blood oozed into her mouth from her cracked lips, but the knot showed no sign of loosening. She gave up and drew her knees toward her, unable to stop herself gasping as she picked at the bindings around her ankles with stiff fingers. This knot put up little resistance, though the ligature left puffy circles in her numbed flesh.

She fell as soon as she tried to stand, bruising her hands and face against the stone. The pain gave her a split second of clarity, and she almost identified the vague thought that was nagging at her, but it faded at once. Letting it go, she staggered to her left, toward the point from which he always approached. She squeezed through the only gap she found and let the fresher air guide her path, a thin breeze that wrapped itself around her skin and set her shivering, even as she sucked in huge, grateful breaths. Leaving the stench of blood, excrement, and urine behind, she threw herself at the wooden pallet wedged into the low entrance point. Kicking at the planks drove splinters into her heels, but the air was growing cleaner still, and she could see flashes of the outside now. One final push knocked the barrier down, the momentum hurling her onto her hands and knees. She crawled over the threshold and then got to her feet, swaying and trembling and surrounded by nothing.

"Oh God, oh God."

Nothing: no lights, no obvious paths, no signs of civilisation. There was just a thin sliver of moon and the wind howling across the moors.

"Somebody help me, please," she whispered. "Please, please."

She was still begging even as she started to run, her feet alternately sinking into the wet peat and tearing on the gritstone. She lost count of the number of times she fell and had to stagger back up. Only once did she stop, to quench her thirst at a small pond. Unable to coordinate her bound hands, she lowered her head and lapped at it like an animal, the water tasting earthy but clean and cold. When she stood again, her head swam, and her vision twisted in dizzying circles. She closed her eyes, listening to the wind whistle through the boulders, their massive silhouettes darker even than the sky. One day, not long ago, she had climbed rocks like that, scrambling for footholds and handholds, reaching up toward...

She shook her head, the memory indistinct and already slipping. No longer able to run, she could only stagger along what she hoped might become a path. Minutes passed, maybe hours, but the sky never lightened, and the path never materialised.

At least I got away from him, she thought, and in that instant, the ground disappeared from beneath her, leaving her in freefall. She landed with limbs entangled, her head striking against a rock. She took a breath, the pain already fading.

"At least I—"

Chapter One

Leaning back in his chair, the young man facing Sanne Jensen picked something from a tooth with a grime-stained finger and then grinned at her. His teeth were uneven, one broken, one missing, and all unbrushed. Sanne didn't smile back.

"No comment," he said, and the machine recording his interview abruptly clicked off, as if it too had reached the end of its tether.

Sanne set her pen down beside her notepad. "Mr. Clark, I'd like to thank you for your time and your illuminating contribution to the investigation."

Callum Clark narrowed his eyes, not quite sure whether she was being sarcastic. He looked at his lawyer, who indicated that they had been given their cue to leave.

"Detectives Jensen, Turay. We'll look forward to hearing from you." Such was the lawyer's haste that he almost bumped into Clark's chest as Clark stopped and turned back to Sanne.

"Name like that"—Clark pointed his thumb at her ID badge— "I thought you'd be—"

"Blonder?" she offered.

"Taller." He tilted his head to one side. "But yeah, now you mention it, blonder too." He sounded disappointed, as if the futile hours of questioning in a stifling room that stank of crappy coffee and his own dubious hygiene habits had had the potential to be far more entertaining.

Sanne took the implied criticism on the chin. "Yeah, I get that a lot," she said, ignoring her partner's snort of laughter.

The lawyer ushered Clark out into the corridor, and the door swung shut behind them. Sanne leaned forward, her vertebrae cracking as she attempted to rest her head on her folded arms. Weariness made her miss her target, her forehead thudding onto the table.

"Fuck." She groaned but didn't have the energy to move. "Four hours, Nelson," she said against the cool plastic. "Four hours of our lives we're never going to get back, thanks to that little shit."

Nelson Turay clapped her shoulder, and she banged her head on the table again. "Fancy a drink? My shout. Abeni's taken the girls round to see her mum."

Sanne pushed herself upright. "Cheers, mate, but I promised to meet Meg, and I need to type up the notes for the Dawkins case, or the boss'll have my arse."

"True."

She showed him her notepad, holding it in front of her like a trophy. "I kept a tally."

"One-oh-one?" He whistled in disbelief, displaying his own pad, which contained a similar series of marks. "Damn. I only got ninety-seven. Sure yours is right?"

"Dead sure."

"Must've wigged out a bit toward the end there."

"Well, you can double-check when you listen to the tape." She winked at him and ducked as he tried to swat her. They had held a rock-paper-scissors tournament to assign that particular task, and he had lost, badly.

"Not tonight," he said. "If you're ditching me, and I have the house to myself, I will be eating pizza and drinking beer while dressed in naught but my underpants."

She stared at him. "Thank you for that image. My day is now complete."

"Don't say I never do nothing for you." Holding the door open, he gestured for her to leave first.

She glanced once more at the scrawled lines in the margin of her notepad and sighed. In four hours, six minutes, and approximately thirty-two seconds, Callum Clark had repeated the phrase "no comment" one hundred and one times.

❖

It was never going to work. The angle of approach was too acute, the pressure too fierce, and the aim slightly off. The man jerked at the first sting of discomfort and howled as the needle dug in deeper.

"You fucking bitch!"

Her reactions honed by years of experience, Megan Fielding stepped calmly into the firing line. She placed one hand on the man's chest, pinning him to the bed, and used her other to pull the startled junior doctor out of his reach. The junior's ID marked her as Foundation Year One, that tricky transitional period between being a medical student and a registered doctor.

"*Enough*," Meg snapped, as the man actually growled at her. "I've had enough."

He held up his arm, displaying blood oozing from a popped vein, and pointed at the F1. "She did that on fucking purpose."

"She did that because she's new and because you moved your fucking arm," Meg said. The F1's face paled, and her mouth dropped open. Meg ignored her. "Now, it's not our fault that—for the fourth time in as many weeks—you've decided to wash down a month's worth of diazepam with a year's worth of gut-rot cider. And it's definitely not our fault that your veins are all shot to shit. Personally, I'd leave you to sleep it off and suffer the hangover, but protocol and a certain oath, yadda, yadda, yadda…" She tightened a tourniquet around his upper arm and prodded the crook of his elbow. "You going to stay still this time?"

"You going to hit the fucking vein?"

She pursed her lips and blew out a breath. "Can't make you any promises, I'm afraid." She palpated one of the few veins that the F1 hadn't ruined, before sliding the cannula into place. "There, that wasn't so bad, was it?" The blood bottles clinked as she dropped the samples into the tray. She turned to address the F1. "Start a litre of saline, and refer him to psych when he's sober enough to talk about it. That is, of course, unless he kicks off and then absconds, like he did on the last three occasions. In which case"—she made a show of checking her watch—"we'll see him again in about seven days."

The man opened his mouth to respond, froze, smacked his lips together, and projectile-vomited all over Meg's scrubs top.

She took a belated step back. "Well, that's just fucking perfect."

❖

As the printer churned out page after page of Sanne's case notes, she stood by the window and let the bleating of sheep and the hum of traffic heading into Sheffield blot out the mechanised drone. Six months ago, a contractor rushing to meet a deadline had painted the window shut, and of the nine detectives in the East Derbyshire Special Operations department, only Nelson had the knack of opening it fully. The warm air wafting in did nothing to temper the stuffiness in the office, but at least it smelled more pleasant. Sanne knelt to push her face closer to the narrow gap.

"I don't recall authorising any overtime for you, Detective."

The sound of Eleanor Stanhope's voice provoked a Pavlovian response. Sanne bolted upright, forgetting about the window and bouncing the top of her head off its frame.

"Ow, fucking hell." She clamped a palm over the injured spot and looked up at the detective inspector. "Sorry. Ow, fucking hell, *ma'am*."

Eleanor smiled. "Were you planning to stay here all night?"

"No, but I'm off tomorrow, and I needed to finish up the Dawkins notes." Sanne quickly gathered the printed sheets and clasped them to her chest. "I was going to have a final read-through before I left them for you."

"Why don't you just give them to me now and go home? It's late. I know you came in early, and I also know you spent the afternoon being no-commented by one of the finest scrotes Halshaw has to offer." Eleanor held her hand out expectantly. "If I were you, I'd be neck deep in a bottle of Scotch by now."

"I'd settle for fish and chips with a cup of tea." Despite the lightness of her tone, Sanne surrendered her paperwork with reluctance, nervous about typos or questionable grammar that she might have overlooked. Even after twelve months, she was still the most junior member of Eleanor's team. She had been selected on merit alone—Eleanor made no secret of her disdain for positive discrimination—but the urge to push herself that little bit harder than most had been ingrained in her from an early age. EDSOP's remit was major crimes—murders, rapes, serious assaults, kidnappings— and they covered a large swath of east Derbyshire. Prior to joining the team, Sanne had worked Response for three and a half years, and she'd never regretted the move.

Eleanor slid the sheaf of papers into her briefcase and snapped it shut. "Go on. Get yourself to the chippy."

They crossed the room together and paused at the door to Eleanor's office.

"G'night, boss." It went without saying that the DI would be working into the early hours.

"Night, Sanne. Enjoy your day off."

That brought a smile to Sanne's face. She had met her deadlines, cleared her outstanding caseload, and triumphed at rock-paper-scissors. For the first time in months, she had nothing work-related left to do.

"Cheers, boss." She grabbed her jacket and leaned over her computer to log out of the system. As she headed for the stairwell, her phone buzzed. Meg's text was brief and to the point.

Running late. Got puked on. Fancy a chippy tea at mine instead?

The hospital's shower pressure left a lot to be desired, but the water was hot and plentiful, and Meg felt herself beginning to relax beneath it. She shampooed her hair and then let her arms fall to her sides, allowing the thin stream to do the work of rinsing for her. Her back ached, and she could still smell a trace of alcohol-laced vomit, even through the body wash.

"Sod it," she muttered, switching the shower off. "Better than it was before."

Her torso was rubbed almost raw where she had tried to scrub herself clean. Already starting to shiver in the cool bathroom, she dabbed the abraded skin with her towel. Once dressed and somewhat warmer, she tossed her filthy scrubs into a clinical waste bag, collected her belongings, and carried everything out into the corridor.

"Bright side, Doc?" one of the porters called to her, as he wheeled a patient past. "Least it happened at the end of your shift."

"Yeah, yeah, laugh it up." She smiled as he over-steered his trolley and bounced it off a doorjamb.

"Bugger. Sorry, Ethel. See you tomorrow, Doc."

Meg turned in the opposite direction and dumped her waste bag in the sluice, before hurrying toward the exit. As she neared the doors, she had to force herself not to run. This was always the trickiest part of the shift: leaving without anyone attempting to waylay her, to ask her for a second opinion or get her to do just this one small procedure that wouldn't take more than a minute, honestly.

The doors shut behind her, and she stepped out into mild evening air, tinged with tobacco smoke as someone hidden behind an ambulance enjoyed a crafty cigarette. She breathed deeply regardless, and smiled when her stomach rumbled. On cue, her phone chirped.

Hurry up, Sanne had typed. *Make mine the usual, and add curry sauce xx*

Sanne moved around Meg's kitchen with an ease born of familiarity. She knew in which cupboard Meg stored her crockery and behind which jar of pasta the condiments were hidden. Tea bags waited in mugs beside the kettle and slices of thick-cut buttered bread, while the oven burred in the background as it warmed the plates.

The end-of-terrace house had beautiful Victorian features, but the living room's large bay window and high ceiling left it draughty and cold even in summer. Kneeling on the hearthrug, Sanne pushed another log onto the open fire and shifted its position with the poker. A rush of heat made her cheeks tingle pleasantly, and she smiled as the scrape of a key in the front door was followed by the traditional hail: "Anybody home?"

Lured by the scent of vinegary chips, Sanne scrambled up and found Meg in the hallway, struggling to untie her trainers with her hands full.

"Plates are in, kettle's boiled, bread's done, fire's lit, and oh, I love your new hairdo," Sanne said. She took Meg's workbag and the chip shop bag, and stood patiently as Meg used her as a prop while she levered the shoes off.

"You've been busy," Meg said, giving Sanne a wet kiss on the cheek. "I knew there was a reason you were my very best friend." She poked experimentally at her hair. "Did I forget to brush it again?"

Sanne laughed. "I would say so, yes."

"Does it look horrible?"

"It certainly looks original."

"Well, you know me. I am all about setting trends."

That just made Sanne laugh harder. Meg adored the hospital's casual dress code of scrubs for its Accident and Emergency doctors, and spent most of her free time wearing combat pants and hooded tops. Her short hair needed minimal styling, and the only colour in her cheeks was a suntan acquired sitting in her back garden with her feet up, while Sanne tended to her plants. Sanne grinned and kissed Meg's forehead. They had been best mates for years, and Sanne adored her.

"You look gorgeous," she said.

"Mmhm." Meg regarded her with customary scepticism. "I think the promise of chips is clouding your judgement slightly."

"That's a distinct possibility. Did you remember my curry sauce?"

"Of course I did."

The protestation might have been more convincing had Sanne not already seen *CURRY!* scrawled across the back of Meg's hand. "How far did you get before you had to go back for it?"

Meg attempted to feign indignation for a moment, before she sighed. "About a mile and a half."

"So, better than that time you came home with nothing but two pickled eggs and someone else's mushy peas?"

It was faint praise, but it seemed to cheer Meg. She opened the paper wrappings and shook vinegar across her fish with renewed zeal. "I even remembered to put the bins out this morning."

"Yeah?" Sanne said through a pilfered chip, as they took their plates into the living room. "Good for you."

"Course, it was cans and paper this week, and I put out household and garden, but at least I got the day right."

They sat together on the sofa. Sanne reached over to tap her fork against Meg's.

"You're bloody brilliant," she said, and took the lid off her carton of curry sauce, to find gravy instead.

"Sorry about the curry." Her expression downcast, Meg proffered a fresh brew and a packet of chocolate HobNobs like a peace offering.

Sanne took the mug and patted the sofa cushions, waiting until Meg had slumped beside her before she replied. "How many times do I have to tell you?" She stroked her fingers through the rough mess of Meg's hair. "The gravy was fine, and you're being a silly sod. Now, eat your biscuits."

Meg made no move toward the packet. Her grip on her mug was so tight that her knuckles were turning white. "Think I'm going to end up like my mum, San?" She spoke in an undertone, her breath whispering against Sanne's cheek.

"No, I don't," Sanne said without hesitation. The possibility was too awful to consider. "I think you've always been a scatterbrain, and your shifts just make it worse." She almost spilled her tea as Meg sat upright, worry stark on her face.

"I wonder sometimes. It can run in the family, you know."

"I know, love, but lots of things can do that, so there's no point fretting about it."

"Hmm." Meg toyed with the packet of HobNobs, looking unconvinced.

"Come on," Sanne chided her gently, not wanting her to slip into a funk. "Get them open before your tea goes cold."

The packet rustled as Meg let out her breath and took a biscuit. She dunked it in her tea, held it for a couple of seconds, and pulled it out the instant before it collapsed. Her success seeming to buoy her mood, she ate the biscuit with enthusiasm. "How's your dad?" she asked.

Sanne bit into her own HobNob, crumbs scattering on her lap as she made a so-so gesture with the remnant. "He's slightly less yellow."

"That's good. Your mum okay?"

"Fine. I'll probably go and see them tomorrow while I'm off."

"Say hello to your mum from me."

"Of course."

The welfare of their respective families adequately covered, they fell into an easy silence, broken only by an occasional pop from the fire and by the satisfied slurping as they drank their tea. Sanne stretched her legs out on the ottoman, her toes kneading the air contentedly. She only realised she had dozed off when Meg's voice jolted her awake.

"So, what happened with Phoebe?" A sharp elbow nudging into her ribcage punctuated the question.

"Phoebe was nice," she said, rubbing the sore spot. "Blond, bubbly, posh."

"Ooh." Meg wiggled her foot against Sanne's. "Tell me more."

"Educated at Oxford. Spoke all proper-like."

"What was she doing up here? Working?"

"Researching." Sanne watched embers rising from the fire. She had really liked Phoebe. It had been a promising date, for the first few hours.

Cradling her mug in both hands, Meg leaned forward, her curiosity piqued. "Researching what? Does she work at the uni or something?"

Sanne let out a short laugh. She wished it had been that simple. "No, she was researching, uh, well, me."

Meg's eyes narrowed as she waited for the punch line. When it didn't come, she sat back against the cushions with a thump. "Are you having me on?"

"Nope. We're sitting there, chatting away over coffee, all very civilised. Then, out of nowhere, she tells me that she's a trainee journalist and that she's researching a piece about women in the police force. She'd managed to find my details through some random Googling, pretty much stalked me to the pub that night we first met, and, oh, would I mind awfully if she asked me some questions?"

"You're shitting me."

"Wish I was." Sanne giggled, Meg's incredulity finally letting her see the funny side. "She whipped out this Dictaphone, set it next to the after dinner mints, and opened up a pad full of notes."

"Oh dear." Meg's cheeks reddened as she tried to remain composed and appropriately sympathetic. When she spoke again, she sounded as if she were being strangled. "Did she at least pay for the meal?"

"Too bloody right she did. Y'know, I hope she's got a day job, because I snuck a peek at her notes, and her spelling was crap."

Meg laughed, inadvertently dropped her HobNob into her mug, and spent the next minute attempting to fish it back out.

"I'm glad my tragic love life amuses you," Sanne said.

Meg gave up and finished her tea, biscuit and all. "At least you have one. I can't remember the last time I kissed a girl that wasn't you."

"Oh, that's just charming." There was no malice in Sanne's words, and she felt the familiar flutter in her stomach as she looked at Meg in the firelight. "No," she said firmly, as much to persuade herself as to dissuade Meg. "I've got plans for tomorrow. Loads of stuff to do."

The plates and mugs clattered as she stacked them up with clumsy fingers. Meg stooped to help her, and the sensation of their arms brushing together sent a thrill right through Sanne. She caught her breath at the same time Meg did and shook her head in despair. It was no wonder their love lives were such a bloody disaster.

"Are you on an early tomorrow?" she asked. The mundane nature of her question was all it took to break the tension. She heard Meg chuckle ruefully as they both turned their attention back to tidying.

"Yep. Seven till whenever, if it's anything like today." Meg straightened, her hands full of sauce bottles, and nodded for Sanne to lead the way to the kitchen. "Have you got anything more exciting planned for your day of leisure than visiting your parents?"

The water that Sanne had set running hit the edge of a plate, and she had to raise her voice above the splashes. "I'm getting up early for a run, and then I need to thin out my radishes, pick some lettuce before it goes to seed, and—" She frowned at Meg. "Why are you shaking your head?"

"Honey, you lost me at 'getting up early for a run.'"

Sanne started the washing up, clattering the cutlery in indignation. "We can't all laze about on our arses on our days off. I like to spend mine running. And do you want fresh salad this summer, or do you want to keep buying those limp, overpriced bits of leaves from Asda?"

"I want fresh salad, please." Meg's response was muffled by the tea towel she was hiding behind, and she squealed as Sanne dashed soapy water at her.

"Come and fix my leaky washing machine for me, and you can have all the salad you can eat. Deal?"

They shook on it, their hands slippery and full of bubbles.

"Text me your route tomorrow," Meg said, her voice suddenly serious. "Because I know you. You'll be up at the crack of dawn, and no one else will be around."

"Sounds perfect." Sanne touched Meg's cheek gently. "I'll have my phone, whistle, water, survival bag, and a first aid kit. I go up on Corvenden Moss all the time. I'll be fine." She dropped her hand away and used a clean tea towel to dry the suds she had left on Meg's face. "But I do love you for worrying about me."

Chapter Two

Moments like this made Sanne grateful she lived somewhere remote. She had woken to soft morning light shining through the gaps around her curtains, while the scent of freshly cut grass and clean air filled her bedroom. She lay still, contemplating the idyllic peace.

It lasted only twenty seconds or so, however, before it was shattered by the raucous *cock-a-doodle-doo* of the rooster in the garden as he imitated a particularly obnoxious alarm clock. He woke all six chickens in his harem, who protested en masse. Sanne stuck her head under her pillow to drown out their squawking and once again thanked her lucky stars that she didn't have any close neighbours. Fortunately, she was a morning person, not that her job gave her much choice in the matter. She lived about half an hour away from the police headquarters, a commute that could easily be doubled in winter, when the roads threading across the Pennines and connecting the cities of Manchester and Sheffield were often closed by snow.

There was a series of creaks as she climbed out of bed: the mattress, the floorboards, both of her knees. At thirty-three years old and with a long history of fell running, she felt as if her joints needed a good oiling first thing in the morning. Confident of her privacy, she opened the window wide and worked through her routine of stretches. Although a shower was somewhat superfluous, given that she would be mud-spattered and sweaty within the hour, she set it as hot as it would go and let it ease the remaining stiffness from her muscles. She dressed herself in front of the mirror, rolling her eyes at her towel-mussed hair. Like Meg, she kept it short, but a wayward, dogged waviness made styling it next to impossible. One gust of wind was all it would take to destroy anything she might achieve with gel or clips, and the weather in the Peak District was seldom placid. She ran a comb through it just for the hell of it and scowled at the result. Maybe next time she had it cut, she would go for broke and get rid of it all. Contemplating such an act of rebellion, however, quickly turned her scowl into a self-deprecating grin. She had no doubt that Meg would have embraced the challenge in a heartbeat, but her own nature was inclined toward conformity. She knew she would never have the guts to go through with it.

Leaving the mirror behind, she headed for the kitchen, with her reflection, captured in a series of framed photographs, tracking her down the stairs. *Bemused* was probably the politest word to describe people's reaction to her. She was only five foot four, with hazel eyes, dark brown hair, and a northern English accent. She couldn't have looked or sounded less Scandinavian if she'd tried, and yet fate and her mum's bloody-mindedness had saddled her with the name Sanne Jensen. Mispronunciations occurred daily, "Sayne" and "Sanney" being the most popular. If someone had given her a pound coin every time she'd said "Actually, it's 'Sanner,'" she'd have been able to retire years ago.

"Fat bloody chance of that," she muttered, toasting her mum's stubborn streak with a mango and banana smoothie.

Sunlight poured into the small, tatty kitchen, hiding its flaws and casting rainbows through the water dripping from the faulty tap over the sink. Sanne had bought the cottage for its views and its land, but she had grown to love the old, weathered building for its sheer resilience. Wind, rain, and snow battered it year in, year out, and the worst it ever did was lose a tile or two from its roof. Beyond the kitchen window, hills dominated the landscape, their wild beauty a far cry from the cluttered streets where she had grown up. The dull browns of a cool spring had finally been replaced with lush shoots of bracken and bilberry, while lower in the valley the pastures were dotted pink with foxgloves. Summer arrived late in the Peak District, and the breeze carried with it the bleating of lambs still much smaller than their lowland cousins.

Surrounded by ever-changing scenery, Sanne was fond of each season in its own way, but this was her favourite time of the year to go fell running. She checked her pack one last time and scooped up her keys. The hens scattered as she jogged down the driveway to her car. The rooster just glared from the car's roof.

"Hop it, Git Face."

He ruffled his feathers but didn't budge an inch.

"Oh, you'll move soon enough, you little bugger," she said and started the engine.

❖

The stretcher collided with the bed, sending a jolt through its patient and forcing Meg to make a grab for the endotracheal tube protruding from his mouth.

"Easy, everyone. We'll get him across on my count, okay?" She had to raise her voice above the mêlée, keeping a grip on the tube as the team around her prepared to slide the unconscious man from the stretcher. According to the ambulance pre-alert, he was only in his forties, but he was morbidly obese, naked aside from a pair of soiled boxer shorts, and had one foot firmly in the morgue. His belly jiggled as he landed on the mattress, a motion inadvertently worsened by the nurse resuming CPR.

"Bit of hush while I check this, please," Meg said.

Squeezing the ventilation bag at a steady rate, she assessed the placement of the ET tube with her stethoscope. They could become dislodged during rapid transfers, but this one was right where it needed to be.

"Lovely." She smiled at Kathy, the paramedic responsible for its insertion, who smiled back in relief. "Go ahead, hon. Everyone else, listen up."

"Okay. Jimmy Taylor, forty-five years old. Found in a collapsed state by his wife at approximately six thirty. She was doing CPR when we arrived, but hadn't been able to shift him off the bed. Initially in VF, shocked once, straight into asystole. He's had"— Kathy checked the back of her glove, on which she'd scribbled her drugs—"four adrenaline. Due another about now. He's a type two diabetic. Sugars are eight point six. High blood pressure and high cholesterol. Smokes thirty a day."

"Cheers," Meg said, wincing as the F1 from her previous shift made another mess of inserting a cannula. "Get him booked in as soon as, will you?"

"No worries. Wife should be here in a mo. She's coming down with the Rapid Response para. Oh, and she said he's allergic to strawberries."

"Right, no strawberries. Probably the least of his worries." Meg shook her head as Kathy laughed. "Go and put the kettle on."

"Rhythm change." A keen-eyed nurse was watching the monitor. "PEA."

"Most likely due to the adrenaline." Still pumping the bag with one hand, Meg peeled open Jimmy's eyelids to find two blown pupils. "He's already fixed and dilated. I don't think we're getting anything meaningful back from this."

A murmur of assent rippled through the team. The F1 looked pale but resolute, under no illusions about the inevitable outcome of their efforts. Meg sighed. Even for one in such lousy general health, Jimmy had died far too young.

"Let's give him the benefit, eh? We'll have a look at his gases and go another couple of loops." She glanced up at the red-faced nurse who was still doing compressions. "And can someone please take over from Liz before she pegs out as well?"

The doors to Resus edged open just as Meg dialled the oxygen down and disconnected the ET tube. She unplugged the monitor, and the alarm that had been sounding intermittently for the last half hour ceased.

Kathy poked her head through a gap in the curtains. "Mrs. Taylor's in the Rellies' Room." She looked at Jimmy Taylor, splayed out and cooling on the bed. "Poor sod. They have three kids: ten, twelve, and fifteen."

"Bloody hell," Meg muttered. "Anyone come down with his wife?"

"No, but her mum's on the way."

Meg took off her gloves and plastic apron and flicked them into the nearest bin. "Cheers, Kathy. I want nothing but nice old grannies from you for the rest of the day."

Kathy snorted. "I'll see what I can do, Doc."

Left alone behind the curtains, Meg brushed down her scrubs and ran a hand through her hair. She didn't have a vain bone in her body, but she did want to appear professional. No matter how badly her own day had started, she was just about to make a complete stranger's day infinitely worse.

"Dr. Fielding?"

Startled by the quiet voice, she looked up to see the F1 making an apologetic gesture.

"Sorry, I…" The F1 cleared her throat and tried again. "I was wondering if I could come with you when you speak to Mr. Taylor's wife." She met Meg's gaze, despite her obvious trepidation. That was all Meg needed to reach her decision.

"Of course you can," she said, and saw some of the tension ease from the F1's posture. "Have you ever informed a relative of a death before?"

"No. Would I be okay just to observe?"

"Best way to learn." Meg held the door for her. "Tell me your name again? I've got a mind like a sieve."

"Emily. Emily Woodall. Yesterday was my first shift in A&E."

"Bit of a baptism by fire today, then?"

"Yeah, you could say that." The admission left her in a rush of breath.

Meg smiled, remembering her terrifying first few days on the job. "Well, at least you didn't end up covered in vomit."

Emily chuckled, but she sobered as they approached the Relatives' Room. The nurse assigned to the role of family liaison opened the door at Meg's knock and stepped aside to allow her to enter. Mellow light replaced the corridor's harsh ceiling neon, and it took Meg's eyes a moment to adjust. When they did, the familiar layout of the room took shape: the cupboard holding a kettle and china cups, and the low table with its vase of dried flowers carefully arranged beside a box of tissues. The chairs were pushed together to form a quasi-sofa, mimicking the design of a living room. As with most of the people who spent time sequestered there, Mrs. Taylor didn't seem reassured by the home comforts. Her cup of coffee was still half-full, and two balled-up tissues rested on her lap. When she looked up at Meg, there wasn't a flicker of hope in her eyes.

"Mrs. Taylor, my name is Dr. Fielding. I've been looking after your husband since he came into the hospital." Meg took a step forward, broaching the gap. "May I sit down?"

Mrs. Taylor nodded, shifting her feet closer together even though there was ample space on the chairs. "He was always 'Jimmy,' never 'Mr. Taylor,'" she said, unconsciously lapsing into past tense.

"'Jimmy,' right." Meg sat at an angle, so she could look at Mrs. Taylor directly. "Jimmy's heart wasn't beating when the paramedics brought him here, and he wasn't able to breathe for himself. Despite all of our efforts, we were unable to restart his heart." She took care to speak clearly, leaving no room for misinterpretation. Mrs. Taylor was already weeping, her shoulders shaking as she tried to remain silent. Meg placed a hand on her arm. "He died, Mrs. Taylor. I'm very sorry."

As if in slow motion, she watched the woman's entire life crumble beneath the weight of those words: plans she and her husband might have made together, the financial security his job might have brought, holidays and Christmases they would never share, and then the realisation that she had three children who didn't yet know their dad was dead.

"Oh God," she whispered. "Oh God, the kids." She buried her face in her hands, rocking and sobbing. "I want my mum."

The liaison nurse gathered her close, pulling her away from Meg. Meg withdrew her hand but didn't leave. Eventually, there would be questions Mrs. Taylor would need answering. Behind her, she heard Emily sniffle, and she surreptitiously passed a tissue. She closed her eyes and tried to block out the raw sounds of grief. Only two hours into her shift, she already felt exhausted. Sometimes, she wished she'd followed in her dad's footsteps and become a plumber.

❖

The route Sanne had chosen up Corvenden Edge was now more of a scramble than a path. That suited her fine. It gave her the opportunity to slow down, catch her breath, and take in the scenery around her. Beneath a bright blue sky, its few clouds mere high balls of fluff, the Peak District stretched for miles in every direction. The rounded shapes of ancient stones were distinct on the various summits, the occasional flash of white among them marking the locations of the more daring sheep.

Easily finding handholds, Sanne made swift progress up the final section. She climbed farther than she needed to and turned in a slow circle atop the highest boulder. To the west, the clough dipped away, the stream winding through its centre sparkling in the sunlight, its soft gurgle inaudible unless she faced it directly. To the east, the weathered rocks of Gillot Tor thrust up from the high plateau of Corvenden Moss. Ahead of her, the Pennine Way cut a line across the peat bogs covering the plateau. The path had been paved with huge stone slabs reclaimed from defunct mills, one of the few concessions made to hikers in that part of the Peaks. Once a walker left the Pennine Way, a map, a compass, and a sense of adventure were essential.

Sanne took a long drink from her water bladder and recapped the tube. The paving would make short work of her next section, but only for a mile or so. After that, it would be a case of veering to the right, trying not to sink too deeply into the bogs, and hoping to connect with the other path, on the far side of Corvenden Moss. At some point, there would be a stile over a fence. All she had to do was find it. The prospect made her grin, and she hopped down off the rocks, keen to get going again.

Though dry and relatively flat, the millstones were unforgiving to run upon, and she was relieved to reach the way-marker signalling her turn. She added a small stone to the marker for luck, before casting an experienced eye over the undulating peat hags and groughs. The ground between the knolls looked firm, but she knew that was deceptive. On a previous run, her right leg had been sucked thigh-deep into a bog, and she had managed to scramble out only because her left was safely on solid ground. She set off more cautiously this time, jumping between thicker patches of vegetation less likely to collapse beneath her weight.

Occasionally she landed short, splashing mud up her ankles, but the recent sunny weather made the traverse less tricky than she had anticipated. With no low cloud to mar her view, she spotted the stile from some distance and adjusted her direction to aim toward it. Across the sheep fence, her route would swing south and climb again, leading up to her favourite part of the run, a stretch along Laddaw Ridge, before finally taking her back down to the reservoir where she had parked her car.

She was slogging up the steepest section of Laddaw Ridge when she heard the whistle. Piercing and panicked, there was no mistaking it for anything but a distress call. At first it sounded in a continuous wail, but then the person signalling seemed to remember the SOS code and blew with more purpose: three long blasts, a gap, another three blasts.

Sanne looked around, the exertion of the ascent and a sudden dread raising goose pimples on her arms. The breeze and the echoing hills made it hard to pinpoint the call's source, but it was close by and somewhere ahead of her. She set off running again, stopping at intervals to listen and alter her course. Soon, though, she realised where the sound was originating, and she slowed to a walk.

"Bollocks," she whispered, preparing herself for the worst. A fall or a suicide leap from the cliffs that edged this section of the ridge. It had to happen one of these days, and dog walkers or joggers were always the ones who found such victims. In all honesty, she was surprised it hadn't happened to her sooner. She left the path and climbed onto the rocks, leaning out as far as she dared and catching a flash of movement below her.

"Hey!" she yelled, and was somewhat bemused to see two youngish lads at the cliff base begin to wave frantically and beckon her down. "Everything okay? Are you hurt?" Neither of them appeared injured, but something had obviously given them a fright. She didn't know if they could hear her. Even straining to listen, she had trouble picking out their response.

"No—us," one of them shouted back. He stepped to his right, pointing down to the grass at his feet, where Sanne saw a third figure, lying motionless. "Need—ambulance. *Please*—no signal."

For a long moment, she just stared, shock addling her thoughts. She couldn't discern much detail from where she was, but she could see enough to know that the woman hadn't simply fallen or tried to take her own life. She yanked off her pack and found her mobile phone.

"Come on, come on, you fucking useless thing." She clambered onto a different rock, watching the phone's signal fluctuate and then hold. "Is she alive?" she shouted down, an unaccustomed tremor in her voice.

The boy's response filtered up to her as she dialled 999.

"Yes. Just."

Her call was answered on the first ring. She interrupted the operator to identify herself and give her police collar number.

"I need paramedics and police to Laddaw Ridge, off Corvenden, north of the reservoir at Rowlee. There's a woman at the base of the rocks."

"Is she injured?"

"Yes. I don't think she's conscious, and there's blood all over her."

"Are you with her, Detective?"

"No, I'm on the ridge above." Sanne dug her fingernails into her palms, trying to be rational when all she wanted to do was get down there and help in some practical, hands-on way. "We'll need Mountain Rescue and Helimed." She glanced over the edge again, needing to be certain of what she had seen. The woman lying in the grass was still half-naked, and her hands were still tied. "Fucking hell," she whispered. Then, louder, "Inform Detective Inspector Stanhope at EDSOP—shit, I mean East Derbyshire Special Ops. Let her know we have a probable kidnapping. She'll want to get a team out here."

The operator stammered a little, but repeated the name and the details. "ETA on Helimed is thirty minutes."

"Right." Sanne was already trying to visualise her path down through the rocks. "Tell them to look for a red survival bag. I'll lay it out for them."

"I'll pass that on."

Whatever else the woman might have said was lost as Sanne scrambled onto a lower slab at the edge of the cliff. She tucked the phone into the pocket of her shorts and re-shouldered her pack to free up her hands. Adrenaline and fear were making her limbs feel wobbly. Breathing through her nose to steady herself, she began to move with more purpose, turning to face the rocks and taking a first tentative step downward. She had never been a climber. She didn't mind taking her chances for a good viewpoint, but that was as far as she went. Often enough, she had watched small groups of men and women suspended beneath the overhangs on Stanage Edge, their lives reliant on thin ropes and metal clips, and had never once envied them. Now, without safety lines or gear, she manoeuvred herself off ledges, into crevices, and through the tightest of gaps. She was only wearing a T-shirt and shorts, and the sharp gritstone soon started to rip into her exposed limbs. Ignoring the pain, she focused on her route and tried to block out the awful scene looming in her peripheral vision.

"Oh, shit!"

A loose stone toppled beneath her foot, and she slid, her hands flailing for a hold as she slipped between two boulders. Her left arm bore the brunt of her uncontrolled descent, losing a layer of skin from shoulder to elbow, before she landed heavily on a grassy outcropping. She doubled over, winded, a fresh bolt of pain making her vision swim.

"You need to come this way a bit. It's not as steep."

Her head shot up at the quiet instruction. About six feet below her, one of the boys was using a stick to indicate a simpler passage.

"Okay." The word came out in a gasp. "I got it, thanks."

He held out his hand to help her off the last rock, and she felt the sweat coating his palm and the fine shivers running through his body. His face was dirt-streaked, with wet smudges on both cheeks as if he had wiped tears away with his sleeve.

"She's over here," he said, setting off at a trot.

Sanne matched his pace without difficulty, and as they neared the woman, she caught hold of his arm to jerk him to a stop.

"Stay back. I'm a detective with the Derbyshire Police, and I need you and your mate to keep clear of her, okay?"

His eyes widened, but he nodded, his throat working as he tried to swallow. He couldn't have been more than fifteen. The second lad must have heard her instruction. He began to tiptoe gingerly through the cotton grass and bracken toward them.

"We were camping. We didn't do nothing to her. We just found her," he said as he approached. He raised his hands as if to protest his innocence, but they were covered in blood, and he dropped them again to wipe them on his trousers, his efforts increasingly frantic. "She's hurt her head. I was trying to stop it bleeding." His voice broke and he started to cry. "I think she's dying."

"There's a helicopter on the way for her." Suspecting he needed distraction rather than comfort, Sanne upended her pack to retrieve her small first aid kit and her survival bag. "You got a knife?"

The boy sniffled but pulled a Swiss Army knife from his pocket. When he offered it to her, she held out the bag instead.

"Cut it open as wide as it'll go, and lay it out flat. Anchor it with stones if you need to. The pilot will be looking for it."

She watched the lads begin their task. Then she started to walk slowly toward the woman, battening down the instinct to rush. As she approached, she noted the trampled vegetation, the rapidly abandoned camping gear, and the small puddle of vomit by the woman's feet. Even at a cursory glance, Sanne was certain the boys were responsible for all of that. The woman was lying in a twisted heap at the base of the rocks and didn't look as if she'd moved since landing there. Whether she had fallen or been thrown over the edge, Sanne had no way of knowing.

Kneeling beside her, Sanne placed two fingers against her throat, pressing with increasing force until she found the faint throb of a heartbeat.

"Jesus Christ," she murmured, relief and revulsion hitting her simultaneously. The young woman was naked but for her bra and knickers, and the skin beneath Sanne's fingers felt cold and clammy. Bright orange rope bound her wrists, and ligature marks stood out in bloody furrows around her ankles. Her features were difficult to ascertain. Her head had been shaved, haphazard chunks of hair clung to her scalp where the razor had skipped, and grotesque blue-black swellings closed both of her eyes. Bruises and lacerations covered the rest of her body, with new and old wounds crisscrossing each other, and her left leg was twisted at such a bizarre angle that it had to be fractured. Deeply unconscious, she showed no reaction to Sanne's presence or touch.

Sanne floundered momentarily. She had never been solely responsible for a crime scene like this, and she was scared of fucking it up. There would be trace evidence all over the woman, evidence that might lead to her assailant being apprehended, so ideally she ought not to be moved or covered, and yet she was freezing and bleeding and completely exposed.

"I'm sorry," Sanne whispered, arriving at a compromise that still made her feel like a ghoul. Using her phone, she took a series of photographs—close-up shots to record the woman's position, her injuries, and the way in which she was bound—and then switched to video for a wider shot that would give context to the scene.

As soon as Sanne was confident she had documented everything, she shouted to the boys to throw her their knife. She scrambled through the grass to collect it from where it landed, picking up one of their abandoned sleeping bags on her way back.

Ensuring that the knot was preserved, she sliced through the ropes at the woman's wrists. The bindings were tight, and there were shreds of flesh stuck to the orange strands when she was finally able to unwind them. She set the rope aside and tucked the sleeping bag around the woman.

"You're okay," she said, her voice breaking, belying her words. "You're safe now. We're going to get you to the hospital. You're safe now." She wrapped a clean bandage around the bloodiest part of the woman's scalp, not even sure where the wound was but hoping for the best. There was blood everywhere, clotted and cool and reeking of metal. She knew she should be doing something: questioning the two boys or working out a way to protect the immediate area. Instead, she crouched by the woman's side and put a hand on her arm, listening to the guttural snore of her breathing and watching her chest lurch with the effort it was taking to stay alive.

"We'll have you out of here in no time." Sanne looked up, searching the sky as she spoke, but all she saw was blue with dabs of white. The colours blurred. She wiped her nose and eyes with the back of her hand. "I promise they'll be here soon. Just keep breathing."

Chapter Three

The two lads had been sitting in quiet consultation, their heads bowed over a small scrap of paper, since Sanne had asked them to provide their details and an account of what they had been doing on their camping trip, but they sprang to their feet when they heard the distant thrum of a helicopter. They looked at her in unison, as if seeking her permission, and she smiled back, having recognised the bright yellow bodywork of Helimed. They began to yell and run around the survival bag, releasing their pent-up tension by waving their jackets one-handed, like fans on a football terrace.

She knew exactly how they felt. Her own pulse quickened as the helicopter circled overhead. She hadn't expected the woman to make it to this point. Fifteen minutes ago, the woman's breathing had faltered, becoming a harsh stop-start staccato as blood frothed at her lips, and with a sense of profound hopelessness Sanne had tilted her chin, preparing to do CPR. Somehow that slight adjustment had alleviated the crisis, however, and Sanne had been frozen in the same position ever since, holding the woman's head in place, terrified of moving in case she made anything worse. Beneath her hands, the woman's jaw churned as she continued to strain and gasp for air, but she had shown no further signs of deterioration.

"The medics are here, and we're going to get you to the hospital in just a few minutes," Sanne said, acutely aware of the cramping in her fingers and arms and how badly her back ached. She leaned forward, sheltering the woman from the helicopter's downdraught.

When she looked up again, two men laden with kit were jogging toward her. From the way they slowed and approached in single file, it was apparent they had been briefed about their patient and the condition in which she had been found.

"Detective Jensen?"

"Yes." She didn't move.

The patches on the speaker's jumpsuit identified him as a doctor. He carefully prised her hands free. "You can let go now," he said. "We've got her."

She shuffled aside but stayed close. With no medical training to speak of, she had not been able to do much for the woman, yet she felt uneasy about handing her over to strangers.

"I think she came off the rocks," she said, watching the doctor and paramedic unravel monitoring equipment and set up an oxygen tank. "But before that..." She shook her head. "Before that, I don't know. You can see she was already hurt. Someone had hurt her."

Her words were as simplistic as any layperson's, but she knew that all the finer details would come as soon as she got a pen and paper in front of her. The medics were barely listening to her anyway. The paramedic had uncovered the woman and was swearing beneath his breath at the damage he revealed. He bowed his head for a second to compose himself and then began to run his hands over and under her body, checking his gloves at intervals for what Sanne assumed was fresh blood. His report to the doctor was concise.

"Her left femur's a mess, but I can't see anything else major."

Keeping one eye on the monitors, the doctor was laying out a pack of sterile equipment. "Airway's lousy," he said. "Sats are only eighty-eight. She'll need tubing before we move her. We'll get her immobilised, get IV access, Kendrick splint on her leg, and run with her. Her golden hour is long gone."

The paramedic, already occupied with an IV line, murmured his agreement. Not for the first time, Sanne wished Meg were there to provide a translation, to explain what the hell the doctor was injecting into the line and why it had just stopped the woman's breathing.

"Shit," Sanne hissed. When no one else seemed to react, she lunged forward to intervene, but the paramedic stopped her.

"It's okay, Detective. We've anaesthetised her so we can breathe for her."

"Oh." Sanne put a hand to her chest, realising that she wasn't doing much breathing herself. "You might've warned me."

"Yeah, sorry about that." He smiled wryly as he secured the tube the doctor had just slid into the woman's throat. "Her oxygen levels are climbing now. See?"

On the monitor, the figure he indicated gradually increased from eighty-eight to ninety-seven, and the woman's chest rose and fell as the doctor worked the ventilation bag. It was strangely peaceful, yet eerie at the same time. Sanne had sat with her mum and watched a similar machine breathe for her dad once. It was the quietest she had ever seen him. He couldn't yell at them with a tube sticking out of his mouth. It hadn't lasted, though. He had got better, the tube had been removed, and they had let him come back home. The day before he was due to be discharged, Sanne remembered, she had hidden under her bed and cried herself hoarse—

"Detective, I need you to take over for me, here."

She blinked at the doctor's instruction, shaking her head when she worked out what he was asking of her.

"I don't think—"

He raised a hand to dismiss her protest. "Squeeze, release. Pause. Then repeat. Nothing to it. Come on."

He couldn't have known it, but Sanne had always responded well to authority. She took the bag from him, allowing him to wrap his hands around hers and demonstrate the process.

"Good. Keep that up."

He left her then, turning his back to help the paramedic with a complicated-looking splint. With her heartbeat thumping in her ears, Sanne did as he had instructed, trying not to feel overwhelmed by the responsibility so casually assigned to her. She could feel the oxygen rushing through the tube, and the reading on the monitor remained reassuringly stable. The woman's face was no longer quite so ashen, a pallid pink replacing the blue tinge to her lips. Sanne counted soundlessly, keeping to an exact rate. She was still counting when a flash of red-clad figures appeared on the horizon: a Mountain Rescue team approaching on foot.

"Thank fuck for that," she said, factoring them into an equation she had been struggling to solve. "Perfect bloody timing."

❖

The Bat Phone rang just as Meg was chewing a bite of toast. She groaned, washed the bread down with a gulp from the first brew she had managed to snatch in hours, and dragged her feet off the staffroom's coffee table. Sometimes she heard that phone in her dreams. It had an unmistakably shrill tone, setting it apart from the myriad other phones in the department, and its job was to link the A&E to incoming ambulance crews and Helimed. Red Standbys (cardiac arrests, major trauma, unmanageable airways, or catastrophic haemorrhage) and Amber Standbys (patients who were poorly but not yet at death's door) were all called through, to pre-warn the hospital staff. Often the crews were mere minutes away, and their patients would invariably go straight into Resus.

Chancing her luck, Meg stayed where she was, hunched forward with her mug clasped in her hand. When nothing happened, she risked another sip of tea, wondering whether someone had decided the call was the result of an overly cautious ambulance protocol, and that the patient could bypass Resus and be seen in Majors.

"Do not pass Go." She licked melted fake butter from her fingers. "Do not take up one of my beds." Her trainers had just hit the table again when she heard the sound of rapidly approaching footsteps. "Ah, bugger."

The staffroom door opened a crack, and a hand appeared around it, waving a sheet of paper like a flag of truce. "Don't shoot the messenger," a voice called from the safety of the corridor. Meg recognised the broad West Riding accent of Liz, the staff nurse currently working with her in Resus.

"ETA?" she asked.

"Twenty. It's coming via Helimed."

"Is it dead?"

Liz poked her head around the door. "No, but it sounds nasty." She consulted the paper. "Female, mid to late twenties. Fall from rocks. GCS three. Possible base of skull. Midshaft femur."

"Shit." Meg got up so abruptly she sent her toast flying. "Fast bleep Neuro and Anaesthetics, and get as many hands on deck as you can."

Liz nodded. "Um, Meg?"

Halfway to the door, Meg hesitated. "What?"

"Got a bit of butter on your chin."

Meg rubbed her palm across her mouth and grinned, the prospect of a time-critical case kicking her weariness into touch. Genuine life-or-death traumas were a rarity, and any A&E doctor who claimed not to get a thrill out of them was a liar.

"How's that?"

"Still a bit smeary, but you'll do."

"Fab. Has Mrs. Jones gone up to Surgical Assessment yet?"

"Yep. The shock room is all yours. That nice F1 is in there, getting things sorted."

They darted around an elderly man, who was failing to steer a wheelchair containing an equally elderly woman into a toilet cubicle.

"Easier if you pull that, love," Meg called. He raised his hand in acknowledgement and rolled the chair into the wall again, prompting a loud tirade from his passenger. Meg only caught the opening salvo of, "You're a bloody useless bugger," before she rounded the corner and the row faded.

"Oh, hello, Eds Up," she said, spotting a familiar figure waiting outside the shock room. She only knew Nelson Turay because he was Sanne's partner, but Sanne chatted about him so much that he felt like an old friend.

On hearing his department's traditional nickname, he turned and gave her a crisp salute. "Dr. Fielding. Just the person I wanted to speak to." Despite the lightness in his tone, his expression was serious. A colleague of his, a man she didn't recognise, nodded politely at her.

She closed the gap between them to avoid shouting across the corridor. "You cop for one on Sanne's day off? That's bad luck, fella."

"Uh, yeah." Nelson leaned back against the wall. "San sort of copped for it first, though. She's on her way in now with the chopper."

For a few seconds, the logic wouldn't connect. Then Meg felt her knees weaken as her mind leapt to a conclusion. Her face must have given her away, because Nelson gripped her arm and kept her upright.

"Meg, it's not Sanne," he said. "She's okay."

"She's okay," she repeated, slowly realising that Sanne wasn't the "female, mid to late twenties, fall from rocks, GCS three." She stepped out of his hold. "What the hell is going on, Nelson?"

"Two lads out camping below Laddaw Ridge came across a young lass unconscious at the bottom of the rocks. Do you know where I mean?"

She nodded. She had been up there hiking with Sanne and suffered vertigo just peeking over the edge. "Yes, I know Laddaw. Jesus."

"Sanne was on the ridge and heard the lads signalling for help. She managed to call it in and then scramble down to them."

"She *scrambled down*? What the fuck was she thinking? I'll bloody kill her when she gets here." Meg only remembered the need for discretion when she realised she was yelling. She let out a long, shuddery breath. "Is she really all right? Have you spoken to her?"

Nelson smiled at her seamless transition from infuriation to concern. "The boss spoke to her briefly, said she sounded fine, but you know Sanne."

"Yeah. She wouldn't tell you if her leg was hanging off." An ambulance crew appeared, pulling a stretcher toward them, and Meg hesitated, waiting out the squeak of its wheels. "I've got to go and get ready for this call coming in. Make San a brew when she gets here, and keep an eye on her, will you?"

"Of course I will."

"Cheers. No doubt I'll be seeing you around, if you're on this case."

"No doubt about that." He guided her into a more secluded section of the corridor and spoke in a guarded undertone. "Meg, that girl—she was bound and half-naked when those lads found her. We're looking at abduction, assault, probably murder if she doesn't make it."

She stared at him. From the information on the standby, she had assumed the casualty was the victim of an accidental fall or a suicide attempt.

"Fucking hell," she said, his demeanour suddenly making a lot more sense. "Out there on the moors? But...who? How?"

"At the moment, we have no idea. Bag everything. Note everything. She'll need a rape kit, and Scene of Crime Officers will be here for photographs at some point."

Meg checked her fob watch, her careful plan of approach for her incoming patient thrown into disarray. "You know the drill, Nelson. All that has to wait until she's stable enough, and that'll probably be Neuro's call, not mine."

"Just don't want anything getting missed."

He was a good foot taller than her. She tilted her head and held his gaze.

"I promise you, mate, we won't miss a damn thing."

As the helicopter gained height, Sanne gripped the arm of her seat. Through the window, she could see the indistinct blobs of red marking the positions of the Mountain Rescue team. If its members had found it strange to be met by a perspiring, muddy, blood-coated detective in running gear, none of them had mentioned it, and they had listened intently to her instructions. At her request, they had spread out, half on the ridge, half on the lower section of the moor where the woman had been found. Until the police arrived, they would prevent anyone broaching the perimeter she had established. She had left the two lads eating the team leader's sandwiches, and he had promised to see them handed safely into the care of her EDSOP colleagues.

Sanne had never flown before, but the impromptu trip in the helicopter wasn't the only cause of her edginess. Leaving the scene and travelling with the woman had been her own decision, and although she could have asked the pilot to let her speak to EDSOP first, she had chosen not to. Eventually, she would have to explain her actions to Eleanor Stanhope, not something she ever relished.

The helicopter banked left, breaking into her train of thought and making her lose sight of Laddaw Ridge. At this distance, the hills blurred into an amorphous mass of green and murky brown, broken by the occasional trail where sheep or hikers had ventured, while glints of sunlight marked the cars weaving along the Snake Pass toward Sheffield. Sanne glanced at her watch, calculating their own ETA at Sheffield Royal: approximately nineteen minutes. According to the pilot, they would land in the hospital grounds and cover the short final distance by ambulance.

One of the Mountain Rescue team had loaned Sanne his jacket, and she pulled it closer around her, glad of its warmth and the fact that it would hide her injured arm from Meg. The abraded skin stung furiously as the cloth rubbed against it, but she could cope with that. From texts they had exchanged earlier that morning, she knew Meg was working in Resus that day and would have enough on her plate without worrying about her.

Sanne turned from the window to study the woman lying insensible on the narrow stretcher. The ventilator and monitor were drowned out by the helicopter's din, so Sanne had to take her cues from the body language of the medics. The strain was evident on both of their faces. When she tapped the doctor on his shoulder and mimed writing, he handed her a spare clipboard and an observation chart before saying something to his colleague, who hurriedly drew a clear drug into a syringe and injected it into one of the IV lines. She nodded her thanks, even though the doctor was too busy to acknowledge it, and flipped the paper onto its blank side. Keen to keep herself occupied, she began to bullet-point the information she would need for her preliminary report.

CHAPTER FOUR

The approaching siren sounded agitated, its tone changing frequently as the paramedic tried to harry drivers out of the way. Meg had enough experience of waiting in the ambulance bay to recognise a bad job when she heard one.

"Let the crew get her out," she said to Emily. "If we start pressing buttons on the bus or mucking about with the stretcher, we're only going to fuck something up."

Emily nodded and scuttled backward as the ambulance raced into the bay, overshot the A&E doors, and had to be reversed again. Its rear doors were flung open by Kathy before the driver had emerged from the cab. "Fucking new starters," she muttered.

"Might have known it'd be you," Meg said.

"Sorry, Doc. I know you asked for nice little old grannies." Kathy, who seemed to be well in the running for Paramedic Shit Magnet of the Month, jumped down from the back and began to work the controls for the tail lift.

"Yeah, you're sacked." Meg couldn't see much of her patient, but judging by the expressions of the Helimed crew, they had had a fraught journey even before they were subjected to the newbie's driving. It was only when one of the men moved that Meg noticed Sanne sitting on the seat by the bulkhead. She looked pale and shaken, and was dressed in running shorts and a jacket far too large for her. Meg raised an eyebrow at the state of her legs, which looked as if someone had taken a cheese grater to them.

Sanne must have caught her reaction, because she straightened her back and shook her head once, warning Meg not to make a fuss. She took the hand Meg offered, gave it a quick squeeze as she climbed down from the ambulance, and then stepped aside to allow Meg to focus on her patient.

The clatter of the stretcher wheels against the lift prompted Meg to follow her lead. "Shock room please, chaps," she said, turning to escort the stretcher down the corridor. Her initial visual assessment of the woman had made her hands start sweating in her gloves. With someone in such a critical condition, everything was against the clock.

Due to its helipad and specialist neurosurgery unit, Sheffield Royal had been a designated Trauma Centre for just over a year: ambulances and Helimed routinely bypassed local hospitals and transported the more severely injured patients to the Royal for expert care. Once the woman had been transferred onto the hospital bed, Meg's team knew to stop what they were doing and listen to the Helimed doctor as he handed his patient over.

He cleared his throat to ensure that his voice carried above the rasp of the vent and the sound of someone moaning in the next bay. "Patient is an unidentified female, found unconscious at the base of a cliff. The exact mechanism of her injuries is unknown..."

Meg scrutinised the woman as she listened, matching the vital signs on the monitors to the physical signs: the rising blood pressure indicating an intracranial bleed; the telltale contusions around her eyes, typical of those caused by a fractured skull; and the slowing pulse and single blown pupil that warned that the woman needed surgery within the next few hours if anything resembling a life were to be salvaged for her. Even though Meg tried to consider the overall picture, the sheer horror implied by the smaller details made them stand out: ligature marks, abrasions around the woman's lips, torn or missing fingernails, and the filthy underwear that was revealed when the blankets were unwrapped. She was gaunt and dehydrated, with a succession of bruises and track marks over the veins at her inner elbow suggesting repeated injections administered by an inexpert hand. Meg added a toxicology screen to a mental list that was growing longer by the second.

"That's great, thanks," she said as the Helimed doctor indicated he had finished speaking. "Sahil, you happy with her airway?"

The anaesthetist nodded. "Tube's fine, but there's resistance to the vent, and air entry is poor on her left side."

"She's got a lot of bruising on that side of her chest," Meg said. "Okay, let's not bugger about waiting for an X-ray series. We'll get a drain in, see if that improves things, and then get her down for a full CT, ASAP. Any word from Neuro?"

"Thirty minutes," Liz said, "but that was twenty minutes since. Dr. Maxwell got held up in theatre."

A clock had been set running at the start of the trauma call. Meg noted its time and added another ten minutes to Liz's estimate. Neuro were notorious for being late to every party.

"Right." She rocked back on her heels as she finalised her plan of action. For some reason, the motion always helped her to think. "That gives us a chance to get the drain in, ABG, catheter, and urinalysis. Type and cross for at least six units, and take the usual bloods, including a tox. Shout up if you spot anything Helimed might have missed, and bag everything, please. We have a detective here waiting for the clothing, so remove it in one piece if possible."

Sanne was at the back of the small room, pressed up against a clinical waste bin and feeling she was taking up too much space even so. When she heard Meg mention her, she stepped forward, arms laden with the evidence bags Nelson had just given her in the corridor. He had offered to do the task himself, but one look at her face had stopped him pushing the issue. The rope she had cut from the woman's wrists was already sealed and tagged. She set the container where she could keep a close eye on it and opened another large paper bag for the blankets a nurse had collected.

"Fold them inward," she said, trying to make things easier for the labs. "That's perfect, cheers."

She scrunched the top of the bag over, recorded the time and date, and added her signature. As she did so, she heard Meg swear, and she looked up to see blood pouring through the wide plastic tube Meg had just pushed into the side of the woman's chest.

"Bollocks," Meg said. "If this doesn't slow, we'll need to get Cardiothoracic down here."

"Her sats are improving, though," the Asian man standing behind the woman's head said with more optimism.

It took at least another minute before Meg responded, but a smile gradually spread across her face. "Tapering off at about seven-fifty mils, so that's a bullet dodged. How are we doing elsewhere?"

Sanne listened to the different voices reporting numbers and procedures. The terminology and the significance of the figures were meaningless to her, but Meg seemed to take it all in her stride, not once asking for clarification or for anyone to repeat themselves. Sanne had never seen her working a major trauma before. Thinking back to the previous night's curry sauce disaster, she was slightly awed by Meg's calm command over her team.

"Detective?"

The same nurse who had given Sanne the blankets held out the woman's underwear gingerly. A pale blue bra went into one evidence bag, and knickers that had once been cheerfully patterned went into another. It was a mismatched set probably chosen at random, the woman never imagining it would be seen by a room full of people fighting to keep her alive.

Sanne closed the bags and rubbed a hand across her eyes, swiping at the tears before they could form properly. It was dangerous to let her guard down and think like that. She couldn't do her job if she fell into that trap. Grateful for the excuse to drop out of sight, she crouched by the door to annotate the bags.

The door nudged against her thigh as someone pushed it open, and a disembodied voice called across to Meg.

"CT are ready when you are, and Dr. Maxwell is on his way down."

"Fabulous." Meg peeled off her gloves and reached for a fresh pair. "Tell Max to meet us at the scanner. We'll be there in five."

❖

Left behind in the shock room, Sanne gathered up the evidence bags and paused, leaning against the wall. Her ears buzzed, and a dull throb behind her eyes warned of an impending headache. She hadn't drunk enough, she had barely eaten anything, and she had been functioning under constant stress for hours. Just another day at the office, then, but she'd never experienced a day quite like this one. She cradled her left arm where Meg had gripped it. When she had winced beneath the touch, Meg had quickly released her. "Don't go anywhere until I've taken a look at you," she had told Sanne in a peremptory tone, before leaving to follow the stretcher to the scanner.

Annoyed at herself for wasting time, Sanne pushed open the door with her backside and carried the bags into the corridor. Two uniformed officers came over to help.

"Thanks," she said, as they added her bags to the pile already stacked on a wheelchair. "Is Detective Turay around?"

"He just went outside to take a call."

Sanne glanced at the exit with a degree of uncertainty. She wanted to check in with her partner, but she was reluctant to leave her post. Meg had told her the scan would take at least twenty minutes, though, so she decided to take the risk.

"If I'm not here when they bring her back from CT, come and find me," she told the officers. Their bemused reaction made her pause, and she shook her head, embarrassed. "Sorry, I'm Detective Jensen."

"Oh." The older of the officers flushed to the roots of his auburn hair. "We heard someone had been out on the moors with the vic, but—"

"But you didn't know to look for a detective in shorts."

"Exactly." He smiled, his flush receding a little. "I'll come and fetch you as soon as she's back."

"Ta. Appreciate it." She was already walking toward the open doors, beyond which Nelson's voice was just about audible amid the chatter of sparrows nesting beneath the ambulance bay's canopy. Sanne knew Meg loved those sparrows and regularly flaunted hospital policy by leaving crumbs for them on the bins flanking the doors. As she waited for Nelson to finish on the phone, she found herself scanning the bins for telltale scraps of bread, but all she found were cigarette butts and a discarded piece of gum. She moved closer to the sunshine instead, wishing her day off had turned into anything but this.

"Hey, San." Nelson spoke quietly so as not to startle her. She hadn't noticed his approach. He tucked his phone back into his pocket. "Where are we up to?"

"Shouldn't that be my line?" They walked into a shadier part of the bay, and she lowered the hand that had been shielding her eyes. "Was that the boss?"

"Yep. She's out on the moors with SOCO."

Sanne licked her dry lips, loath to ask anything else. Forewarned was forearmed, though. "Is she…?" She swallowed and tried again. "Did I—"

"Is she coming here to haul your arse over the coals?" Nelson offered. "No. And you did fine, so don't look so bloody terrified." He barely gave her time to process that before he continued. "I uploaded the photos and video from your mobile and sent them to SOCO and the boss. They looked good. You picked out some useful details. SOCO, EDSOP, and a team of uniforms are going over the immediate scene. The boss is planning to get volunteers involved, too, so we can widen the search."

"The victim was held out there somewhere," Sanne said. "The state she was in, she can't have run far."

"That's one possibility. The other is an escape from a vehicle crossing the high routes or off-roading," he countered. "Or, the perp got bored with her, took her out there, and chucked her off the ridge."

Sanne felt a familiar exhilaration as she weighed up the theories. She and Nelson always worked well like this, bouncing ideas off each other. She had barely had a chance so far to think any of this through, but she loved these first, analytical hours of processing a new case.

"National Trust rangers and Mountain Rescue are helping to pinpoint the closest roads," Nelson said. "Roads, and any areas with vehicular access."

She nodded. If her original supposition was correct, the woman's assailant would have struggled to get her onto the moors, unless she had been hiking out there at the time of her abduction. Which begged the question: was he an opportunist, or had he planned this in advance? Sanne wasn't sure which was the more frightening answer. She frequently jogged alone up there and had never considered herself in danger from anything but the weather and the terrain. "Are the two lads okay?" she asked, changing the subject.

"They're upset, understandably, but their parents met them at HQ, and they've both managed to give detailed statements."

"Already?" She squinted at her watch. "God, is that the time?"

"Time for lunch. The boss said to get a statement off you, but I'm sure she meant to say that you were to eat something first."

Sanne shook her head and tried not to grimace at the pain the motion caused. "No, I can't do a statement yet. I want to stay at the hospital." It came out more desperate than she had intended, but to his credit Nelson just nodded.

"How about two ibuprofen and a cup of tea?"

She smiled and leaned into him briefly. "Now you're talking."

If Meg had been a betting woman, she'd have just won herself a fiver. She found Sanne, as predicted, exactly where she had last seen her, pushed up against the shock room wall, waiting to continue her task, with more empty evidence bags at her feet. She had been scribbling in a notepad, but as the team returned, she lowered the pen and cast Meg an expectant glance.

"Not good," Meg mouthed. Surrounded by colleagues, she was unable to break the news gently. "Give me a few minutes, okay?"

Ever the professional, Sanne nodded, her face betraying nothing, but her pen slipped unnoticed from her fingers and rolled beneath the bin. Meg turned away, quelling a sudden impulse to wrap Sanne in a blanket and march her into a cubicle for some much-needed TLC.

With perfect timing, someone thrust a Polystyrene box from the blood bank into her hands and motioned that she should sign for it.

"Thanks," she muttered, crosschecking the contents and scrawling her name. "Max, you want a unit of this up now?"

"Lovely. Yes, please," Max called back.

The scan results had made this Neuro's show to run, and they were finalising arrangements to take the woman to theatre. Their plan was to cut into her skull to try to relieve the pressure from the intracranial bleed. They might remove a section of bone to create extra space for the brain or to suck out the clot that had formed, or they might open her up and realise their efforts were futile, that all they could do was try to make her comfortable. The skull was essentially a closed box. Either the swelling from her injury would subside, or it would squash her brain until her vital functions failed. For someone who had survived so much trauma already, such a death seemed particularly vindictive.

Meg took her fury out on the tangled IV tubing in her hands, snapping it taut and daring it not to fall into place. The woman's arm was cold and slack beneath Meg's fingers, as if her body was already coming to terms with her prognosis and beginning to shut down. The blood ran through the line when Meg opened it up, but there was no miraculous transformation as it hit the vein, no flush of healthy colour or twitch of movement—not that Meg had expected one.

"We're good to go," Max told her.

"Right." She pulled the blanket back over the woman's arm. "Anything else you need me to do?"

"No, thanks. We're as ready as we'll ever be. I'll give you a call when we're done, okay?"

"Okay." She didn't move as the bed was wheeled from the room. Within a few minutes, most of the team drifted away to clean, restock, or write up retrospective notes. It was only when the last person had left that Sanne approached her.

"Hey," Sanne said.

Meg let out a shaky breath. She felt weirdly disconnected. She knew she should be doing something but couldn't figure out what. "Hey, yourself."

Sanne's fingers closed around hers. "Come on, love. I'll make you a brew."

❖

Half a mug of tea and a shortbread finger consumed in the refuge of the staffroom had Meg feeling more like herself again. From behind the rim of her mug, she watched Sanne alternate between tea and biscuit, never using both hands.

"So, where are you hurt?"

In a series of guarded movements, Sanne set down her mug and brushed invisible crumbs from her knees. "Nowhere. What do you mean?" she mumbled, looking at the floor, her ears turning pink.

"Sanne Jensen, you're a terrible liar. This is why Mr. Kincaid always used to give us detention, because you were bloody useless at telling a simple fib."

Sanne paused mid-sweep. "I never wanted to take that shortcut! I loved running cross-country. You were the lazy arse who insisted we go across the turnip field."

The memory made Meg grin. Unbeknownst to them, Kincaid had been lurking on the section of route they had bypassed, and he had rumbled their shortcut fair and square.

"Always such a swotty little thing." She smoothed Sanne's unruly hair from her forehead. "You want a hand taking your coat off?"

Sanne shook her head, excuses already tumbling from her lips. "I'm fine. I need to get back to work, start writing everything up. The boss will be wondering where I am. You'll have to give a statement—I can ask Nelson to take it—and you'll phone me as soon as you hear anything, won't you?"

She tried to stand, but all her strength seemed to desert her. Her shoulders sagged, and tears brimmed in her eyes. She wiped her nose heedlessly on the sleeve of her borrowed coat.

"God, Meg, I thought she was going to die on me. It felt like forever out there before the chopper came, and I couldn't do anything for her. All I could do was keep her fucking head still and tell her she'd be okay." She ran out of breath and gave a single sob. "And she's going to die, isn't she? So I *can* tell a fucking lie after all, can't I?"

She tensed when Meg reached for her, but then she pressed her face against Meg's neck and let herself be held. Meg rocked her gently, the aimless motion calming them both. It was less than a minute, however, before the sound of voices in the corridor made Sanne pull away. She took the tissue Meg offered her and blew her nose.

"What did the scan show?" she asked, using the same tissue to dry her eyes.

"Multiple skull fractures." Meg stroked the back of Sanne's head, surreptitiously checking for bumps. "And a clot from a bleed. Maxwell—the neurosurgeon you saw in the shock room—he's going to try to remove it, but it was pretty big, San. Even if he's successful, it may have caused irreversible damage."

Sanne sat up properly, pulled her knees beneath her chin, and wrapped her right arm around them. She was staring at her muddy trainers when she spoke again.

"Was she raped?"

"I don't know." Meg saw Sanne's confused glance. "There wasn't time for a rape kit. We'll need to get someone over from St. Margaret's to do that. The nurse who catheterised her didn't note any signs of trauma to her genitals, though—no bleeding or discharge. None of the typical injuries you'd see in a sexual assault, either. No bite marks or bruising to her thighs or breasts."

"I don't get it," Sanne said. "Why else would someone have taken her? Personal grudge? Ransom?"

"I'm glad it's not my job to figure that out. I'm not sure I want to know."

"I want to know. It's the only way we're going to catch this bastard. If she escaped from him before he was done, chances are he's already looking for another victim. Shit, I need to speak to Nelson." Sanne stood too abruptly and swayed on the spot, her flush of anger vanishing, leaving her face pallid and clammy. "Whoa, what the fuck?" she muttered, grabbing the hand that Meg flung out to brace her.

"Sit your arse back down." Meg pushed her into the chair. "Apart from half a piece of shortbread, what've you eaten today?"

"Does a smoothie count?"

"Sort of. What else have you had?"

"Some water. That tea."

"And how far had you run before you embarked on your impromptu rock climb?"

"About eight miles." She peeked up at Meg. "Who told you about the rock climb?"

"Nelson." Meg didn't try to disguise her exasperation. "You're probably dehydrated, and even an idiot could see you've hurt your arm. So, drink the rest of your tea and get that coat off."

Sanne shuffled in the chair like a scolded child. "I can't."

"Can't what? Tea or coat?"

"Coat. I think it's stuck."

"The zip?"

"No, the sleeve."

Meg touched Sanne's forehead, checking for warmth. "You, my darling, are not making much sense. Did you bump your head?"

"No, but I sort of bumped my arm."

"You *bumped* it?"

"On the rocks." She had the grace to look guilty. "It was more of a flaying, really, if you're being picky."

"Ah." Meg nodded in sympathy. Raw skin and dry fabric did not make for a happy marriage. "Come on, then. Let's find a nice secluded cubicle and a bucket of warm water."

Sanne stood up, with more caution this time. "Can't refuse an offer like that, can I?"

❖

"Ow," Sanne said, with a certain amount of understatement. She had never been one for making a fuss, and she had a commendable pain threshold, but the warm water burned like acid on her wounds. She swallowed repeatedly, trying to breathe through her nose, and when those tactics failed she closed her eyes and thought of nothing. Nothing, just blackness and silence. It was an old childhood trick, honed in the hours she used to spend hiding beneath her bed. It buried the sound of yelling, or crying, or flesh pounding into flesh, or a fist pounding against her mum, and it still worked. By the time Meg's hand cupped her cheek, the coat was gone, and Meg had positioned her arm on a dry sheet.

"You okay there?" Meg asked carefully, as if rousing someone from hypnosis.

"Yep, I'm fine."

Meg tapped the mattress, and Sanne swung her legs onto the bed. The pillow beneath her head felt luxuriously soft. She eyed the tweezers laid out on a tray beside a collection of dressings, but was too weary to care about what came next.

"Do your worst."

"Might sting a bit. Sure you don't want anything stronger than paracetamol?"

"I'm sure. Codeine wipes me out." Sanne spoke with more confidence than she felt. Half of the Dark Peak appeared to be embedded in her upper arm, and Meg was not renowned for her bedside manner.

"Probably because you don't drink." Meg dug into Sanne's arm without further ado and snared her first piece of grit. "Ooh, that's a big one."

Her wholly inappropriate enthusiasm made Sanne smile, even through her clenched teeth.

"Feels like the worst skinned knee in the world."

"Wait till I add antiseptic to it," Meg said. "I'll kiss it better, though, if that'll help."

Sanne's toes curled as another chunk came free. "Wouldn't that violate some sort of doctor-patient rule?"

Meg grinned. "I've kissed you in far naughtier places than your elbow, Detective."

"Jesus, Meg!" Using her good arm to cover her burning face, Sanne silently thanked the old woman next door for choosing that moment to tell the entire department that she needed a wee. "You'll get me sacked. You'll get yourself sacked."

"Probably." Meg didn't sound at all troubled by the notion. "Not for kissing you, you berk, but I do still have a tendency to swear at patients."

"I thought you'd agreed to work on that."

"Yeah. It's hard, though, sometimes. Some wanker will sneak in under my defences, and out it comes."

As Sanne lowered her arm, a smell of sweet copper hit her, and she noticed the woman's blood still caked beneath her fingernails. "Lot of wankers out there," she said quietly.

Meg hesitated, the tweezers poised in mid-grab. "Yes, there are." She patted the back of Sanne's hand and resumed her task. "Let's get you patched up so you can go and catch this one, eh?"

Chapter Five

When a uniformed officer met Sanne in the police HQ car park and handed her her car keys, she could almost have kissed him. There were spare clothes in the boot of her car, which meant she wouldn't have to walk through HQ in the ill-fitting pair of scrubs Meg had found for her. Her running gear and the soggy coat were currently folded up in one of her evidence bags.

"Nelson asked me to pick your car up from the reservoir," the officer said. "I've left it over in A3."

"Appreciate that. Thanks very much."

The keys were hot against her palm, the sun still beating down, reflecting off the four-storey building that housed the main administrative infrastructure of the East Derbyshire police force. EDSOP had been relocated there during a recent modernisation process. They were secreted away at the rear of the building, but their technology was top of the range, the main office had a pleasant view of fields, and the female locker room was a purpose-built facility instead of a toilet cubicle next to the urinals. The little kitchen annex even came with a geyser, negating the need to boil a kettle. Fred Aspinall, one of the older detectives on the team, had welcomed that innovation with a wonder more suited to the discovery of life on Mars.

Tracking the numbered bays, Sanne found her Vauxhall Corsa parked between an expensive-looking Audi and a really expensive-looking Range Rover. Neither vehicle evoked a shred of envy in her. The Corsa was nippy, practical, and surprisingly effective in the snow, and it was also the best form of transport she'd ever had. Most of her family still walked or relied on the bus. Sheltered behind the open boot, with the high wall of the car park boxing her in, she stripped off the scrubs and pulled on her spare outfit. The jeans were too casual for the office, and the shirt's short sleeves didn't cover the bandages swathed around her arm, but it was a definite improvement. Remembering Meg's advice, she drank half a bottle of water. Then she damped her hair down with a cupped handful and headed for the main entrance, clipping her ID badge onto her shirt as she approached. The badge and her warrant card were always somewhere about her person. She even carried them in her pack when she went out running. No one out on the moors had questioned her authority that morning, but it had been reassuring to know her credentials were there, just in case.

She displayed her badge to the officer on the front desk and took the stairs two at a time. The muscles in her legs complained, reminding her that she had started the day with a lengthy run and then added bruises. She persevered, though, and by the time she reached the fourth floor the short burst of exercise had left her feeling much less decrepit. She walked straight into the chaos that traditionally accompanied the early stages of a case: phones ringing, paperwork cascading onto the floor as people brushed against fragile piles, a variety of ringtones announcing incoming texts, and Fred in the corner, kicking the photocopier.

"It's this drawer, mate. It's always getting stuck there." Sanne flipped open the offending part and teased the sheet of paper through. "There, try that."

Fred hit the green button and beamed as the machine sparked into motion. "You bring sunshine to my life," he sang, to a tune only he would ever recognise. "I'd make you a brew, but the boss wanted to see you as soon as you got in."

"Right." She rocked back a little, and he placed a steadying hand on her shoulder.

"You done a statement?"

"Yes, at the hospital. Nelson's faxed it over here already."

"Got nothing to fret about then," he said, and she smiled, almost believing him.

As she went over to Eleanor's door, George Torren—Fred's partner—crossed himself and raised his eyes heavenward. She stuck two fingers up at him, knocked, and walked into the office. It smelled like apples. She had no idea how Eleanor did it, since she had never seen her eat one, but the room always brought to mind a crisp Granny Smith.

Mid-sentence on a phone call, Eleanor acknowledged Sanne but continued her conversation. Her nose and forehead were bright pink. Evidently, she hadn't expected to spend hours exposed to the sun that morning, and her fair skin had paid the price.

"Yes, sir." She tapped one fingernail on the desk. "I can get that to you within the hour. No, there's been no word yet. She's still in surgery. Yes, I will, as soon as SOCO have been allowed access."

Sanne couldn't hear the reply, only that it was curt and swiftly followed by the dial tone. Eleanor placed the receiver back into its cradle with admirable restraint.

"Well, you look like you've been in the wars." An uncommon softness in her voice took Sanne aback. "Are you okay to work?"

"Yes, boss." Sanne's answer was as absolute as she could make it. The thought of being sent home and kept off the case was anathema.

"Just checking." Eleanor gave her a sly smile. "Welfare of my team, and all that crap. I'm sure there's a manual on it somewhere." She waved a hand toward a shelf full of white lever-arch files so rarely handled that they were still pristine. "I've read your statement. It's very thorough. Images were excellent too. They've already gone to the lab for enhancement."

Her mobile phone rang. She checked the caller ID and flicked the call through to her voicemail. When she looked up again, Sanne felt the full force of her scrutiny. "Did you consider staying at the scene instead of accompanying the victim to the hospital?" she asked, in a tone that gave no hint as to the right answer.

"Yes, ma'am, I considered it, but the victim was our most valuable piece of evidence, and I wanted to maintain a documentable chain." Sanne paused for a breath, providing an opportunity for correction or contradiction, but when Eleanor remained silent she pressed on. "I don't believe that area of the moor is our actual crime scene, ma'am. I think the victim was held somewhere else, or perhaps escaped as she was being moved, so I made the decision to arrange the Mountain Rescue team in a wide perimeter and to travel with the victim myself."

She held Eleanor's gaze, letting her know she had finished. It was an explanation that she had mentally rehearsed until she could deliver it verbatim, and it was as clinical and analytical as Eleanor's standards demanded, even if it didn't begin to scrape the surface of Sanne's actual reasoning. She wondered whether something in her expression or her posture would give her away, a flicker in her eyes or a twitch in a muscle that would betray her emotions.

If Eleanor saw or suspected anything, however, she made no comment. She clicked the nib of her pen and made a short note in an open file. "You did a good job out there, Sanne."

Sanne licked her dry lips and waited for the inevitable "but." To her astonishment, it never came.

"I've scheduled a team briefing for four p.m.," Eleanor said. "That gives you ninety minutes to prepare your account. Is that enough?"

Sanne just about stopped herself from saluting. "Yes, boss."

Eleanor smiled. "How is it that I'm glowing like a bloody lobster and you're not?"

"I had a cap on, boss. And sun cream."

"Yes, I imagine that would do it." She touched the tip of her nose, making it blanch beneath the slight pressure. "Get something to eat before you start your report, Sanne. You look peaky."

"I'm fine," Sanne said, and for the first time in hours, she did feel fine. Relief and pride had dispelled all of her aches and pains.

Eleanor made a non-committal noise but didn't push the point. "I'll see you in ninety minutes, then," she said, and swore as her mobile and desk phone began to ring simultaneously.

Sanne took that as her cue to leave, shutting the door behind her. Fred met her with a cup of tea and a Double Decker. She took the mug and the chocolate bar, and pecked him on his cheek, laughing as he fake-swooned and cupped the place where her lips had touched him.

"You're a daft bugger, Fred." She sipped the tea as she went over to her desk. The clock on the wall told her she had eighty-six minutes to meet Eleanor's deadline. It was a good thing she thrived under pressure.

❖

Despite her daunting task and the ticking clock hanging over it, Sanne was thankful for the opportunity to review her mobile phone footage before presenting it to the team. She hadn't taken many photographs, but the ones she had were graphic and unflinching in their focus, and she had to go to the bathroom to wash the sweat from her face and neck as soon as she finished her notes. Fortunately, her reaction went unnoticed in the commotion around her, and half an hour later, she was composed enough to stand in front of her peers and talk through the events of that morning.

Everyone had made it back for the meeting, which Eleanor opened with a short précis before handing over to Sanne. Her fingers tight around the computer's remote control, Sanne outlined her findings, actions, and initial thoughts, her words punctuated by the sharp click of the images changing. She saw the anger on her colleagues' faces harden into determination as they watched. As a junior member of EDSOP, she was used to being the butt of jokes, but on this occasion, no one interrupted to make a glib comment or inappropriate remark. This was the first time most of the detectives had seen the images, and they too seemed rattled. Sanne's hand trembled as she paused to drink her water. Her nerves had dissipated within the first few minutes, but she still found the photograph of the woman's feet hard to bear. She heard Mike Hallet swearing beneath his breath. She knew he had two daughters, both in their early twenties.

Once she was sure she could continue without her voice shaking, she set her glass down and glanced at her notes to find her place. As she did so, something caught her eye, and she turned to look at the projected image again.

"Boss, could those be splinters?" She aimed the red dot of the laser pointer at the woman's heel. Marks that had been indistinct on her computer screen now appeared to be slivers of wood embedded in the peat-smeared sole. She crumpled her paperwork in her fist as she picked up the thread of a theory and began to follow it. "Only, I've run that route a few times, and there's nothing that'd cause injuries like that. There's a wooden stile within a mile of where she was found, but unless she'd stood there and stamped on it with both feet—"

"Why the hell would she do that, Jensen?"

Sanne tried not to react to Duncan Carlyle's withering tone. One of these days, she would tell him where to shove his criminal psychology degree, but this definitely wasn't the right time.

"Well, she wouldn't," she said, as if explaining something very complicated to someone quite dim. "She might have climbed over it, but that's all she'd have done."

She leaned back on the desk, imagining herself up on the moors, sick with terror and not knowing where to go for help, knowing only that she had to get as far away as possible. Adrenaline would have cut through the pain and lent her strength, at least at the beginning. Strength enough, perhaps, to untie her bonds and escape from wherever she had been imprisoned.

"Maybe she had to kick her way out when she first got herself loose," she said, with the calm certainty of having fathomed the answer. "If he'd kept her in a disused building, it might've had a boarded-up entrance or just a wooden door. Her hands were bound, swollen, so she was limited with what she could do with them, but her legs were free." Perching on the desk, she raised her feet and kicked out in demonstration. "She hammers at the wood, driving the splinters into her heels, but she smashes through it and runs."

"That makes it likely she was held out there somewhere," Fred said, and Eleanor raised a hand as everyone began to speak across each other.

"Okay, thank you," she said as the babble of voices faded. "It's still useful to bear the other possibilities in mind: that the victim was intentionally thrown over the ridge, or that she escaped onto the moors from her abductor's vehicle. We'll know more once SOCO have been able to examine her. Right now, we have an unidentified victim. Finding out who she is is an absolute priority." She took the remote from Sanne and switched to an image of the woman's face. "And here's what's going to make that an absolute ball-ache."

Sanne saw several heads bob in understanding. The woman's features were so distorted by her injuries that it was likely even close family would struggle to recognise her. Meg had found no distinguishing marks during her examination—no birthmarks, tattoos, scars, or piercings—and the CT scan had failed to detect any surgical metalwork that might have helped.

Eleanor consulted the file in front of her. "Fred and George, you take missing persons reports. Chase up anyone who matches or comes close to matching her description, and start fitting together details for a press release. Scotty, Jay, you're on access roads, rest stops, and lay-bys, with one of the rangers and as many officers as Traffic can spare. Plot the closest routes to Laddaw Ridge and start there. If he drove her out to the moors last night, he must have parked somewhere. Talk to anyone and everyone you come across. Show them her picture. Even if they didn't see her yesterday, they might recognise her if she walks up there regularly. Sanne, Nelson, Duncan, and Chris"—she ticked off the names as she went along, like a schoolteacher trying to coordinate an impossible project—"I want you up on the moors at first light, to organise the uniforms. A grid has been blocked to cover a realistic area, based on the vic's physical condition, and we need as detailed an examination of that area as possible. Bag and tag anything that looks to have been discarded recently, and if anyone finds a series of bare footprints that we can follow back to some kind of lair, that would be very helpful." Eleanor paused to acknowledge the wild improbability of that, and Sanne heard Carlyle mutter something beneath his breath. When she glanced at his notepad, it was completely blank. He hadn't even taken the lid off his pen.

"We've been in touch with Derbyshire Cave Search and Rescue, who are going to start a systematic check of the cave formations in that neck of the woods. Apparently, these hillsides are riddled with potholes and tunnels, so if she was held out there the perp may have utilised one. Try to steer clear of them yourselves. A number of them are structurally unsafe, and the department can't afford the liability damages at the moment. Now for the good news: we have a group of locals who are willing to help out tomorrow."

A predictable chorus of groans welcomed that revelation. It would be a difficult enough day without the added burden of supervising amateur sleuths. Above the protests, Eleanor continued to speak.

"Bear in mind that the perp could well live locally, and we all know how many of these idiots get their jollies assisting the police after the fact. The Mountain Rescue truck can get you within two miles of the scene." A smile twitched at the corner of her lips. "Dress appropriately, chaps. I think Sanne would recommend that you wear a cap."

The disdain on Carlyle's face tightened into a scowl as he watched George pull at the neck of his shirt and fan himself with his notepad.

"Saw the forecast earlier," George told him. "Ouch. Full sun and eighty-one degrees. You're going to need more than a cap, Sarge. You're going to need a bloody miracle."

Carlyle was a redhead, with a ghostly complexion that broke out in freckles and acne the instant it was exposed to sunshine, but Sanne suspected something more lay behind his reaction. He was a city boy, living in the centre of Sheffield and making no secret of his antipathy toward the rural villages and their small-fry criminals. He had submitted several applications to transfer to Manchester and London, but each time he had failed at interview level. Eleanor actively encouraged his ambition to move on from EDSOP. His swift promotion to sergeant had owed a lot to a well-placed uncle, and she had played little part in his being selected for her team. His insistence on addressing everyone by surname, possibly because two names per person was one too many for him to remember, was not appreciated either. The team, in return, called him a grudging "Sarge" to his face and all kinds of names in private. Sanne knew he would perceive tomorrow's task—being forced to work in an area familiar to her, and to defer to her local knowledge—as an insult to his seniority, and he would either sulk or attempt to reassert his authority by behaving like an arsehole.

As Eleanor finished dividing up the workload, Sanne caught Nelson crossing his eyes at her, and she had to hide a smile behind her hand. If Carlyle was the team bully, she and Nelson were the kids who hid his lunchbox in revenge and stole all his pens when he was away from his desk. She had once overheard him refer to them as "the dyke and the darkie." She had never dared to repeat that to Nelson, but concocting covert ways to torment Carlyle was the only form of insubordination in which she ever participated.

Back at her desk, she and Nelson pored over Ordnance Survey maps and local guidebooks, trying to find farm buildings or shelters within the area Eleanor had identified. There was nothing. The dearth of roads and accessible tracks made it unfeasible for anyone to live so far from civilisation.

"You could get a four-wheel-drive up here, but it only goes to these grouse butts." Sanne traced a line demarcating an unmade road. "Then where would he go? Did he carry her, or maybe force her to walk?"

Nelson angled the map so that he could look at it without tilting his head. "These are hiking trails, right?"

"Yep. All of the dotted green lines are some sort of footpath." She pointed to a bolder pattern of green diamonds. "That's the Pennine Way. It goes right up to the Scottish border, and it's a busy route, especially in good weather. If he'd planned to abduct a hiker, he's more likely to have gone off the beaten track. It's open country, so people can go anywhere. They don't have to stick to the paths."

"Needle in a haystack," Nelson muttered. He wasn't good with maps and usually relied on Sanne for navigation while he drove.

"Let's hope the rangers will come up with some ideas. In the meantime, have one of these for bedtime reading." She arranged the four guidebooks in a row and let him take first pick.

The buzz of her mobile interrupted his offer of a brew. She flipped it open, saw Meg's name, and answered immediately.

Meg didn't bother with a greeting. "She made it through the operation. Max is 'cautiously optimistic' about her chances."

"Bloody hell," Sanne whispered. That was the last thing she had been expecting to hear. "What happens now?"

"She's in an induced coma, to try to control the swelling to her brain. When Max is happy with her progress, he'll wake her up. We won't know much more until he does that. The tox screen found traces of diazepam, ketamine, and flunitrazepam—that last one's Rohypnol—so even if she does come through this, the chances are she won't be able to remember what happened."

The toxicology results were no surprise to Sanne. Ever since Meg told her about the track marks, she had been trying to predict what the perpetrator might have used. All three of those drugs—reasonably easy to obtain, for someone who knew where to look—had been on her list. She looked across the room, to where enlarged copies of her photographs had been displayed sequentially on a whiteboard. Beyond the board, the window framed wisps of cloud, tinged pink by the setting sun.

"You're working late," she said.

"Yes, I am." The exhaustion in Meg's reply was almost palpable.

Sanne closed her eyes, wanting nothing more than to climb into Meg's bed and hold on to her until they both fell asleep. She sighed. "Thanks for letting me know, love."

"No problem. Max is phoning your boss. Drive safe, San."

"You too. I'll see you soon." Sanne ended the call, stared at the screen of her mobile until it went blank, and then gathered her books.

Nelson had obviously overheard most of the conversation, because he picked up her keys and held them out to her. At the last second, however, he kept hold of her car key and looked at her sternly.

"You should get yourself home." He knew her too well. The concern in his voice showed he had sussed out her intention not to do anything of the sort.

"I will. I just…" She shook her head, unable to explain.

He nodded his understanding anyway and spread his fingers to release the key ring. "Okay. I'll see you in the morning."

His compliance, together with the relief that Meg's news had brought, lifted her mood immeasurably. "I know you're going to be tempted tomorrow, mate," she said, "but stop and think of me when you open your wardrobe."

"'Think of you?' What the hell does that mean?"

She grinned at his confusion. "It means please don't wear shorts."

CHAPTER SIX

Sanne held her badge in front of the tiny fish-eye lens and informed the disembodied voice that she was a detective. She didn't need to say anything else. The light beside the buzzer turned green, and a subtle snick of the lock told her that the door was open.

Beyond the door, the corridor was deserted, with only a rack of advice leaflets and a cage full of medical supplies giving any hint as to what lay farther along. Twenty years had passed since Sanne's dad had been brought here, but as she reached the open-plan section of the Intensive Therapy Unit, she couldn't stop herself glancing into the second bay, the one where her hopes had been raised and then dashed so completely.

The unit smelled and sounded the same as it had that week. It was always hushed, the whispers of machines and voices broken only by the occasional wail of an alarm. The patients were passive bodies, largely silent, too ill or sedated to object to the tubes and wires and invasive procedures. Their relatives would sit vigil, holding the patients' hands, rubbing their feet, sometimes weeping, but they too seemed governed by some unspoken rule, and everything they did was quiet and tentative. It was like being in church, except that the odours of sickness replaced those of incense and musty hymnbooks, and that no one would ever have dared to sing. For long stretches of time, very little happened, improvement and deterioration being for the most part gradual processes. It was no wonder, then, that a buzz of excitement surrounded the unit's newest patient. Sanne spotted a group of nurses chatting in low tones to two Scene of Crime officers they appeared to have waylaid en masse.

One of the officers took his elbows off the ledge around the nurses' station and nodded to Sanne as she approached.

"We've just finished." He sounded defensive, as if she might reprimand him for slacking on the job.

"I'm not here officially," she said, choosing not to go into detail. "Which room is she in?"

"Three. Bottom of the unit, on the left."

She was tempted to ask what his examination had found and how long the labs would take to process the trace evidence, but that could wait until tomorrow. There was nothing she would be able to do with the information now.

"Am I okay to go through?" She didn't aim her question at anyone in particular, but a young nurse with a cute dimple pointed her in the right direction.

Outside room three, Sanne squirted a blob of sanitising gel onto her hands and swore as it seeped into the broken skin on her palms.

"You kiss your mum with that mouth?"

Sanne smiled at the familiar voice and pushed the door open fully, not at all fazed to find that she would have company. She crossed the small room and kissed the top of Meg's head.

"So much for going home, eh?" she said.

"Yeah, so much for that."

"Any change?" She sank into an empty chair and tried to answer her own question by examining the woman. There weren't many differences. Her face was slightly cleaner, but the swelling around her eyes was far more pronounced than Sanne remembered, the bruising now such a livid purple that it was almost black. Bandages swathed her head, and there was a piece of sticky tape across one section of her skull bearing the warning *NO BONE*. Various tubes hydrated her and carried away her waste, and a mess of colourful wires put numbers on the monitors. The ventilator presided over it all, as if aware that without its input everything was lost.

"Her blood pressure has stabilised," Meg said.

The interruption made Sanne blink. She rubbed her eyes, trying to erase the number 63 that was still vivid in red on her retina.

"The head injury was making it rise, but they've got it under control now." Meg turned the woman's hand over and gently straightened the fingers, each marked with ink. "SOCO were in here when I arrived. Why hasn't anyone missed her? Some of her injuries were almost healed, so he must have taken her a few days ago."

"We don't know that they haven't," Sanne said. "Hopefully, something will come up on the database."

Meg was still holding the woman's hand. "I spoke to the specialist from St. Margaret's. The rape kit was negative."

Sanne wanted to say "that's good" or "thank fuck for that," but all she managed was a nod.

Meg waited a moment before asking, "You okay, San?"

A shake of the head this time. "I told another lie. To my boss." Sanne heaved in a breath that made her dizzy. "Well, not a lie, not really, but I didn't tell her the whole truth."

"About what?"

The room was dimly lit, leaving Meg no more than a silhouette in her peripheral vision. If the ITU was a sort of church, maybe this was confession.

"About why I left the moors. I could have stayed behind at the scene, but I got into the chopper instead. I told the boss I'd been preserving the chain of evidence, but that didn't even occur to me until we were in the air. The only thing I was thinking was that I couldn't leave her with strangers. When we were in here with my dad, they told us that unconscious people can sometimes hear your voice, and I'd been talking to her and reassuring her, and I didn't want her to think that I'd abandoned her. It was bloody stupid, because once we were in the helicopter no one could hear a damn thing anyway." She plucked up enough courage to look at Meg. Green and blue from the monitors were flashing across her face, giving Sanne something to focus on. "The boss reckons I did the right thing, but it was just luck, not judgement, and I can't tell that to anyone, not even Nelson."

Meg cupped her cheek. "I won't say a word."

"Because we're supposed to keep everything at arm's length and not get involved."

"Yeah. Sometimes it just doesn't work like that."

Sanne hummed low in her throat as Meg caressed her face. "No, it doesn't," she said. "Sometimes stuff sneaks up on you and bites you on the arse."

"I know what you mean. It's been a proper shitty day." Meg sounded as heartsick as Sanne felt.

Some unspoken cue made them lean back in their chairs. They sat in silence for a few minutes, lulled into stillness by the regularity of everything around them: falling drops of saline, a breath every five seconds, the pattern of spikes on the monitor.

After a while, Sanne put her hand on the woman's arm, the first time she had touched her since the moors.

"I wonder what her name is," she said.

"Come on, sleepyhead. Bedtime."

The insistence in the voice was reinforced by hands unwrapping Sanne's blanket. She screwed up her face. If it was bedtime, why wasn't she being left to sleep?

"Five more minutes," she mumbled, and heard Meg chuckle.

"You can have five more hours, sweetheart, but I think they'd be better spent in a bed, don't you?"

That gave Sanne pause, and she cracked open an eye. "Aw, fuck." The back of her neck burned as she lifted her head from the chair's headrest. She ran her tongue around her dry mouth and wiped the drool from her cheek. "What time is it?"

Meg liberated the blanket and folded it up. "Just gone nine. I gave you an hour. I didn't think you'd make it past twenty minutes in one of these things, but I'd overlooked your ability to fall asleep on a clothesline."

"Hmm. How is she?" Sanne squinted at the monitors surrounding the woman's bed, but couldn't remember what their original readings had been.

"She's stable." With one arm shoved beneath Sanne's, Meg hoisted her to her feet. "You, on the other hand, look like crap."

"Thanks."

"You're coming to mine tonight, so I can keep an eye on you."

"No, I'm fine," Sanne protested. "I'll go home." Her heart wasn't really in it, though, and one stern glance from Meg made her capitulate.

"I'll drop you back here in good time tomorrow and get your neighbour to feed your hens," Meg said. "I've told security that you're leaving your car. Okay?"

"Okay." Sanne stood and tried to pat her hair into some semblance of style.

"Don't know why you're bothering with that. Half the department has been in and out of here while you were snoring."

"Terrific."

"At least you slept through the ridicule."

"Oh, very droll."

They shared a quick grin, but as they reached the door Meg's expression sobered.

"I asked a nurse to call me if anything happens," she said quietly.

That was better than nothing, but as Sanne left the unit she still felt she was letting the woman down.

Meg put her arm around Sanne and fell into step with her. "You'll be no good to her if you don't take care of yourself, San."

"I feel like I should be doing more. Hell, I've barely done *anything*."

"You saved her life."

That would have been a comfort, had Sanne been able to look beyond the woman's dire prognosis. Was any kind of life better than no life at all? Her mum, with her lapsed Catholic sensibilities, might have had an answer to that one, but Sanne was too tired to consider the debate. She allowed herself to be steered into Meg's car, felt the seatbelt latch into place, and didn't open her eyes again until Meg was driving past the *Welcome to Rowlee Village* sign.

"Bugger." Sanne repeated the neck-stretching, drool-removing process.

Meg sniggered and then swerved wildly to avoid a duck dozing in the road. "Damn, I wish they wouldn't do that." She didn't appear to be troubled by the close encounter. "Food, bath, and bed for you," she said without missing a beat.

Sanne groaned and dug her fingers into the muscles of her back, which were clenched round her spine like a vice. "Can't I skip the first two and just go to bed?"

"Will you promise to eat a proper breakfast and change my sheets in the morning?"

It was a fair question. Sanne still had a day's worth of muck and blood clinging to her. She had never been a Brownie Guide, but she flashed Meg an improvised version of their salute. "I'll sort out your sheets, and I promise to eat breakfast, if you promise to let me make it."

Meg gave her a look. "You're a cheeky sod."

"You're a crappy cook."

A second duck asleep in the road curtailed Meg's answering gesture, but Sanne was sure it wouldn't have been one approved by the Girlguiding Association of Great Britain.

The blackbird singing down the open chimney sounded a lot more chipper than Meg felt as she cancelled the alarm clock seconds before it was due to go off.

Half-sprawled above the quilt, with a leg thrown over Meg's thighs, Sanne scratched her nose, mumbled something inaudible, and smacked her lips together as if she'd eaten a bug. She didn't wake, though, and Meg's hand on her forehead was all it took to settle her back into a deeper sleep. It was barely light outside. Meg made a unilateral decision that another half hour would make no difference to Sanne's schedule and all the difference to her general health.

"And I am sort of your doctor, so I know what's best," Meg whispered, smiling as Sanne snuffled softly in response.

It hadn't been a good night. At Sanne's insistence, Meg had cleared a small mountain of textbooks, journals, and un-ironed clothes off her spare bed and let her sleep there. It had seemed easier not to argue, but less than an hour later, Sanne's screams had brought Meg running into the room, and the only way to stop them had been to get into bed with her.

"I'm making a mess of *you* now," Sanne had sobbed, still mainly asleep, her face sticky with snot and tears. Then, undeterred by her own protests, she had tucked her head onto Meg's chest and started to snore through her blocked nose.

Meg knew from long experience that Sanne's sleep was the first thing to suffer when she was stressed. Her legs would jump, she would talk or cry out, and occasionally she wandered, waking up in random rooms with no memory of how she had got there. Meg hadn't heard her scream like that in years, though. The last time, they had been in secondary school, just turned thirteen, and squashed together in a single bed, after their respective parents had finally allowed them to sleep over. Remembering the way she had quieted Sanne on that occasion made her smile broaden. She kissed Sanne's brow, feeling the crease of frown lines ease away beneath her lips.

They were both idiots, Meg decided, as she listened to the blackbird choosing another tune and watched sunlight brighten the pattern on the curtains. They were inseparable, they knew every secret that was worth telling, and they had seen each other through their lowest moments. If they fought, they reconciled the next day. They made each other laugh, shared enough of the same interests that they always had something to chat about, and could even tolerate each other's families.

Given that they were absolutely not in a relationship and hadn't been since those first teenaged fumblings, the sex was no doubt ill-advised, but, Meg thought, as she sighed and inched over onto her back, putting some distance between herself and Sanne's sleep-warmed curves, it was always bloody good sex. So why didn't they just agree they were made for each other? Why did they continue seeing other people, when swapping stories of their bad dates was more fun than the dates themselves? Maybe because they were a pair of cowards, so comfortable with what had become routine that they were scared of messing it up.

"Fuck me sideways!" Sanne sat up so suddenly that she almost punched Meg in the face. "Look at the time! Why did you let me oversleep?"

Meg rubbed her cheek where Sanne's elbow had glanced off her, grateful for the change of subject, even if it came with a bruise. "Because I knew how charming you'd be upon waking?" she offered. She watched Sanne launch herself out of bed and start searching for clothes. "Do you feel any better for it?"

Sanne held up two pairs of knickers from Meg's laundry pile. "Yeah, a little. Are either of these mine?"

"No, but you wore the spotted ones the last time you stayed over."

"Oh." She looked sheepish. "Sorry. Can I steal them again?"

"Be my guest. Bras are—oh, you know where they are. Help yourself."

That prompted a moment of obvious befuddlement as Sanne spun around, trying to find Meg's chest of drawers and then noticing for the first time that she was in the wrong room.

"Hey, why…?" She inclined her head toward Meg's bedroom. "Uh, what did I miss? Because I can't…Did we…?"

Meg put her out of her misery. "No, we didn't. You had a nightmare, and I played pillow, that's all."

"Oh God, sorry. You must be knackered."

"I'm fine. I was tired enough to sleep through your snoring."

"I was snoring?" Sanne slapped a hand over her mouth.

"Just a little. You turned over if I poked you in the ribs."

"I don't remember any of that."

"Probably for the best." Meg wriggled out of bed and went to check Sanne's dressings. The rough start to the night had left them speckled with blood in numerous places. "I'll change these after you've had a shower."

"It feels much better," Sanne said, flexing her arm. "Actually, *I* feel much better." She trotted into Meg's room, where Meg heard her set the shower running and begin rummaging for underwear.

Meg wandered onto the landing so she didn't need to shout over the splash of the water. "You've got a bit more colour in your cheeks."

"Most of that's probably dirt," Sanne called back cheerfully.

Her lack of self-consciousness made Meg laugh. "Don't block my bloody drains up. I don't have time to fix them again."

The boiler whirring into life drowned out Sanne's reply. Meg checked her phone for messages, found none, and concluded that no news was good news. She pulled on an old sweater and carried the first aid kit down into the kitchen. As the kettle boiled, she found bacon, eggs, and bread that wasn't yet visibly mouldy, and set them all by the stove ready for Sanne. The last time Meg had attempted a fry-up, she had wandered off to find a book she thought Sanne might like and had become distracted by a bee trying to get out of her living room window. Oil had set itself on fire, smoke alarms had screeched, and Sanne had saved the day with a wet tea towel. The book had been a success, though, and the bee had flown off into the sunshine, so it hadn't been an unmitigated disaster.

"This got a bit soggy." Sanne walked into the kitchen, holding up her arm, displaying her sagging bandages like a bargain basement mummy.

"Come out here, and I'll look at it." Meg unlocked her patio doors, opened them wide, and beckoned Sanne into the garden. The patio was directly south facing, and she could feel the warmth of its stone flags begin to chase the chill from her bare feet. Catching the scent of the rose trained across the trellis, she tilted one of its flowers upward to smell it properly.

"I love this. It's gorgeous." She held the rose for Sanne. "Which one is it again?"

"It's 'The Pilgrim.'"

Like most of the plants in Meg's garden, Sanne had chosen and planted it herself, and often returned to prune it. Among many things, she had inherited her green fingers from her mum. In a stroke of good fortune, the majority of her paternal genes seemed to have been recessive.

It was too early for any of Meg's elderly neighbours to be awake, and the middle-aged couple at the far end of the terraced row were away on holiday, so birdsong and the steady play of water over rocks were the only sounds to break the stillness. Neither Meg nor Sanne spoke as Meg took the scissors from the first aid kit to snip away the dressings. They both craved peace and quiet, in the way that newly paroled junkies craved a fix.

At times, when the doubts crept in, Meg would come out here regardless of the weather, just to reassure herself that the past sixteen years of hard graft had paid off, that she really was a doctor who owned a house that didn't stink of cigarette smoke and cheap microwave meals, and didn't have its windows smashed every other month. These days, the only police she encountered were the ones who came to the hospital, where they spoke to her as a professional and not because her brother was one of their prime suspects. The thought gave her pause as she stuck down a flap of bandage and tapped the back of Sanne's hand to let her know she was finished. There was, of course, one police officer she saw on a very regular basis, but then Sanne was an exception. She had always been an exception.

"It's beautiful out here," Sanne said. Still suffused with heat from the shower, she looked healthy and content, but there was a sadness underscoring her words. Meg suspected she was contemplating the day ahead.

"There was nothing on my phone." Meg displayed its blank screen.

Sanne nodded. She had probably been afraid to ask. The news, or rather the lack of it, seemed to lighten her mood. "You up for bacon and eggs, then?" she asked.

"Yep. Do you need a hand?"

Sanne pretended to give the offer due consideration. "Think you'd be safe making the toast?"

Meg followed her into the kitchen. "Oh, I don't know. That's an awfully big responsibility."

"So long as you shout for me if it starts smoking, I think we'll be okay."

"Smoke. Shout," Meg said slowly. "I can do that."

Sanne sparked up the gas ring and slid the pan into place. The bacon rashers sizzled and shrank as they hit the hot pan. Busy slicing bread, Meg took a deep, appreciative breath. Fresh roses and greasy bacon: was there any more perfect start to a day?

Chapter Seven

A thin, early morning mist rose lazily from the valleys. Beads of dew made the grass and moss glisten beneath Sanne's boots, giving the hills an otherworldly atmosphere that was at once enchanting and sinister. The height her team had gained since abandoning the Mountain Rescue trucks had left the air cool, and she pulled her shirt closed, trying not to shiver. Nelson must have heard how ragged her breathing was, but he said nothing, merely staying close during their slog uphill and insisting that she eat half of his muesli bar. Having left Meg's place in good spirits, she was annoyed at how difficult the hike was proving. Her legs felt stiff and clumsy, and her rucksack dragged on her back. Her fitness level was above average, but the events of yesterday, followed by a disturbed night, had taken an unanticipated toll on her.

Ahead of them, Carlyle marched with the Mountain Rescue team and two National Trust rangers. His partner, Chris O'Brien, trailed a little behind, chatting to a uniformed officer and a small group of local volunteers. More officers and volunteers brought up the rear, their excited voices carrying easily across the open terrain and allowing Sanne to catch odd snippets of speculation: "Found naked," "That lady copper there with the short hair," and a confident announcement from an older male that he'd "stick the bastard's balls" in his thresher if he was the one to apprehend him. She glanced over her shoulder to see whether she recognised the speaker. Grundy, she thought, though she couldn't remember his first name. He ran the corner shop in Rowlee with his wife Doreen. A number of the other faces were familiar, too, but she had no names to go with them. During the day, a register would be taken of all the search participants, along with surreptitious photographs to record their identities. Even if background checks on the volunteers failed to yield anything useful, it would begin the process of elimination. Of the local villages, Rowlee was the closest to the scene, but numerous isolated farms, cottages, and small businesses would make the investigation's door-to-door enquiries a challenge, to say the least.

Threads of mist curled around the lower reaches of the cliffs at Laddaw Ridge, making them loom in and out of the landscape. Sanne couldn't believe she had managed to climb down them without breaking her neck. With hindsight, her efforts had been almost suicidal. Nelson was obviously thinking along the same lines, because he halted and whistled.

"Jesus, San."

She rubbed her sore arm, reassuring herself that that was the only damage done. "Yeah. I wouldn't even know where to start now, but at the time I just didn't think about it."

"No, I don't imagine you did."

They continued walking in silence, until Carlyle called a halt midway along the ridge. Before setting off from the rendezvous, he had split the group into two: a small number had taken a track leading below the ridge, to liaise with SOCO, while the bulk of the party had followed him onto the upper moors to scour for any evidence of the woman's route or that of her assailant, and for any structure in which she might have been held.

The instant everyone was assembled, Carlyle whipped out his map and proceeded to re-divide the remaining group.

"You, you, and you."

The three men he'd indicated looked across at him, bottles of water and half-eaten snacks poised at their lips.

"I want you to cover this sector," he told them. "See? I've marked it A1 on your plan."

They nodded slowly, one of them mopping his face with his T-shirt. They were all in their fifties and looked worn out before they had even started.

Nelson bowed his head and whispered directly into Sanne's ear. "It's no wonder he's so loved. His people skills are second to none." Carlyle was still pointing his finger at officers and volunteers, getting them to shuffle into an order based on their designated grid references.

Sanne smiled, but her focus was on her own map. "Sensible thing to do would be to head over here, to Gillot Tor." She kept her voice quiet, so that only Nelson could hear her. "It's a little beyond our boundary, but there are caves marked all along its lower section, on the same elevation as us. There are caves here at Laddaw, too, but they're down at the base of the cliffs, and Meg said the woman's injuries were consistent with a fall from height. If she was trying to get to safety, why would she run up onto the ridge?"

"She wouldn't," Nelson said. Then, before she could stop him, he raised his hand and his voice. "Sarge?"

Carlyle looked over in irritation. "What is it, Turay?"

"Are the cavers going to Gillot Tor today?"

The question seemed to wrong-foot Carlyle. He fumbled with his notes, flicking the pages so quickly that they snagged on the wire spiral at the top. "No. They'll be here around Laddaw, today and probably tomorrow. There's a number of potholes leading into limestone caves, about half a mile back that way." He pointed in the direction from which they had just approached. "I spoke with DI Stanhope last night, and she agreed that in all probability the perp took the woman up onto the ridge and pushed her over the edge. If the cavers find evidence to confirm she was held nearby, we can abandon the wider search." He gave Nelson a look that a parent might give a particularly stupid child. "Besides which, as you can see, Gillot Tor is not within the specified parameters."

"No," Nelson said. "It's all of a mile outside them."

Carlyle misinterpreted the sarcastic response as acquiescence. "You and Jensen are to lead a small group through sectors C3, 4, and 5, and I think that will just about cover it."

"What about you, Sarge?" one of the officers called out. "Your name on that list anywhere?"

Carlyle closed his notepad and slipped it back into his rucksack. "I'm going to lead the fingertip search at the cliff base where the woman was found. Apparently, there's a path down from here that will save me from having to re-enact Detective Jensen's heroic climb."

His announcement was greeted with muted catcalls and a general air of disbelief, which he ignored as he settled his bag on his back and drank from a canteen of water. Sanne contemplated the vast area he had delegated to her and Nelson, and wondered at what point he had realised their task was insurmountable. Had he already been hatching a plot to abandon them as he walked up here? Or was it only on arriving at the ridge that he had decided to switch his own efforts to a search already half completed and with a far greater likelihood of finding something? She couldn't bring herself to ask the questions, though. If he was going below the ridge, he would be nowhere near her, and that could only be a good thing.

He shouted across to her as the group began to break up. "You got your whistle, Jensen? I'd hate to have to tell the boss we lost the little one."

She smiled sweetly at him. "No chance of losing you, is there?"

Several of her team sniggered as he jammed a cap over his conspicuous red hair and turned his back on them. Nelson managed not to react, but when no one was looking he grinned and dropped a toffee into her palm.

She stuffed the sweet into her mouth and spoke around it. "Are we set then?" An urge to get started and see what was out there had replaced her earlier weariness.

Nelson opened his arms, encouraging her to take the lead. "Ready when you are, partner."

Sanne took the tea from Nelson and sipped at it where she stood. Aching, sticky all over, and thoroughly disheartened, she felt like sinking onto the nearest peat hag instead.

"You okay?" he asked quietly.

"Yep." She swallowed the dregs from the plastic cup and gave it back to him. Other officers and volunteers were nearby, so she was reluctant to stop for long.

"You can take a break, you know. Most folk have already had a sandwich or something."

"I'll eat mine in a bit."

Her tone ended the exchange. She didn't want to tell him she was afraid that she would never get up again if she sat for any length of time.

It was late afternoon, and the haze had burned off hours ago, leaving the skies blue and the sun tempered only by a brisk but tepid wind. With nowhere for the team to shelter, energy levels were flagging. Nelson had already called up for fresh water supplies and then for a Mountain Rescue medic to treat two volunteers who were verging on heat exhaustion. The morale, so high at the outset, had been quashed by the enormity of the task: mile upon mile of inhospitable terrain, which had so far yielded no clues, but which was liable to snap ankles on a whim. Many of the volunteers were familiar with the moors and had known what they were letting themselves in for, but even they were stopping for more and more frequent breaks.

A perspiring young woman jogged over to present Nelson with an evidence bag containing a weather-faded crisp packet. As he nodded his thanks, the woman strode away, her head held high.

"I blame Gil Grissom," he said, dropping the bag into his rucksack. He unwrapped a Twix and shared it with Sanne. "Everyone thinks a crime can be solved in forty-five minutes or less."

The Twix melted all over Sanne's fingers. She sucked them clean before she spoke. "You mean that the telly lies about us? That we're not all stunningly photogenic and accompanied by a thumping soundtrack and moody yet flattering lighting?"

Nelson grinned. "Have you taken a close look at some of the SOCO lads recently?"

"I try not to. A couple of them scare me."

They stopped laughing as someone waved them over to a dirty mass of white fluff, wedged among rocks near a small pool.

Sanne sighed. "Sheep or hare?"

"Sheep," Nelson said without hesitation. "Unless it was a bloody massive hare."

The volunteer was evidently pleased with his find. "Think it might mean something?" he asked as they approached. To their credit, the three older men standing with him rolled their eyes and smirked. The ewe had met her demise some weeks ago, and little other than teeth, bones, and fleece remained.

"You're a bleedin' halfwit, Ned," one of the men said.

Ned looked hurt. "Lots of violent criminals start off by slaughtering household pets," he said piously.

Sanne crouched by the carcass. "I think she probably lost her footing on these rocks, maybe trying to get to the water." The position of the skeleton suggested the poor creature had ended up trapped between two of the boulders and died a slow, terrible death, but Sanne kept that to herself. She stood and clapped Ned on the back. "You've got a good eye, though, mate."

His sunburnt face glowed even hotter. "Thank you, Officer Sanney."

"It's Sann-er," she murmured, but she was already turning away, a familiar colour having drawn her attention. "Everybody just stay still," she said, and they all froze like statues. "Nelson, look just to the left of the pool. The orange strand. Do you see it?"

"Got it." He herded the men off the peat and onto the low rocks.

Taking a roundabout approach, her focus on the crumbling ground, Sanne walked over to the bog-fed pond. Beside two pronounced indentations in the mud, a shred of bright orange rope undulated gently as the wind played around it. Like the unfortunate sheep, one end of it had been trapped between two rocks, and she could clearly imagine the woman kneeling at the pond's edge, lowering her head to drink, and placing her hands in such a position that the rope binding them became snagged.

"Get SOCO up here," Sanne said, but Nelson was already making the call.

"Did you find something?" Ned asked her. "Was she here?"

"Yes, I think so." The rope was securely held in place, so she left it for SOCO to document and collect and went to join the men on the rocks. With a boost from Ned, she climbed onto the highest boulder and surveyed the section of moor that surrounded them. None of the volunteers had made it beyond this point, about two miles west of Laddaw Ridge, well away from the path she had been running along yesterday. Several sheep tracks meandered across the moor, any one of which the woman could have been following, but given her condition it was unlikely she could have reached Laddaw from anywhere much farther than this.

"Well, that pisses on Carlyle's chips a bit, doesn't it?" Nelson said, hauling himself up to stand beside Sanne.

"It does." She looked out at the wild, windswept plateau. "But where on earth would she have come from? You can't drive here, and there are no buildings, not within our agreed boundary. So what the fuck did he do? Pitch a tent?"

"For all we know, that's exactly what he did. If he hid it in one of these ditches, no one would have heard or seen a thing."

"They're called groughs," Sanne said absently, trying to revise her theories to incorporate a portable crime scene. She couldn't do it—the idea seemed ridiculous—and she found herself half-agreeing with the notion that the woman had only been brought to the moors once her captor had decided to get rid of her.

"What are?" Nelson asked, and it took Sanne a couple of seconds to realise he hadn't moved on from her original statement.

"The ditches. They're groughs, and the mounds of peat are called hags." She formed the corresponding shapes with her hands, but her thoughts were elsewhere, wondering where the splinters in the woman's heels could have come from if she had been marched out here to die, and why, if that was the case, she had been allowed to kneel by the pond to drink.

Sanne made a quiet noise of frustration and decided to go with what her gut had been telling her all day: that Carlyle's cavers were looking in the wrong caves. She pointed to the sheep tracks, the easiest way to cross the bogland and knee-deep heather between her and Gillot Tor. "Is it worth regrouping and focusing on these paths? Maybe just use the uniforms? They'll be less liable to wander over footprints or signs of a struggle. Half the volunteers are done in, anyway."

"I'll call everyone together," Nelson said. "We've got, what? About five, maybe six hours of daylight left?"

She shifted around and gauged the position of the sun, already some way over to the west. "If we want to get back to the trucks in one piece, we've got less than that."

"You didn't pack a torch?"

She smiled. "I'll be fine. I packed a *head* torch, mate. It's you I'm worried about."

They heard Ned's voice raised in warning and jumped down to the lower rocks. He had run to greet the first arrivals, urging them to stay well away from "his" discovery.

"Do you want to tell them, or shall I?" Nelson asked in an undertone.

Sanne winced. No one would be happy about this. The officers would be nearing the end of their shift, while the volunteers were being disbanded just as things got interesting.

Keeping their hands out of public view, she and Nelson played a covert game of rock-paper-scissors.

"Bollocks," she whispered, as Nelson's "paper" wrapped over her "rock."

Nelson's attempt at a sympathetic expression failed gleefully. "I promise to intervene if they try to chuck you in the pond."

She punched him in his biceps and strode over to break the news to the gathered crowd.

The three-year-old boy looked directly at Meg and emptied his cup of blackcurrant juice all over the bed sheets. His mum, who seemed barely old enough to tie her own shoelaces, let alone procreate, tittered and ruffled his hair.

"Oh, Bailey-Kaden, that's naughty." Her protestation was as impactful as a butterfly chastising a lion. "He must be feeling better," she said to Meg and beamed at her son.

"Yes, it's amazing what a dose of paracetamol will do," Meg said with only the faintest hint of sarcasm. "I'm guessing you hadn't given him any before you phoned the ambulance."

"Oh, no!" The young woman looked aghast, as if Meg had just made the most outlandish of suggestions. "When I rang 999, they told me not to give him anything to eat or drink."

Meg nodded. It was the same old song, over and over. The tune never varied, and it irritated the hell out of her. "And in the hours before that, when he was feverish and miserable, you didn't think to give him any then, either?"

The girl stared at her, arms folded, her mouth curled into a sulky pout. "I didn't have none in."

"Of course you didn't." Meg only just managed not to snap at her. A bottle of generic paracetamol suspension cost about £1.50, was readily available in the supermarkets, and was a commonsense mainstay for anyone with a young child. "We'll send you home with a bottle and one of these advice leaflets." The girl needed an advice *anthology*, not a leaflet, but it was the best Meg could do. The child was well dressed and obviously loved, so there were no concerns regarding neglect. If she referred every dim parent to Social Services, she would singlehandedly collapse the system.

"A nurse will be in with the extra medicine in a few minutes," she said, and left Bailey-Kaden splashing his hands and his mum in blackcurrant.

Outside the cubicle, she checked her pager, her phone, and her watch. It was almost five p.m., and she had no messages. She sank into a chair at a free computer terminal and began the process of discharging the child.

"Did you read her the riot act?" Liz called over. She was busy squirting blood into culture bottles at the sink beside the nurses' station.

Meg hit *enter* and snarled as the screen froze. "No." She tapped the key repeatedly and with increasing force. "I don't know what's wrong with me today. I just don't think my heart's in it."

"Your heart wandering out there on the moors, by any chance?"

Liz probably didn't mean anything by that, but it was such a lovely, apt turn of phrase that Meg smiled, despite her dark mood. "You might have hit the nail on the head there."

The needle tinkled in the sharps bin as Liz discarded it. "I've got a friend works up on ITU. She told me our mystery woman is as well as can be expected."

"Max said as much this morning." Meg began to type rapidly as the computer decided to behave itself. "He said he might try waking her in the next couple of days." She hit the wrong key and erased everything she had just entered. "Oh, for fuck's sake."

Liz's hand closed over hers, stilling her fingers. "Have you had a break today?"

Meg answered with a shrug. She honestly couldn't remember.

"Why don't you take one when you've finished that? There are only four patients in the waiting room, and they're all heading to Minors."

The computer saved the discharge summary at the second attempt. Meg glanced around. The department had several beds empty and a number of medics chatting or trying to look busy. She was senior to many of them, but she wasn't indispensable.

"You'll page me if the Bat Phone goes?" she said.

"If it's something we can't cope with for half an hour, then yes," Liz replied in her stern mum voice, her hands planted on her hips. It had the dual effect of making Meg laugh and realise how ridiculous she was being.

"I'm bloody starving," she said, and hit *print* before she could jinx herself and make the phone ring.

The hospital canteen was on the verge of closing when Meg skidded to a halt in front of its counter. They'd run out of everything savoury, with the exception of a limp corned beef sandwich. Unwilling to risk it, she asked for apple crumble and custard, and came away with a portion generous enough to sustain her for the rest of the week. A glare from a cleaner warned her not to try sitting at any of the canteen's tables, so she wandered back toward the A&E staffroom, but as she reached the stairs, she changed her mind and headed for the ITU. The nurses there were all familiar faces, who turned a blind eye to her carton of pudding, but the sight of someone far more unexpected made her pause on the threshold of room three.

"Hey," she said, and Emily jerked her head up. She began to stand, but Meg waved her down and walked to the foot of the bed. "Great minds think alike, eh?"

"Apparently so." Emily was perched uneasily on the edge of her chair. She touched her fingers to the bed sheets, several inches away from the woman's hand, and then leaned back again without making contact. "I'm on my break."

"Yeah, me too." Meg felt a twinge of guilt. She had been so intent yesterday on running the trauma and keeping an eye on Sanne that she hadn't thought to check how Emily was. Judging by the dark shadows beneath her eyes and by her presence in the ITU, she was far from all right. She also appeared to be on the verge of bolting, so Meg shifted her scrutiny to the woman's chart instead, which provided her with a conversation opener.

"Did you read this? She's a hell of a lot better than I expected."

Emily's demeanour brightened a fraction. "I know. Dr. Maxwell was here when I came in. If she continues to improve at this rate, he's going to try waking her tomorrow afternoon."

Meg nodded, her finger tracking the lines of figures and notes. After coping well with the surgery, the woman had responded to the drugs treating the cerebral oedema and shown no further signs of bleeding. She was running a mild temperature, but otherwise her observations were within normal parameters, and her latest blood results were promising. Taking the opportunity to look at her without having to focus on her injuries, or what treatments might be necessary, Meg saw a woman who must have been slim even before her recent weight loss. Her broad shoulders spoke of an athleticism probably associated with swimming or climbing, but whatever her sport, her fitness had stood her in good stead. It would have allowed her to quickly metabolise the drugs her assailant had pumped into her, given her the strength to escape, and helped her to survive the additional insult of her severe injuries.

"Have you ever seen anything like this?" Emily's soft question cut into Meg's train of thought. There were tears brimming in her eyes.

Meg gave her a canteen napkin and sat in an adjacent chair, watching her try to avoid smearing her mascara. "I've treated rape and assault victims, but nothing where the suffering has been so prolonged or so fucking vindictive." She took a breath that smelled incongruously of crumble and antiseptic. Although the arm lying across the woman's abdomen was wrapped in bandages, Meg couldn't forget the damage concealed beneath. Like an animal trapped in a snare, the woman had almost degloved her hand trying to undo her bonds.

"I couldn't sleep last night," Emily whispered. "I couldn't even lie in bed. I just walked, room to room. I tried to watch something or read something, but mostly I just walked."

"Didn't do too brilliantly myself," Meg said. "Do you need to speak to someone? There are counsellors in the department, peer support…" She trailed off as Emily shook her head.

"It's okay. This has helped. Thanks." Emily began to collect the pieces of the napkin she had unconsciously shredded. "They won't let me come in here again if I leave a mess."

Meg gathered a couple of strips from the floor and dropped them into Emily's palm. "If they're okay with me bringing my lunch in, I think they'll overlook a bit of tissue."

"It smells really good. What did you get?" Emily asked, and then looked mortified when her stomach rumbled.

"Enough apple crumble to feed the five thousand. I'll go and cadge another spoon and dish from the nurses." Meg tapped the overbed table with her plastic spoon to overrule Emily's weak signs of protest. "You'll be doing me a favour by helping me eat it. If you make me finish all this by myself, I'll curl up in the corner there and sleep through the rest of the shift."

"G'back, g'back, g'back!"

A tan-and-white ball of feathers shot up from the heather in front of Sanne and hurtled out of harm's way, its warning screech giving an air of foreboding to hills blazing beneath a glorious sunset.

"What on earth was that?" Nelson had his hand on his heart, as if checking for a terror-induced arrhythmia.

"Grouse," Sanne said. "I think they get a kick out of scaring folk half to death." The birds were a common feature of the moors, lying out of sight until unwitting hikers happened upon them, and then flying to safety in a clamour of wings and cackling.

Nelson dabbed his brow with his hanky. "No wonder people shoot the buggers."

Her answering smile faded as Carlyle's voice came across the comms.

"Jensen, Turay. Status report, please."

Nelson gesticulated in a way that would have made his mother blush. Sanne slapped his arm.

"At least he said please," she mouthed silently. Then, speaking aloud, "Just reached the tarn, Sarge. Nothing found so far."

"Copy that," Carlyle said, and Sanne listened to similar negative updates from the remaining officers on Corvenden Moss.

After hearing about their earlier find, Carlyle had become keen to lead the second stage of the search. The team up top hadn't wasted daylight waiting for him to join them, but as soon as he had made it onto Laddaw Ridge, he had taken great delight in interfering. On his orders, Sanne and Nelson had followed a path that meandered through rocks for twenty minutes before trying to lead them off a precipice.

Considering that particular assignment at an end, they had spread their map out across the heather, and, on Sanne's prompting, decided to take a narrow track toward a tarn near the base of Gillot Tor. The tarn itself wasn't large enough to warrant a name, and the area around it appeared isolated, hemmed in by a succession of rock formations and the cliffs of the tor. On the map, a sporadic rash of red triangles to its west marked blocked-off potholes and unsafe entrances to a rudimentary cave system.

The warning icons pulled Sanne in like a siren's call. She knew there were other possibilities, most of them more likely than this one, but she couldn't move away from the thought that, somewhere close by, the perp might have constructed a makeshift dungeon. Although

Gillot Tor was a mile beyond the established search boundary, that boundary was only an estimate. Another mile might not mean much to someone running for her life.

Afraid that Nelson would advise caution, Sanne hadn't voiced any of this to him. One word of dissent and she would have had to cede to his better judgement. But it wasn't as if she was planning to go potholing. She just wanted to get near enough to Gillot Tor to get a feel for it, and if they got to the tarn and then decided to go a little farther, where was the harm in that?

In the end, Nelson's ineptitude with a map had made things simple for her. He had followed her lead without question. All that remained for her to do was convince Carlyle it had been his idea.

Her toes just touching the spongy shore of the tarn, she knelt and dipped her fingers into its water. This one was clearer than the last. Instead of disappearing in its murky depths, her hand remained visible, tinted brownish-orange and coated with tiny flecks of peat. The water was warm on the surface, so she plunged her hand deeper, allowing the chill to numb her fingers, before pulling them out and placing them onto her forehead. She closed her eyes in pleasure as the heat there dissipated. The crack of Nelson's knees and a soft splash of water told her he was following her example.

They didn't rest for long. There was no obvious path, so they used the patches of vegetation as stepping stones to circle the tarn without soaking their boots. The air was cooler here, the rocks and the steep hillside channelling the wind and casting the moor into shadow. The droplets of water at Sanne's hairline soon made her face cold, and her damp shirt clung to her unpleasantly.

"Never thought I'd say this, but I miss the sun." She could see goose pimples rising on Nelson's arms as he nodded.

"That poor girl," he said. "Escaping from God only knows what and finding herself in the middle of this."

Sanne had spent the day trying not to think about such things, and the unwelcome reminder sent a prickle of goose pimples across her own skin. If the woman had screamed, the only response she would have heard was an echo. It must have been terrifying.

Shaking off the image, Sanne returned her attention to the ground, scanning for signs that anyone had recently passed that way. The cotton grass and heather sprang back into shape the moment she lifted each foot, making it unlikely they would find a discernible trail, but there was a chance that the peat would hold a footprint.

"This is bloody daft," Nelson muttered, pulling his leg from a bog he hadn't spotted. The peat made an obscene sucking sound as it released his foot. "We're both knackered, we can't see properly any more, we're miles away from the pick-up point, and I need a wee."

"Go for a wild one." Sanne consulted the map, altered her heading slightly to aim for the caves, and set off again. "I promise I won't look."

"Of all the people on this moor, San, you're the least likely to sneak a peek."

"True. Carlyle would probably insist on comparing sizes."

Nelson let out a bark of laughter. "He'd lose," he said and ducked between two rocks.

Leaving him to it, Sanne scrambled into a grough that threaded up toward the side of the hill. Wind gusted through the passage, blowing grit into her eyes and lashing the straps of her rucksack against her. She heard Nelson shout her name, and as she took a breath to reply, the cold air made her cough. Her eyes watering, she sneezed twice and fumbled for a tissue to blow her nose.

"Nelson?" She pulled the tissue away from her face and sneezed again. "Fuck. Nelson?"

"San? You okay?" He appeared over the ridge of the grough. Crouching down on its edge, he regarded her with a concerned expression.

"I can smell smoke," she said. "Can you see a fire?"

He scrambled quickly up out of sight again, no doubt sharing the same thought: that the recent hot weather had left the moor as dry as a tinderbox, and one carelessly discarded cigarette would be enough to spark it up.

"I can't see anything," he yelled back. Then, softer and closer, as if he'd got down from a high vantage point, "No smoke. No fire. Are you sure?"

She had walked farther up the grough, and she was sure. Her pulse beat against her temples, and she cried out when a hand closed around her arm.

"Fucking hell!" She whipped around, leading with her fist and forcing Nelson to step hastily out of her range.

"Easy, partner."

She bent over, panting. Somewhere beyond the sound of her own gasps, she heard him sniff the air experimentally.

"Definitely smoke," he said as she straightened. "I'll call it in, just in case."

She put her hand on his, stopping him from activating his radio. "And then what? We just wait for Carlyle's Cavalry to arrive?"

That gave him pause. He allowed her to lower his hand.

"Why don't we see what there is to call in, first?" She could hardly believe she was making the suggestion, but they were going to get summoned back to the pick-up point within the hour, and she couldn't bear the thought of going home empty-handed, when they might be on the verge of a genuine break in the case. "Ten minutes? If we don't reach the source by then, or we spot a moor fire, we'll call it in."

He checked his watch and nodded slowly. "Okay. Ten minutes. Go."

She set off before she could second-guess her decision. The gully was gently sloping and easy to negotiate. Keeping to its centre and away from its friable edges, she broke into a trot. The smell of burning gradually became stronger even as she became less convinced that the moor was on fire. In her earpiece, Carlyle barked an order to regroup on Laddaw Ridge. Ignoring him, she dragged herself above the lip of the grough and crouched there, coughing against the irritation in her throat. By the time Nelson joined her, she had her torch pointed at a thin plume of grey.

"Bingo," she said.

The torch picked out a dark circle, half buried by a rock fall, almost invisible except for the thread of smoke guiding the eye.

Without speaking, Nelson helped her up, and they walked toward the narrow gap. She could hear him breathing heavily as they drew closer, and wondered whether he too was afraid that someone might be lying in wait to attack them. They had no weapons, nothing with which to defend themselves, and their backup was currently heading in the other direction, toward Laddaw. She strained to listen for any sounds that were out of the ordinary, but there was only the crunch of heather beneath their boots, and the rustle of wind through the cotton grass. She was beginning to relax, when Nelson grabbed her arm.

"Jesus! What?"

"Look." He swirled his torch beam to direct her attention.

She saw what he was indicating, and dismissed her fears of ambush. Whoever had started this fire must be long gone, otherwise he would have ensured that nothing was left for them to find.

"I'll have to call it in now, San."

"I know. I guess he didn't pitch that tent after all."

She felt like crying, not out of sadness but out of anger that someone could have dragged another human being to a place like this, bound her, abused her, and then left her alone. She stared at the hole that led into the depths of Gillot Tor. In front of it, smoke drifted and danced in the breeze. A little came from the cave itself, but most was rising up from the remains of a wooden pallet by the entrance. The wood was charred but not destroyed, and even from a distance Sanne was certain of one thing: it would be a match for the splinters SOCO had pulled from the woman's feet.

Chapter Eight

The rock was coarse and unforgiving beneath Sanne's buttocks. She wondered whether the old wives' tale was true, whether sitting on cold, hard surfaces for a prolonged time really did cause haemorrhoids, and, if so, what exactly a haemorrhoid was and how she would know if she had one. She made a mental note to ask Meg, whenever she was finally allowed to go home.

"So, can either of you explain that to me? Jensen?"

In front of her, his hair aflame in the glow of a torch, and his face only a shade less red, Carlyle seemed to be waiting for a response. As she had missed the first part of his question and couldn't tell him why she'd not been paying attention, she looked to Nelson for assistance.

"Because Sanne had already smelled the smoke by then," he said, and she realised Carlyle must have been asking why they'd disregarded his order to head back to the ridge.

"And you took it upon yourselves to wander blindly across the moor on a wild goose chase?"

"Wild grouse," Nelson murmured, and feigned innocence when Carlyle glared at him.

Sanne ran her fingertips across the gritstone, letting it wear away her skin like an over-keen emery board. Such distractions were a coping method she had used for as long as she could remember. They stopped her from flinching and cringing at raised voices or raised fists, and from yelling back and getting herself in even more trouble. Not that she and Nelson were really in trouble now. They might have pissed Carlyle off by proving him wrong and stealing his glory, but he wasn't stupid enough to report them for persevering and actually finding something.

Whatever else he might have said was cut off by the roar of the police helicopter, swooping low on its final approach. Someone much higher up the pecking order than Carlyle was evidently convinced that the crime scene had been located, and had increased the budget for the case accordingly. In a fraction of the time it had taken Sanne's group to cover the distance by truck and on foot that morning, the chopper had already completed two round-trips to drop off equipment and personnel, and it was currently on its third. Powerful floodlights, brought in on the first flight, illuminated the mouth of the cave, and for the past two hours, forensics officers in Tyvek suits had been scurrying in and out like termites.

Experienced enough to leave the scene undisturbed, Sanne and Nelson had stayed out of the cave, but one of the younger lads from SOCO had stopped to speak to them and confirmed that an accelerant had been used to start a fire in a chamber close to the entrance. It had burned poorly in the damp atmosphere, leaving hair, fibres, and bodily fluids, which were being collected for analysis. Until SOCO cleared the scene, there was nothing more that Sanne and Nelson could do, but Carlyle hadn't yet given them permission to leave.

As the helicopter landed and the beat of its rotor blades slowed, Sanne bent forward, her eyes closing of their own accord. She forced her head up again as she sensed Nelson take a step toward her, but he merely sat by her on the rock. She leaned into him, grateful for his support.

As if disgusted by this show of solidarity, Carlyle strode away to greet Eleanor, the only person to leave the helicopter's landing zone.

She, however, went straight past him, making a beeline for Sanne and Nelson. "Well, if it isn't Nancy Drew and her favourite Hardy Boy," she called.

Sanne got to her feet. "I think Nancy Drew had better hair than me, boss."

"And the Hardy Boys were white," Nelson chipped in.

Eleanor took a moment to observe the activity at the cave. "Nice work," she said, turning back to them. "But I'm assuming you're not just sticking around for me to get here and pat you on the head."

"Not really, boss." Nelson shrugged but offered no further explanation, and Sanne developed a keen interest in her bootlaces.

"The helicopter's waiting for you." Eleanor laughed at their startled reactions. "I need you at your desks bright and early tomorrow, so I'm not going to ask you to walk back."

"Oh." Sanne swayed and felt Nelson pull her back into position.

"What about Carlyle?" he asked.

"He can't go anywhere until he's briefed me, can he?" Eleanor's tone implied she already knew everything there was to know about the day's events. She smiled, her teeth gleaming in the moonlight. "So he'll just have to stay out here a little while longer."

Three and a half years of working shifts as a uniformed officer had taught Sanne to function on very little sleep. She could also demolish a hot meal in less than five minutes, and catnap while sitting bolt upright with her boots on, although those were more questionable talents. Nelson was proficient at the latter skills, but not so adept at the first, so Sanne made coffee strong enough to stand the spoon up in and put it on his desk the moment he arrived.

"Got three sugars in it," she said, her voice making him recoil like a drunk with the mother of all hangovers. "I also got you this."

His expression shifted from pained to blissful as he took the paper bag. "Runny egg?" he asked, breathing in the scent of artery-clogging fat.

"Of course. I thought you might need a treat, so I got you bacon *and* sausage."

"Don't ever leave me." He spoke through the first bite of his sandwich, making egg-yolk drip onto his chin.

"The boss is briefing us at seven thirty." Sanne checked her watch. It was 7:22. "Plenty of time to get that down your neck."

A third of the barm cake already devoured, Nelson gave her a thumbs-up and mumbled a question that she interpreted as "any news on the vic?"

"She's 'stable,' which Meg reckons is one up from 'critical but stable.' They might try to wake her later today. Meg's on a twilight, but she's going in early if the neurosurgeon gives her a shout."

Nelson washed down his mouthful with a gulp of coffee. "Any word from SOCO?"

"I've not heard anything yet, but I think that's what the briefing will be about. Speaking of which…" Her prompt made him cram in the last of his breakfast and grab his mug. She shook her head at his bulging cheeks. "One of these days you're going to make yourself sick."

The office had filled up during Nelson's speed-eating feat. Teaspoons clinked against mugs, and the smell of coffee, toast, and microwave porridge drifted through from the kitchen. With such early starts, people tended to wait until they arrived for their shift before eating breakfast.

Sanne and Nelson filed into the incident room ahead of George and Fred.

"I've put in an application to swap partners," Fred announced loudly. "I want to work with Detective Jensen, so her women's intuition rubs off on me."

Sanne looked back and arched an eyebrow. "I'm not rubbing anything off on you, Detective Aspinall."

Fred's ears turned pink as Nelson and George laughed. Thrice divorced, with six children, he was in his mid-fifties, but that didn't stop him from flirting with Sanne at every opportunity. Nor was he deterred by the fact that she was, as he put it, "a big old lezzer." The first time he said that, he might have been trying to push her buttons and gauge his limits, but they had got along just fine after the only thing she objected to was his use of the words "big" and "old."

He linked his arm in hers. "Sit next to me, love, so we can compare notes."

Squeezing his arm, she allowed him to lead her to a couple of spare chairs. "I love what you've done with your hair," she said.

He rubbed his head and made a show of preening. He was as bald as a coot.

The chatter faded when Eleanor walked in. She opened a file on the computer and perched on a desk just to the right of the overhead screen, which now showed a wide-angled exterior shot of the cave at Gillot Tor.

"Okay, this is where we're at." She waited out the clicks and crackles as her team readied pens and notepads. "SOCO have been at the scene overnight and through the early hours. The labs are expected to take three to four days to come back with DNA and fibre analysis, but it's looking certain that the vic was held in a small, well-concealed chamber, approximately forty metres from the cave entrance. A thread of rope matching the one she was bound with has been recovered, along with several hairs, and traces of blood, vomit, faeces, and urine."

George raised his hand and cleared his throat. "No semen?"

Eleanor switched to an interior shot before answering. "SOCO went over the area with a Wood's lamp, but nothing showed. Obviously, the labs will be taking a close look at the fluid samples. Conditions in the cave are far from ideal. There's standing water, the walls are wet, and the perp covered as much as he could with petrol before he sparked it up. No prints have been recovered, and my gut feeling is that all the DNA will point to the vic. But there is a bit of light at the end of the tunnel, so to speak."

Another image, taken at dawn, showing a rough dirt track down a rugged hillside.

"One of the Rangers took SOCO out here this morning. The track meets up with an access road for a long-abandoned barn, a road that in turn connects to the Snake Pass. It tapers out a little under three miles from the scene, and yes"—she smiled at George as he began to lift his hand—"we found tyre treads, which are being cast as we speak. The use of this route—and I think we have to assume this is his access and egress—points to a perp with in-depth knowledge of the area. That he took the time to return to the scene to destroy evidence suggests we're looking for someone with a certain amount of acumen, even if he only managed a half-arsed job in the end."

She flicked through a series of images, before alighting on one that made Sanne avert her eyes.

"This is the photograph we've released to the press." Eleanor let that sink in for a few seconds.

Sanne steeled herself to look again and managed not to react this time. The photograph had been taken in the ITU, with a harsh light rigged to provide the necessary detail. The woman's eyes, temporarily relieved of the tape that had kept them closed, were mere slits amid balloons of bruising. The tube in her mouth distorted her lips, and bandages concealed what remained of her hair.

"I know, I know," Eleanor said, in response to the general discord. "We're pissing in the wind with this, but somewhere a parent or a partner might be missing her, and there's always a chance we'll get lucky." She shut the computer down, and the image vanished.

Sanne slowly uncurled her toes, and the pain from where they had rubbed against her hiking boots began to ease. When she looked at the notepad in front of her, she could still see the shape of the woman's face in silhouette. She stared at it as she listened to Eleanor switch Carlyle and his partner to door-to-door enquiries, leaving George and Fred with Missing Persons and the new telephone hotline that was to open that morning. By the time she heard her own name, the paper showed nothing but her notes.

"Sanne, Nelson, the chopper will pick you up from the playing field in twenty-five minutes."

Snapping to attention, Sanne hoped her jaw hadn't dropped as far as she feared. Her reaction made Eleanor smile.

"One of the SOCO chaps is going to take you on a walk-through of the scene," Eleanor explained. "I want to know what your impressions are."

"Haven't you been in there, boss?" Nelson asked.

"Yes, but three opinions are better than one, don't you think?"

Nelson nodded, no sign of tiredness now as he sat up straight and beamed at Sanne. They both understood that this was their reward for their efforts the previous day. In her eagerness to get going, Sanne almost bolted from her seat the moment Eleanor ended the briefing.

Eleanor's voice stopped her in her tracks.

"Sanne?"

"Yes, boss?"

"You heard from your doctor friend today?"

Sanne nodded uneasily. She felt as if she had been caught cheating on an exam, conferring with someone who had insider knowledge. "She called me this morning," she admitted.

"Did she tell you they might be waking our vic up later?"

"Yes."

"Good. I want you there with me when they do."

Sanne clamped her teeth shut before her jaw gave her away again. "Okay," she said, once she was certain she had a modicum of control.

"I don't go in for all this touchy-feely bullshit, but you spent a while talking to her on the moors." Eleanor indicated that Sanne should walk with her. "So, there's a chance she might have heard you and might respond to you when we try to interview her."

"Pretty slim chance, boss." Sanne didn't want to talk Eleanor out of her decision, but her reasoning seemed out of character.

Eleanor lowered her voice. "That's the official reason, at any rate. Unofficially, sitting in a hospital room with Sergeant Carlyle holds all the appeal of going for a root canal."

Sanne laughed and then put a hand over her mouth. "Message received and understood, boss," she whispered.

❖

The hand Meg took hold of felt fragile, the bones delicate beneath its tissue-paper skin. She rested her fingers against the wrist's visible pulse, counting out its irregularities and trying to gauge whether they were more pronounced than on her last visit.

Down the corridor, someone wailed, then began to weep, then stopped to wail again, the sound setting Meg's teeth on edge. She left her chair to pace to the small window, which looked out onto a patch of dry grass adjacent to the car park. Crates of milk were being delivered from a lorry, and a sparrow was vying with a goldfinch for the best nuts on the bird feeder.

"She had a settled night, and there have been no problems this morning."

The nurse's voice pulled Meg away from the uninspiring view. She had never seen the woman before, though that wasn't unusual; staff turnover on the unit was an ongoing problem. She adjusted the bed's pillows before she took her seat again, and the nurse smiled in approval at her apparent devotion.

"Did she manage her breakfast?" Meg asked. She fought the urge to return to the window and open it wide. The room was unpleasantly hot, and the lingering smell of a water infection pervaded its every corner.

"Most of it." The nurse checked a fluid balance chart and closed the file with a snap. "She likes scrambled eggs."

"Funny. She always used to hate them." Meg ran a hand through her mum's hair, making her mum beam at her with wet, pink gums. "She needs her teeth in. They keep leaving them out. There was supposed to be a note about it in her file."

"Sorry, Miss…" The nurse checked the nameplate on the door and took a chance on Meg's surname. "Fielding. I don't usually work on this floor, but I'll get someone in to sort that for you."

"Not for me," Meg said as the nurse left the room. "I've got teeth. See?" She smiled, baring hers.

Her mum chortled. "Teeth," she said, and then looked forlorn, as if she had only just realised hers were missing.

"I'll have a look for them, Mum. Stay there, okay?"

Meg left the bathroom door open so she could hear if her mum tried to get up. When Connie Fielding had been only sixty-two years old, she had started to grow uncharacteristically forgetful. Within eighteen months, her vascular dementia had advanced to a stage where she could no longer care for herself. She forgot to eat, even when the food was in front of her, and she became doubly incontinent. She would allow strangers into her home, and leave the door wide open when she ventured outside. She still wandered now, but the doors at each end of the Unit for the Elderly Mentally Ill required a code to unlock them, which meant that Meg no longer had to field calls from the people living in the house where her mum had grown up, letting her know that her mum was sitting on their garden swing again. The nursing home fees were a small fortune, but for the last two years her mum had been safe and clean and as happy as anyone could be who had lost all sense of herself.

"Right. Open wide." The bottom teeth clacked against the top set as Meg fitted them into her mum's mouth. "Much better."

"Meg." Her mum drew the word out, obviously grappling for the right information.

"Yes, Mum, it's Meg." Meg raised her mum's hand and kissed the back of it, taking genuine pleasure in the tactility of their relationship. On a good day, her mum recognised her. On a bad day, she sat politely indifferent to Meg's company and attention. For years, Meg had only spoken to her through her brother, and—thanks to his lifestyle choices—those conversations had been ill-tempered and sporadic at best.

The last time Meg had seen the sound-minded version of her mum, the hand she was currently holding had slapped her so hard she had gone to work with a swollen jaw. Nothing had really improved until the dementia had taken hold. Occasionally, the hours she spent with her mum felt like recompense for the time she had missed out on. At other times they made her feel devious, as if she were stealing comfort from an infant who couldn't defend herself. Her mum remembered random things—a dress Meg had worn for a friend's birthday party, the recipe for macaroons, the name of the teacher who had taught her to play the piano—but in the past three and a half years, she had never remembered the day that Meg had come out to her. Meg hoped she never would.

❖

Standing closer to the cave's entrance than on the previous night, Sanne was reminded of that awful thrill of being suspended at the top of a roller coaster, waiting for the drop. She had sweated through her Tyvek suit within minutes, and the way it clung to her body made her movements awkward and slow.

"Keep to the centre of the tunnel and don't touch anything." The forensics officer was too spent to put any inflection into his voice. He had probably been at the caves all night. He issued Sanne and Nelson hardhats with torches attached. "Twiddle this to adjust the size," he told them, indicating a dial that tightened the interior mesh. He wandered away to consult with a colleague, and Sanne took the opportunity to correct the angle of Nelson's torch.

"Try that," she said. "Perfect."

He looked as ridiculous in his outfit as she was sure she looked in hers, but he didn't seem inclined to joke about it, and she certainly wasn't in the mood to do so. Instead, she peered into the jagged opening. Beyond the scant reach of her torch, she couldn't see a thing, and the cool air filtering toward her dried her lips and left them tasting of smoke. By her feet, forensic tags identified where the pieces of pallet had lain. The wood was still undergoing analysis in the lab, but she had heard through the grapevine that smears of blood had been found on two of the fire-damaged slats.

She stood up as the officer returned.

"All set?" he asked, already hurrying past them. "Passageway is uneven, so take it nice and steady. Cavers say there hasn't been a collapse in this section for at least a month, so we should be okay."

On that note of dubious optimism, he led them forward in a line. Sanne brought up the rear, trying to ignore the rasp of her breathing as it echoed through the tunnel. Above her, the stone glistened where water beaded and dripped, and there was little traction underfoot. She heard Nelson swear and then warn her about a puddle. In avoiding it, she slipped and bumped her leg on the wall. She shook her head as she righted herself. They had lights and a guide, yet they were struggling to make progress, so how the hell had the woman managed to find her way out?

Within a couple of minutes, the mounting odour of smoke and something unmistakeably putrid told Sanne they were close to their destination. She rounded a corner and found Nelson preparing to pass through a narrow gap in the side wall. He had waited for her to catch up to make sure she didn't continue straight on.

"Just when you thought it couldn't get any worse," he said, ducking low and squeezing himself into the opening.

She took his hand, as much for the comfort of his touch as his assistance, and allowed him to steer her through.

"Jesus," she whispered.

The enclosed nature of the chamber limited the circulation of the air and concentrated the smell to an almost unbearable degree. Foul smoke and the fumes from an accelerant did little to mask the stench of loosened bowels, stale urine, and vomit. Sanne tasted bile at the back of her throat, but she waved away the proffered mask. Knowing she would grow accustomed to the smell, she was reluctant to exacerbate the sensation of suffocation by covering her face.

As the nausea slowly faded, she began to look around with more confidence. The cavern was a naturally occurring space approximately fifteen feet across, with a ceiling she could graze with her fingertips if she stood on tiptoe. Clusters of smooth stalagmites and stalactites had formed in the dampest sections, giving an incongruous fairy-grotto appearance to a place that had evidently been utilised for torture. The only way in was the gap through which they had just crawled. The temperature was uncomfortably low, and there was no source of natural light. Sanne's primary school had once taken her class on a visit to the Castleton caverns as an end-of-term treat: deep underground, their tour guide had flicked a switch and extinguished all the lights, plunging them into absolute darkness. He had turned them on again within seconds, of course, but she still remembered the disturbing impression of staring into the void, and the way Meg had clutched her hand and shrieked. Without their torches and the Forensics generator that kept a series of small lamps burning, this chamber would be as dark as the Castleton mine. She didn't want to think about someone being imprisoned for days here. She didn't even want to stay half an hour.

"All of the forensic samples were gathered from this corner," the officer said, pointing to the area closest to the entrance. "Our medical exam of the vic detected signs of lividity that suggested she spent most of her time lying on her left side. The distribution of faecal matter and vomit would support that."

For a long moment, Sanne stared at the forensic markers. Following the officer's example, she detached herself from her knowledge of the victim in order to visualise the scene.

"Huh…" Nelson began, and Sanne spotted the anomaly at the same moment.

"So, if she was over here, why was the seat of the fire right over there?" she asked, crossing to a sooty area of rock on the far side of the cavern. "He must have known it wouldn't burn well. If he came back to cover his tracks, why risk leaving potential clues?"

"We don't know that he has," the officer said. "The only prints we've lifted have been partials belonging to the vic. There was no semen, and I'm guessing she was the only one forced to use this place as a toilet. We've found no trace of him at all. Maybe he just stored stuff in that corner that he didn't want to get covered in shit."

The beam from Nelson's torch created a lively shadow display on the walls as he walked over to Sanne. "He comes back to continue where he left off and finds she's already gone," he said. "He has no idea where she's run to, so he cuts his losses and focuses on hiding the evidence of his own involvement, because he knows that at some point she's likely to be found."

"That weird smell," the officer said, "that's bleach. He scrubbed some of the surfaces down before he resorted to torching them."

"He's not stupid, then," Sanne said. "Somehow he's managed to kidnap a woman and get her here without anyone seeing or hearing anything. Plus, he has basic forensic know-how."

"Every bugger has, these days," the officer muttered. "I went to a scene on Halshaw the other week, and some scrote who was barely out of nappies asked me why I wasn't using luminol."

"*CSI* effect," Nelson said.

The officer scowled at him. "I fucking hate that show."

Sanne squatted and touched her gloved hand to the fire-darkened rock. A filmy residue gathered on her fingertips: petrol, bleach, water, she couldn't tell which, but the perpetrator clearly hadn't left anything to chance. She took her notepad from her suit and sketched a rough outline of the chamber, estimating the dimensions and highlighting the two areas.

"He went to a lot of trouble, didn't he?" the officer said, as she tucked away her pad. "The vicious bastard."

Sanne exchanged a troubled glance with Nelson. Whatever the perp had been doing, the woman had ended it prematurely by managing to escape, but it was probably only a matter of time before he tried again with another victim, and men like him tended to learn from their mistakes.

CHAPTER NINE

The Quad was a well-loved haven for the staff of Sheffield Royal. A square of landscaped grass with a generous allocation of benches, it was tucked away behind the Outpatients block and accessible only by those lucky enough to have a swipe card. When the weather was fine, it was the perfect place to eat lunch, and staggered shifts with unpredictable break times meant that people were almost guaranteed to find a seat. At four thirty, with the hum of traffic already building on the main roads around the hospital, Meg had the Quad to herself. She chose a bench in a sunny spot and unwrapped the foil from her sandwich. The limp white bread looked wholly unappetising, but she crammed a handful of cheese crisps on top of the ham filling and took a bite regardless. Fitting the sandwich into her mouth without losing any of the crisps was such a tricky endeavour that she didn't realise someone was standing beside her until she noticed a pair of pink Crocs.

"Oh, hey," she said, and dabbed crumbs from her lips. "Did you want to sit down?" She shoved her bag onto the grass to make space.

Emily sat next to her. "Thanks. I'm not disturbing you, am I? We had a sixty-five-year-old go off in Resus, and everyone's breaks got pushed back."

Meg waved away her concerns. "Not at all. How's the patient?"

"On her way to HDU." Emily began to unpack a series of Tupperware boxes, and Meg watched, mesmerised, as she produced a napkin-wrapped knife and fork. As the lids came off the picnic,

Meg squashed her sandwich between both hands, hoping to disguise the fact that its main ingredient was half a packet of crisps.

"She was a status asthmaticus," Emily added, spearing a cherry tomato with her fork.

"Nasty business." Over her sandwich, Meg took a surreptitious peek at the spread Emily had laid out. It smelled delicious, but the only thing she could identify was a tub of salad. Never having had much pride to swallow, she just went ahead and asked. "What the hell have you got there? Because it beats my ham-and-Quaver butty hands down."

Emily laughed. "God, I love Quavers. I've not had them for years, though. My last partner was a bit of a health nut, and I got out of the habit of buying junk." Meg offered her the crisp packet, and she dug her hand into it. "I have hummus, carrot sticks, and celery," she continued, between crunches, "and three-bean salad with pitta."

Meg pulled a sceptical face. Suddenly, her sandwich didn't seem so bad. Emily must have noticed, because she scooped up a blob of mush on a carrot stick and held it out.

"It looks like baby food," Meg said, but she took it anyway, just to be polite. It was palatable, despite its weird texture. "Hmm. Actually, that's not bad."

"Tin of chickpeas, lemon, garlic, spices, and a bit of olive oil. Throw it all in a blender, and Bob's your uncle."

"Of course, you made it yourself." Meg wasn't really surprised. She had been pleased with her own lunch-making efforts until then. It was a good day indeed when she had a filling other than jam. "I'm not much of a cook. I like trying, but San says I'm a danger to myself and others."

Emily arranged the food so that Meg could help herself, and dipped a Quaver into the hummus. "Who's San?"

"It's Sanne, really, Sanne Jensen. She's the detective from the shock room yesterday. The one at the back with the evidence bags?"

"Oh, the cute one in the shorts?"

Meg choked on a piece of celery and felt her cheeks redden as she coughed. Apparently, there was more to Emily Woodall than her clipped BBC tones and prim fashion sense might suggest.

Emily grinned as she passed Meg a bottle of water. She seemed delighted to have wrong-footed her unflappable mentor. "Sanne Jensen…Is that Swedish? She didn't look very Swedish."

The familiar misconception made Meg smile. "I think it might be Danish or Dutch. Her parents are English through and through, though, and San's never been out of this country." There was a story behind the name, but it wasn't hers to tell. She wasn't even sure if Sanne's siblings knew it, and it had taken Sanne a good few years before she shared it with Meg.

"I like it. It's unusual," Emily said. "It beats some of the idiotic things parents are calling their kids these days."

Meg raised her water in a toast. "To Bailey-Kaden: may you grow up to outshine your moniker."

They tapped their bottles together and settled back on the bench. Meg closed her eyes and relished the sun on her face.

"So, you and Sanne." Emily spoke hesitantly, and Meg kept her eyes shut, knowing what would come next. There was a long pause, followed by the rapid-fire snaps of Emily replacing the tub lids. "No, never mind. It's none of my business."

"I don't know what we are," Meg said, and the sound of movement stopped. "I love her to bits, but"—she floundered for the rest of the thought, before deciding to keep things simple—"but we're not together." She wondered whether she should offer to set Emily up with an introduction or even a date, but a possessive little stirring of jealousy kept her quiet.

Emily chose to change the subject entirely. "Why are you here so early? I didn't think you were on till six."

"I'm not. Dr. Maxwell rang me. He's going to stop the sedation on our mystery woman."

"You think she'll actually wake up?"

"Not straightaway, no, but Sanne's going to be there…" Meg sighed and left the sentence hanging. It was unlikely that Sanne would expect any kind of miraculous recovery as soon as the drugs were discontinued, but Meg still wanted to be with her when that failed to happen.

"She's lucky to have you," Emily said ambiguously.

Meg smiled, offered Emily the last Quaver, and waived her own right to ambiguity. "I think I'm luckier to have her."

❖

Sanne took a gulp from her plastic cup of machine-dispensed tea. It tasted foul, but it was marginally better than nothing. Eleanor had chosen coffee and was having an even worse experience. There was a murky slick on the drink's surface that neither of them could identify.

"I reckon he lives somewhere round here," Sanne said. "I doubt she would have had the chance to escape unless she'd been left alone for a while. Maybe he'd gone home for supplies, or to sign on for his benefits, or to meet a friend at the pub."

Eleanor added another sugar to her coffee and used her pen to stir it. She and Sanne had been bouncing ideas off each other for the last half hour, and this was her second cup. "You think he was trying to establish an alibi?"

"It's possible. He's not an idiot, boss. He could be a complete loner, who nobody missed for the days he held her in that cave, or he could be someone who carried on with his life in between visits to abuse her."

"He might be married with kids, for all we know," Eleanor said. "Look at Paul Farnworth: loving family, new baby, yet he managed to rape and murder three women in six months. I saw his wife on telly again the other week. Even with his confession, she still swears he's innocent."

"I know." This time it wasn't the tea that made Sanne wince. The garden shed on Farnworth's allotment had contained shelves crammed with preserved body parts, and his compost heap had tested positive for human remains. Through the observation mirror of the interview room, she had watched him relax back in his chair as he described each of the murders in explicit detail. She hadn't slept properly for a month afterward.

Propping her chin on her clasped hands, she thought about what she had seen at Gillot Tor that morning and tried to reconcile it with her own experience of the moors. One obvious fact stood out above all the others.

"Y'know, boss, there are easier ways of abducting someone. Farnworth's methodology was far more typical: two prostitutes to hone his skills on, before he stepped up a gear with the lass from his night school class. I've been running on those moors for years. Some days I go past a few people, but more often I don't see anyone. If I were a perp wanting to find a victim, the hills are the last place I'd try. Why bother with the hassle?"

"Unless he already knew her," Eleanor said. "We're only assuming this is a stranger abduction. Maybe he took her up there on a date—nice walk in the hills—and the next thing she knows, she's drugged up to her eyeballs in a cave."

Sanne nodded and drained the dregs of her tea. It made her teeth feel furry. "Option two is that she'd caught his attention at some point, and he stalked her up there."

"Either way, the bastard had it planned. You don't pack rope, knives, and half a pharmacy's worth of drugs if you're heading out for a picnic."

They ruminated upon that in silence for a while. Sanne watched the clock tick around to five. "You think he'll do it again?" she asked quietly.

Eleanor's grim expression was an answer in itself. "Without a doubt. Unless we catch the little shit first."

The sound of voices outside made Sanne twist in her seat, but the door remained closed. She tapped her foot with mounting impatience. They had been waiting for almost an hour, and still no one was telling them anything. She should be out with the rest of the team, chasing leads, instead of being stuck in an airless box with a crappy cup of tea and nothing useful to do. She was about to text Nelson when there was a knock on the door, followed by Meg poking her head into the room.

"Hey, Meg, what are you doing here?" Sanne rose to greet her and then remembered that she and Eleanor had never actually met. "Sorry, boss, this is Dr. Fielding. Meg, Detective Inspector Stanhope."

Meg stepped forward to shake hands. Sanne held her breath, waiting for her to say something embarrassingly personal, but she was all business.

"Dr. Maxwell sends his apologies. His theatre list overran, but he'll be down in five minutes. He asked me to take you through." Meg ushered Eleanor out of the room ahead of them, before sticking her tongue out at Sanne. "Bet you thought I'd say something dreadful," she whispered.

"Not at all," Sanne said, and gave herself away by tripping over a wheelchair.

Laughing, Meg tugged her upright again. "I do love her boots, though. Remind me to ask her where she bought them."

"I most certainly will not." With Eleanor a safe distance ahead, Sanne linked her arm through Meg's. "So, you checking up on your patient or on me?"

"Well, technically you're both my patients, and I am nothing if not a very committed doctor."

Sanne squeezed her arm and then released it again before the police officer on duty outside room three spotted them. "Either way, I'm glad you're here."

The officer checked their identification and held open the door for them. A familiar wave of fury and sorrow hit Sanne as she walked toward the hospital bed. Hours after leaving the cave, she could still feel its filth crawling on her skin, and she wanted to grab the insensible woman by the shoulders and implore her to get better so they could find the sick fuck who had done this to her.

Nothing was ever that simple, though. She stopped a short distance from the bed, privately resigned to the fact that, even without the drugs keeping her asleep, it was unlikely the woman would wake up.

"She's breathing for herself," Meg told Sanne in an undertone. "That's something."

Sanne nodded, never taking her eyes off the woman. When the anaesthetic had been discontinued, the woman had instinctively gagged against the tube down her throat, but nothing else had happened since the removal of the ventilator, not even a blip on the monitors.

"Without the head injury, she might have been expected to regain consciousness quite quickly. As it is"—Meg opened her hands helplessly—"it's a complete crapshoot."

"How long might we be talking about?" Eleanor asked.

Glancing up from checking the woman's pupils, Maxwell answered on Meg's behalf. "How long is a piece of string? It could be minutes, hours, days, or months."

"Bloody hell." Eleanor rubbed the bridge of her nose where her glasses had left a red mark, something Sanne only saw her do when she was under extreme duress. "I need someone in here with her twenty-four seven from now on. I can't risk missing anything she might say."

Maxwell gathered his paperwork. "Providing they stay out of our way, I don't have a problem with that. I believe you wanted to speak to one of the trauma specialists about her other injuries, too. He's over by the desk."

"Excellent, thank you." Eleanor picked up her bag. "Sanne, you're on first watch. Page, text, or call me if anything changes. I'll send someone over to relieve you at eight."

Sanne wrenched her gaze away from the woman's face. "I can stay a bit later if you want, boss."

"Ten, then?"

"That's fine."

"Okay. I'll leave the uniform posted outside for now, so you can switch out if you want a break. Keep in touch." The door clicked shut behind her.

Sanne pulled two chairs up to the bedside. "Déjà vu," she said.

"Only with less drool this time," Meg said, sitting next to her.

Sanne punched her lightly on the arm. "Shouldn't you be downstairs getting puked on?"

"I've got half an hour." Meg lowered her fob watch, her expression turning serious. "How did it go today?"

"It was horrible," Sanne said without hesitation. It was a relief to be able to speak about it. "I showered when we got back, but I still don't feel clean. The smell…" She shook her head. "I can't even begin to describe it. It would have been so dark in there, too. It scared me, and I was with other people, and we all had torches."

"Do you want to sleep at mine tonight? I'll be in late, but at least you won't be on your own all night."

"Thanks, but I'll be fine." Sanne gave a self-deprecating smile. "I might sleep with the light on, but I'll be fine."

"Well, you've got a key if you change your mind."

The woman's assigned nurse entered the room, nodded at them, and began a series of basic checks.

"I saw my mum this morning," Meg said as they watched the nurse's methodical progress.

"She have her teeth in?"

"Nope. She'd managed to gum her breakfast, though. Good job it was only scrambled eggs. And she remembered my name."

"Excellent. Did you give her my love?" Sanne had been genuinely fond of Meg's mum throughout her childhood. It was only as an adult that their relationship had turned sour. She suspected Connie blamed her for Meg's sexuality, as if Meg would have been straight had Sanne not led her astray. It was nonsense, of course, but people always looked for explanations or excuses when their children disappointed them. In Connie's case, her sense of devastation had overridden any ability to be rational.

"Of course I did," Meg said. "Oh, hell, I better get going." She kissed Sanne's cheek, causing the nurse to fumble with and then drop an empty IV bag. "Text me if anything changes."

"Won't that muck up the monitors or something? I don't want to set all the bells and whistles off."

"Naw, it's bullshit. I use my phone in Resus all the time. Haven't killed anyone yet." She blew Sanne another kiss and set off down the corridor at a jog.

The nurse caught the door before it could close. "I'll be back in a moment to bathe her," she told Sanne. "Please don't set any bells or whistles off while I'm gone."

Sanne did her utmost to look responsible. "I won't."

The nurse tried to leave the door ajar, but it swung to, leaving Sanne in the glow of a single lamp and surrounded by the room's artificial sounds. One by one, she studied the switches on the wall, and when she was certain she had identified the dimmer for the lights, she turned it up a notch. She didn't want to dazzle the woman, but she couldn't bear the thought of her opening her eyes to darkness.

"There, that's better." The hand she took felt warmer, which she supposed must be encouraging, even though it lay limp and unresponsive to her touch. "You're safe here," she said, echoing what she had told the woman on the moors and willing her to show some sign that she was listening. "He can't hurt you anymore. You're safe. But we really need you to wake up and help us."

❖

Sanne ran the damp cloth between the woman's fingers, the way the nurse, Alice, had just shown her. She doubted it was approved procedure for police officers to help out in the ITU, but the door was closed, the blinds were drawn, and Alice didn't seem to mind. Through every stage of the bed bath, Alice had been chatting to the woman, explaining what was happening, reassuring her, but mainly providing a friendly voice to go with impersonal procedures. Sanne found herself doing the same, no longer shy about talking to someone who was comatose.

"Do you really think there's a chance she can hear us?" she asked Alice.

"I think it's more habit than anything. Every now and again, I've had patients tell me they could hear voices while they were anaesthetised, but they can never give specifics, so they were probably just dreaming."

Sanne dipped the cloth, wrung it out, and continued scrubbing at the woman's hand. SOCO had trimmed the fingernails, but the dirt and blood around the nail beds was proving stubborn.

"My dad was in here once," she said. "The doctors told us we should talk to him." Unlike her mum, Sanne had never heeded the advice, not because she felt scared or uncomfortable, but because she hadn't wanted to do anything that might speed his recovery. When her mum asked him afterward if he'd heard anything, he told her not to be "so fucking stupid."

"Did he get better?" Alice asked. Then, with professional curiosity, "What was it, an accident?"

"He got better, yeah, but it wasn't an accident. He had varices in his throat, and they ruptured."

Alice nodded without comment and then lowered her head. Sanne had seen many people react like that over the years, the polite acknowledgement, the refusal to make eye contact. Any nurse would recognise oesophageal varices to be a complication of chronic alcoholism. Sanne had found her dad collapsed against the bath in a growing pool of his own blood, and when she had tried to help him, she had slipped on the tiles and ended up covered in gore. Even after another gout had poured from his mouth, he had slapped at her and called her a useless bitch. She had been thirteen years old. Since then, he had survived two further, less severe ruptures, and he still drank five litres of cheap cider a day.

"Are you finished there, love?" Alice had her hand held out for the cloth. Sanne wondered how many times she had asked for it.

"Yes. Sorry."

Soapy water slopped over the side of the washbowl as Alice took it to the sink. "Can I get you a brew?" she said, busy scrubbing her hands.

"Tea, no sugar, would be great, but only if you're making one for yourself."

Alice folded the damp towels into a pile, balanced the washbowl on top, and carried everything to the door. "I'll get your young colleague to help me. Let him stretch his legs a bit and work off a few of those biscuits he keeps pinching."

Sanne feigned shock. "A copper pinching brews and biccies? I've never heard anything so outrageous."

Alice grinned at her and let the door swing shut.

Sanne stayed by the bedside, kicking her feet idly and watching the woman sleep. After a while, she noticed a mark she had missed, and she leaned forward with a scrap of damp paper towel to dab at it. Finding the spot of blood firmly ingrained, she repositioned the woman's arm so that she could scrub a little harder. Satisfied with her efforts, she was about to reach for a dry cloth, when the woman's finger suddenly twitched.

Sanne froze, staring at the hand in hers and trying to convince herself that she hadn't just imagined the movement.

"Can you hear me?" she whispered. Then, louder, "You're in the hospital. Squeeze my hand if you can hear me." She gasped as she felt the faint pressure renewed. When she returned it, the woman's eyes opened a crack.

Sanne's heart was pounding so hard she felt dizzy. She knew she should go and get a doctor or press something to summon Alice, but she was terrified of doing anything that might disrupt this breakthrough.

"My name's Sanne," she said. "I'm a detective with the East Derbyshire Police. Honey, I know you're scared and hurting, but can you tell me your name?"

The woman's eyes opened slightly wider, two flashes of hazel against the deep purple. Her throat worked as she swallowed, and Sanne realised it was probably sore from the tube. There was no convenient glass of water on the bedside table; no one had expected the woman to need it. On the monitor, green changed to amber as her heart rate rose.

"I'm going to get a nurse," Sanne said. She had managed to find the light switch earlier, but she didn't have a clue which button called for help. "Just try and stay awake for me."

The grip on her hand tightened.

"Rachel." The woman barely managed a whisper. Her chest rose and fell rapidly, and her nostrils flared.

"Rachel? Rachel what? What's your surname?"

The woman's eyes were already closing, tears leaking down her cheeks. The name she repeated was half-buried in a sob. "Rachel."

Sanne felt the fingers around hers grow slack and watched the numbers on the monitor climb back down into green. "Fucking hell," she whispered. The emergency buzzer above the bed was obvious, now that she no longer needed it. She pressed it anyway, and then pulled out her phone. Eleanor answered immediately. Sanne sat down. Her legs were shaking.

"Boss, I think I have her name."

Chapter Ten

The patter of rain against her bedroom window and the indignant clucking of wet hens greeted Sanne when she woke. She rolled onto her back and draped her forearm across her face until she grew accustomed to the dull morning light. Her head had hit the pillow at midnight, but she had lain awake for at least another hour, tossing and turning and trying to get Rachel's voice out of her head. She couldn't remember her dreams, only a vague sense of claustrophobia that made her grateful to have woken up to daylight, however dismal. Her lack of sleep did nothing to curb her anticipation of the day ahead, though. Now that Rachel was conscious, there was a good possibility they would be able to interview her, and—as she was their only real lead—almost anything she could tell them would propel the investigation forward. Eleanor had already asked Sanne to assist with the interview.

The prospect made her bounce out of bed. After a few stretches to shake off the stiffness of sleep, she opened her window, letting the cool air turn to mist on her face. Drizzly rain and a dip in temperature had chased away the mugginess of the last week, and the hills wore caps of thick cloud. She waved at the bedraggled rooster and closed the window again. She showered and dressed quickly, unplugging her phone from its charger as she headed for the kitchen. Once the kettle was boiling and the bread was in the toaster, she flipped open the phone's cover and entered her security code.

"Shit."

The phone had been charging all night, which meant its ring tone had been muted, and four messages and two calls had gone unnoticed. The first message was from her mum, its preview showing an invitation for tea. She bypassed it and opened the thread from Meg.

Are you awake? Call me.

Call me when you get this.

Guess you're asleep. Call me when you're up.

One of the missed calls was from Meg, the other Eleanor, so the crisis must be work-related. After a moment's hesitation—it was still only a quarter past five—Sanne sat at her kitchen table and phoned Meg, who answered on the second ring.

"Hey. I thought you might beat my alarm clock." Meg sounded tired, but too cogent for the phone to have woken her.

"What happened? What's wrong?" Sanne blurted out the questions before her courage failed her. She shrank back in the chair, expecting a blow.

Meg duly delivered one. "Max paged me at a quarter to one. Apparently, Rachel's nurse called him to the ITU because Rachel was becoming increasingly agitated. Just before he got there, she had a seizure. The CT showed a small re-bleed on her brain, so he took her back to theatre to fix it. She's okay, San, the bleed was minor, but—"

"But we're back to square one." Sanne slumped against the table.

"Yeah. He had to intubate her for surgery, and he's wary about lifting the sedation again until she's completely out of the woods. He thinks the bleed was connected to a post-traumatic reaction. She was screaming, distressed, and her blood pressure spiked."

"What was she screaming? Did she say anything?"

"No, just her name over and over. They had to restrain her. She was trying to get up."

"Jesus." Sanne ran a hand through her damp hair. A jumble of questions went through her mind, but in the end she asked only one. "Have you been to bed yet?"

The wry humour in Meg's voice was unmistakeable. "Well, I lay in it for a few hours."

"You should go back. Try again."

"I might. Are you okay?"

"Yep, I'm fine," Sanne said, with more assurance than she felt. "Thanks for letting me know."

Meg yawned. "Sorry it was such shitty news."

"Bed," Sanne told her. "Sleep. I'll call you later."

"Okay. Night, love." Meg hung up.

"Fucking terrific," Sanne muttered, slapping the phone's cover back into place. Seconds later, her toast shot out of the toaster. It was burned to a cinder.

Waterlogged potholes littered the track leading down to the penultimate address on Sanne's list. Her teeth snapped together as the car caught the edge of a rut.

"Bloody Nora," Nelson said. The muscles on his forearms stood out as he tried to keep the car level. "So, who've we got at this one?"

Rain had blurred the names on the paper, but Sanne had already committed the details to memory. "Mrs. Edna Clegg, seventy-eight, and her son, Derek, forty-five."

"Does he work?"

"Only on their land. He was a painter and decorator, but he gave that up when his dad died and his mum was left with the farm."

A large stone cottage came into view, and Nelson slowed the car to a crawl. "Sounds promising. Elderly mum, lots of time to duck out and get up to no good. Did he ever get married?"

"Not according to this."

"Maybe he prefers helping himself to hikers off the moors." Nelson took the keys from the ignition and rubbed his sleeve over the condensed windscreen. Rain and a thin mist were obscuring the surrounding buildings. Sanne pulled her jacket tighter around herself and then wondered why she'd bothered; the material was soaked through.

"Not sure I want to go out in that," she said.

The look he gave her was little short of incredulous. "You were the one who volunteered us for this. We could've spent the day tucked up in the office, tracking down illicit drugs online, or Rachels on the Missing Persons database, or local suppliers of fluorescent rope."

"I know, I know." She held up her hands in surrender. "I wanted to be out in the fresh air. Come on. Let's get this one done, and then I'll buy you a cuppa."

He took a moment to consider the deal. "And a pasty," he added.

"Fine, you can have a pasty. There's a good bakery in Rowlee. I'll take you there."

He smiled, grabbing his umbrella from the back seat. "Last one to the door's a rotten egg."

With her own umbrella offering little protection against the wind-driven rain, she ignored the challenge, picking her way carefully instead through the puddle-ridden farmyard, noting its rundown outbuildings and the machinery abandoned to rust. Hens clucked in one of the barns, and somewhere close by a dog began to bark furiously.

"That thing better be on a chain," Nelson said.

"I'm guessing it'd have its jaws clamped around your ankle by now, if it wasn't."

He knocked on a door that bore a sticker warning off *Hawkers, Canvassers, Religious Types, and Politicians.* "*My* ankle? What about your bloody ankle?"

"Yours are meatier." She rang the bell for good measure, as she felt rain seep beneath her shirt and into her bra.

A few seconds later a man shouted, "Who is it?"

Sanne left Nelson to answer. His deeper voice carried better.

"It's the police, Mr. Clegg. Would you mind opening the door?"

There was a long pause before a figure appeared behind the dirty glass window. When it did, Nelson sighed and Sanne shook her head in dismay.

"Bollocks," she said.

Derek Clegg opened the door wide, enabling him to step fully into view. Approximately five feet in height, his grossly obese figure was still clad in grimy pyjamas. He gave them an excited smile and scratched his overhanging belly.

"Is this about that girl found up Laddaw?"

Sanne pocketed her ID badge. "Yes, it is. Could we come in and ask you and your mum a few questions? It shouldn't take long."

"Course, no problem. Excuse the mess. We're in the middle of a clear-out."

He turned and lumbered down a darkened hallway. Stacks of newspapers and general detritus lined the narrow corridor, and the carpet felt sticky beneath Sanne's boots. It was apparent from the layers of dust that nothing resembling a clear-out had happened this side of the millennium. The smell of cat piss and boiled vegetables grew stronger as they followed him farther into the house. Sanne tried and failed to get the sound of "Dueling Banjos" out of her head.

"You owe me a really big pasty," Nelson whispered.

The room Derek took them into looked out over a poorly maintained plot of land, with a pig wallowing in the fresh mud. The pig, at least, looked content to be living in squalor.

"Visitors, Mum! Police officers!" Derek yelled, and then, quieter, "She's a bit deaf."

"Just a minute," his mum shouted, over the sound of a flushing toilet.

He busied himself shifting food wrappers, magazines, and what might have been the remains of a pizza from the sofa.

"Sit down, sit down," he said, beckoning them forward. When Sanne lifted her boot, it had a piece of pepperoni stuck to its sole. She eyed a suspicious-looking stain on the closest sofa cushion and then gave Derek her best conciliatory smile.

"We're fine as we are, thanks. This won't take a minute. And we're dripping wet—we wouldn't want to ruin your sofa."

Derek might have insisted, had his mother not chosen that moment to make her entrance. Her walking frame appeared first, propelled by chubby hands. She stopped dead and gaped when she saw Nelson, but covered her reaction by launching the frame another inch.

"Aren't you handsome?" she said, regarding him like an exotic zoo exhibit. "Have you offered them a drink, Del? Has he offered you a drink, Officers?"

Nelson stepped backward as the frame almost clipped his shins. "Please don't go to any trouble. We had a coffee at the last house."

Edna lowered herself into an armchair and used its remote to adjust the footrest. "We heard about that girl on the news. Terrible thing."

"Yes, it was," Sanne said. She waited until Derek had settled on the sofa before continuing. There was no point asking him to account for his recent whereabouts—not when the short walk down the hall had been enough to leave him panting for breath—so she moved directly to the second set of questions, which focused on strangers in the area or locals who had been behaving oddly. Had Derek or his mum spotted anything out of the ordinary, over the past week or so?

It soon became apparent that Edna and Derek didn't get out much. They had their shopping delivered, and the only other person they saw on a regular basis was Ned, who came to help Derek on the farm. Due to their health problems, they were planning to sell up and buy a bungalow closer to the village.

"What's Ned's surname?" Sanne asked, wondering if it was the same man who had discovered the dead sheep on the moors.

"Moseley," Derek said. "He told us all about the search. Said he'd found something very important."

"Yep, he certainly did." She scribbled Ned's full name into her notebook. "Has he been around much lately? Worked his usual hours?"

Derek crinkled his brow, obviously trying to remember. When nothing was forthcoming, he looked to his mum for help.

"He skipped Tuesday and Thursday last week," she said. "Went fishing, instead of mucking our chickens out."

Sanne sensed the shift in Nelson's stance as the detail caught his interest.

"Is that unusual for him?" he asked. "To leave you shorthanded like that?"

"Depends on where the fancy takes him." Edna sniffed. "Would've liked more notice if he was going to bugger off and leave our hens, though. Them and the pig are all we've got left." She tapped a walking stick on the floor to attract Derek's attention. "Make us a cuppa, pet. I'm spitting feathers here."

"Just a second." Suspecting that Edna's cooperation was waning, Sanne opened her bag and took out a photograph. "I know this is an upsetting picture, but have either of you seen this woman before? Maybe shopping in the village, or out and about around here? We think her name is Rachel."

Derek's double chin quivered as he stared at the image. He quickly passed it to his mum, who placed her glasses on the end of her nose and peered through the fingerprint-smudged lenses.

"Poor little mite," she said. "I don't recognise her. Do you, Del?"

"No, Mum." He turned to Sanne. "Am I okay to make her tea now?"

"Of course. Thank you for your help." She gave him her card. "If you think of anything, anything at all, give me a ring on this number."

"Detective Sar-ner Jensen," he read aloud.

"Aye, that's close enough." She zipped up her jacket, longing to be back in the rain. "Thanks again. We'll let ourselves out."

She headed into the corridor, forcing herself not to sprint for the front door. Drizzle washed over her as she left the porch, and she drew in deep lungfuls of manure-scented air.

Once in the car, Nelson opened the windows wide and stuck his head out of the closest one. "I reckon that rates at least a seven on our shithole scale," he said.

"I was thinking more of an eight."

"Ooh, controversial. That puts it on a par with Flat 4C, Smackhead Terrace, from Assault with a Deadly Weapon."

Sanne fastened her seatbelt. "Yeah, you're right. Maybe a seven."

He manoeuvred the car onto the track and began to weave around the potholes. "I think we can safely say that Mr. Clegg is not a person of interest."

"No, but Ned Moseley might be worth a closer look. Right age, good level of fitness, potential holes in his whereabouts, and an enthusiastic participant in the investigation."

"I totally agree," Nelson said. "But I'm having my bloody pasty first."

❖

The line at the bakery was halfway out the door. Sanne joined the rest of the prospective pasty buyers, her hood drawn up against the rain. It was always a nightmare trying to find a parking spot in Rowlee's tiny, overcrowded back streets, so Nelson had dropped her off while he looked for one.

As the queue edged forward and she crossed the shop's threshold, she pushed her hood down and ran her fingers through her matted hair. The gesture made the man beside her smile in recognition. He had obviously only just seen her face.

"How do," he said. "I thought that wreck of yours was due in for a service?"

Geoff Cotter owned the local garage, out on Lower Bank Road. He was reliable, he didn't try to rip his customers off, and he was fastidious about keeping up to date with scheduled work. He was also supposed to be Sanne and Nelson's last house call of the afternoon.

"Hey, Geoff. I meant to book in on Monday, but this case…" She left the rest of her explanation hanging. She didn't want to go into detail in front of a crowd of locals who were now paying her their undivided attention. Some of them undoubtedly knew her—she did most of her shopping in Rowlee, and the village was small and insular enough that the sight of lesbians still turned heads—while even those unfamiliar with her had visibly pricked up their ears at her mention of "the case." There was only one case around Rowlee in which anyone was interested right now, and the village grapevine was extraordinarily efficient.

"I understand, pet. Just don't leave it too long. One of your tyres was borderline on your last MOT."

The woman behind the counter interrupted to take Geoff's order, and another assistant prompted Sanne for hers. Sanne added sausage rolls to the pasties, and on a whim bought three jam and cream scones as well. Nelson would probably eat his straightaway, but the other two she intended to save.

She caught up with Geoff as they were leaving. "Are you around this afternoon?" she asked. "Only, we're doing house-to-house enquiries, and you're on our list. I could kill two birds with one stone: ask our questions and arrange a date to bring my car in. Say, in half an hour or so?"

The church clock in the centre of the village chimed twice, saving him the trouble of checking the time. "That'd be fine," he said. "Make sure you have your dinner first, though. Billy and Joan will be home as well, if you need them."

"Perfect." Her phone began to ring as she returned his farewell wave. She had to fumble in her pocket for it and answer it while attempting to keep hold of her carrier bag. "They only had cheese and onion, so I got you a sausage roll to go with it," she said.

"That's lovely, dear." It was Meg, sounding very amused. "I do like a nice sausage roll."

Sanne laughed. "Bugger, I thought you were Nelson. The sausage rolls are all spoken for, but I did buy you a cream scone. Did you get any sleep?"

"Four hours. Could've been worse."

"Could've been better. Are you okay?"

"Bit mopey," Meg admitted. "I've got the day off, but I don't know what to do with myself. Fancy coming round for tea?"

"Of course I'll come round for tea," Sanne said. "I already bought dessert, remember?"

"You should try this," Nelson said. "Seriously, it's a taste sensation. It'll be on *MasterChef* before you know it." Sitting in the driver's seat with his sausage roll in one hand and his pasty in the other, he was taking enthusiastic, alternate bites of each.

Sanne gave him the special look she reserved for moronic criminals who were caught in the act and still trying to blag their way out. She supposed she should be relieved he hadn't yet added his scone to the mix. "I'll stick to my pasty, thanks," she said. "You're lucky to have that sausage roll. Meg was all for pinching it, a few minutes ago."

She opened her window a crack, letting out the steam and the smell of grease, and feeling cooler air brush her cheek. Nelson had managed to find a parking spot beside the river. The rain had stopped, and the clouds were breaking up, letting flashes of sunlight through. On the near bank, a child was beginning to wail as a swan strayed too close to her fingers. The swan honked as the child's parent shooed it away, and that in turn set all the ducks off quacking. Ignoring the feathered mini-riot, Nelson raised the last piece of sausage roll, but then he set it down untouched on the bag.

"San? Can I ask you something?"

"Yep." She poured tea from their flask and offered him a cup. "What's up?"

"You don't have to answer if you don't want."

"Will anything I say be taken down and used in evidence against me?"

He laughed. "No."

"Right, then. Go ahead."

"Okay." Now looking nervous, he sipped his tea. "Okay. So, why the hell aren't you and Meg a couple?"

The directness of the question caught Sanne off-guard. She choked a little on her tea and spent the next minute spluttering and coughing. Nelson slapped her on the back before offering her a napkin.

"Thanks." She blew her nose. Then she wiped her mouth and blew her nose again. When she had run out of other ways to stall, she propped her feet up on the dashboard and hooked her arms beneath her thighs. "Did you know Charles Darwin made a list of pros and cons before he decided to get married?"

"No, I didn't."

She smiled. "You should look it up online. It's quite funny. Meg and I sort of did the same once: we made a list of the pros and cons. Y'know, for moving in together or trying to make a go of it as a couple."

"What happened? Did you end up with more cons than pros?"

"It was actually pretty balanced. She'd do the plumbing, I'd do the gardening. I'd cook, she'd wash up. We both wanted pets, and neither of us wanted kids." Sanne poured herself more tea and refilled Nelson's cup. "We weren't taking it that seriously—Meg had had a lot of beer—but I think we were trying to figure it out for ourselves, all the same."

"How long ago was this?"

"Just after we'd graduated. We were twenty, maybe twenty-one, and toying with the idea of sharing a flat."

"Did you?"

"No, we've never lived together. We'd probably end up killing each other. She'd steal all my bloody clothes, laze around, mess up my books, and leave her journals everywhere. And I'd drive her mad, making to-do lists, trying to clean around her, or dragging her out for exercise. It just seems to work better for us the way it is. We might see other people, but we still manage to keep this status quo between us." She hugged her legs closer. Nelson wasn't daft. He was accustomed to a traditional family setup, but he must know that she and Meg were more than just friends. She wondered for how long he had been trying to puzzle their relationship out.

"Don't you risk wrecking that status quo when you date other people, though?" he asked.

"I suppose, but it hasn't happened yet. Maybe we set such an impossible standard for prospective partners that no one measures up."

"Unless one day someone does," Nelson said quietly. "What happens to the one left behind then?"

The prospect brought a lump to Sanne's throat. It was exactly what she lay awake fretting over, especially when she knew Meg was on a date.

"I'm not sure," she said. "I try not to think about it. I know we could commit, make ourselves exclusive, and still live separately, but even that would change things."

"If it ain't broke…"

"Precisely. Don't rock the boat." She rolled her eyes at her mangled proverbs.

"You're not mad at me for asking, are you?"

Sanne shook her head. Sometimes it was a relief to try to work the logic through, even if all that did was emphasise the illogicality of it all. "To be honest, mate, I'm surprised you waited this long."

Chapter Eleven

A n automatic plug-in air freshener sprayed the reception area of Cotter's Garage every ten minutes, but its pungent floral bouquet did little to mask Joan Cotter's chain-smoking. Nicotine tinged the wallpaper, and a phone that had once been cream was now a tarry yellow.

"A week on Wednesday. Would that be okay for you?" Joan spoke around her cigarette, puffing out smoke like a carcinogenic dragon.

Eager to retreat to a safe distance, Sanne agreed to the date and jotted it in her diary. "I'll drop it off as soon as you open. Are you three able to spare us ten minutes now?"

In lieu of an answer, Joan opened the door connecting to the workshop and bellowed for her son and husband. Her lips never lost their grip on her cigarette. Sanne saw Nelson's eyes widen in appreciation.

"Hey, Sanne." Wiping his hands on a grease-stained rag, Billy Cotter greeted her warmly. "My dad's on his way. Can I get you a drink?"

Keen to get back to the office and type up their reports, she and Nelson declined the offer. When Geoff joined them, they pulled up chairs in the office, Joan lighting another cigarette from the stub of her last. Sanne introduced Nelson and began to run through the questions. The family's answers were simple and unembellished: Billy spent most of his days in the garage or on call outs, and in the evenings he was either at home or at the pub. Geoff's routine followed an even more straightforward pattern: garage, home, and a visit to the Working Men's Club on a Tuesday. None of them recognised Rachel, and no one but locals had used the garage in the past two weeks. Both men were willing to volunteer DNA samples if that would help exclude them from the enquiry, and Billy offered to double-check the diary and computer records, to make absolutely sure they hadn't dealt with anyone from out of the area or who might fit Rachel's description.

The Cotters already had Sanne's mobile phone number on their database, but she was in the middle of giving them her work number as well when her phone rang yet again.

"Excuse me," she said, remembering to check who was calling this time. It was Eleanor's mobile. "Hey, boss. We're just finishing—"

Eleanor cut across her. "Scotty and Jay found the vic's car, shoved into a riverbed off the Snake. They tracked it back to a rental agency in Sheffield. The manager there confirmed that a Rachel Medlock had signed the rental agreement. He couldn't give a positive ID from the photograph, but she'd provided a local address for the paperwork: a holiday cottage out in the sticks."

"Jesus." Acutely aware that she had an audience, Sanne turned away from the Cotters. "What's the address?" Trapping the phone with her shoulder, she scribbled down the details.

"You're closest," Eleanor said. "The owner of the cottage has agreed to cooperate fully and will meet you there in twenty minutes. I'm en route with Duncan and SOCO, but the traffic's gone to shit in the rain. Approx ETA is one hour. Update from scene ASAP, please."

"Yes, boss." Sanne was already gathering her paperwork. She hung up and turned to Nelson. "We have to go."

He didn't stop to ask why. "I'll bring the car around," he said, heading for the door.

"Is everything all right?" Joan asked.

"Uh, yeah." Functioning on autopilot, Sanne fell back on her training. "Sorry to have to cut this short. Please get in touch if you remember anything you might have overlooked."

Nelson pulled up the car outside the office. She heard him rev the engine in an unsubtle hint.

"Did something happen on the case, Sanne?" Billy sounded intrigued.

"Yes, you could say that." Giddy with the promise of real progress, she smiled at him and ran out into the rain.

❖

Rowan Cottage was a picture-perfect example of a holiday retreat. Pink roses arched across its whitewashed exterior, and a gravel path meandered through a well-tended garden, whose flowers filled the air with scent and the buzz of bees. Its owner, Mrs. Martindale, had met Sanne and Nelson with trepidation, and taken two attempts to unlock the front door. It was little wonder she was nervous, having watched her visitors don Tyvek suits, gloves, and protective booties. Sanne politely requested that she stay outside and then followed Nelson into the hallway.

The door clicked shut behind them, leaving them in the beams of multi-coloured, late-afternoon sunlight shining through the door's stained-glass panels. Dust motes danced in the air, and the pendulum of a grandfather clock marked time in a soothing rhythm.

"You okay to take the upstairs, and I'll stay down here?" Nelson asked quietly.

"Fine," she said, impatient to get started before SOCO arrived en masse and claimed ownership of the scene.

At the top of the stairs, she pushed open each door in turn, finding a double bedroom, a tiny single, and a bathroom. The single bedroom had obviously not been used. Its patchwork quilt was folded back to welcome a guest, and complimentary toiletries were arranged on an untouched stack of fresh towels. She left everything as it was and went across to the double room, stopping just through the doorway to observe its layout and contents. As she did so, her heart rate sped up, and she took an unconscious step forward.

Rumpled sheets and pillows told her that both sides of the bed had been slept in. The pillow on the left bore a folded pair of plaid pyjamas, but the occupant of the right side had discarded their nightclothes in a more haphazard fashion. Sanne knelt by the bed and picked up the satin nightdress, the fabric slipping in her gloved hands to reveal its mid-thigh length and the intricate lacing on its straps.

"Jesus," she whispered, all her theories around a stranger-abduction beginning to unravel. If Rachel's husband or boyfriend was the culprit, EDSOP would have a face to look for, and the case might be solved within days.

With mounting urgency, she started to search for whatever might help identify Rachel's companion. The clothes in the wardrobe were a mix of casual trousers, shirts, and sweaters, plus a couple of dresses kept separate to stop them creasing. Two empty, matching holdalls provided more evidence of a couple on holiday. Wondering at what point it had all gone so wrong, she shut the wardrobe and opened the nearest bedside cabinet. She pulled out a collection of guidebooks and maps, and then felt farther back until her fingers touched upon a purse. Four pound coins and a fifty-pence piece dropped onto the floor as she hooked out a collection of plastic cards: one debit card, two credit cards, Boots and Nectar points cards, and a driving licence in the name of Rachel Medlock. The mugshot was too small for Sanne to distinguish much detail aside from blond hair, but the notes section of the purse contained a larger photograph, folded in half and tucked away behind a ten and two twenties. In red pen, an inscription on the back recorded the date as 14th February and beneath it: *She said YES!*

Sanne took a deep breath and unfolded the image.

"What the fuck?"

For a long moment, all she could do was stare. Then she grabbed the driving licence and set both images on the floor in front of her.

"Oh, no. Fucking *no*."

A background of bright blue sky and a vast aquamarine lake had made the light perfect for the photographer. Rachel Medlock's cheeks were pink with cold, but she was smiling broadly at the camera, her arms wrapped around a taller woman whose eyes Sanne recognised even without the bruising and the swelling she was accustomed to seeing.

"Nelson!" She ran to the top of the stairs, both photographs clasped in her hands. She could hear him hurrying down the hall.

"San? You okay?"

"You need to see this. Fuck. Fucking shit, we've got it all wrong."

He met her halfway, and she handed him the images.

"That's Rachel." She pointed to the blue-eyed, fair-haired woman.

"Poor kid. She's pretty, isn't she?" He studied the larger photograph. "So who's the other one?"

She wiped a hand across her face. Her glove came away wet. "The other one is the woman I found at the bottom of Laddaw Ridge."

It took Nelson a few seconds to register that. She watched his jaw slacken as he scrutinised the two women again. Uncertain whether he was convinced, she pulled out the photograph they had used for the interviews.

"It's difficult to see it, I know, but look here, at the shape of her face, her chin. I saw her eyes when she woke up, Nelson. They're hazel, almost brown. Rachel's are blue."

"Bloody hell," he muttered. "There are two sets of dishes on the draining board. Were they both here?"

She nodded. "I think they're a couple. They shared a bed, and you can just…Well, look at them."

Nelson returned his attention to the lakeside photograph. He tapped his finger just above Rachel's head. "Do you think she's our perp?"

"No." Sanne's voice betrayed her, cracking on that one word. "I think he took them both. I think that when he came back and realised our woman had escaped, he moved Rachel somewhere else. That would explain why he started the fire where he did. We assumed he was destroying evidence of himself, but maybe he was blitzing the spot where a second woman had been lying."

Nelson's eyes widened. "Jesus Christ."

"The woman at the hospital tried to tell me," Sanne said. "She wasn't saying her own name, she was asking for her partner."

"You couldn't have known that, San."

"No, I suppose not." She shivered. "But all this time we've been looking for him, when we should have been looking for a second victim."

"One will probably lead to the other," he said, though he must have known as well as she did that the wasted days might have cost Rachel her life.

He tilted Sanne's chin and made sure she looked at him. "You okay?"

"Yes." She might not be okay later, when she was alone with time to think, but right now she just wanted to do her job. "We should call Eleanor, give her a heads-up."

Nelson offered her his mobile. She managed a small smile and began to dial on her own phone.

"Wish me luck," she said.

Sanne discovered a second pile of bankcards and store cards hidden in a sock in the wardrobe. She had often done that herself before going hiking: emptied her purse of everything but a few quid for parking and an emergency tenner. The cards were similar to Rachel's, except that they belonged to a Ms. Josie Albright. Sequestered among them was a bus pass, complete with photograph.

There was nothing else of interest upstairs, no other helpful documents, no signs of a disturbance or a break-in, no indication that anything out of the ordinary had occurred. Satisfied that she had finished her sweep, Sanne met Nelson in the kitchen, where she swapped Josie's pass for two unsent postcards he had found propped up against the toaster.

"Definitely the same woman," he said, holding the pass alongside the lake photo. "See the addresses on the postcards? Her parents live in Australia. Rachel's are a bit closer, though. Up near Loch Lomond."

"And the cards are dated seven days ago, which fits our estimated timeline," Sanne said. The scribbled messages were standard holiday fare: *having a lovely time, weather is great, Josie got chased by a cow, Rachel fell into a bog, the fish and chips are amazing.* Nothing hinted at any kind of tension or relationship breakdown, and both women had promised to Skype their parents as soon as they were "back in civilisation." They had booked the cottage for two weeks, which would explain why no one seemed to have missed them yet.

"Pity the parents," Nelson said. "Should be getting these, and instead they'll be getting a phone call from the boss."

"Can't imagine that, can you?" Sanne murmured. Everywhere she looked she saw traces of the couple: odd socks left to dry on the radiator, the *Guardian* newspaper spread over the kitchen table and scattered with crumbs, a note reminding them to buy stamps and milk. There was no outdoor gear in sight, which suggested they had gone for a hike, taking their boots, rucksacks, and raincoats with them. Had they been followed onto the moors, or had their assailant acted spontaneously once he had seen them up there?

A timid knock on the front door brought her out of her reverie. She hadn't noticed the cars pull up, but she could hear their doors opening and voices calling to one another.

"There goes the neighbourhood." Nelson placed the photograph and the pass on the kitchen table. "I think that was Mrs. Martindale trying to warn us."

"Yeah, SOCO aren't likely to knock." Sanne went to the window in the living room. An SUV and a Crime Scene Investigation van were parked behind Nelson's car. She saw Eleanor greet Mrs. Martindale with a distracted smile and head for the front door.

"Evening, boss," Nelson said as Sanne joined them in the hallway.

Eleanor shook her head. A flush of stress coloured the tip of her nose. "You two certainly know how to kick up a fucking shit storm," she said.

❖

Nursing a bottle of water, Sanne watched Eleanor talking to an overweight man in a smartly pressed, navy blue suit. She didn't recognise him, but from the way Eleanor deferred to him, he was probably one of the top brass, dragged out of his office just as he was contemplating going home, to come and stand instead on a muddy driveway in the middle of nowhere. He held up a hand, cutting Eleanor off mid-sentence to answer his phone. She waited for no more than twenty seconds before going back into the cottage.

"That didn't look very encouraging," Nelson said. Predictably, SOCO had requested that he and Sanne leave the house so they could begin to process the scene.

"It didn't. Do you think someone's head will roll for this?"

He ran a hand over his chin, scratching at his five o'clock shadow. "Who the hell knows? I wouldn't want to be the one who has to stand in front of the press and admit that we only just realised another woman is missing, and that, by the way, we still have no idea who our perp is."

A crunch of boots on gravel warned them of Carlyle's approach.

"I've got a damn good idea who our perp is," he said. His thin smile made his lips look purple.

Nelson settled onto the bonnet of his car, folding his arms. "Care to share with the rest of the class?"

Carlyle's smile widened. He ignored Nelson and directed his answer at Sanne. "One lesbian in the hospital, one lesbian AWOL. You do the maths."

Sanne blinked slowly and counted to ten before she responded. "You're considering Rachel Medlock a suspect?"

"Obviously." He frowned. "Although you'd expect it to be the other way around: the butch one on the run, not at the bottom of the rocks."

Sanne felt Nelson shift closer to her, as if afraid she might go for Carlyle's throat. She held herself perfectly still and started another count. While it was true that Josie's hair had been shorter than Rachel's, neither woman adhered to a butch or femme stereotype, judging by the clothing Sanne had examined.

"Most lesbian relationships don't work like that, Sarge," she said quietly.

"No?" He lowered his voice. "Hey, if you ever feel like giving me some pointers…"

She smiled sweetly, wishing she could knock his teeth out. "There's not enough time in the world to teach you half of what I know."

His face turned scarlet, his obvious discomfiture making Nelson chuckle. Sanne was grateful Nelson had left her to fight her own corner. He knew she was capable of holding her own against Carlyle.

As Eleanor left the cottage and began to walk over to them, Carlyle fired a parting shot. "Just because they're gay doesn't mean they're special, Jensen. Cases like this, nine times out of ten it's the boyfriend. Or, in this instance, the girlfriend." He turned to leave, calling back in a singsong voice, "You don't want me to be right, but I am."

Nelson waited until he was out of earshot before speaking. "Ignore him. He's a prick."

Sanne was proficient at ignoring Carlyle, but part of what he'd said had hit home. She wondered whether she really was following the evidence in believing Rachel a victim rather than a suspect, or whether other factors—including her own sexuality and preconceptions—were clouding her judgement. There was little about Josie's abduction that would point to Rachel being the culprit, though. The use of drugs, the knowledge of the local caves, the prolonged torture, and the sheer physicality required to subdue Josie initially—all seemed to suggest a premeditated crime by a male perp, not a woman of slender stature who was writing light-hearted postcards in the hours before she disappeared.

Sanne shuffled over to make room for Eleanor, who slumped beside her on the car bonnet, plucked her water bottle from her hand, and drained half of it.

"What a fucking mess," she said, screwing the lid back on. "You two get home. There's nothing more you can do here tonight. Team briefing is at six a.m. sharp. I've pulled everyone in from leave and rest days, so we'll have an overnight team to start following up on leads. Rachel's parents are on their way from Scotland, and the shit will be hitting the fan with a live press conference in about an hour."

"Did you manage to speak to Josie's parents?" Nelson asked.

"Yes. They're trying to arrange flights."

Sanne raised her head, though she couldn't look Eleanor in the eye. "Is Rachel a suspect?"

Eleanor sighed. "I think we'd be remiss not to consider that, but from what we've already established, it seems unlikely. Her parents are devastated. They're coming to sit with Josie until her own family can get here. According to Josie's mum, the two were inseparable—Rachel was the reason Josie stayed in Scotland when the rest of the family emigrated—and she wouldn't even entertain the possibility of Rachel being responsible. They've been together for eight years and got engaged in Italy this last Valentine's Day."

Sanne chewed on her lip, thinking of the women's gleeful embrace by the lake, "*She said YES!*" commemorating the moment in red ink.

"Ready to call it a night?" Nelson said.

She nodded, though the thought of going home to an empty house filled her with dread. As he unlocked the car, she dug out her phone. Earlier she had sent Meg a text, apologising for missing tea and promising to catch up with her soon, but now she typed a second message. With the phone balanced on her knee, she reached for her seatbelt, glancing down at the draft text as she did so: *Can I stay with you tonight?*

"Fuck it," she whispered. The words were swallowed by the noise of the diesel motor kicking in and the tyres spinning on the driveway. She snatched up the phone and pressed *Send*.

Meg set down her book at the first sound of a car pulling into her driveway. The heavens had opened, and she could barely distinguish the hunched figure through the downpour, but she recognised the shape of the car. She watched with concern as Sanne, seemingly oblivious to the storm, trudged toward the front door. Although the unexpected text had already set Meg's alarm bells ringing, it was the sight of Sanne's beaten down demeanour that made her run for her keys and yank the door open before Sanne had the chance to knock.

"San?"

Sanne raised her head. Rain was beading on her eyelashes and dripping off her nose, and her eyes were bloodshot with exhaustion.

"I brought you these." She held out a soggy bakery box, but when Meg put an arm around her, guiding her into the hallway, her face crumpled and she started to cry.

Abandoning her questions, Meg pulled her into a tight hug. Sanne's body, initially rigid with resistance, gradually relaxed as Meg murmured soothing nonsense and ran her fingers through strands of sodden hair.

"I'm sorry, I'm sorry." Sanne sniffled but stayed snug in the embrace, and the tremors that had been wracking her eased. It was a long time before she took a shuddering breath and pulled away slightly. "I ruined our scones," she said, the words hiccupping through her tears. At some point, the box had fallen unnoticed to the floor.

Meg laughed, relieved to find an outlet for the tension. She knew it took a lot to make Sanne drop her guard to such an extent, but this wasn't the time to delve into the reasons, not while Sanne had the potential to bolt.

"No matter. If they're all smushed up, we'll just have to eat them with spoons." She curled her fingers around Sanne's cold hand. "Let's get you out of these wet things." She tugged once, not sure whether to be relieved or even more worried when Sanne followed her upstairs to the bathroom without a protest.

Sanne stood pale and listless, allowing Meg to undress her, as if the stamina that had kept her going through a sixteen-hour shift had simply run out.

"You're not hurt, are you?"

Sanne shook her head, her teeth chattering. Meg could see scattered bruises and scrapes on her arms and torso, but nothing that appeared recent.

"Are your mum and dad okay?"

"They're fine," Sanne said, watching Meg as she set a bath running and poured lotion into the water. The bathroom began to fill with lime-scented steam.

"So what happened at work, then?" Meg asked quietly. She sloshed the water with her hand, encouraging bubbles to form and giving Sanne time to answer. She looked up again as she felt the first button on her pyjama top being unfastened.

"Come in with me," Sanne said.

❖

The water was just on the wrong side of hot, but Meg was already in the bath and holding her arms out, so Sanne lowered herself beneath the suds and leaned back against Meg. Goose pimples covered her skin as ripples washed over her. She closed her eyes, concentrating on the slow, steady thud of Meg's heart. Under the foam, Meg's hands fumbled for hers and interlaced their fingers.

"Can you tell me now?" Meg murmured.

Sanne nodded, but the thoughts that had tormented her during the drive over were still too close to the surface. Fresh tears trickled down her cheeks. She licked her lips, tasting salt and citrus, and felt Meg give her hands an encouraging squeeze.

She took a deep breath. "The woman in the hospital is called Josie, not Rachel." Setting out the facts was a technique she often relied on at work. It allowed her to speak without emotion, relaying information but not identifying with it. "Nelson and I went out to search a holiday cottage she had rented, and it was obvious that two people had been staying there. Then I found a photograph of her with her partner, Rachel."

She felt Meg's reaction, the sudden rigidity in her limbs, and the increased rate and force of her heartbeat.

"Oh no," Meg whispered, and Sanne wondered whether she had figured the rest out.

"Whoever did this, Meg, I think he abducted both women, and he's still holding Rachel somewhere. He's had her for all this time, and we weren't even looking for her. God, I don't know if we're looking for her now, not like we should be, anyway, because Carlyle thinks she was the one who hurt Josie."

The heat of the water was too oppressive. She let go of Meg's hands and shoved herself upright, gripping the cool porcelain instead.

"I can't stop thinking about them," she said. "I know Carlyle's wrong, and I can't stop thinking of that fucking photograph, and Josie, waking up in the hospital and screaming because somehow she knew—she *remembered*—that she'd got out of there and left her partner behind. And then I think, what if? What if it had been us out hiking that day? We've been up on those trails loads of times. What if I'd escaped and you were still missing?"

Saying the words aloud had acted as a simple form of catharsis, but she could still hear her breath coming in short, sharp gasps. Making an effort to compose herself, she turned around to face Meg. "I know I need to be tougher, or I'm going to end up looking like a right tit. Fucking hell, I almost sat down and lost it, right there at the scene. Can you imagine the boss seeing me in that state?"

"Come here, you daft bugger," Meg told her, and she went willingly, tucking herself into Meg's arms, as water sloshed over the floor. "You can't do this to yourself, San. What's happened is horrendous, but we're not that couple, and you need to keep your head clear, or you won't be able to help them."

Sanne stroked her fingers across Meg's chest, swirling patterns in the soapsuds. "It's not so scary now I've told you."

Meg's quiet laugh rocked them both. "Out of your nightmares and straight into mine, eh?"

Sanne winced. "Sorry."

Meg kissed her forehead, and she instantly felt forgiven.

"Shall we get out of here before we go all pruney?" Meg said, waiting for her nod before reaching for a towel. "Grab yourself some pyjamas. I'll put the kettle on, and we'll see about resurrecting those scones."

Sanne took a plate and raised an eyebrow at its contents.

Ignoring the bait, Meg bumped down onto the sofa with her own plate. "It'll get even more mushed up when you chew it, and I bet you skipped your tea, so get it eaten." She peeked over the rim of her mug, watching Sanne take a first, dubious bite of the mangled scone and then settle in to eat with more gusto. The wavering firelight enhanced the healthy glow that the bathwater had given Sanne's face, and she seemed more herself as she licked jam and cream from her fingers.

"Did you speak to Dr. Maxwell today?" she asked, claiming a piece of scone that had slipped from Meg's fingers onto the No Man's Land of the sofa cushion.

"You're a thieving git, Sanne Jensen," Meg said, avoiding the question. She had thought her news good, but wasn't so sure after what Sanne had told her.

"What did he say?" Sanne pressed.

With a sigh, Meg put her mug onto her empty plate and turned to face her. "He told me she's showing strong signs of recovery, and he's hoping to wake her again in the next day or so."

Only the crackle of the fire broke the stillness, as Sanne took her time chewing her last mouthful. "At least we're prepared now," she said at length. "We know her name and how she might react, and Rachel's parents are coming to sit with her, so she'll have familiar faces there."

"Someone needs to reassure her that what happened wasn't her fault," Meg said. "The drugs in her system would have left her so disorientated that it was a miracle she escaped. She can't be held responsible for Rachel not escaping as well. She might not believe that at first, but she needs to be told."

Sanne banged her mug down, spilling tea and rattling the crockery. "I'll tell her. I don't give a shit what Carlyle thinks. If the boss still wants me to help with Josie's interview, I'll tell her."

The flash of fierce determination in her eyes made Meg smile. This was the Sanne of old, the one who had marched into Meg's kitchen in her welly boots and pyjamas, loudly declared that her dad was a "drunken fucker," and kissed Meg full on the lips as soon as Meg's mum had gone to phone the Jensens.

"What are you grinning at?" Sanne poked her in the side, her tone full of suspicion.

Caught red-handed in reminiscence, Meg laughed. "You, that night when you came to our house in your wellies and those jammies with the little purple elephants on them. You were so pissed off at the world, but you gave me the sweetest kiss."

"Our first." Sanne shuffled closer.

Meg put an arm around her. "Your lips were all blue, and you tasted of raspberry ice pop."

"I just remember you squeaking in shock, and that you used your tongue a surprising amount for a twelve-year-old."

"You taught me! You gave me all my theory lessons round the back of the bike sheds. 'Make sure you use your tongue,' you said."

"I was so scared that you might like boys," Sanne murmured, her voice thick and drowsy. "Even then, I knew I didn't, but I couldn't think of a way to tell you."

Meg stroked her cheek. "I guess you improvised in the end."

"Hey, it worked. You got the message, didn't you?"

"Oh, yeah. Loud and clear."

Sanne exhaled and settled her head on Meg's lap. "I'd seduce you now, if I wasn't so bloody tired."

"Ever the romantic. How about a rain check?" Meg put her feet up on the coffee table and draped a throw rug over them both.

"Mm, well, it *is* raining."

"That it is. I do have a bed, you know."

"Can't be arsed moving." Sanne's toes were clenching and unclenching like a cat kneading a blanket, a sure sign she would be asleep within minutes. Conceding defeat, Meg set the alarm on her mobile phone, leaned her head back on the sofa, and closed her eyes.

CHAPTER TWELVE

Sanne's commute was slightly longer from Meg's house, so she left herself extra time to get to headquarters. It was exactly 5:30 a.m. when she entered the office, to a glare from Carlyle, and a mug of tea and a cinnamon swirl from Nelson. She carried the impromptu breakfast to her desk, where Nelson pulled up a spare chair and sat sipping from his own mug.

"What crawled up Carlyle's arse this morning?" she asked. She bit down on her pastry, dabbing up errant flakes with her fingers. Nelson was concentrating on his coffee, but his eyes were full of mischief as he procrastinated.

"Nelson!" She smeared icing on his nose. "Spill the beans, *now*."

"You didn't hear this from me," he said in an undertone, "but rumour has it that you were right last night, and that Carlyle was barking up the wrong tree, as usual."

"Oh." She put the cinnamon swirl down, her appetite fading. "Damn. How did that come about? Did forensics find something?"

"No, Josie woke up a couple of hours ago. Mike was on duty at the hospital. He says they were weaning her off the sedation, and she started to fight the vent. Rachel's mum was there, though, and managed to keep her calm—calm enough to confirm that our perp is a male, and that Rachel was abducted with her."

Sanne took a gulp of her tea, welcoming the scalding heat. "Did she say anything else?"

"I don't think so. She wasn't awake for long. But it means we can narrow the focus of the investigation, instead of chasing around after Carlyle's shadows."

The office was starting to become noisy, as detectives heading for home swapped updates with those arriving for the day shift. Fred winked at Sanne—news had obviously travelled fast—but she didn't return his smile. Her being proved right just meant that Rachel was either dead or still held captive by a sadistic and dangerous individual. She wrapped her hands around her mug, wishing that there could have been a third explanation for Rachel's disappearance.

"San?" Nelson waited until she acknowledged him. He looked sombre and guilty, as if he had only just remembered what was at stake. "We'd better go and get a seat."

She followed him into the incident room and sat on a desk beside George and a man she didn't recognise. The room was crammed with people drafted in from other departments. Uniformed officers mingled with plain-clothes detectives, some pensive, most looking excited to be involved in a major case. A second whiteboard, displaying various images of Rachel Medlock and of Josie prior to her injuries, stood next to the one dominated by Sanne's pictures from the moor.

"You seen the papers this morning?" George asked.

She shook her head. Meg's newspaper hadn't arrived by the time she left the house, though she could imagine the scathing headlines.

"All the tabloids ran it on the front page," he said. "We're either incompetent, arrogant, or just plain stupid. The *Mail* is after the boss's head, and one of its reporters was caught trying to sneak into the ITU disguised as a nurse."

"Arseholes. I wouldn't piss on their newsroom if it was on fire." Sanne doubted Eleanor would bow to the media pressure, but the top brass weren't renowned for their patience, and there was a real danger they would hand the case to an external review team.

When Eleanor walked in, a hush rapidly descended. Wasting no time on pleasantries, she handed a pile of briefing notes to the closest officer to pass around. She held her own copy aloft.

"This summarises everything we know so far. Read it, digest it, and read it again. In the early hours of this morning, Josie Albright managed to describe a white male, indeterminate age, indeterminate features. She said that he wore a mask of some kind. Bugger-all to go on, I know, but we have another interview arranged, and she has at least eliminated Rachel Medlock as a suspect." She paused to indicate the photographs on the second whiteboard. "Copies of these are contained within the briefing material, and they are being widely circulated. Use them to jog people's memories. We've already seen an increase in calls to the incident line now that we have better images. The labs bumped this case up their schedule, and the forensics from the cave have just come back. However, as predicted, Josie's DNA is the only match. The results are documented in the notes. Take time to catch yourselves up, and see the list on the bulletin board in the main office for your assignments. EDSOP detectives, stick around for a minute, please."

Sanne waited with the rest of her team as the majority of the officers filed from the room. Eleanor shut the door behind the last to leave, a subtle shift in her body language betraying how worn out she was.

"None of you have fucked this up," she said. "*None* of you. But the press are having a field day, and the brass want results. Go over everything again. Re-interview anyone who fits the profile in the notes. Mrs. Martindale rents several other cottages through an agency, and she's given us a list of everyone involved in the building and garden maintenance. Fred and George, ditch the Missing Persons and start chasing down these names. Josie couldn't think of anyone who might be holding a grudge against her or Rachel, but, Mike, I want you to double-check their background, contacts, and colleagues. If that proves too big an ask, choose a couple of unis to help you out. Sanne, you're with me at the hospital this morning."

Sanne saw Carlyle open his mouth to object, but Eleanor didn't give him a chance.

"That's all for now. If you've been assigned a group of uniforms for the door-to-doors, keep them organised, and for the love of God, keep them away from the bloody press." She began placing her papers into her briefcase, an obvious cue for the detectives to leave. "Ten minutes, Sanne," she called out as Sanne reached the door.

Sanne nodded and joined Nelson in the crowd around the bulletin board. She was unlikely to be at the hospital all day, and she wanted to know what the rest of the shift had in store. Scotty Ramsden stepped aside, allowing her to squeeze into a space between Nelson and Carlyle.

"What've we got?" she asked.

"Six unis and the south side of Halshaw," Nelson said, tapping their names with his pen.

Carlyle laughed. "What's the boss doing sending her little pets to that shithole?"

Sanne had a very good idea what Eleanor was doing, but she merely gave him an enigmatic smile and walked back to her desk.

"I'll give you a call when I'm finished at the hospital," she told Nelson.

"No problem. I'm going to run a background check on Ned Moseley first, to give the good folk of Halshaw a chance to get out of bed."

"That's probably wise." On the other side of the office, she saw Eleanor waiting. "I've got to go."

"I'll leave Windermere Avenue till last, so we can get a cuppa."

Sanne grabbed her bag and coat. "Mate, if I'm with you by then, we'll be able to get more than a cuppa."

Even without the presence of a police officer outside Josie's room, visitors would have suspected there was something unusual about its occupant. Unlike every other bay and cubicle in the ITU, room three blazed with light, illuminating a wide section of the surrounding corridor and making Sanne squint as she and Eleanor drew closer.

Once her vision had adjusted to the fluorescent glare, the first thing she registered was the room's quietness. The automated noise of the ventilator had been replaced by Josie's soft snoring, and there were fewer drips or pumps to set off alarms. With her breathing tube removed and the swelling around her eyes less pronounced, Josie was starting to resemble the woman in the lakeside photograph again. She appeared to be sleeping comfortably, her hand held in a loose grip by a slight, grey-haired woman sitting at her bedside.

Eleanor told the uniform on duty that he could take a break, and at the sound of their voices, the woman looked up.

"Mrs. Medlock." Eleanor greeted her with a familiarity that suggested they had already met. She beckoned Sanne over and introduced her. Mrs. Medlock's handshake was firm, but grief and pain were etched across her face, and her eyes were swollen from crying.

"Please, call me Helen," she said, gesturing to two empty chairs. She regarded Sanne steadily, as if trying to piece together half-forgotten details. Then she brightened as she made the connection. "Oh, Sanne Jensen. It's good to meet you. I wanted to thank you for helping Josie."

Sanne glanced at the floor, uncomfortable accepting gratitude from someone whose daughter was still missing. "I just happened to be in the right place," she said quietly, pulling one of the chairs closer and sitting down. "I'm sure the boss has told you we're doing everything we can to find Rachel."

"Yes—yes, she has." Fresh tears broke into Helen's reply. She wiped her eyes with a tissue and looked over to Eleanor. "Would you like me to wake Josie up for you?"

"I'd appreciate that," Eleanor said. Despite her reluctance to rush the start of the interview, she had been unconsciously tapping her foot since she sat down.

Helen laid her hand on Josie's cheek, her thumb stroking the discoloured skin as she spoke to her. Within seconds, Josie made a guttural sound and smacked her lips in confusion. She blinked against the light, her body frozen, until she recognised her surroundings and sagged back onto her pillows.

"Helen?" she whispered.

"It's just me, sweetheart. Alec went to get some sleep."

"Rachel?"

Helen shook her head. "Nothing yet. There are two detectives here who need to speak to you. I told you they were coming. Do you remember?"

Josie's eyes had closed, but she forced them open again. "Mm. Not really." She tipped her head, searching for her visitors and flinching at the pain.

Sanne leaned forward to make things easier. "Hey, Josie. My name's Sanne. I'm one of the detectives working your case."

Josie nodded slowly. "You were here before." Like Helen, she spoke with a mild Scottish accent.

Sanne smiled, surprised she had any memory of that. "I sat with you a couple of times, and I was here when you woke up the other night."

The continued intensity of Josie's stare suggested that something about the explanation didn't quite fit. Helen must have sensed that as well, because she took Josie's hand in both of hers.

"Sanne was the one who found you on the moors," she said.

Josie seemed to take the unlikely coincidence in her stride. "I think I owe you a beer."

Sanne chuckled. "Technically, you owe two young lads a beer. They found you first. Do you remember any of that?"

"No. I just…Maybe your voice, but that might be from when you've visited. I asked the docs to stop putting shit in my IV, and I thought that would make things clearer"—anger started to eat into her words—"but they're not, and that fucker still has Rach."

Her breathing rate had shot up enough to make an alarm wail. Her nurse, who had been an unobtrusive presence in the corner of the room, sprang to her feet, but with a visible effort, Josie slowed her breathing, and the nurse resumed her seat without intervening. Sanne would have given Josie another minute to compose herself, but she saw Josie was looking at her expectantly again, so she took out her notepad and uncapped her pen.

"Can you take us through exactly what you do remember?"

Josie gave a faint nod. "I'll try, but it's all in pieces."

"Start with the first piece. What's the earliest thing you remember clearly?"

"Toast." The answer came out tinged with self-loathing. "I can't tell you much about who took us, but I know we had toast for our fucking breakfast. Is that going to help you, Detective?"

Sanne decided honesty was the best policy. "No, probably not. What's the next piece?"

"We're walking, and it's hot. Bright sunshine." Josie spoke slowly, her accent more evident as she tried to remain coherent. "Rach was lagging behind. I don't know why. She took lots of pictures, so maybe she'd stopped to do that. I always made fun of her for taking too many." She caught her breath on a sob. "I didn't hear him, didn't know he was there. He must have hit me with something. I fell, and Rach shouted out."

She reached for a cup of water, and Sanne held it for her until she indicated she was done.

"Can you describe him?"

"Not really. I keep trying to see him, but all I get is a blur. He was tall, taller than me. He wore a mask, but it had gaps, so I could see he was white."

"What about his eyes, or his hair?"

Josie shook her head. "I don't know. I'm sorry."

The misery in her voice made Sanne glance up from her notes. "You're doing a great job. Don't be apologising."

Obviously unconvinced, Josie licked her dry lips, her tongue lingering over a sore-looking split. "It's like I have this image of him, but it's all hazy, and I don't know if it's real or if I'm making stuff up, just so I can feel like I'm helping."

Eleanor cleared her throat, halting Sanne's notes mid-bullet point. She had been so focused on the interview that she had forgotten Eleanor was there.

"You're consistent with these details, Josie," Eleanor said. "What you've told Sanne is the same as you told the detective last night, and in my experience that's always a good sign. We just need you to dig a little deeper. Can you remember what he was wearing?"

"Only that it was black, and that it covered him. We were in shorts and T-shirts, and he was dressed like a fucking ninja." Josie's voice dropped, and she shivered. "He had black gloves on, and the sun hit his knife, and Rachel was crying, and he wouldn't let me go to her."

Sanne resumed writing, trying not to put images to Josie's rapid monologue. An ache in her chest warned her she was breathing too fast.

"I felt sick, but he made us walk. And then I think there were rocks, and it went dark. After that it was cold, and something was dripping." Her right hand tapped the bedrail, sounding out the rhythm. "And all I have is flashes: pain, and being scared shitless, then feeling as if I was floating, and everything was pitch-black. I was so thirsty, but I couldn't move, couldn't get over to whatever was dripping."

"Was Rachel with you?" Sanne asked.

Josie nodded, her eyes full of tears. "I can still hear her screaming. How could I forget about her?" Her body shook with the force of her sobs. "How could I leave her in there with him?"

The questions were directed at Sanne, but her gaze went to Helen, and Sanne realised that it wasn't her place to offer explanations or the absolution Josie needed. Without a word, Helen sat on the edge of the bed, gathered Josie into her arms, and held her as she wept.

Feeling like an intruder, Sanne averted her eyes, her pen still poised above notes that told her almost nothing and more than she had ever wanted to know.

❖

Built in the Sixties by Sheffield Council as an overspill housing development, Halshaw estate was a sprawling conglomeration of rundown council-leased properties and the occasional privately owned home. Five miles west of Rowlee, it was a blight on an otherwise picturesque landscape, and its troubled regeneration project had been stalling for several years. With high rates of unemployment, drug use, and alcohol dependency, Halshaw had a significant number of residents with criminal records, and its populace was familiar with unannounced visits from the police.

A uniform dropped Sanne off on the estate, and she met up with Nelson outside the small parade of shops where he'd parked his car. As they headed to the next street on his list, she updated him on the morning's events.

"We managed to finish the interview once Josie had settled down a bit, but she blanked on his accent or any other distinguishing features, and on whether they'd encountered him prior to their abduction. There didn't seem to be any pattern in what she could and couldn't recall." She paused to check a road sign, avoiding a pile of dog shit that someone had already stepped in.

"Given what she's been through, I'm amazed she was able to remember anything," Nelson said, happy as ever to leave the navigating to Sanne.

"Me too. I know it's not helping us, but a big part of me hopes she never gets those memories back." She pointed out the start of Keswick Walk. "Right, this is our next one to cover. There's ten or so houses on it. Top end's okay, but the three at the bottom are notorious for drugs, drink, and Granny Sedgely."

He caught hold of her arm before she could cross the road. "Granny Sedgely? Are you having me on?"

"Nope. She's probably knocking on for eighty now. Mean old bird. Used to have this baseball bat with razorblades stuck into it. Everyone, and I mean *everyone*, was terrified of her, even the dealers."

Nelson eyed the forlorn terrace with a wariness he rarely allowed Sanne to see. The first and fourth houses flew tattered St. George crosses, a national symbol that had become synonymous with far-right racism. Although he'd not told Sanne much about his morning, she could guess from his subdued mood that it hadn't been pleasant.

"Fuck it," she said. "Windermere's just around the corner. Let's go there instead and leave Granny S to the unis."

For once, he capitulated without protest. "I'll call up the closest team and ask them to swing by here." When he had finished on the radio, he smiled his thanks at her. "Lead the way, partner."

Number thirty-two Windermere Avenue looked a lot like most of its neighbours: a dour semi-detached with small windows to deter burglars, rickety garden fencing, and a front lawn in need of a trim. It was only on closer inspection that a visitor might realise the fence had been carefully painted and the flowerbeds bordering the lawn sported a well-tended, colour-coordinated display. The lawn was looking tatty only because Sanne hadn't had the time to come round and mow it recently. She went up the drive, plucking out a couple of weeds en route, and rang the doorbell. A child shrieked in response.

Sanne rolled her eyes. "Sounds like the gang's all here. We can go back to the razor-toting granny if you prefer."

Nelson laughed. "How many kids is it now? I've lost track."

"Four, and the eldest is five. I keep telling her to get a television—" The door opened and she smiled. "Hey, Mum."

For a split second, Teresa Jensen looked like a deer caught in headlights, or—more apt in her case—a house-proud sixty-two-year-old who preferred to vacuum her home top to bottom and dust her mantelpiece before she welcomed guests.

"It's okay," Sanne whispered in her ear as they embraced. "We're just here to pinch a brew. I promise we won't be checking for cobwebs."

Her mum relaxed and kissed her cheek. "You look peaky," she said. Then, to Nelson, "Don't you think she looks peaky, dear?"

"A little." He shook her hand in both of his. "You, on the other hand, look as lovely as ever."

She tugged at her apron and blushed. "Flattery will get you everywhere. I just made a Battenberg cake. Come on in, and I'll fetch you a slice." As they took off their boots, she shouted down the hallway. "Keeley, put the kettle on! Sanne's here."

At the mention of her name, Sanne's niece and nephew came racing out of the kitchen. She scooped up the smaller one, Kiera, and left Kerby hanging on to her trousers. Although she despaired of her sister's choice of names, she adored the children, and the feeling was mutual.

Her mum led the way into the kitchen, where the smell of fresh baking made Sanne's mouth water, and where her sister eyed Nelson with blatant appreciation. Keeley was between boyfriends, having finally split up with Kiera's dad two months ago. There was a rumour that Kyle's dad was back in the picture, not that anyone would guess that from the way Keeley chewed her hair and batted her eyelids at Nelson.

Sanne gave Kiera a biscuit and set her on the floor, watching her as she toddled through the patio doors into the garden, dropped her biscuit in the mud, picked it up again, and gnawed on a damp corner. Sanne didn't try to interfere. She had eaten countless muddy biscuits during her childhood, and they had done her no harm.

"Sorry I couldn't make it for tea the other night," she said, adding milk to her brew and then passing the bottle to Nelson.

Her mum paused in the middle of cutting thick slices of cake. "That's all right, love. We know how busy you are. Those poor girls…Have you heard anything yet?"

"No, not yet. That's why we're round here: house-to-house. We can only stay a few minutes."

Keeley slurped at her tea and grabbed the first piece of cake. "You missed a nice leg of lamb. But then Michael tried to convert Dad again, so Dad tried to clout him with the serving spoon." She paused for a breath, broke her cake into chunks, and popped one into her mouth. "You should speak to Pete Farris. He was always a dodgy little shit."

"Keeley! Language!" her mum hissed, shooting an apologetic look in Nelson's direction.

"This is really good cake," he said into the awkward silence.

Sanne nibbled a bit of marzipan, torn between amusement and despair. "Pete Farris only has one leg, Keels. Remember? He injected into his groin and got that abscess."

"Yeah, right. He gets loads of disability." Keeley spoke with unmistakeable envy. She was endlessly bitter about her own government handouts, despite the fact that they totalled almost as much as Sanne's salary, but a well-timed wail from the garden prevented her from launching into one of her tirades. "Oh, those fucking kids." She slammed down her mug and stamped out through the patio doors, leaving her mum shaking her head in dismay.

"Is Dad in?" Sanne asked quietly.

"Aye, usual spot," her mum said.

Sanne sighed. She didn't want to leave the kitchen, with its warm lighting and its bakery scent, but she knew her mum would be made to pay later if her dad found out he'd been ignored. "I should probably go and say hello."

She left her tea and half-eaten cake and went into the living room. It was barely four p.m., but the curtains were drawn, the only light coming from the muted television. She stopped just over the threshold, grimacing at the stink of stale booze and unwashed clothes. This room and the man sitting in its far corner were her mum's perpetual shame. He rarely allowed her to clean anything in there, and he refused to clean himself. A pall of cigarette smoke hung in the air. As Sanne watched, her dad lit another roll-up and took a swig from the can in his hand.

"Hi, Dad." She walked forward slowly, kicking an empty two-litre bottle of White Ace cider from her path. Her dad grunted in acknowledgement and peered up at her, smoke rushing from his nostrils. She couldn't bring herself to touch him, so she stopped at a safe distance, focusing on the framed picture of a cruise ship that took pride of place on top of a nest of tables.

He ran a grimy hand over his beard and belched. "What are you doing here?"

"House-to-house enquiries for a case. Thought we'd drop in for a cuppa."

He took a drag on his cigarette, indifferent to the ash falling on the carpet. "That coon with you?"

She gritted her teeth. There was a reason Nelson had stayed in the kitchen. "His name is Nelson, and yes, he's with Mum."

Her dad scoffed, flicking more ash on the floor. "Don't know what this bleedin' country's coming to."

She stared at the photograph until the crystal blue of the ocean blurred with the white of the ship. She had nothing to say to him that wouldn't provoke an argument. In truth, she couldn't stand the sight of him. She was holding her breath and counting to fifty, when she heard her mum call her name.

"I'd better go. Sounds like I'm needed."

He grunted. "Shut the fucking door behind you. Keep them kids out of here."

Sanne ran upstairs to the bathroom, where she locked the door, filled the sink with scalding water, and scrubbed her hands and face. She felt calmer when she was done. Her mum's soap was sweet with lavender, and she had found a tub of moisturiser in the cabinet that erased the smell of nicotine and dirt completely. She flushed the toilet, hoping to explain her long absence.

Back downstairs, she found Nelson drying pots. Her mum handed her a fresh mug of tea, ushered her into a seat, and put a sandwich in front of her.

"Nelson said you missed your dinner."

"Mm." Suddenly ravenous, Sanne took a mouthful and spoke around it. "I was busy with an interview."

"You need to eat, San. You've lost weight. Is Meg not taking care of you?"

"Meg takes care of me just fine." She winked at her mum. One of her mum's biggest regrets was Sanne's and Meg's refusal to do the decent thing and get married.

"Bring her for tea one night. It's weeks since I saw her."

Sanne toasted the idea with her mug and wrapped the rest of her sandwich in a napkin. "We should make a move."

"I tried to answer Nelson's questions," her mum said, "but I really haven't seen anything that might help, and your dad's not left the house in two weeks." She added a slice of cake to Sanne's picnic and carried the rest into the pantry.

"What about Keeley?" Sanne asked Nelson.

He consulted his notes, biding his time to ensure her mum was out of earshot. "She said she hadn't been into Rowlee for almost a month, because, and I quote, 'that prick Nathan who works in the butcher's keeps trying to cop a feel.'"

"Perfect," Sanne said. "Thanks for trying, anyway."

Outside, they found a light rain had started to fall, making the streets look even less inviting. They waited until a young man had ridden past on his bike, dodging potholes and broken glass, and then crossed the road. Music was blaring from the window of a nearby flat, but beneath the relentless bass an argument was clearly audible. Sanne hated coming back here, hated the claustrophobic feel of the streets: too many houses and too many unhappy people, crammed into too small a space. Of her colleagues, only Nelson and Eleanor knew she had grown up on Halshaw. She wouldn't lie about it if someone asked her directly, but it wasn't something she wanted to shout about. Meg had lived two streets over, and somehow they had both managed to avoid the trap of unemployment and reliance on government benefits that had ensnared their siblings. Not many people truly escaped from the estate—not unless you counted those who found a new home in a prison cell—and Sanne's mum had been delighted the first time she had visited Sanne's cottage.

Knowing that the DI rarely did things by chance, Sanne suspected Eleanor had assigned her that patch of Halshaw to ensure that no other members of EDSOP would happen upon her family.

"Okay, cheers for that," Nelson said into his radio, and Sanne realised that an entire conversation had taken place over the comms without her hearing a word. He held out his list for her to consult. "We have Scafell Walk and Thirlmere Avenue still outstanding."

She pulled a face and handed Nelson the piece of cake. The quizzical look he gave her made her laugh. "Eat it. Trust me, mate, if we're going to Scafell we'll need the sustenance."

Three hours later, footsore and soaked to the skin, Sanne was attempting to question a lethargic nineteen-year-old with heroin-narrowed pupils, when the comms buzzed.

"Excuse us a minute," she said. The lad tutted and folded his arms, as if the delay kept him from attending to something of vital importance.

She ignored his tapping feet as Eleanor's voice greeted her and Nelson with a terse, "Where are you?"

"Halfway down Thirlmere Avenue. Is something wrong?"

"Nelson, you requested a background check on a Ned Moseley this morning?"

"That's right," he said. "Preliminary came back clean. I left Scotty chasing down the rest of it."

"It was all clean," Eleanor said, "but guess who's come up as the general handyman and caretaker of Rowan Cottage?"

Sanne and Nelson reacted in unison. "Bloody hell."

"My sentiment exactly. He lives on the outskirts of Rowlee, about three miles from Halshaw. George and Fred are on their way over, but the address is a terrace with a back alley, so we need someone to cover that in case he does a runner."

"What about Tactical Aid?" Nelson asked. The TAU were far better equipped to apprehend potentially dangerous criminals than EDSOP were.

"They're at an EDL rally in Sheffield. You're on your own."

"Well, we've both got our big-boy boots on," Sanne said.

Nelson apologised to the lad and turned a blind eye to the answering gesture. He and Sanne hurried away from the house.

"Keep me up to speed, and be careful," Eleanor told them.

Sanne signed off, breaking into a trot as she plotted the quickest route back to Nelson's car.

"I'll toss you for it!" Nelson had to shout to be heard above the thudding of their boots on the pavement.

"Tails," Sanne shouted back.

Reaching his car, he flipped a coin and whooped when it landed heads-up. "Next time, San, I promise." Grinning like a child, he got into the driver's seat, stuck his blue light onto the roof, and activated the beacon as he pulled away from the kerb. "Oh, I'm getting chills. It's been way too long since we did this."

He skidded to a halt at the junction, set the siren wailing, and sped out onto the main road.

Chapter Thirteen

The drizzle had turned into a downpour. It bounced off the windscreen as Nelson extinguished his blues and turned onto Prospect Road.

"Name seems a bit cruel," Sanne said, craning her neck to look at the street of scruffy terraced houses suggesting little in the way of good fortune.

"It was probably nicer when they built it." Nelson eased the car into a gap between a Micra with a flat tyre and a knackered Fiat with a huge exhaust and a ludicrous body kit.

"Yeah, maybe." Far from convinced, she raised her hand to acknowledge George.

Minutes later, they were crammed into Fred's car, steaming up his windows while peering through the darkness at the middle house on the row. There was nothing to distinguish it from the others: a two-up, two-down, it opened directly onto the street, and its downstairs curtains were drawn as if to shut out the miserable weather.

"Lights have been going on and off, so someone's in. The woman at the rental agency reckons he lives alone." Fred had offered around a bag of humbugs and was picking caramel from his teeth as he spoke.

"Right, what's the plan?" Nelson asked.

"At the moment, he's nothing more than a 'person of interest.'" Fred wrapped the phrase in air quotes. "We knock and invite him down to the office for tea and a chat. With a bit of luck, he's all obliging, grabs his coat, and offers to provide the KitKats. You and

Sanne just need to hang out round the back in case he decides to play hard to get."

Sanne grinned, making her mint rattle against her teeth. "Who could possibly resist your charms, Fred?"

"My first, second, and third wives, love." He gave a theatrical and slightly camp sigh. "Sometimes I wonder about switching to your team."

In a flash, George had his door open. "I think that's our cue to leave. Buzz us when you're in position."

At the entrance to the alley, Sanne flicked her torch on and panned it across the narrow passage. The houses on Prospect Road and those on the road running parallel had backyards instead of gardens: depressing concrete squares devoid of flowers or trees, some still dominated by air-raid shelters, and all surrounded by high brick walls. Hemmed in on both sides but unsecured at the entrances, the alley between them provided the perfect opportunity for illegal rubbish dumping.

Sanne negotiated a careful path through the heaps of debris. "Shame no one's been bothered to gate the alley."

"I might write an angry letter." Nelson tripped over a rusted toy scooter before stopping on Sanne's cue. "Is this us?"

"Yep, eighth house down." She keyed her radio. "Ready when you are, Fred."

"Roger that."

A minute passed, then another. Standing to one side of the yard gate, Sanne adjusted her weight from foot to foot while Nelson kicked two squashed cans and half a loaf of bread back toward a gnawed-open bin bag. In the next street, a car alarm blared. He swung around toward it and then shook his head at his own edginess.

Sanne put her torch beneath her chin and pulled a face, making him laugh. "Maybe Ned didn't answer the door," she said.

Nelson flicked a crust from the toe of his boot. "Maybe he invited them in for coffee, and they've forgotten all about us."

"Knowing those two—"

"Bloody hell! *Stop!* Oh, arse!" Fred's yell cut across the comms, swiftly followed by another. "Nelson, San! Incoming!"

That was all the warning they got before the gate slammed open and a dark shape barrelled into the alley. Ned Moseley led with his fists, hitting out repeatedly at Nelson and forcing him against the wall. With no time to consider the consequences, Sanne threw herself forward, trying to put herself between the two men, but Nelson was already slumping to the floor. Seeing his escape route almost clear, Ned punched her once—a sloppy hit that caught her shoulder—and set off at a run. She took half a step after him before hesitating and looking back at Nelson.

"I'm fine." He waved her away, urging her to give chase. His nose was bleeding, and more blood dribbled down his chin as he coughed.

"Back in a minute." She turned to cast her torchlight down the alley.

Hampered by the near-total darkness, Ned hadn't got far. As he floundered over an upended sofa, she ran after him, skirting the torn bin bag and then sprinting down the centre of the alley, where less rubbish had collected.

"He's heading west, west, west," she shouted into the comms.

"Backup's seven minutes out." Fred's voice, puffing for breath. He sounded as if he was running but already winded. "He slammed the front door on us. We're coming round the side."

"Shit," she whispered, and swore again as she lost her footing and collided with a gate swinging from its hinges. She quickly righted herself and charged onward, spotting Ned on his hands and knees about fifty yards ahead.

"*Police!* Stay where you are! Oh, for fuck's sake…" She'd put everything behind her command but wasn't surprised when he ignored her. Although she was faster than him, he definitely had the advantage in build, and she doubted her torch would double as a cosh.

The orange glow of streetlights brought the end of the alley into focus. Ned ran across the dividing road beyond it and into another unlit passageway, this one overgrown with weeds. She heard a sudden shriek and saw him hopping over to the left side of the path. For the first time, she realised he was wearing only boxer shorts and trainers. His progress became a halting dance around clumps of nettles and brambles.

"Seriously?" she muttered, slowing to a jog and then a cautious walk. Fifty yards narrowed to ten, until she was close enough to hear his yelps every time something snagged him. "Cross the street at the west end of Prospect," she said into her mike, struggling to keep the tremor from her voice. "We're in the ginnel immediately after that, and I don't think we're going much further."

An affirmative response and the wail of sirens reassured her somewhat—until Ned abruptly stopped and turned to face her. She held one hand up in an attempt to placate him, using the other to direct her torch at him.

Shielding his eyes, he took a step forward. "Officer Sanney?"

She stood her ground, angling the light to impede his vision. "Yeah, Ned. We met on the moors."

He nodded, and his bottom lip began to quiver. "I didn't mean to hurt anyone."

She instinctively moved closer. "Who didn't you mean to hurt?"

He pointed back over her head. "That cop. I was just watching *Emmerdale*, and those blokes scared me. I wasn't doing nowt wrong."

In the corner of her eye, she saw blue and red flashes. "It's okay, Ned. We just need to have a chat with you, that's all. Shall we get out of these nettles?"

"I'm allergic to nettles." He was staring past her, mesmerised by the strobes, and without being prompted, he held out his hands in surrender. Technically, they hadn't come to arrest him, but that was before he assaulted a detective, so she snapped her cuffs around his wrists and recited his rights as they picked their way back to the street.

"Sorry I hit you," he said. He tripped over his flopping shoelace, and she had to grab his arm to right him, keeping hold of it to steer him toward the closest police van. When he saw the officers charging over to meet them, he hid his face in his hands and started to cry.

"This our chap?" one of the officers asked. He kept glancing over Sanne's shoulder, as if waiting for something more exciting to emerge from the shadows. His team was obviously geared up for a scrap, not for a compliant, blubbering perp wearing nothing but boxers and nettle rash.

"Aye." Sanne handed him over and waited until the van pulled away. "Fuck me," she whispered to herself. Her legs felt like jelly, and she had to keep her mouth shut to hold back a hysterical bubble of laughter. Still shaking her head in disbelief, she went to find Nelson.

❖

Meg injected the morphine into Hilda Ratcliffe's IV and watched as her eyes flickered before finally closing. Even in sleep, the patient continued to mumble, her words nonsensical and tangled. Meg took hold of her hand, nodding at Emily as she did so.

"You should be okay, now that she's more settled. Soon as you're done, we can get her up to Ortho."

Emily opened a suture kit and picked up a syringe of local anaesthetic. "Right. Are you sure about this?" The back of her wrist bore vivid scratches where Hilda's fingernails had raked across it. Her multiple attempts to insert the IV had not been appreciated, and Hilda's screeches had brought Meg running to the cubicle.

"I'm sure. She's pretty out of it." Meg touched a hand to Hilda's brittle hair. Blood matted a large area where she had hit her head, but it was the fractured hip that would probably prove fatal. For a ninety-one-year-old already in fragile health, a general anaesthetic would be high-risk and her recovery fraught with complications. She was unlikely to be able to fight off any kind of post-operative infection. Her nose twitched as Emily began to inject the lignocaine, but she remained asleep.

"Poor old sod," Meg whispered. The woman was covered in bruises and scars from previous falls, and her skin tented where Meg pinched it, showing how dehydrated she was. "We'd put a bloody dog down if it ended up in this state."

Emily stiffened slightly but didn't contradict her. "Which home is she from?"

"Juniper Bank. It's a proper shithole. Care Quality have threatened to shut it down twice, but somehow it keeps rising from the ashes. The manager couldn't even be bothered to send an escort with her." Meg encircled Hilda's wrist with her index finger and thumb. The woman was so emaciated that Meg's fingers easily met. Alzheimer's had left Hilda utterly dependent on care home staff, and it was evident that they were failing her. "The paramedics are going to report the home again. They think she'd been on the floor for a few hours before anyone found her."

"That's awful. I could never put a member of my family in one of those places."

In retrospect, Meg wasn't sure if it was the pious tone of Emily's voice or the bald naivety of the statement that made her hackles rise, but she replied without thinking.

"My mum's in one of those places."

The sharpness of the retort made Emily hesitate midway through tying off a suture. A flush crept up her neck, but she didn't apologise; she just looked at Meg in curiosity.

"She is? Why?"

Meg had to give her credit for audacity. She might still be useless at cannulation, but she had apparently developed a backbone during the last few days of Meg's unofficial tutelage.

"Early-onset dementia." Meg shrugged off Emily's sympathetic wince. "I couldn't afford to give up work and look after her, my brother's an idiot who can barely look after himself, and I've not seen my dad in years, so full-time care was the safest option. San helped me check out all the homes in the area, and we picked one with an excellent rating. It's not perfect, but it's better than the alternative."

Emily placed a dressing over her neat row of sutures and started cleaning the blood from Hilda's neck. "My dad's been screwing his secretary for five years, and my mum pretends she doesn't know." She continued to scrub at the blood, her tone that of someone chatting about the weather.

Meg blew out a breath that rippled her fringe. She didn't know what to say to that, which wasn't a situation she often found herself in.

It was Emily who cracked first. A hint of a smile broke into a full grin. "With families this messed up, how did we turn out so normal?"

"Damned if I know." Meg held up a hand in apology as her phone began to ring. Seeing Sanne's name on the caller ID, she ignored the department's rules and answered it. "Hey, you. What's up?"

There was a short delay before Sanne spoke. When she did, Meg had to strain to hear her over the noise in the background.

"Hiya. You're on a late today, aren't you?"

"Yes. Are you all right?"

"I'm fine." Sanne's sigh was cut short by the unmistakable sound of someone vomiting. "You couldn't free up a cubicle for Nelson, could you?"

For the second time in less than a week, Meg met Sanne in the ambulance bay. On this occasion, however, Sanne pulled up in an unfamiliar car. She gave Meg a quick hug before going over to the ambulance she had been escorting, and as they waited for its doors to open, Meg took the opportunity to eyeball her. She was a little rumpled, and her coat-sleeve was torn, but she seemed hale enough.

"Dare I ask?" Meg said.

"We went to bring a chap in for questioning, but he didn't take too kindly to us. Nelson took a couple of punches. He didn't want to come here, but he's bleeding like a stuck pig."

Meg pulled her to one side. "What about you?"

"I'm fine." Not only did Sanne look Meg in the eye as she answered, but excitement had her practically bouncing on the spot. She put her lips to Meg's ear and whispered, "I ran after the bloke and arrested him on my own." Her grin stretched from ear to ear.

Meg's kneejerk horror quickly turned to pride. She slung an arm around Sanne's shoulders. "How the hell did a tiddler like you pull that off?"

"I used my feminine wiles."

"Yeah. You don't really have any of those, love."

Sanne tilted her head, considering and then conceding the point. "Okay then, I chased him into a shitload of nettles." She displayed hands sporting a mass of raised welts. "Don't suppose you have any calamine lotion?"

"I'll see what I can do." Meg smiled at Nelson as he stepped off the ambulance, holding a wad of gauze to his nose.

"The boss insisted he get a check-up," Sanne said. "Then I'm taking him back to HQ so we can watch the interview."

Meg nodded, but she was only catching occasional words, and even those weren't making much sense to her. Exhilaration had left Sanne's cheeks rosy, and the flecks of green in her eyes were glinting brightly, a combination that was very pretty and extremely distracting. When she smiled at Meg for no reason, Meg had to have a stern word with herself about maintaining her professionalism.

"Cubicle four," she told the paramedics, with all the authority she could muster.

"Righto."

Meg took a breath, satisfied that no one had noticed a thing. She caught Sanne's eye and swiftly corrected herself: no one, that was, except for Sanne.

Even walking down a noisy, over-lit hospital corridor, Sanne couldn't mistake the expression on Meg's face. Everyone else appeared to be oblivious, but it made nerves that were already humming pleasantly begin to sing in full-throated chorus. When she poked out her tongue to wet lips that had suddenly gone dry, Meg arched an eyebrow at her, making her stumble.

"You okay there?" Meg's voice was hoarse but amused.

"Yep." Looking up, Sanne saw Nelson and the paramedics rounding a corner and took the opportunity to slap the back of Meg's hand. "Will you bloody behave yourself?"

Meg widened her eyes, feigning innocence. "I am behaving in an impeccable manner."

"You're incorrigible."

"I may well be that too."

Upon reaching the cubicle, Sanne watched Meg smoothly return to doctor mode, running Nelson through a brief but thorough assessment. Envying her ability to compartmentalise, Sanne took a seat in the corner, where she plucked a leaflet from a collection on the wall and began to educate herself about otitis media. She was halfway through the section on treatment, when a young-looking doctor poked her head around the curtain.

"Sorry to interrupt, Dr. Fielding, but I wondered if you needed any help."

"We're just about finished, thanks." Meg beckoned the woman into the cubicle. "Sorry, Emily, this is Sanne Jensen. I think you've met Nelson already."

"Yes, he took my statement after Josie went to surgery." Emily smiled at Sanne and extended a hand. "Good to meet you."

Her grip was warm and firm, and she held on a little longer than Sanne thought necessary. She was attractive, in a well-brought-up, designer-clothing, perfect hair and makeup kind of way. She didn't make Sanne's nerves tingle, though. She just made her wonder whether there were any straight people left in the NHS these days.

The buzz of Sanne's phone came as a welcome interruption. Emily took it as her cue to leave, and Meg followed her out to collect Nelson's painkillers.

Sanne leaned forward on her chair and accepted the call. "Hey, boss."

"Everyone still alive down there?" Eleanor asked.

"Alive and kicking. Nelson's got some sort of Tampax thingy shoved up his nose, but he'll be fine."

"Good. George and Fred got here about fifteen minutes ago, looking quite sheepish."

Sanne tried not to laugh. "They ran the wrong way. Could've happened to any one of us."

"Any one of us who doesn't know their west from their east," Eleanor said dryly. "Anyway, I'm sending you Ned Moseley's mugshot. Could you take it up to Josie and see if it rings any bells?"

"No problem. Are you interviewing him tonight?"

"We'd planned to, but the bastard really is allergic to nettles. The doc gave him an antihistamine, and he's in one of the holding cells, sleeping like a baby."

"Sorry, boss."

Eleanor scoffed. "What the hell are you sorry for?"

"Um. Chasing him into the nettles?"

"Don't be a berk. We're going to leave him till first thing in the morning, so once you've seen Josie and finished your report you can head home."

"Wilco," Sanne said, but the line was already dead. She dropped her phone back into her pocket and turned to Nelson. "Looks like we've got the night off." Relief flitted across his bruised face. She patted his shoulder. "Sit tight, and I'll see where Meg is."

Outside the cubicle, she checked the image Eleanor had sent her: a standard mugshot of Ned that perfectly rendered his confusion at the booking process. With tear-smudged cheeks and a hangdog expression, he hardly fitted the stereotype of a cold-blooded kidnapper, though Sanne knew better than to be fooled by appearances.

Meg approached with pills in one hand and a cup of water in the other. "What've you got there?" she asked.

Sanne showed her the photo. "Prime suspect Ned."

"He's the one who kicked the crap out of your buddy?"

"Yep."

"And the one you followed into an unlit alley?"

"Uh, yeah." She ran a hand across the back of her neck. The height marker by Ned's head indicated he was six foot two.

Meg touched her knuckles to Sanne's chin. "Hey, I'm just relieved you came out the other side, that's all."

"Me too," Sanne admitted. After the high of the chase, the reality of the risks she had taken was beginning to set in. Putting thoughts of a bath and bed out of her mind, she steeled herself for another hour or two of work. "I have to go and speak to Josie. Will you get Nelson a coffee?"

"Sure."

"Two sugars."

"You know I'll forget that."

Her nonchalance made Sanne smile. "Yeah, I know you will. Just try not to make him tea."

❖

The doctor in the ITU wasn't happy about Sanne's request for another interview with Josie only hours after the first, but he grudgingly gave permission, along with a stern warning not to cause undue stress.

"Fifteen minutes," he said, escorting her to the room. "She started physio this afternoon, and she's exhausted."

Sanne knocked out of habit, expecting Josie to be asleep or with company, but she was alone, staring at a book that lay unopened on her lap. At some point during the day, the dressings had been removed from her head, leaving her surgical scars exposed.

"Hi." Her greeting was subdued. She had probably worked out that a solo, junior detective would not be conveying any significant developments.

"Hi." Sanne walked to the side of the bed. Then, for want of a better opening, "You suit the non-bandagey look."

It was such a daft thing to say that it made Josie smile. She touched the bristle of new hair. "Apparently, I'm a brunette. I didn't remember until Helen let me have a mirror." Her fingers approached the edge of a sutured wound but stopped just short. "I thought they'd cut it for the surgery, but it was him, wasn't it?"

There was no point in lying. Sanne needed to gain her trust. "Yes, he cut it. We're not sure why."

Josie nodded, swallowing repeatedly as if something was blocking her throat. For a while she kept her eyes fixed on the door, but when she seemed sure they wouldn't be interrupted she turned back to Sanne. "No one will tell me much or talk to me about this shit. They keep bringing me stuff—books, magazines, fucking Sudoku—but all I can think about is Rachel and what he might be doing to her. And then I think, what if she's dead? What will I do then?"

She started to cry, rocking back and forth in her effort to keep quiet and avoid alerting the medics. Sanne sat on the bed and took hold of her hand, and Josie clung on as if it were the only thing keeping her from going under.

"I should never have run." Her breath hitched between her words. "I should've stayed with her."

"You didn't even know she was there. You did what anyone would have done in those circumstances. You got the hell out when you had the chance. Do you think she will blame you for that?"

Josie coughed and sniffled. Sanne freed up their hands to pass her a tissue.

"She might." Josie wiped her face, but she was becoming more composed, and her expression softened. "She's terrible for holding grudges."

"Well, I don't think she'll hold on to this one." Mindful of her deadline, Sanne fished out her phone. "Josie, we brought someone in for questioning tonight. Do you feel up to looking at his photograph?" She chose her words carefully. Ned had been arrested for assault, not on suspicion of kidnapping.

Josie studied the image for a long time, tapping the screen to reawaken it when it timed out. Sanne surreptitiously watched the monitors, but they registered no signs of distress, and Josie's face gave nothing away. Eventually, she allowed the screen to shut itself down and handed back the phone.

"I don't think I recognise him." She gave a derisive laugh. "But I wouldn't take my word for it. A friend of mine sent me a text this afternoon, and Helen had to remind me who she was. I had a stroke after I woke up that first time. Did they tell you that?"

"No, no one told me that." Sanne had guessed, though. Josie was using her right hand for everything, her left lying in a stiff claw on the bed sheets. It was little wonder that she was vacillating so wildly between anger and grief. It was a miracle she was functioning at all.

"Will the physio help?" Sanne asked, aware how intently Josie was gauging her reaction.

Avoiding pity and shock appeared to be a sound tactic. Josie slung her bad arm across her lap and slowly unfurled her index finger. "Better than nothing, right?"

"Damn right. That's bloody impressive after one session."

A smile seemed to catch Josie unawares, and for a couple of seconds Sanne glimpsed the young woman who had written postcards about falling into bogs and being chased by cows. The smile didn't last, but it was reassuring to know that that person was still in there.

"You should probably go," Josie said, covering her left hand with her right. "You must be busy."

Sanne thought of the report she had yet to start, the fourteen-hour shift that awaited her the next day, and the sixteen-hour one she was coming to the end of. Then she looked at Josie, who was determinedly studying the bed sheets.

"Do you want me to stick around for a bit?" she asked.

Josie nodded.

Sanne shrugged out of her coat and arranged it over the back of her chair. "I have to warn you though," she said, taking a bar of Dairy Milk from her bag and snapping it into chunks, "I'm crap at Sudoku."

"Me too. I think I was better at concentrating before I whacked my head. Well, I must have been, because I have a degree in classics from Edinburgh University. First class, apparently."

"Clever clogs." Sanne offered her a piece of chocolate, holding it patiently as Josie struggled to take it in her left hand. She managed to curl her fingers around the chunk, but then gave up and used her good hand instead.

"Dr. Maxwell says it will all come back to me in time. The swelling in my brain is getting better, and most of the early things are there. They're just jumbled."

Sanne settled in her chair and crossed her legs at the ankles. "Did you meet Rachel at university?" she asked.

Josie's face brightened at the mention of Rachel's name. "Yes. She was studying environmental sciences, but we're both cinema geeks, so we met through FilmSoc. She works for the National Trust now, and I'm a curator at the National Museum in Edinburgh. Have you ever been there?"

"No, I've not." Sanne had never really been anywhere. She could have afforded to travel abroad now, but staying at home seemed kinder to her mum. Woe betide her if her mum ever worked that out, though.

"You should come for a long weekend. We could give you a tour. Arthur's Seat in Holyrood Park is—" Josie stopped suddenly, realising what she had said. She bowed her head, her fingers screwing the bedding into a knot. When she continued, her voice was little more than a whisper. "Helen sounds just like her. Their voices, their accents, they're so similar. I can close my eyes, and it's as if Rachel's here in the room with me. Helen was reading to me earlier, and I fell asleep thinking everything was fixed, that you'd found Rachel and she was fine. I didn't ever want to wake. I couldn't bear the thought of coming back."

She looked up, and Sanne almost recoiled from the raw anguish on her face. There was nothing Sanne could say that wouldn't sound trite or falsely hopeful. She rested her hand on Josie's arm and sat silently for a while, listening to someone humming off-key in the next room and to the gradual deepening of Josie's breathing as she began to fall into a doze.

Half asleep, Josie fumbled with the sheets. Sanne straightened them for her, pulling the blanket under her chin. Josie turned on her side and opened bleary eyes.

"Sanne?" Her voice was slurred with drowsiness.

Sanne leaned closer. "What's the matter?"

"Please don't tell Helen what I said."

"I won't breathe a word of it, I promise." Sanne stroked a hand through the short fuzz of Josie's hair.

"She'll think I've given up on Rachel, and I haven't. I *haven't*."

"Neither have I." Sanne couldn't speak for the rest of her team, but she could speak for herself, and that seemed to be good enough for Josie. With Sanne's hand still on her forehead, her eyes drifted shut.

Chapter Fourteen

Never sure when she would be home, Sanne had an automatic light timer in her living room, but, pulling up at the rear of the cottage that night, she wasn't surprised to see another lamp burning in her study. She parked behind Meg's car and drew her collar closed before making a dash through the rain to her back door. The first thing she spotted as she untied her boots was the bottle of calamine lotion sitting in the middle of her table.

"Very funny." She stuck out her tongue as Meg peeked around the kitchen door.

"And you're very late." Meg held out her hand for Sanne's coat. Her hair was still damp from the shower, her hands warm where they touched Sanne's clammy skin, and she smelled like fresh summer herbs. Sanne closed her eyes and rested her head on Meg's shoulder.

"How was she?" Meg asked quietly.

"Up and down. I stayed for an hour, in the end. The doc chased me out when she finally fell asleep. I can't imagine what it must be like for her. I don't think I want to imagine."

"Shh." Meg silenced her with a soft kiss, her lips making the barest contact.

Sanne pressed closer, feeling Meg's lips part and the tip of her tongue flick out. Smiling at the unspoken promise, she cupped Meg's face with both hands. "I need a shower."

Meg turned her head so she could kiss Sanne's left palm. "Need me to doctor anything?"

"No." Sanne blew out a breath, pushing away her exhaustion and the day's stress. "I just need you."

It was a very quick shower, just enough to wash off the sweat of the chase and the grime of the alley. She found Meg sitting in the centre of her bed, wearing pilfered pyjamas and fidgeting like a toddler with a sugar rush. Meg's wide eyes followed the towel as Sanne dropped it to the floor.

"You seem to have forgotten your clothes," she said. She was obviously flustered, which amused the hell out of Sanne.

"Yeah, I think someone pinched them." Sanne climbed onto the bed and knelt in front of her. "Do you have any idea as to who the culprit might be?"

"Uh, no?" Her breathing quickened as Sanne popped the first button on her pyjama top, but when Sanne went no further, she changed her plea. "Maybe?" That earned her another button, and she squirmed, apparently in no mood to play hard to get. "Okay, okay, it was me."

"Well, that was my easiest interrogation ever." Sanne kissed her forehead. "Please don't ever commit a crime."

"I won't. I promise." Meg shook her head fervently, groaning when Sanne's mouth met hers. There was nothing tentative about this kiss, and Sanne dealt with the rest of the buttons as she felt Meg nip at her bottom lip. She opened the shirt wide and used one finger to trace a line from the hollow of Meg's throat down to her belly button. Meg squeaked, her body jerking in response to Sanne's knuckles brushing over the sensitive skin of her abdomen.

"Gets you every time," Sanne whispered.

"Yeah, yeah." Meg lay back and attempted to wriggle out of her pyjama bottoms in a series of graceless and increasingly convoluted manoeuvres. Mesmerised by her complete lack of coordination, Sanne watched her effectively hobble herself.

"Bugger." Meg laughed as Sanne kissed each of her knees in turn and then freed her legs. With a contented sigh, Meg let them fall open, pulling Sanne down on top of her and kissing whatever came within easy reach.

The touch of heated skin against hers made Sanne shiver in anticipation. She played her hand across Meg's chest, her fingers following a familiar path that took in a pale birthmark, the rippled scar from an emergency appendectomy, and the ticklish bit on top of Meg's clavicle. Beneath her, Meg shifted restlessly, urging her lower, so she dipped her hand between Meg's legs and kissed her when she gasped.

"Oh, Jesus." Meg raised her hands to Sanne's breasts, teasing the nipples into peaks as Sanne entered her.

"That's very distracting," Sanne murmured, slowing the movement of her fingers until Meg whimpered in protest and dropped her hands back to the bed. Wasting no time, Sanne slid back into her. "Like this?" she asked, smiling at Meg's vigorous nod. In the lamplight, Meg's face was damp with sweat, her eyes heavy-lidded as she guided Sanne's pace. When they kissed, Sanne tasted salt and mint toothpaste, before moving her mouth to join her hand, and tasting only Meg.

"Bloody hellfire!" Meg's head hit the pillow with a thud, and her toes curled into the sheets.

Her yelp was enough to make Sanne pause and look up. "Such a pushover," she said, feeling Meg's legs shake as she laughed.

"*Please* stop talking." Meg's tone held more than a hint of desperation.

Sanne grinned and for once in her life obeyed her doctor's orders.

With timing honed by years of shift work, Sanne woke five minutes before her alarm and cancelled it to stop it from disturbing Meg. Sensing the movement, Meg shuffled closer, but the furrow creasing her brow disappeared as her sleep deepened again. Sanne tucked the sheets around her and crept reluctantly from the bed.

She ran the shower hot, letting the water pound her muscles while she tried to work out which were stiff from sprinting after Ned and which were aching because of Meg. Right on cue, the bathroom door opened.

"Oh God, you broke me," Meg said, limping to the toilet.

Sanne shut off the water before the toilet flush could turn it into a trickle. "If you'd like to make a complaint, I can give you an address." She grabbed her towel and began to rub her hair. "It's number five, You-Bloody-Started-It Road."

Meg cackled and came over to plant a wet kiss on Sanne's lips. Then, as if regretting her haste, she kissed her far more thoroughly.

"No. *No.* I'll be late…"

Sanne's resistance got lost somewhere in the midst of the tongue circling her breast and the fingers slipping between her legs. Unable to do much but stay on her feet, she allowed Meg to steer her back into the shower. The water was already warm when Meg turned it on again. Sanne shuddered with pleasure as it cascaded onto her and Meg trailed kisses down her torso.

"I'll be in so much trouble," she whispered, raising her head into the spray and trying not to hyperventilate. She felt hands spread her legs wider, felt a heat between them that wasn't from the water, and gave up thinking about anything but what Meg was doing to her. Within minutes, she came hard and fast, her hands sliding down the glass as she searched for something to grip on to.

Meg caught her, keeping her steady until the tremors stopped and then cradling her to the floor. She reached for a discarded flannel to dry Sanne's face.

"I think I might need to learn self-restraint," she said.

"Where would the fun in that be?" Sanne curled against her. She didn't want to move, didn't want to open the shower door and let the day back in. Instead, she entwined Meg's fingers with her own and wondered how long it would be before the water ran cold.

❖

With most of the detectives following leads or interviewing, the EDSOP office was quiet for once. The rain pattering on the window and the rhythm of Nelson's four-forward, two-back typing were the only sounds breaking the peace.

Chewing the last bite of her late lunch, Sanne straightened her spine to ease out a kink and sent another completed report to the printer. Although she would have preferred to observe Ned Moseley's interview, she had spent most of the day in Halshaw, finishing the enquiries there, and had resigned herself to watching the recording in her own time. At the desk opposite, Nelson dry-swallowed two painkillers and squinted as if the light hurt his eyes.

"You should go home," she said. "No one expected you to be in today."

"Funny. That's what Abeni told me."

"Talks a lot of sense, your missus." She clicked open a new e-mail headed *Rope Analysis*, her attention already diverted by the details. The rope used to bind Josie had been a 10mm multi-purpose utility type, widely available in DIY, auto, and boating stores. It could even be bought through Amazon. As there were several sailing clubs and a multitude of farms in the area, the officers attempting to trace local purchasers weren't making much headway.

A sudden intrusion of animated voices in the corridor made Sanne raise her head. She exchanged an intrigued look with Nelson, recognising one of the voices as Eleanor's but unable to distinguish the words.

"I guess the interview's over," she said. She could hear Carlyle now. As a Tier Three interviewer, he had been selected to question Ned alongside Eleanor.

"Sounds like someone's happy," Nelson said.

The door slammed back against the wall as Carlyle bounded into the office. Evidently pleased with himself, he collected his briefcase from his desk and marched out again with it swinging by his side. From just inside the doorway, Eleanor watched him leave.

Sanne waited for his footsteps to fade. "How did it go, boss?"

Eleanor looked tired, but there was something of the usual spark in her eyes. Instead of answering directly, she set a memory stick on Sanne's desk. "I'd like your opinion, without prejudice. We're seeking an extension from the CPS."

With that, she left them alone again. Her office door shut, and a phone that had started to ring fell silent. Sanne picked up her mug and held out her hand for Nelson's.

"Think we're going to need a brew with this," she said.

❖

Ned Moseley didn't seem to know what to do with his hands. Within the first five minutes of the recording—as Carlyle introduced himself and Eleanor, and explained the structure of the interview— he had sat on his hands, shoved them beneath his armpits, and then hidden them in the sleeves of his police-issued sweatshirt. Fifteen minutes later, he was crunching on his fingernails and pulling at the loose skin around his cuticles. His lawyer, a woman with a cheap dye job who was probably nudging retirement, looked as if she might clip him around his ear if he continued to fidget.

"I don't know," he kept mumbling. "I don't know…"

Leaning closer to the screen, Sanne adjusted the volume. The notepad in front of her was still blank. Carlyle, apparently keen to make Ned squirm, had barely started the questioning.

"You don't *know*?" he repeated. "You don't *know* why you assaulted a detective and fled from your house?"

Failing to grasp Carlyle's scepticism, Ned shook his head earnestly, his thumbnail tapping on his teeth.

"Did your actions have anything to do with this?"

Ned's chewing became hesitant as he stared at the evidence bag Carlyle slid across to him.

Hunched beside Sanne, Nelson pointed at the screen. "Is that a joint?"

Sanne tipped her head at an angle. It didn't help, so she hit *pause* and zoomed in on the bag. "Yep," she said. "Personally, if I were watching *Emmerdale* I'd want to be stoned, too."

"Good point."

When she restarted the video, Ned was sitting on his hands again, his face pale and shiny with sweat.

"I was smoking it in my own home. That's not a crime."

"Tell me about your job at Rowan Cottage." Carlyle's change of subject was deliberate, ignoring the joint and Ned's loose grasp of the law, and it worked. Wrong-footed, Ned stuttered, a muscle in his jaw twitching.

"I'm like a caretaker," he said at length. "I have the keys, and I go and fix stuff when Mrs. Martindale tells me to."

"When was the last time you went there?"

Sanne watched Ned's eyes flick to the camera and back. He must have known that they would have spoken to Mrs. Martindale, and the gravity of his situation seemed to be dawning upon him. He took a gulp of water, almost knocking over the glass when he put it down.

"About ten, maybe twelve days ago. One of them girls said the sink was leak—" Realising what he had just revealed, he snapped his mouth shut. His chest heaved as he tried to regulate his breathing.

"Did you meet them, Ned? Were Josie and Rachel there when you went to the cottage?" It was Eleanor who spoke, keeping her voice calm and controlled, in direct contrast to the young man across the table from her. As she said each name, she placed the women's photographs side by side on the table.

Ned nodded miserably. "They made me a brew."

"Did you speak to them?"

He frowned, toying with the edge of Josie's photo. "Not much. They were going out. Asked me if I knew any good pubs, so I told them the Crown and Anchor did the best sausage and chips. They were nice. They said I could help myself to biscuits."

Sanne swung her chair back, balancing it on two legs as she considered Ned's answer. He had relaxed incrementally as he spoke, warming to his theme and showing no indicators of stress or subterfuge. There was an innocence to his short sentences and simple diction that seemed genuine, as did the tears that filled his eyes when Carlyle threw down two further pictures of Josie.

"Those are nasty," he whispered, trying to cover them with his hands, before turning them facedown. One was from the moors, the other from the ITU.

"Why didn't you come forward when Josie was found?" Carlyle phrased the question like an accusation. Ned looked to Eleanor and his lawyer, as if beseeching them to intervene, but Carlyle wasn't finished. "You'd met her, spoken to her, yet you didn't tell a soul."

"I didn't know! I didn't know it was her! How could I, when she was all messed up like that?" Trying to emphasise his point, he shoved the photos back toward Carlyle, who took them and studied them calmly.

"What made you decide to help with the search?" Carlyle asked. Ned drew in a breath to answer, but Carlyle didn't wait for his response. "Is that how you get yourself off, Ned? Leading everyone on a run-around? Watching the police chase their tails, and knowing that you'd moved Rachel and left nothing for us to find?"

Ned shook his head repeatedly, his expression full of horror. For a moment, Sanne thought he might be sick, but he swiped tears from his face and managed to reply.

"I wanted to help find out who done that to that girl. I watch a lot of telly, so I thought I'd be good at finding clues, and I helped find that rope. You ask Detective Sanney." He ended on an indignant note, as if annoyed that his contribution was being overlooked.

The self-satisfied smirk that spread across Carlyle's face made Sanne's skin crawl. "Telly isn't all you like watching, is it?"

Ned stiffened, every inch of him on guard.

Sanne glanced at Nelson, who shrugged, apparently as confused as she was.

On the recording, Carlyle had opened a plastic folder and carefully laid out a series of magazines, to which he added a small pile of silver discs and the sleeves from four DVDs. Ned closed his eyes, and Sanne felt like doing the same. Though rendered in grainy quality on the computer screen, it was still possible to distinguish the violent nature of the pornography, and the titles of the DVDs left little to the imagination.

"We know these are yours, Ned," Carlyle said quietly. "We found them in your house."

Ned swallowed, his Adam's apple bobbing up and down as his throat worked. He seemed on the verge of attempting a denial but said nothing.

Sanne felt as blindsided as he looked. She had been sucked in by his blank face and his childlike answers, almost to the point of feeling sorry for him. Now she found herself wondering exactly what he was capable of and how accomplished an actor he might be. She blinked, refocusing her eyes, when Carlyle began to speak again.

"Tell us what you've done with Rachel." His tone was soft and persuasive. "Things will work out much better for you if you tell us where she is."

Heedless of the snot streaming from his nose, Ned let out a single sob and turned his head away, refusing to acknowledge the display on the table. When his lawyer placed a hand on his arm, he yelped as if scalded.

"I'd like to request a break," she said, and seconds later, the recording stopped.

Sanne minimised the video and stared at her desktop wallpaper for a few seconds, drawing comfort from the image of the Peak District covered in deep snow.

"Didn't see that coming," Nelson said with considerable understatement.

"Me neither." Sanne tapped her mouse, making the cursor jump. There was something about Ned's reaction to the pornography that felt off, though she couldn't put her finger on it. "No wonder Carlyle looked so bloody smug."

"I suppose he has to get something right every now and again, and he did a good job there."

"Yeah, he did," she said. As Nelson reached for his jacket, she checked the clock, surprised to find it so late in the evening. "You heading off?"

He nodded. "I'll write up my impressions at home and e-mail them in. You?"

One click of her mouse reopened the video. She hovered the cursor over *play*. "I think I'll stick around for a while," she said.

❖

With each hour that passed, Sanne's handwriting deteriorated. Neat, precisely formed letters became a scrawl, and her hand was cramping every few minutes. She had rewatched Ned's interview in its entirety and then flicked through it several times more, trying to debunk or add weight to her initial reactions. From a circumstantial viewpoint, things didn't look good for him. By his own admission, he had been in contact with both women. He had volunteered to aid in the search and bragged about his forensic know-how. According to the Cleggs, he had skipped two days of work during the period the women were missing, and his whereabouts at that time could not be accounted for. The cannabis proved he had access to illegal substances, and the pornography found at his address implied a fascination with violent and non-consensual sex. Sanne had tagged "resisting a reasonable request for an interview" and "putting a detective in the hospital" onto the end of her list, but those seemed almost incidental in comparison.

Her eyes felt gritty, and the ache in her back had spread to her bottom and thighs. Sighing, she shifted the marker to thirty-two minutes and fifty-seven seconds, and restarted the recording. By now, she knew exactly how the sequence of events played out: Ned averted his eyes and flinched away from the table, stress making a florid rash creep up his throat. When he spoke, his voice was hoarse and tremulous. "Those are nasty."

Jumping ahead to thirty-eight minutes and twelve seconds, she watched him react to the pornography in exactly the same manner. His facial expression, the rash, and the way his body edged backward mirrored his response to the graphic images of Josie. In both instances, his revulsion seemed instinctive, and the unease Sanne had felt upon her first viewing was developing into full-blown doubt.

She slapped a hand on the mouse, minimising the video, as she saw Eleanor approaching her desk.

"You stay any later, and you may as well sleep here," Eleanor said.

Sanne flipped her pad to a clean page before Eleanor was close enough to read it. "I was just shutting stuff down. I'll finish it tomorrow." She dropped the pad into her bag, hoping that that might discourage Eleanor from asking questions. She didn't want to say what she thought. She didn't want to be the one who undermined what looked to be a significant development in the case, particularly when she wasn't sure she was right.

"The CPS are happy. They've granted us a twenty-four-hour extension." Eleanor gestured at the computer screen. "How many times have you watched it?"

Sanne slowly drew the zip on her bag shut. "A few," she said, her heart sinking.

Eleanor sat down heavily in Nelson's chair, eliminating the height difference between them. "Doesn't strike you as a criminal mastermind, does he?"

"Not really." The zip reaching its end seemed like a sign. It left Sanne with nothing to do but bite the bullet. "Circumstantially, everything looks great, but when you study him properly, his body language, his expressions and reactions, they just seem wrong. And that rope on the moor, he didn't find that. He found a dead sheep that happened to be nearby, and he was so excited by it."

"He's all we've got at the moment, Sanne." Eleanor made it sound like a warning. "And I don't think we know enough yet to dismiss the evidence out of hand. We've only scratched the surface in terms of interviewing him. The brass are pleased, the press are coming onside, and I need my team to back me."

Sanne nodded and hated herself for it, but Eleanor looked equally uncomfortable pulling rank. Deciding that she couldn't make matters worse, Sanne broached an issue that had been troubling her since Ned's arrest.

"If he really has done this, and we keep him in custody for forty-eight hours straight, what will happen to Rachel, assuming she's still alive?"

The question gave Eleanor pause. She opened her mouth to reply and then shut it again to consider. "He'll tell us where she is," she said finally, but it must have sounded inadequate even to her own ears, because she rubbed at the bridge of her nose. "You should go home. We've got a warrant to search the land around where he goes fishing, so I'll need you in early tomorrow."

As soon as the office door closed, Sanne covered her face with her hands. "Bollocking fuck," she whispered.

There was no light in the study window and no other cars parked outside the cottage. Frowning at the uneven feel of the steering as she pulled into the driveway, Sanne made a mental note to check her tyres in daylight. The wind had strengthened, lashing loose leaves and twigs across the gravel, and she had to kick her car door to open it fully. When she stepped inside the cottage, the kitchen was cold, the creak of the roof beneath the force of the storm giving it an eerie air. She fumbled for the light, dispelling the creepiness with the flick of a switch. As her vision adjusted, she saw the bottle of calamine lotion still sitting on the table and two sets of breakfast plates on the draining board. Meg must have washed up before leaving.

Her every movement dulled by fatigue and an unfamiliar pang of loneliness, Sanne stacked the crockery and put it away. She was hungry but couldn't summon the energy to make anything, so she opened a packet of biscuits and filled the kettle. While she waited for the water to boil, her eye strayed to the phone, and she had to tamp down the urge to call Meg. Instead, she shoved an entire biscuit into her mouth in the hope that a sugar rush would banish her maudlin mood. The first biscuit having failed to yield a miracle cure, she tried a second and then a third, washing them down with tea.

Half a packet and two mugs in, she was more inclined toward contemplation than self-pity, and able to accept that she sometimes missed coming home to Meg. Although she loved having independence and her own space, after a day like today there would have been comfort in knowing she wasn't going to spend the night alone.

"Maybe I should just get a cat," she said, despairing at her habit of talking to herself. At the very least, a cat would make her feel less crazy. Still toying with the idea, she dunked another biscuit, waiting until the last moment before rescuing it. Two chocolate chips escaped and floated on top of her tea.

"Come here, you little buggers." Using a teaspoon, she scooped them out. As they melted, sweet and warm on her tongue, another pang—this one far more pleasant than the first—reminded her of that morning. She smiled, feeling her ears turn hot. Although she occasionally coveted a more conventional relationship, there were definite advantages to an unofficial and unpredictable one.

Dunking a final biscuit in Meg's honour, she tried to decide whether she could be bothered having a shower. She grinned as she walked upstairs. Another benefit to living alone: no one complained if you went to bed mucky.

CHAPTER FIFTEEN

It felt like a dance, though a strange one. The stick would swish through grass, more grass, slightly longer grass, and then hit a solid object, making Sanne drop to her knees. For a few tense seconds, she would dig around in the weeds, until she found a piece of metal or a plastic carton that someone had tossed into the undergrowth, and the routine would start all over again. To her left, Nelson swore as brambles snagged around his legs. To her right, a line of detectives and uniformed officers, all making the same halting progress, stretched the width of the field adjoining the reservoir. Wind whipped across the vast body of water, driving sharp showers before it and making conversation difficult. The line was approaching a patch of woodland, and Sanne eyed the trees with apprehension. Finding anything significant in the field had been unlikely, but the forest was a far better place to conceal a body.

Nelson touched her arm, making her jump and drop her stick. Using her foot, she levered it up so she could grab back hold of it.

"Sorry," he said. "Looks like we're taking a break before we head into there." He nodded toward the pines swaying in the wind.

"Right." She scanned around for somewhere dry to sit, before giving up and flattening out the plastic charity bag she always kept in the pocket of her hiking jacket.

Nelson sat on it with her and offered her a packet of crisps. "You're quiet today. Late night?"

"Late enough." She hadn't slept well. Every time she'd shut her eyes, she'd heard screaming. It had taken hours to persuade herself that the noise was only the storm, shrieking around the eaves. She crinkled up the half-finished packet and stuffed it into her rucksack. "I saw Eleanor before I left the office."

"And?"

"And I told her I wasn't sure about Ned Moseley." She wiped her greasy fingers on the grass, savouring the feel of the cool stems instead of meeting his eyes. She and Nelson were the ones who had raised initial suspicions about Ned and been instrumental in his arrest. Now she felt her lack of conviction was letting their partnership down.

"I spoke to one of the lads from SOCO this morning." Nelson screwed his own packet into a tight ball, and his fingers were still clenched around it as he continued. "He'd been tasked to log that porn they found, after the first bloke they asked lost his breakfast over it. Most of it's imported from Eastern Europe, and he says it's the worst sort there is. If Ned gets off on that kind of thing, there's no telling what he might have done to those girls. He's sick, San. Don't be taken in by his lost little boy act." He offered her a hand and pulled her to her feet.

"You're probably right," she said. Then, quieter, her eyes fixed on the tree line, "Do you think she's still alive?"

In her peripheral vision, she saw the faint shake of his head.

"I think he killed her the night he dragged her out of that cave."

The shout made the hairs stand up on the nape of Sanne's neck. Frozen in place, she strained to pick out further calls amid the racket the trees were making in the strengthening wind. In the hours since lunch, she had scoured her designated patch of forest, tripping over concealed roots and snarling at the tangles of undergrowth. The continuous tension had given her a throbbing headache, but she had found even less among the trees than she had in the field, and now the light was beginning to fail.

A stranger's voice crackled in her earpiece. "We've found some sort of hut, and it smells fucking rancid. Request EDSOP and SOCO. Over." A volley of details followed, including coordinates.

Sanne heard Nelson yell her name. Her hands damp around the wood, she drove her stick into the ground to mark her place, before picking her way in his direction. Each step she took felt leaden, as if she were a condemned prisoner making her final walk. It reminded her of taking the long way back from school so that her dad might be in the pub before she got home. She had often stumbled into the hallway, tired out and freezing cold, but still feeling victorious because she had seen through the window that the television in his room was off.

Realising belatedly that Nelson had stayed behind to wait for her, she fell into step with him. He didn't ask if she was okay. She knew one glance at her face would have answered that question. Ahead of them, a group of men crowded close to a wooden hut barely the size of a garden shed. Its rough finish implied it had been constructed on the spot using timber from the forest, and two large holly bushes gave it excellent camouflage.

"Wasn't meant to be found, was it?" she murmured. The woodland was privately owned, and the lack of rubbish and tracks suggested that few people trespassed.

Nelson made a grunt of assent as he broke a path through the bracken. Ten yards farther along, the smell reached her, an insidious, foul yet sweet odour of decay that hit the back of her throat with such intensity she felt as if she were chewing on it.

"Jesus," Nelson said, clamping his sleeve across his nose and mouth. He kept walking, though with more caution, and Sanne forced herself to follow, trying to get used to the stink before she had to deal with her colleagues.

"It's locked, but we just spoke to the landowner," Scotty Ramsden told her, as soon as she and Nelson were within earshot. In contrast to the hut's dilapidated nature, the padlock securing its door was new. "To his knowledge, the only buildings on this area of the estate are fishing shelters and barns closer to the lake. He gave us permission to bust it open. Everyone on board with that?" He made the question sound general, but he looked to his EDSOP colleagues for their consensus. "Right, then. How the hell are we getting in?"

In the absence of battering rams and crowbars, brute force was the only option. Standing off to the side, Sanne watched Nelson and Jay Egerton shoulder-charge the door. They crashed into it twice before a panel in the middle splintered, allowing them to peel back half of the wood. A swarm of black flies rushed out through the gap, and Jay recoiled, turning to retch into the nearest bush.

Without giving herself time to think, Sanne went up until she was shoulder to shoulder with Nelson. Holding her breath, she shone her torch alongside his.

"Gamekeeper taking the law into his own hands?" he said quietly, and she nodded, too relieved to be angered by the carnage in front of her.

At the far side of the room, a glut of flies crawled across a table thick with blood, guts, and patches of fur. Fox pelts hung from nails in the walls, and carcasses of a buzzard and a goshawk had been flung into a corner. Traps and snares were neatly stacked against the table, along with a wooden box, which Nelson drew toward him and flicked open to find a set of butcher's knives. Every inch of the room was visible, and there was no sign of Rachel.

Leaving Nelson to call in the find and decide whether forensics were necessary, Sanne stumbled away from the hut. A fly crawled across her cheek. She batted at it with numb fingers and then scrubbed the skin with her fist. Nausea threatened to embarrass her, so she found a spot hidden behind a standing stone and sank to the ground, hugging her knees to her chest and waiting for the sickness to fade. Gradually, her stomach settled, but the smell seemed to have seeped into her pores, her hair, and the fabric of her clothing, making her feel filthy. She stood up and used rainwater collected in a concavity in the rock to wipe her face and hands. With the scents of moss and earth counteracting that of putrescence, she retraced her earlier route, looking for where she had left her stick. Just as she reached the spot, her radio buzzed, the display showing Nelson's number.

"Just checking in." His voice was soft with concern.

"I'm okay. I'm back on my patch."

"Me too. If I grin, you might just be able to see me."

She laughed. "Idiot. We calling it a day soon?"

"I think we'll have to. You ready to go home?"

"Yeah." She leaned on her stick, using it to prop herself up. "If I never come back here, it'll be too soon."

Sanne dropped her phone on top of her bag and thumped her head back against the driver's seat. According to Joan Cotter, Geoff was off work with a tummy bug, and jobs at the garage were stacking up fast, which meant at least another week of driving around on tyres that barely gripped the road. After the day she had had, the prospect of finding somewhere else to deal with them seemed like too much effort, though, so she scribbled the date suggested by Joan into her diary.

As if determined to push her over the edge, her phone rang the instant she turned the key in the ignition. Leaving the engine running for warmth, she flicked off the windscreen wipers, and rain obscured her view within seconds. Although the number on her screen had been unfamiliar, she recognised the panicked voice on the end of the line.

"Sanne?"

"Hey, Josie. Everything okay?" There was no response, but Sanne could hear Josie sobbing in frantic bursts. "Josie, listen to me. I can't help you if you don't tell me what's going on. Are you on your own?"

"Yes, I didn't…" Josie trailed off, her breath heaving over the line. "I can't talk to my mum or Helen about this."

"Talk to me, then."

A gust of wind rocked the car. Sanne peered up at the swaying trees that surrounded the small car park, and was about to reverse out of harm's way when Josie began to speak.

"I saw the news. Everyone's been trying to stop me from watching it, and they never bring me papers, but I've got my phone

back, and the Internet works in here, so I know he's still in custody."
She was crying again. "What'll happen to Rachel if you keep him
in there? Hasn't anyone thought of that? She'll die if he doesn't tell
you where she is. Please, Sanne, you've got to make him tell you
where she is. Please don't let him leave her on her own. Oh God,
she'll be so scared." It was a child's plea, hopeless and unrealistic,
and punctuated by the high-pitched tone of an alarm.

"Fuck," Sanne whispered, all too aware of what had happened
the last time Josie had been so distressed. "Josie? Josie, say
something, love."

There was no answer. Despite repeated attempts, Sanne
couldn't get a response. Eventually, in desperation, she ended the
call. Not knowing the number for the ITU, she selected the name at
the top of her directory instead.

Meg answered on the second ring.

The rapid thump of Sanne's boots echoed in the almost deserted
corridor. A young nurse turned to stare, four cartons from the canteen
stacked precariously between her hands and chin. Trying not to look
like an escapee from the psychiatric block, Sanne gave her a wide
berth and headed for the stairs. She hit the staircase door with both
hands and took the steps three at a time. Her imagination had been
working overtime as she careened along the Snake Pass, but she
found the ITU in its usual tranquil state, and the nurse at the desk
waved her through without checking her ID.

Room three was also peaceful, with all but one of its lights
extinguished and the sound of deep, regular breathing telling her
that Josie was asleep. Sitting close by the bed, Meg was keeping a
loose grip on Josie's fingers. She smiled as Sanne walked over.

"Is she all right?" Sanne asked. The monitoring equipment
had been scaled back since her last visit, but the numbers on the
remaining machines were a reassuring green.

"She's better than she was when I got here," Meg said. "An old
bloke had just arrested, which meant that half the staff were jumping

up and down on him, and no one had noticed Josie having a meltdown. I'd paged Max on my way up. He came and gave her a mild sedative, and she was so knackered it knocked her out in minutes. I did tell her you were coming, but she probably won't remember."

Sanne ran a trembling hand over her face and sank into the closest chair. She bent low, leaning her head on her folded arms. There was a rustle, followed by a hollow thud, and she opened her eyes to see a vomit bowl set strategically by her feet.

"Don't think I'll need that," she muttered.

Meg reached for her wrist and palpated her pulse. "You're tachy, and you look like crap. Keep your head down for a minute."

"It's been a bad day, and she gave me a fright, that's all." Despite her protests, Sanne stayed where she was. The fact that she couldn't see Meg or Josie made it easier for her to explain. "We were searching the woods around Long Edge reservoir, and I thought we'd found her. There was this hut and a terrible smell." She gagged involuntarily, though nothing came up.

Meg rubbed her back. "What was it?"

"Gamekeeper, illegally trapping predators. But, Jesus, for a few minutes I was so sure it was Rachel."

"Did you speak to Eleanor?"

"Yes, she—"

A cough from the bed made Sanne break off and raise her head. In the dim light, Josie was beginning to look around. Her lips moved, but she didn't yet seem capable of speech. Reacting first, Meg dropped a straw into a cup of water and held it for her to take cautious sips.

"Shit," Josie whispered, wiping up a dribble of water with her good hand. "Did I have another bleed?"

"No. Dr. Maxwell gave you something to help you sleep," Meg said. "You were only out for an hour or so."

"You're Meg, aren't you? From A&E." Josie shaped the words slowly, obviously struggling to recall the details. She relaxed a little when she noticed Sanne. "Hey. Sorry if I scared you."

Sanne waved away the apology. "I'm just glad you're okay. Do you remember why you called me?" At Josie's nod, she left her chair and sat on the edge of the bed. "I spoke to my boss on the way here, and she's decided not to ask the CPS—that's the Crown Prosecution Service—for another extension on Ned Moseley's custody."

"What does that mean? Are you letting him go?"

"It means he'll be granted bail tomorrow and released." She held up a hand to stop Josie from interrupting. "I'm telling you this in strictest confidence. DI Stanhope will speak to you tomorrow, but she gave me the go-ahead to come and see you tonight. We'll be keeping him under surveillance twenty-four seven, and the hope is that he'll slip up and lead us to Rachel."

The operative word there was "hope," and it was a slim hope at that. All too aware of previous kidnap cases where victims had starved to death after the arrest of their assailants, however, the brass were keen to give surveillance a chance. Three teams would monitor Ned around the clock, with Sanne and Nelson supervising the first night shift. The investigation and searches would continue in the meantime, but Ned Moseley remained their only suspect.

Josie had pushed herself up, her eyes bright and alert as she digested the information. Sanne didn't warn her that Eleanor doubted Ned would leave the house and suspected that, even if he did, all he would lead them to was a body. For the sake of Josie's health, Sanne wanted her to think positively until she had a definitive reason not to.

"No blabbing, I promise." Josie mimed zipping her mouth shut. "Oh, hey, you'd better warn your boss that I'm being downgraded to High Dependency in the morning. I think I should've gone today, but they didn't have a free bed."

The news lightened Sanne's mood. "Congratulations."

"Yeah. I don't care where they put me as long as it has a window." Josie grimaced at the four blank walls surrounding her.

"HDU definitely has windows," Meg said. "And I know a few of the nurses on there, so I might be able to get you a bed with a view."

It was such a simple proposition, but it made tears shine in Josie's eyes. "I can't remember the last time I saw the sky," she said.

❖

"Has your bum gone to sleep, or is it just mine?"

The car rocked as Nelson slid the driver's seat backward and shuffled around until he was satisfied with his new position.

"I'll give you half an hour." Sanne set the alarm on her phone and propped it on the dash. "If you can keep still for that long, you win a bag of Haribo."

"Half a bloody hour? That's not fair, San. My legs are longer than yours."

"Half an hour, or no little jelly eggs for you." She placed the sweets next to her phone, settled back into her seat, and crossed her legs at the ankles. "We've only been here for ninety-seven minutes, and your wriggling is already doing my head in."

Nelson hid his face in his hands. "Ninety-seven minutes? Is that all?"

"How long did you think it was? It's not even dark."

"Hours. It feels like it's been hours."

"Well, it hasn't. Have a nap or something. I'll keep watch."

Satisfied that an accord had been reached, she turned her attention back to Ned's house. As planned, he had been released on bail mid-afternoon, and a taxi had brought him straight home. He had remained in the house for two hours before walking to the corner shop, buying a pizza and four cans of lager, and walking back again. The most exciting event the surveillance team in the alley had observed was Ned throwing the pizza box into his bin. At no point had he appeared to realise he was being monitored. The trace on his phone showed that his mum was the only person he had contacted since his release, and no one but his lawyer had called him. Although he had a full driving licence, the only vehicle registered in his name was a scooter, which would have been completely impractical for moving Rachel. One of the uniforms was looking into his access to off-road or four-wheel-drive vehicles, but as yet nothing had come up.

Parked on Prospect Street, Sanne and Nelson were keeping watch at the front of his house, while also managing the two units situated in the back alley. A new team would relieve them at seven a.m.

Two hours of unrelenting tedium later, Sanne was watching the light of Ned's television flickering behind his living room curtains, when a spicy aroma made her mouth water and reminded her that half a bag of Haribo made a poor substitute for an evening meal. She looked around to find Nelson sharing out two portions of curry and rice onto plastic plates.

"Is that what I think it is?" She took the napkin he offered her and stuffed it into the front of her shirt.

He grinned. "Abeni thought our first all-night stakeout would be the perfect occasion."

For months, he had been promising to bring in a flask of his wife's famous goat curry, but the opportunity had never arisen. The aversion of Sanne's dad to anything foreign meant she had been raised on a strict English-food-only diet, and she had consequently spent her adulthood sampling the cuisine of as many different cultures as she could, but she had avoided Caribbean food for the past year, after Nelson's boast early in their partnership that no one cooked it as well as Abeni.

"It smells amazing," she said, scooping a generous amount of rice and meat onto her fork.

Nelson laughed at her enthusiasm, holding off on his first taste to await her verdict. It came with two thumbs up and another forkful stuffed into her mouth.

"Good, isn't it?"

"Fab." She chewed more slowly, savouring the spices and the tender meat. "She'll have to give me her recipe."

He waggled his fork at her. "I'll ask, but it might be a family secret."

"Fair enough." She found it very difficult to hold a grudge with a full stomach.

"Maybe we can do a deal." He popped the top off a can of ginger beer and held it out to her. "You tell me how you got your name, and I'll get hold of the Balewa family goat curry recipe for you."

She narrowed her eyes at him, and for a moment he seemed on the verge of recanting, afraid that he had broached too sensitive a subject. Then she smiled and tapped her can against his.

"Okay, deal. But I'm finishing my tea first."

They took their time eating, as the setting sun turned the sky purple and pink, making even the grotty terraced houses look appealing. Sanne washed down her last bite with ginger beer and dabbed her mouth with her napkin.

"Please pass my compliments to your lovely wife."

"Will do. Can I interest you in an after-dinner mint?" Nelson asked in a ridiculously posh voice, while proffering a packet of Polos.

"Thank you, kind sir." She sucked her mint for a couple of minutes, letting him put away their plates.

"So…" he said, once he had settled in a comfortable position.

"So." She stuck her feet up on the dash and cracked her knuckles in preparation for her tale. "'Twas a dark and stormy night…" She paused for effect and bit her mint in half.

He laughed. "You've missed your calling. You could've been an actor."

"Yeah, yeah. Where was I? Right, dark and stormy, blah blah, back in nineteen-eighty-something or other, when my mum and dad got married. You know my dad's an inveterate alky, don't you?"

"You have mentioned that on occasion."

"Well, he hid it pretty well when my mum first started to date him. I'm sure she was aware that he liked a drink, but she didn't really have a clue what she was getting herself into. A year later, they were engaged, and my mum had her wedding all planned— nice ceremony, lots of friends and family, dress like a meringue, bridesmaids in turquoise, and a dream honeymoon cruise to the fjords of Norway."

"Ah," Nelson said, a connection obviously beginning to form.

"Yeah." She sighed and tucked her hands between her thighs, no longer able to maintain her jocular tone. "Mum got her wedding, but the reception was at a crappy local pub, her dress was a hand-me-down, and my dad had already drunk all the money she'd saved for their honeymoon cruise. He took her to Blackpool for a weekend instead, and she ended up pregnant with me. I'm not sure he was even there when I was born, but I know he told my mum that he didn't give a shit what she decided to call me. So, she chose the name Sanne because that's what her beloved Norwegian cruise liner was called." Sanne looked up at Nelson and shrugged hopelessly. "I'm named after the honeymoon my mum never got to go on."

"Oh, San." He sounded mortified, but she shook her head and managed a smile.

"I asked her once if I made her sad—y'know, reminding her of what she'd missed—but she just said, 'I have no regrets about anything your dad has done, because without him I wouldn't have you.'"

"Your mum's a remarkable lady."

Sanne stared at a streetlamp, letting the orange glow fill her vision. "She's too bloody proud to take any money from me, so I've never told her that I'm putting fifty quid aside for her every month. She's going on that cruise as soon as that bastard finally kicks it. Maybe she can take his ashes and dump them into the North Sea."

Nelson snorted. "There'd be something poetic about that."

"Aye." She thought of her dad, huddled by the gas fire even in the height of summer, his pinched fingers stretched out to the red-hot bars. "It'd be perfect for him. He fucking hates being cold."

CHAPTER SIXTEEN

The uneven path crunched beneath Sanne's trainers, so that she had to concentrate on where she placed her feet, rather than on the weariness pervading her body. She had managed to snatch only a few hours of sleep after her night shift, before the warmth of her south facing bedroom had combined with an unsettling, barely-remembered dream to force her awake. Reluctant to lie there tossing and turning, and eager to get back into the office that afternoon, she had opted for a run to clear her head. Now, six and a half miles into the eight-mile loop, her head did feel clearer, but her legs were on the verge of mutiny.

Slowing her pace as the path widened, she looked up at the hills that rose out of the valley. Bright sunshine lit their summits and sparkled off the brook alongside her track. Swelled by the recent rain, foamy streams zigzagged through the vegetation, and sheep roamed freely, helping themselves to bilberries. She wiped sweat from her eyes and pushed on. The serenity of her surroundings couldn't distract her from the fact that this was her first run since she found Josie. There was no doubt that she was more cautious now. She kept scanning the horizon with a wary eye, and her phone— something she rarely carried on a low route—was tucked into her pocket. Whenever a grouse broke for cover right under her feet, it frightened her half to death. She couldn't bear to sacrifice the moors, though. It would be too much like admitting defeat. Instead, she considered every step a small victory, a chance to reclaim the peaks for those who loved them.

Thinking about the case reminded her of an idea she had had during the previous night's fruitless stakeout. Techs working on Ned Moseley's computer had unearthed no history of any pornographic sites or mail-order companies related to the stash discovered in his house. He had no PayPal account, as far as they could tell, and his debit card statements indicated that nothing but a few harmless video games had been purchased over the Internet. The DVDs and magazines had been found wrapped in supermarket shopping bags, as if they had been delivered in person rather than mailed. It made Sanne wonder about a local supplier. That part of the investigation had been handed over to the Sexual Offences and Exploitation Team, but they were an under-resourced unit unlikely to drop everything in order to give it precedence. She hadn't discussed any of this with Nelson, who was also unlikely to consider it a priority, but at this point even the slightest lead was worth following up on. Fortunately, she happened to know someone very well connected. She made a mental note to call Keeley about it when she got back to the cottage.

The plan gave her a burst of energy. She leapt across a puddle stretching the width of the path and made quick work of the last mile, sprinting along the home straight. At her gate, she bent double to catch her breath, and as she panted for air, a hint of smoke caught in her nostrils. She raised her head to see a grey cloud drifting from her kitchen window, which would have been more alarming were Meg's car not parked in the drive.

The shrill bleep of a smoke alarm halted her at the back door. "Raise your hands and step slowly away from the stove," she said, attempting to sound stern, though too breathless to carry it off.

"Just in time! Go and have a shower." Meg silenced the alarm by knocking the battery out of it, and slid the over-heated frying pan from the gas ring.

"Just in time for what? And are you planning to burn down my house while I wash?"

"Eggy bread, and no, I don't think so." With a dubious expression, she surveyed the oil sizzling in the pan. "I hope not, anyway."

Sanne filled a glass with water and took a long drink. "How about we eat first and then I shower?"

"Fine, but I'm cooking. I wanted this to be a surprise."

"Consider me surprised."

Meg looked downcast. "I fixed your washer and that dripping tap for you."

Swallowing the last of her water, Sanne took a proper look around the kitchen. Meg's tool kit was still open at the side of the washing machine, with a towel spread out beneath the cupboard that housed the plumbing. On the unit, a dish held eggs cracked in readiness beside a fresh loaf and two mugs.

"You're a love." Sanne planted a sweaty kiss on Meg's cheek and grinned when Meg shooed her away. "Thank you. I owe you salad."

Meg picked up a fork and began to scramble the eggs. "I crept in, thinking you were still asleep, and spent over an hour being as quiet as I could. It wasn't until I nipped to the loo that I realised you weren't bloody here."

"I'd have left a note, only I live on my own."

Meg laughed. "Touché."

Sanne gave her a little bow. "Can you hold off on breakfast for a few minutes while I phone Keeley?"

"Sure. Anything wrong?"

"No. I just want to pick her brains about something."

"About what?" Meg's voice followed Sanne into the hallway. "Crap names beginning with K? How to filch from the system without breaking your false nails?"

"She speaks very highly of you, you know," Sanne called back. Meg's hoot of laughter was swallowed up by the whistle of the kettle.

Out of habit, Sanne checked the time before she dialled. It was almost noon—late enough for Keeley to be back from the post office if it was benefits day. The phone rang repeatedly, but just as Sanne had resigned herself to leaving a message, Keeley answered.

"Oh, hey, San. What's up?"

"Nothing much." Sanne floundered. She and Keeley usually met on the neutral turf of their parents' house, where they got along fine for the few hours it took to eat a Sunday roast. She couldn't remember the last time they'd spoken on the phone. "How're the kids?"

"Loud, annoying, snotty, and at school. In that order. San, you didn't call to ask about the kids. What's wrong?"

"I just…" This time she hesitated for a different reason, unsure whether Keeley would take umbrage. She decided to make her request seem official, hoping Keeley might be flattered rather than offended. "Okay, I need your help on this case."

She heard the spark of a lighter and, seconds later, Keeley sucking on a cigarette.

"Cool." Keeley exhaled. "I don't know nothing, though."

"Never say never, Keels. We're investigating a porn link, nasty hardcore DVDs, and I remembered Wayne used to dabble in that kind of thing."

"Wayne never made pornos!" She sounded outraged.

Sanne winced at her own poor choice of phrasing. Wayne was Kasper's dad, or was he Kerby's? She could never keep track. "No, sorry, I didn't mean he made them, but he sold a few pirated films, didn't he? He's not in trouble. I just wondered if he knew anyone local who was dealing in the really hard stuff. Maybe bringing them in from abroad and copying them to sell on?"

"He probably wouldn't tell me, San. He knows you're a bobby." Keeley paused, and the turning cogs were practically audible as she mulled over the pros and cons. "He has been sniffing around a bit lately, though. Maybe if I promised to meet him for a drink…"

"That'd be great, Keels." Sanne pre-empted Keeley's next question. "I'll send you some cash to pay for a meal out. Okay?"

"Nice one, sis." Keeley took another long drag on her cigarette. "I'll give him a ring now and let you know."

She hung up without saying good-bye. Sanne took the handset into the kitchen, where the smell of frying eggs had replaced that of burning.

"Perfect timing," Meg said. "Grab a plate."

❖

"I think this is one recipe I've mastered to perfection." Full to bursting after two slices of fried bread, Meg was now sipping from a mug of tea. She slid a third slice onto Sanne's plate and watched her pour on a generous quantity of maple syrup.

"Can't really go wrong with eggy bread." Sanne paused, as if considering the myriad ways in which Meg could make it go wrong. "Hmm…"

Riding high on the success of her breakfast, Meg merely smiled. "I think, as adults, we're supposed to call it French toast."

"Bit lah-de-dah for us, love."

Meg sniffed. "I'll have you know I can be very lah-de-dah when I want to be."

"My arse! My bloody rooster's got more decorum." Sanne laughed as Meg flipped her the bird.

The phone rang just in time to prevent things escalating. Clearing the plates away, Meg listened to a one-sided conversation that culminated with Sanne agreeing on a time and place to meet Keeley. Sanne was still clutching the phone when she came back into the kitchen, and she appeared to be on the verge of dialling again.

"Problem?" Meg asked.

"No. Well, yes." Sanne sat at the table. "I'm not sure. An ex of Keeley's knows a bloke who sells legit DVDs on Halshaw market and not-so-legit ones to a chosen few. She doesn't think he's got access to the sort of stuff we found at Ned Moseley's, but her ex reckons he might know who has."

Meg dried her hands and hoisted herself onto the countertop. "So what's bugging you?"

"The market's only on today, and we have no other contact information for this bloke. He'll be shutting up shop in a few hours. If we miss him, it could be another week before we get a chance to speak to him."

"Too late in the day to get this authorised by the boss, is that the problem?"

Sanne nodded, her teeth worrying her bottom lip. "Yeah, and also…I still have some issues with Ned Moseley as a suspect, and

I'd like to shore up this link. No one else is really considering this angle. With the surveillance and the searches, there's too much to do. Keeley said she'd come with me and point out the right stall, but I should tell Eleanor what I'm up to, all the same."

"Why? What difference would it make? And what if she refused to give her permission?" Meg's voice rose. Sometimes Sanne's aversion to taking the initiative frustrated the hell out of her. "Are you going in all guns blazing to arrest him?"

"Well, no." Sanne put the phone down and then picked it up again.

"And you're on a bit of a deadline, aren't you?"

"Obviously, yeah. And it might take ages to obtain this chap's home address from the market managers and bring him in for questioning, even if Eleanor thinks it's worthwhile."

"And that's if he's registered the right address. If he's flogging illegal stuff in his free time, it's unlikely he'd be forthcoming with his details."

"True. I don't even know where Eleanor is. She might be with Josie or interviewing. And after working last night, I'm not expected to be in today, anyway." She glanced up at Meg. "You're a bad influence on me."

Meg flashed a grin. "Want some company on your illicit mission?"

"Keeley's bringing three of the kids," Sanne warned her. "And Kerby's full of a cold."

"I'm completely immune to germ-riddled children." Undeterred, Meg ushered her toward the doorway. "Time's a-wastin'. Go get a shower and find yourself something scruffy to wear."

Fine weather and an appetite for bargains seemed to have emptied most of Halshaw estate onto the market. Young mums hurried around the outside stalls, cramming cheap meat and bumper packs of nappies into prams before they had to go and collect their elder children from school. Vendors yelled their knockdown prices, and the air was thick with the smell of bacon butties, greasy burgers, and cigarettes. As teenagers, Sanne and Meg had both worked on stalls during the long summer holidays, but the place hadn't been so bedraggled then, nor the shoppers so downtrodden. A few of the older, more established stalls had survived the recession, and Sanne was watching Meg buying crumbly Lancashire cheese from one of them when she heard Keeley's irate yelling. A thin wail rose above the clattering of plates from the neighbouring cafe.

"Hark, I think I hear the dulcet and loving tones of your sister," Meg said, dropping the cheese into her bag.

"We're meeting her at the sweet stall." Sanne turned toward it, guided by the sound of disconsolate sobbing. She waved at Keeley's brood as they approached, and Kiera's tantrum ceased abruptly.

"Hey, sweetie." Sanne picked her up and blotted the tears from her face with a tissue. "Have you been eating dirt again?"

Kiera chortled, her grubby fists clutching at Sanne's hair.

Rolling a double buggy back and forth, Keeley tried to keep the older toddlers, Kasper and Kerby, asleep. Her lips smacked together as she chewed a piece of gum. "She wanted jelly babies, but I don't get paid till tomorrow."

"Oh, did you get a job?" Meg said brightly.

Sanne shot her a look, warning her to behave. They both knew the likelihood of Keeley finding gainful employment was akin to gold falling from the sky and gilding the pavements of Halshaw.

"No. It's when my bennies come in." Keeley's tone implied that the question had been particularly stupid.

"Ah, right, my mistake." Meg sighed and offered her fingers for Kiera to chew on. "I guess someone ought to buy you some sweets then, eh, kiddo?"

Leaving Meg to deal with Kiera's requests, Sanne surveyed the outdoor stalls. "Which one is he on?" she asked. A number of the booths sold CDs, DVDs, and mobile phone accessories. Each was doing brisk business.

Keeley had tucked herself into a corner with her back to the market. When she spoke, she barely opened her mouth. "Third from the end, between the wool and the bloke selling fake leather bags."

"He can't hear you, Keels. Hell, from here he can't even see you."

"Good. I have to come here every week. I don't want people to know I set the coppers on to him."

"I'll be discreet, I promise." Sanne crossed her heart. She knew it was hard for Keeley to live on Halshaw and have a sister in the police force. While their mum was nothing but proud of Sanne's achievements, it must have been difficult for Keeley to gain the trust of friends, though unfortunately, the useless men she fell for never seemed deterred.

"Here." Sanne fished out a tenner and passed it to her. "Take the kids to the chippy. I'll come and find you when I'm done."

The money was in Keeley's pocket before Sanne could blink.

"You said you'd send some cash for me and Wayne, remember?" Keeley's eyes were fixed on Sanne's wallet.

"Aye, I remember." Sanne gave her another thirty pounds. If Keeley's tipoff helped with the case, it would be money well spent. "Don't get too drunk."

Keeley blew a bubble in her chewing gum and popped it over her grin. "You're such a goody two-shoes, San." All smiles now, she took hold of Kiera and cooed at the bag of sweets she held up. "Say thank you to your auntie Meg."

Not quite adept at speech yet, Kiera waved a beheaded jelly baby instead.

"How much did that cost you?" Meg asked, watching Keeley head for the chippy on the corner of the high street.

"Forty bleedin' quid."

Meg whistled. "I think I got away lightly." She offered Sanne a black-and-white mint. "Fancy a bit of DVD shopping?"

They wandered toward the stall, attempting to remain incognito by detouring via the bakery, where Meg bought Eccles cakes and chattered casually with the cashier. Sanne caught herself tapping her foot as she waited for Meg to count her change. She should have asked Eleanor before she came out here. This wasn't her investigation to run. She couldn't just go off tracking down her own leads. She had never wanted to be a loose cannon.

"Oh, hey, have you seen this? It's supposed to be great."

Caught by the sleeve, Sanne found herself staring at the cover of a random action film Meg had plucked from the first rack of DVDs. The man behind the counter nodded at them but continued to chat on his phone. Approximately forty years old, he was of slim build, with receding hair, a compensatory beard, and pockmarked skin. She didn't recognise him, and she hoped that meant he had no idea who she was either. As Meg continued to extol the virtues of Vin Diesel, Sanne scanned the rest of the shelves. She was no expert, but none of the films or box sets looked like rip-offs. Most were labelled as second-hand, and an advertisement above them offered "excellent" rates for used discs.

"These are all old," Meg said. The stallholder had just finished his call, and she was standing close enough for him to overhear. "Maybe you should ask him about the other stuff." She elbowed Sanne in the ribs, making the gesture obvious.

The man turned the pages of a tabloid newspaper while using his little finger to pick his teeth, but he was clearly listening. Sidling over to his counter, Sanne didn't need to act nervous. Her face felt warm, and the inside of her mouth was as dry as sandpaper. He looked her up and down as she approached, his eyes lingering over the curve of her chest. She quelled the urge to slap the leer from his face.

"Our Wayne reckoned you had better films than this," she said, laying on her thickest Halshaw accent. "Reckoned we had to ask for them special."

"Did he now?" He folded his arms. "Wayne who?"

"Peters. He's my cousin." She took a gamble on his not knowing Wayne except as a casual DVD-laundering acquaintance.

"Ambleside Walk?"

She sidestepped the trap with ease. "Nah, Browbeck. He still lives with his mam."

"Yeah, Browbeck. That's the one." He slapped his own forehead in fake remembrance and lowered his voice. "So, what is it you're looking for? I can get brand new releases before they're even in the cinemas over here. Downloads from iTunes and Netflix? Or maybe you and your bird are after something with a bit of kink?"

Wrong-footed by the accuracy of his gaydar, she let the latter comment slide. "What've you got in?"

He delved beneath the counter and slid out an indexed box of thin plastic sleeves, each containing a single disc. "Seeing as you know Wayne, I can do you a bit of a deal. Four for five quid."

Sanne took her warrant card from her pocket and laid it open on his newspaper. "How about I do you a deal instead?"

"Fucking hell." He stared at the card and then at her, as if trying to reconcile the smartly dressed officer on her ID badge with the scrubber in front of him. "I'll fucking kill Wayne."

"I doubt that." Built like a brick shithouse, Wayne was a nightclub bouncer and more than capable of snapping the man's neck. "And he only gave me your name to save his own skin. Now I'm going to give you a similar opportunity."

Her doubts and trepidation forgotten, she slipped easily back into her role as a detective. She'd been dealing with small-time criminals for years—interviewing them, visiting them at home or in the cells, arresting them on the streets. The one thing they had in common was their ability to figure out what was in it for them. The man in front of her was doing that now—studying her face, mulling over her words, trying to determine her angle.

"I need a name," she said.

"Terry Thorpe," he blurted, before she could go any further.

She raised an eyebrow. "Is that your name? I don't need your name, you pillock, but thanks anyway." She took her pad from her back pocket and made a note. "I'm looking for someone, possibly local, who's dealing in illegal, hardcore pornography—DVDs, magazines, still images. I'm not talking about a 'bit of kink,' Terry. Most likely they're imported, and there are quality sleeves on the discs, so it's not an amateur operation."

Terry toyed with the edge of his newspaper. "I don't know nobody doing that."

"No?" She sighed. "You know I've got enough cause to search your house, Terry. Confiscate all your gear, your computers and discs. Bang you up for a few months. Slap you with a huge fine and a criminal record. What would your missus say?"

The hand sporting his wedding ring vanished beneath the counter, and his bottom lip began to tremble. "Mal Atley," he muttered. "Malcolm Atley. He lives on Lower Ulverston. I don't know what number. He brings stuff to the pub. Sells it out of his car. Proper dodgy shit—rape, kiddies. Says he gets it from Poland and Romania. I've heard he does drugs as well. He can get his hands on all sorts of crap."

"Which pub?" Sanne asked, frantically scribbling notes. The drugs connection was an unexpected bonus. If Atley had supplied Ned Moseley's pornography, who knew what else he might have sold him?

"Coach and Horses, but he also does the Working Men's and the Crown." Terry gripped her arm. She saw Meg take a step toward them and held up her free hand to stop her from intervening. "You won't tell him I snitched, will you?" he asked.

"No. I strongly suggest you don't either."

Her forearm stung as he released it. She didn't recognise Mal's name, but Terry was obviously petrified of him.

"I think I'll close early today," he said, his eyes flitting from side to side as he tried to gauge who might have witnessed the exchange.

The shutter on his stall was clattering into place as Sanne met back up with Meg in the market's main aisle. Meg grinned and linked her arm through Sanne's.

"What are you smiling at?" Sanne asked. She felt Meg's grip tighten and Meg lean into her.

"You are such a badass," Meg whispered.

Sanne laughed. "Don't be a twerp."

"I can't help it. You gave me chills. Look." Meg displayed arms covered in goose pimples.

"You must've been standing in a draught."

"Did you get your name?"

"A name, most of an address, and three pubs." Sanne took a deep breath. "All I have to do now is tell Eleanor what I've been up to."

Chapter Seventeen

The mood in the office was subdued when Sanne walked in. Fred and George were at their desks, and Jay Egerton was over at the copier, but no one spoke beyond a perfunctory greeting, and they all looked dog-tired.

"The boss around?" Sanne asked.

Fred nodded toward Eleanor's office.

Sanne knocked on the office door and waited for a response before she entered. During the drive over, she had given herself a pep talk, reassuring herself that she had investigated the lead in her own time. In any case, EDSOP had never identified the source of the drugs used to subdue Josie. If Atley confirmed he had dealt to Ned Moseley, they might have their first concrete piece of evidence linking Ned to the abductions. This additional possibility gave Sanne the assurance to stand in front of Eleanor's desk and explain where she had spent the afternoon, although she didn't disclose that it was nagging doubts about Ned that had led her to the market in the first place.

Eleanor listened, jotting the occasional note, but it wasn't until Atley's name came up that she showed any reaction.

"Mal Atley," she repeated. Her lips twisted as if at something foul. "Vile individual. Did time for GBH, but it's difficult to make anything stick to him. Are you sure about this?"

"As sure as I can be. Thorpe was scared to death of him. I don't think he'd have given me the name lightly."

"Definitely not." Eleanor pushed her glasses onto her head and folded her arms. "I should let you out on your own more often."

Sanne shrugged, but the praise buoyed her immeasurably. "I have connections in low places, that's all."

That brought a smile to Eleanor's face. "We're stretched too thin as a unit to set up a stakeout, so I'll push this up the chain and let them decide who brings Atley in. Have you ever met him?"

"No, boss."

Eleanor's smile broadened. "You're in for a treat."

The previous night's vigil had been the first night shift Sanne had worked in months, and she had forgotten the hung-over, disorientated feeling of having her body clock completely disrupted. Slouched on her sofa in her pyjamas after a late supper, she scrolled through the case reports, repeatedly adjusting the glare of the laptop, and absorbing little of the information. She opened a medical file that listed Josie's injuries in stark, emotionless terminology—*"base of skull fracture, large subdural haematoma, multiple superficial lacerations (most likely inflicted with a razorblade or small knife), contusions consistent with being kicked or punched, fractured left femur"*—and a forensics report with next to nothing of any import. Nine days into the investigation, EDSOP had an entirely circumstantial suspect; a young woman missing, presumed dead; and a trail that was growing colder by the minute.

The buzz of Sanne's mobile stopped her from taking her frustration out on the computer. Expecting Meg to be the only other idiot awake at such an hour, she frowned when she saw Eleanor's number instead.

"Hey, boss, you're up late." She heard Eleanor sigh and guessed she was still in her office, heels off, blouse untucked and unbuttoned at the neck. The bottle of Scotch she kept for dire emergencies or the successful closure of cases had probably taken a battering.

"I could say the same about you." There was a rustling noise as Eleanor shifted the phone, and seconds later, a fanfare signalled the shutdown of her computer. "I'm just about to leave, but I thought you'd want to know that Mal Atley was arrested a couple of hours ago."

Sanne dropped her legs off the sofa and sat upright, as if a teacher had rapped her knuckles. "Bloody hell, that was fast."

"I know. Either Sex Offences have too much time on their hands, or they didn't want to risk Thorpe cracking and warning him. I would suspect the latter. They set up surveillance at each of the pubs Thorpe had mentioned, and they arrested Atley in the car park of the Coach and Horses. He was too busy flogging a bag of DVDs to a local school governor to notice the officers approaching him."

"Is he talking?"

"Not tonight. I think they want him to stew a while in holding first. Plus, they have a warrant for his house, so they'll wait and see what they find there before interviewing him."

"That makes sense." Even so, Sanne couldn't resist looking at the clock on her mantelpiece. The arrest had happened far sooner than she could have hoped, yet nothing seemed to be moving quickly enough.

"I spoke to DI Anderson," Eleanor said. "He agreed to let you speak to Atley once he was done with him."

Sanne almost lost her grip on the phone. "Boss, I'm only Tier Two."

Eleanor didn't miss a beat. "And perfectly capable of dealing with a toe-rag like Atley. It'll be tomorrow afternoon at the earliest, which means you'll have the morning to warn Nelson and prep."

"Right. Okay." Sanne started pacing across her living room. "I'll let Nelson know."

"Sanne?" Eleanor sounded amused.

"What, boss?"

"Get some sleep."

"Yep. Will do."

Eleanor hung up and left her listening to silence. Peering out into the pitch-blackness, Sanne wondered whether she'd break her neck if she went for a jog. She dropped her mobile on the sofa and headed into the kitchen to make a brew. If she couldn't run, tea was her only fallback.

❖

Sanne glanced at the file on the table in front of her and then looked across at Malcolm Atley. He pursed his lips to blow her a kiss, filling the space between them with the pungent odour of cigarettes and aftershave. If he was at all concerned about the eight charges filed against him that morning, he was hiding it well.

"Aren't you two just the poster children for Affirmative Action?" he said pleasantly.

Dressed in a smart suit, he was clean-shaven and handsome in a bland, boy-band way. Living on Halshaw for the past ten years had knocked the edges from his well-bred Cheshire accent, but it was still audible beneath the flattened vowels and hint of Yorkshire. The thirty-one-year-old son of a self-made millionaire, Atley had had a privileged public school education and had apparently inherited his father's business acumen. An unfortunate cocaine and amphetamine habit had eaten into his earnings, however, and since arriving in the area he had moved from petty offences to more organised, serious crime. A small stash of ecstasy, cocaine, and ketamine, bagged and ready to sell, had been recovered from the water tank on his toilet, and his pornography distribution racket had turned out to be far more extensive than Terry Thorpe had thought. The Sexual Offences squad had found a schedule in Atley's bedroom listing a dozen people recently employed to trade the DVDs and magazines, suggesting Atley himself now focused on product acquisition and reproduction. The only reason he had been caught red-handed the previous night was that the school governor had insisted on dealing with him in person. Sanne doubted Ned Moseley would have commanded the same respect, though there was no harm in asking. Atley might even have been a viable suspect in the abduction case, had airline tickets and a travel itinerary not placed him in Bucharest for fifteen days out of the past three weeks.

"Mr. Atley, I'd like you to tell me if you recognise this man." She slid Ned Moseley's mugshot toward Atley, studying his face for any twitch of reaction, but he remained utterly impassive, even as he picked up the photograph to make a show of giving it close attention.

"Nope." He set the image down again. "Never seen him before."

Sanne tried to catch him in a lie. "You don't watch the news? Read the papers? He's had a real rise in his profile of late."

"Got better things to watch and read, Detective." He played his tongue lewdly over his lower lip. She fought the urge to shudder.

"His name is Ned Moseley. Still not ringing any bells?"

"Not a one."

"That's funny, because we found a stash of your special brand of porn in Mr. Moseley's house, and someone's been supplying him with ketamine, among other substances."

Atley relaxed back in his chair and clasped his hands behind his head. "No comment."

Turning to Nelson, Sanne sighed. "I guess we'll just have to cross-check Mr. Atley's client list, then."

"Good luck with that." Atley smirked at her.

She met his cocky expression head-on. "Oh, what, you mean because it's encrypted?" For a second his smile faltered, and she seized on this hint of uncertainty. "Our techs have had less than twelve hours to work on it, and we already know it's a set of initials and phone numbers. I'm thinking a lot of people are going to be very unhappy with you, Malcolm. Never write this shit down, isn't that what they say?" She looked to Nelson for confirmation.

"Schoolboy error," he said, nodding gravely.

She slotted Ned's photo back into the file. "I thought you might be able to save us a little time, Malcolm. Judges and juries like that kind of crap, especially if you're looking at a long sentence. And, believe me, you're looking at a long sentence." She stood up to leave.

Atley lowered his hands. "Don't know him," he muttered.

"Excuse me, I didn't catch that," she said, even though her pulse had fluttered in response.

"I. Don't. Know. Ned. Moseley." He enunciated each word with precision. "But then"—he opened his palms in mock innocence, as if thousands of pounds' worth of computer equipment, explicit material, and drugs hadn't just been found in his home—"whatever makes you think that I might?"

Sanne smiled at him, privately wishing him the sort of hell reserved for prisoners who dealt in child pornography. "Thank you, Mr. Atley. That's cleared everything up beautifully."

Nelson held the door open for her. Atley slammed his fists on the table, his expensive public school manners forgotten as he called after her.

"Yo, you fucking bitch faggot, when do I get to go for a cigarette?"

Cold sweat poured off the elderly man's forehead as he repeatedly yanked the oxygen mask from his face.

"I can't breathe," he said, his eyes wide with fear. "I can't breathe."

Bert was breathing, but Meg could hear the fluid filling his lungs even before she put her stethoscope to his chest.

"The paramedics get a line in?" she asked Liz.

"Yeah, left wrist. His wife called their doctor yesterday, but the doc couldn't be bothered coming out, and just prescribed antibiotics for a chest infection over the phone."

"Because everyone knows antibiotics work wonders for heart failure." Meg didn't bother to disguise her sarcasm, but her voice was gentle when she turned back to Bert. "Your heart's a bit tired, Bert. That's why you feel as if you're drowning. I'm giving you some medicine to get rid of all that fluid on your chest, but it'll also make you piss like a racehorse, so you'll need a catheter. Is that okay?"

Her candour surprised a smile out of him. He nodded and stopped grappling with the mask.

"Good man," she said. "I promise I'll warm my hands first. What's your missus called?"

"Doris."

"I'll get her in as soon as we've finished up the business with your plumbing."

"Righto."

His oxygen level began to climb steadily once the diuretic was administered. He still looked poorly, and his breathing sounded like bubbles blown through a milkshake, but the terror had started to fade from his eyes.

"Dr. Fielding? Meg?" The voice was quiet, but it came with an unexpected tap on Meg's back, sending her pen scrawling across Bert's chart. "Sorry, I didn't mean…" Emily managed to look simultaneously embarrassed and worried. "Could I have a word with you about a patient?"

"Have to be a quick one," Meg said. "I've got an unstable LVF here. You're in Minors, aren't you?"

"Yes, but it's not really a medical thing. I've got a lad saying some weird stuff about that abduction case, and I don't know what to do."

"Weird how? What's he come in with?"

"Lac to his palm. He'll need stitches. He got a bit overly friendly when I examined him—trying to chat me up, bragging about his new car. I wasn't really listening, and he stinks of booze anyway, but then he started playing the big man, and that's when he mentioned the case."

"And? Oh, just a minute." Meg scanned the ECG trace Liz held out to her. "How're you doing, Bert?"

"Better than I was, love."

She checked his observations. All looked stable, so she turned back to Emily, her head humming with everything she was trying to keep in order.

"This lad reckons there's a lock-up," Emily said. "And that the suspect, Ned something-or-other, keeps a Land Rover in it."

"Ned Moseley."

"Yes." Emily clicked her fingers. "That's the one."

"Bloody Nora." Meg heaved out a breath that whistled between her teeth. A lock-up could conceal a vehicle, but it could also be an excellent place to hold a captive. "Did he tell you where it is?"

"No, he clammed up when I showed a bit too much interest. I think I spooked him. He's got a curfew tag, so I doubt he and the police are on the best of terms." Emily moved to her left, allowing Liz to position a small trolley at Bert's bedside.

"Shit," Meg said. " I can't leave Bert just yet. You're going to have to stall this lad."

"Stall him how?"

"I don't know. Hell, bat your eyelashes, tell him you're just a junior and you've asked me to come and supervise your suturing."

Emily smiled demurely. "I can get a bit tearful, if it'll help."

"Perfect. We should have his name and address anyway, if he's booked in at reception, but it'd be useful to get a bit more information out of him before I drag Sanne and the rest of Eds Up over here." Meg washed her hands, letting the water warm them, and pulled on a clean pair of gloves. "Give me a shout if he looks like he's going to scarper."

"Will do." Emily hurried out, leaving Liz staring after her quizzically.

"What on earth are you up to?" Liz asked.

"Absolutely nothing." Meg drew the curtains around the bed, and picked up a tube of anaesthetic gel. "Bert, close your eyes and think of England. I'll have this done in a jiffy."

With Bert stable and sneaking sips of his wife's tea, Meg left him in Liz's hands and went to the Minor Injuries bay. She found Emily at one of the computers, chewing on a pen as she studied an X-ray.

"Impressive," Meg said. "Fall off a bike or a trampoline?"

"Skateboard, actually. She was screaming blue murder when she came in, which gave me a good excuse to leave our mystery informant for a while."

Meg eyed the five cubicles, each with its curtain drawn. "Which one is he in?"

"Three. Once I'd treated him to a Mars and a bottle of Fanta, he seemed happy enough to wait."

"What's his name?"

"Callum." Emily checked his notes. "Callum Clark."

"Right."

Meg tugged the curtain aside, revealing a mucky-looking lad in his early twenties slouching on the bed. Using his unbandaged hand, he stuffed his mobile phone back into his pocket. There was chocolate coating his teeth as he grinned at her, and the tiny cubicle stank of artificial orange flavouring and alcohol. Taking shallow breaths, she stepped closer.

"Dr. Woodall has asked me to take a look at your hand with her. Do you mind?"

"Nope," he said, ripping off his bandage before she could stop him. He poked a finger into the laceration. "Smashed a glass while I was washing up, miss. Thought I'd chopped summat off, it bled that bad."

"Hmm." Meg decided not to challenge his story, although the ingrained dirt on his hands suggested that they hadn't seen soap and water for several days. She ran him through the usual sequence of tests to assess circulation and sensation, trying all the while to remember whether she had seen his face before. She couldn't. He looked like most of the lads she had grown up around, the mates her brother brought home, the ones who smoked dope outside the chippy or tried to get her drunk so they could hit on her. He had an electronic tag half-hidden by his sock, and his unthinking referral to her as "miss" implied he was no stranger to prison.

"That all looks good, Callum. I'm going to stick around while Dr. Woodall stitches you up."

"Fill yer boots." He settled back on the bed and crossed his legs at the ankles, though within seconds he was scowling at his tag and uncrossing them again.

Emily began to lay out the contents of a suture kit, taking her time, giving Meg a chance to skim through Callum's notes. A resident of Halshaw, in the last four years he had racked up three A&E attendances for alcohol and drug intoxication, and two for injuries sustained while fighting. A suspicious-looking gap in the pattern probably denoted time in prison. As a potential witness, he didn't seem very promising.

"Which school did you go to, mate?" Meg asked.

"Halshaw County," he said, without taking his eyes off the needle approaching his hand.

"Hey, me too." She perched on the end of the bed, ignoring the rank smell of his socks. "Was Mrs. McNeil still there when you went?"

He looked at Meg as if she had suddenly grown a second head. She sensed a similar reaction from Emily, who tried to disguise hers by jabbing local anaesthetic into Callum's palm.

"Fucking hell!" He glared at Emily, but Meg still had most of his attention. "Yeah, she was still there. Gave me loads of detentions. Are you from Halshaw, then?"

"Ennerdale Close."

"No shit, that's just around the corner from my flat. You still live there now?" He rolled his eyes. "Course you don't. Got somewhere nice, I bet."

She shrugged but saw a hint of an opening. "It's okay. Bit safer, y'know, what with everything that's been going on around here lately."

He pushed himself forward until he could whisper directly into her ear. "I might know summat about that."

"Really?" She kept her voice low. "Have you told anyone?"

"Don't know that I should. Coppers never do me no favours."

"Suppose not. There could be a reward, though." Meg had no idea whether there was one, but it certainly made his ears prick up. "And I know a few bobbies, from working here. You tell me, I pass it on to them, and then you don't need to do anything but collect your money."

His eyes glinted, and he licked his lips, leaving orange spittle at the corners of his mouth. He capitulated sooner than she had expected, but then drink and drugs didn't come cheap, she supposed.

"Ned Moseley keeps a Landie in a lock-up two streets over from Prospect, near the fields." He glanced nervously around the cubicle as if afraid the conversation was being recorded. "One of them old types. I don't know the reg. He's not had it long, but I seen him driving around in it. It's the middle garage. I think it's got a blue door."

From the corner of her eye, Meg saw Emily jot a note on her glove.

"Blue door, near the fields. Got it." As Meg pushed up from the bed, he grabbed the hem of her scrubs top.

"Hey, how do I get my reward?"

She waved his paperwork. "All your details are on here, pal. Don't you worry about a thing." Poised to leave the cubicle, she remembered her original ploy and bent to study Emily's sutures. "You're doing a lovely job there, Dr. Woodall. Carry on."

She added a patronising pat on the shoulder and forced herself to leave the cubicle at a walk, not a run. Once out of sight, she jogged down the corridor until her mobile picked up enough signal to call Sanne.

"Hey, you, what's up?" Sanne sounded tired and distracted. The beep of a fax's modem indicated she was still in the office.

"Grab a pen, love," Meg said. "I think I've got something for you."

❖

"Callum Clark?" Nelson repeated the name as one might say "Bubonic plague?"

"The very same," Sanne said.

"'No comment' Callum?"

"Yep."

Nelson pushed his chair back and flung his pen onto his desk. "And, what? He just suddenly remembered seeing Moseley in this Land Rover and decided now might be a good time to help us out?"

Sanne shook her head. "From what Meg said, he'd probably never have breathed a word about it, if he hadn't been trying to impress the alluring Dr. Emily."

Nelson retrieved his pen and used it to scratch his chin. "Think Clark might be our man, and this is a ploy to throw us off the scent?"

"Unlikely." It was the first thing she had considered. "He's tagged, and I already spoke to his probation officer, who confirmed he's been obeying his curfew. Electronic records prove he barely left his flat for three days around the time Josie escaped. The farthest he travelled was here, to chat to us for the afternoon. He can't have been up on Gillot Tor, moving Rachel."

Nelson's eyes gleamed with renewed enthusiasm as he mulled the information over. "Did we just get lucky?"

She nodded, at first with uncertainty, but then with mounting confidence. "Let's rally the troops, mate."

Chapter Eighteen

It took four hours of phone calls and wrangling with the local council and the brass to establish that no one paid rent on the middle garage with the blue door. That—in all likelihood— whoever had commandeered it and fitted a new lock had acted opportunistically, making use of an abandoned space. Which was fortunate, given that the word of an intoxicated repeat offender would never have been sufficient basis for a search warrant.

As the shadows lengthened and coalesced in the dusk, Sanne stood beside Nelson, watching a uniformed officer assess the best angle of attack for his battering ram. In a nearby tree a thrush was singing its heart out, while a yapping dog sprinted across the playing fields. A gang of children shrieked and then swore at the dog, and the officer smashed through the blue door with a single, precisely aimed strike.

Someone closer than Sanne thumped the officer on the back and began to help him strip the shattered remnants. When the two men had cleared an entrance and stepped aside, Sanne and Nelson followed Eleanor into the garage. Their torch beams crisscrossed each other, glinting back off the dilapidated Land Rover Defender occupying most of the small space. It was a model favoured by many of the local farmers, and this one appeared to have been in recent use. Mud and grit caked its wheels, and its dull green bodywork was similarly splattered.

Sanne heard Nelson's quiet, amazed murmur and shared his sense of wonder that Callum Clark had been telling the truth.

"No plates," Eleanor said, the words muffled behind her paper mask. She had squeezed into the narrow gap between the front grille and the far wall.

"What's the betting the VIN's missing as well?" Nelson said. Along with the masks, they were all wearing forensic Tyvek suits, booties, and gloves, and there was no chance of their contaminating anything, so he tried the handle of the passenger door. Sanne found herself holding her breath as it swung open.

"Anything in there?" Eleanor asked.

"Odd bit of litter. Crisp packet, chocolate wrapper. Nothing else that I can see without getting in."

"Leave that to SOCO. Sanne, try the back."

Sweat crept down Sanne's spine as she nodded. The rear compartment was solid metal, its windows set in and around the back door and obscured by a large spare tyre. If Rachel was anywhere in the garage, it had to be there.

The handle gave easily, and Sanne tugged the door open before she could think about it. Her mask was dragged in against her face as she hyperventilated, but her torch illuminated only an empty space. She staggered a little, grabbing hold of the bodywork for support.

"It's empty," she called, and heard Eleanor's answering curse. Even as Sanne spoke, though, she moved closer and dropped to a crouch by the back step. Vague details became clearer as her eyes adjusted to the poor light—a large, incongruously clean patch on the floor of the compartment, and a tiny, rust-red smear on the green paintwork. The smell of bleach burned in her nostrils. Whoever had tried to clean the interior hadn't done a very thorough job, however. Once SOCO got hold of it, they would probably unearth a treasure trove of DNA evidence.

"Got something over here," Eleanor said. "Looks like fishing tackle."

"Bingo," Sanne whispered.

Ten days into the case, they had their first real breakthrough.

❖

No one went home. Those members of EDSOP not involved in a second search of Ned Moseley's house grabbed hot drinks and any sugary foodstuffs they could find and crowded into the observation room to watch his interview. This time around, he had surrendered without a fight and immediately requested his lawyer. He wasn't yet under arrest, but Carlyle had recited the official caution prior to starting the interview.

Perched on the edge of a chair, Sanne stared at Ned through the one-way mirror. He was obviously unnerved. His eyes were flitting around the room as if seeking an ally or an escape, and he could barely speak to confirm that he had understood the caution.

Carlyle pushed a glass of water closer to him and waited while he drank. "What can you tell me about the garages near the playing fields on Turner Street, Ned?" he said as Ned set the glass down.

Picking at a piece of loose skin on his palm, Ned glanced at his lawyer for guidance. She gave him a nod.

"I started keeping my fishing tackle in one because my mum says it makes my kitchen smell bad otherwise, and the air-raid shelter in the yard is damp." His posture relaxed as a thought seemed to occur to him. "Did the owner complain? It looked abandoned, see? That's the only reason I used it, but if he needs it back then that's fine." He smiled, a good citizen doing his best to abide by the law.

Carlyle wasn't smiling. "Just fishing tackle? Nothing else?"

"I put my scooter in there when it snows."

"What about your Land Rover?" Carlyle asked the question so quietly that Ned had to strain to hear it. His forehead crinkled in confusion.

"I don't have a Land Rover, just a scooter."

"That's funny, Ned"—one by one, Carlyle placed a sequence of photographs on the table—"because we found this parked up in your garage tonight, with traces of blood and bleach all over the back of it. We've already got people working to compare its tyre treads to those we found near our crime scene up on Corvenden."

Ned edged away from the images as if afraid they might contaminate him. "It's not mine," he whispered. Then, louder, "It's not mine. I never seen it before." His lawyer laid a hand on his forearm, urging him to remain calm. He shook it off. "No, fuck off! *Fuck off!*"

Behind the glass, Sanne flinched, but Carlyle ignored the outburst and took an item from his briefcase.

"What the hell?" Nelson said, and Sanne shrugged, equally mystified.

"Maybe the lads at the house found something," she said. It had taken three hours for Ned's lawyer to arrive at headquarters, plenty of time for the search to get under way.

Carlyle set the evidence bag on top of the photographs. "If the vehicle doesn't belong to you, explain why we found this crammed beneath the driver's seat."

The bag contained something green and woolly. Upon seeing it, Ned blanched.

"We'll be sending this to the labs for DNA analysis," Carlyle said. "You understand what I mean by that, right? You watch a lot of television. I'm pretty certain that all the hairs on this are going to prove a match to you. Do you know why I'm so certain?"

Ned's only response was a cold glare. Carlyle smiled at him and held up a large, framed photograph, the type that would take pride of place above someone's mantelpiece.

"Caught yourself a whopper that day, didn't you?"

Sanne leaned forward and sensed everyone else in the room do likewise. Behind her, George let out a whoop. In the photograph, Ned was kneeling at the side of a lake, with a huge carp cradled in both hands, and the same green woollen hat askew on his head.

"Talk your way out of that, you perverted bastard," George said.

"Here, Sanne darling, I saved you my last strawberry bonbon." Fred blew her a kiss and threw her the sweet.

"Cheers, Fred. I can't tell you how much this means to me."

"Anything to see a smile on your face."

She put the toffee into her mouth, though it was too sticky, the taste cloying and rich. Forcing herself to swallow it, she rested her elbows on her knees and dropped her head into her hands. Ned's lawyer had requested a half-hour break, and the interview was due to recommence shortly.

"Tired?" Nelson asked.

"Knackered." She looked up at him. "We've been watching Ned for three days now, and he'd been in custody for two before that."

"I know." His tone told her that she didn't need to say another word.

In those three days of being monitored, Ned had remained within walking distance of his house, retreading a familiar triangular route between the corner shop, the precinct with its chippy and kebab shop, and Prospect Street. Unless he had left Rachel with provisions, the chances of her still being alive were slim to non-existent. Although Sanne knew Nelson had long since reconciled himself to that inevitability, she had refused to give up hope. Now, with the evidence stacked against Ned Moseley, she felt broadsided by a truth she should have acknowledged days ago.

Nelson rested a hand on hers. She smiled at him, and then turned back to the mirror as the door to the interview room opened.

This time Eleanor took the central seat, and Ned eyed her warily as she arranged her paperwork on the table. She began by recapping what he had already discussed with Carlyle—his whereabouts on the days he should have been working for the Cleggs—fishing, alone, in a spot he hadn't shared with anyone, because the best carp were there. No, he still didn't know what a vehicle identification number was, even though both VINs on the Land Rover had been scoured off. And no, he couldn't think of anyone who might have "fitted him up" for the abductions, as he had claimed just prior to the break. He had mates, but no enemies.

"Can you provide us with a list of your mates' names?" Eleanor asked. EDSOP had already spoken to many of the people Ned had mentioned in the course of his first interview, but they had turned out to be casual drinking acquaintances. Either he didn't have any close friends, or he wasn't willing to identify them.

"Already told you their names." He directed his answer to the table.

"Any you might have forgotten?"

He shrugged and then shook his head. She leaned closer, broaching the gap between them.

"Ned, I want to help you, but I need you to cooperate. At the moment, I'll be honest, things are looking bad for you. You've admitted to having contact with both victims. You involved yourself in the case and seemed familiar with the area where the victims were held. You were found in possession of illegal pornographic material and drugs. You assaulted one of my detectives and fled when we attempted to bring you in for questioning. Your alibi has more holes in it than the average sieve. And now, a vehicle that was most likely used in the abductions has been located in a garage you appropriated, and although you deny that the vehicle belongs to you, an item of your clothing has been found within it. " She paused. "Sorry, am I going too fast for you?"

Ned glowered at her. "What's 'appropriated' mean?"

"It means to take something without permission or consent." Eleanor allowed the definition to hang between them for a pointed moment.

Behind the glass, the observation room had fallen silent. Sanne couldn't even hear anyone breathing.

"Where's Rachel, Ned?" Eleanor asked quietly. "You've not been back to her in five days. Help yourself out, here. Tell us where she is, and give her family the closure they deserve."

Ned startled when his lawyer touched his arm. He hugged himself, rocking back slightly, his eyes wide.

"No comment," he said.

Sound seemed to return to Sanne in a rush. Fred swore and kicked the back of her chair, and George punched the wall before stalking out. Almost at once, there was a knock on the door of the interview room, and for a second, she thought George was about to barge in there and take matters into his own hands, but it was only one of the SOCOs. Eleanor ushered him back outside and returned a couple of minutes later to throw an evidence bag onto the table. Something within gave a clank as it landed.

"Go ahead," she said, encouraging Ned to reach for the bag. Her voice sounded strained, and the veins were standing out on her neck. She wasn't upset, Sanne realised, she was furious.

"Those are the keys for the Land Rover, and the padlock key used to secure the garage." She didn't sit down, forcing Ned to look up at her instead. "They were found behind a loose brick in your air-raid shelter." Ned opened his mouth to protest, but she didn't let him speak. "Fingerprints found in the rear of the Land Rover have been matched to those taken from the cottage and identified as Rachel Medlock's. Ned Moseley, I am placing you under arrest for the abduction and assault of Josie Albright and the abduction of Rachel Medlock. You do not have to say anything, but it may harm your defence if you do not mention when questioned something which you later rely on in court..."

Ned hid his face in his hands as Eleanor repeated the caution Carlyle had earlier delivered.

"The time is two thirty-four a.m.," she said. "Interview halted at the request of the defence counsel." As she switched off the tape recorder, applause rang out in the observation room.

"Beer," Fred announced. "I need beer."

Sanne watched two uniformed officers lead Ned away. She was too stunned to feel like celebrating. She stood with Nelson, peering into the now empty room and trying to work through the consequences of what had just happened.

"We have to tell Josie before she sees it on the news," she said. "Once the press learn about the length of surveillance, they'll put two and two together."

"San, *she'll* put two and two together."

Sanne nodded, suddenly cold in the stuffy little room. "I know she will, but someone should be with her when she does."

Snowed under with paperwork, forensics, and preparing a statement for the press, Eleanor was happy to let Sanne speak to Josie. Nelson volunteered to go as well, but Sanne persuaded him to go home. He had seen little enough of his family over the past ten days.

The doctor eating toast at the desk of the HDU dabbed crumbs from her lips and directed Sanne to the Neuro Rehab ward.

"She was still awake the last time I looked in on her," a nurse told Sanne, when she eventually found the ward. He lowered his voice as he escorted her between two rows of sleeping patients. "Have you found her partner? Is that why you're here?" He sounded genuinely concerned, but Sanne couldn't bring herself to break the news twice in quick succession.

"I should speak to Josie first," she said.

His expression turned grim. "Should I phone her mum?"

"Yes, thank you. I think that would be a good idea."

He left her at the door to Josie's room. On a ward dominated by elderly stroke patients, it seemed a kindness that Josie had been allocated a single room. In the ward's last bed, a twenty-something lad with vacant eyes, a large, stapled scalp wound, and a tube in his nose gave her an infantile wave and then pulled his sheets over his head. She wondered how fast he had been driving, or who had provoked the fight that had landed him here. Screwing up her nose against the smell of disinfectants and sweet, artificial feeds, she tapped at Josie's door.

The hand Josie had been using to hold a book flew to her mouth when she saw Sanne.

"Oh God." Her eyes filled with tears. "Did you find her?"

All of Sanne's carefully rehearsed words deserted her. Shaking her head, she went to sit on the end of Josie's bed. "About an hour ago, we charged Ned Moseley with abduction and assault," she said. "Do you remember who he is?"

"Yes. He's the man you've been watching."

It didn't take long for Josie to work through the ramifications of that short statement. Sanne gauged the subtle change in her expression, from relief to fear to utter horror. Josie's face paled, and her left hand began to twitch uncontrollably. She grabbed hold of it with her right, tears splattering on the sheets with each movement.

"How many days is it?" she asked. "I can't count them."

"Five. Josie, we're now treating this as a murder enquiry."

Josie sobbed, a choked, inhuman sound that curled her in on herself. "I can't do this," she said. "I can't do any of this without her."

The sudden surge of grief seemed to overwhelm her, two weeks of misery breaking free and obliterating the barriers she had managed to build around herself. When Sanne reached for her, she tried to pull away, her fist thumping weakly against Sanne's back, but within a few seconds, all the fight had left her. She buried her face in Sanne's neck and wept as if her heart had shattered.

Birdsong and the first touch of sunlight on the treetops met Sanne as she stumbled out of her car. She barely remembered driving, and it took her several attempts to select the right door key. The door caught on a pair of boots left lying behind it. She tugged them free and set them on the shoe rack, placing her own in a space beneath. She was already half-undressed by the time she reached the bathroom, her clothes in a crumpled pile under one arm. Unable to face the effort of a shower, she washed quickly and brushed her teeth.

The sheets she slid between were fresh and cool, but grew warmer by degrees as she inched across the bed. Without speaking, Meg opened her arms and gathered Sanne close. Sanne was too weary to cry, to explain, to do anything but lie still and let Meg hold her. As she felt Meg's hand trace a never-ending figure of eight on her back, she finally allowed her eyes to close.

Chapter Nineteen

Meg set the cup of tea by Sanne's side of the bed, counted to five, and blew carefully in her ear.

"Sanne."

Sanne's face screwed up in irritation. She batted ineffectually at the strand of hair Meg had disturbed, but she didn't open her eyes.

Meg tried again, her voice soft. "Sanne, time to wake up."

"Mmhm."

"So much for the subtle approach." Meg stood up, her hands on her hips, and bellowed, "It's twenty past seven!"

That had the desired effect. Sanne bolted upright. "Please be kidding me." She looked at the clock and half-fell out of bed as the sheets became tangled around her ankles. "Fucking hell!"

"Easy, tiger." Meg knelt by her. "I've already spoken to Eleanor."

"You have? You did?" Rubbing her eyes with her fingertips, Sanne took a deep breath. "Meg, what's going on?"

Meg tugged her hand, encouraging her to sit back against the wall. "Promise you won't be cross with me?"

"Oh God. What did you do?"

"I sent Eleanor a text telling her that you hadn't got home till half four, and she replied to say check your e-mails for the morning briefing and sort yourself out from there."

"You shouldn't have done that." An unfamiliar flatness to Sanne's voice was the only indication of her anger.

"Would you have been any use to the investigation, running on an hour's sleep?" Meg couldn't feel guilty for interfering, not when the skin beneath Sanne's eyes was so purple and swollen that it looked bruised, and when the wall seemed to be the only thing stopping her from toppling over. Meg had seen other cases take their toll in the past few years, but never to the extent of this one.

"Probably not," Sanne said. "But none of us will have had much sleep last night."

"And half of them also missed the briefing." Meg patted Sanne's knee, cutting short her agonising. "Have a shower, and I'll sort breakfast."

Sanne nodded but didn't get up. "You know what happened, then?"

"I saw it on the news." Even as Meg spoke, she made a connection that shed more light on Sanne's beaten-down demeanour. "Did you go to tell Josie?"

"Yes." Shivering, Sanne pulled the sheet closer around herself. "She was devastated, obviously."

"I'll bet she was, the poor kid. I'm on lates the next couple of days. I'll drop in to her ward and see how she's doing."

Sanne leaned her head back against the wall. "I'm so tired," she whispered.

"I know you are." Meg put an arm around her. "When all this is over, I reckon you should use a few weeks of that annual leave you never take. You should go on a holiday, and I'm not talking a stay-at-home and fix-something-on-your-cottage holiday, but one where you fly someplace sunny."

"Sounds nice. You coming with me?"

"I might just do that." Meg ruffled her hair. "Now, come on, best foot forward. Go and get that shower."

Piece of toast in one hand, Sanne scrolled through her e-mails with the other. The briefing notes were concise: Carlyle and Eleanor would continue to interview Ned Moseley throughout the day and should only be contacted in an emergency. The labs were still analysing the forensics and tyre treads from the Land Rover, but the blood had been type-matched to Rachel Medlock. Hers were the only fingerprints found so far, the assumption being that Ned had worn gloves. Scotty and Jay were tracking the origin of the Land Rover, drawing up a list of local auction houses and used car dealerships, and cross-referencing reports of stolen vehicles. Meanwhile, the searches would remain focused on Ned's known haunts, with the addition of the Cleggs' farm and two further reservoirs. Police divers were continuing to trawl the reservoir where he did most of his fishing.

Crumbs fell onto the keyboard as Meg—reading over Sanne's shoulder—bit into her own toast. "Why'd he only do half a job?" she asked, indicating the forensics bullet point with a jammy finger.

"You mean with the cleaning?"

"Yeah. He was handy enough with the bleach in the cave. He managed to erase all trace of Rachel there, yet he leaves evidence in the Landie."

It was a good question, and Sanne stirred her tea while she contemplated it. "Maybe he sussed the surveillance. He's not the brightest of sparks, but in those three days he stayed so close to home that it seemed deliberate. It's safe to assume he hadn't finished cleaning the car before his arrest, and he couldn't risk going back, not if he knew he was being watched. All he could do was hope we never found the garage."

"I guess we owe Callum Clark for that. I told him there might be a reward, y'know."

"I'll send him a tenner," Sanne said dryly.

Meg laughed and licked her fingers. "Right, I'd better get dressed, or the neighbours will start to talk," she said, ignoring the fact that only birds and squirrels could see into her kitchen. "Are you heading off soon?"

"No, I have some work I can do from here. There's a search scheduled at the Cleggs' farm after lunch, so I'll head straight there. Nelson and I copped for that one, since we were the ones who interviewed them in the first place."

"You sound thrilled."

"I can't smile wide enough."

She listened to Meg's footsteps hammer up the stairs and then opened the rest of her e-mails. Little else had happened during the night, it seemed. Nelson had written to express his joy at the prospect of spending more time with the Cleggs. She sent a quick reply, before honing in on a message from the computer techs working to decrypt Mal Atley's client list. Crunching another slice of toast, she read through the initials, alongside which sat fragments of phone numbers. "NM" was nowhere to be seen, but six lines remained encoded at the bottom of the list, and it appeared to be ordered alphabetically. At the time of the update, "GE" had been the last entry. The majority of the numbers shared an 07 prefix, identifying them as mobile numbers, and the remainder had the local dialling code. Even a partial number would be enough to identify Ned Moseley if his initials turned up, and Sanne shook her head at the thought. Only two days ago, she had been unconvinced of his guilt. Now all she wanted was for him to crack under interrogation and give Josie and the rest of Rachel's family a modicum of peace.

With one eye on the time, Sanne swigged the remainder of her tea and headed into the utility room, to see whether Meg had a pair of wellies that she wouldn't mind getting covered in pig shit.

Derek Clegg slapped a meaty hand onto a precarious-looking dry-stone wall and bent double to catch his breath. Having managed to walk all of a hundred yards past the pigsty, toward the first of his fields, he was now giving Sanne and Nelson an unwelcome view of his arse crack, as the waistline of his sagging trousers finally lost its battle against gravity.

Averting her gaze, Sanne watched the pig rolling in a pile of manure and hoped that Derek's theatrical wheezing meant he would renege on his promise of a guided tour. He owned approximately forty acres, much of which had been lying neglected as his health and that of his mother deteriorated. Ned Moseley's role on the farm had largely involved tending the remaining livestock, but Derek had trusted him to take care of whatever else might need doing, and he admitted that Ned knew the land better than he did.

"There's this field, and four more after it." Derek pointed with the handkerchief he had just used to mop his brow. The wind caught the cotton, revealing a colourful patchwork of stains. "Not many outbuildings. Sheep barn in the second field, and something in the fourth, might've been a barn once, but now it's mostly rubble and weeds."

"Right, thanks," Sanne said, but seeing Derek's intent stare she took out her pad and scribbled a note.

"Think you'll manage from here?" he asked. "Only, I best get back and see to Mum."

"We'll be fine." Nelson nodded gravely. "We appreciate you taking the time to come out with us."

Apparently satisfied that he had fulfilled his duties as host, Derek tucked away the hanky, hitched up his trousers, and headed back to the house.

Once certain that Derek was out of earshot, Nelson gave a low cheer and radioed the officers waiting in the driveway, directing four of them to help him search the outbuildings round the yard while the rest joined Sanne at the gate to the first field.

Sanne recognised most of them from the moors and the reservoir, and the automatic way they spread themselves across the width of the field spoke of their recent experience. Tagging onto the edge of the line, she nodded at the man next to her, and they slowly walked forward.

The weather began to turn as the search team approached the second field. They had watched the rain rolling in across the valley, a mass of grey vertical stripes suspended between the thickening cloud and the hills below. It allowed them to judge, almost to the second, the moment when they needed to pull up their hoods, zip their coats, and prepare for the onslaught. Visibility narrowed to a couple of yards as the downpour hit, and within minutes the field was a mess of puddles and slippery tractor ruts. Sanne answered her buzzing radio, knowing without looking that it would be Nelson.

"You want to call everyone back to the yard?" he said. "There's a barn here that's big enough to shelter in. It stinks, but at least it's dry."

She climbed up onto the dry-stone wall, trying and failing to catch a glimmer of brightness behind the pall of clouds. The rain appeared to have settled in for the foreseeable future.

"I think we'll keep going," she told him, almost shouting to make herself heard. "We're close to the sheep barn Derek mentioned, so we can head for that."

"No worries. Let me know if you change your mind. Nothing to report here."

"Ditto. We've got nothing but muck and mud." Rain dripped from her nose as she spoke. She checked the time. Given the weather, they probably had another three and a half hours of daylight left, at most. "Do you need a lift back to the office when we're done?"

"That'd be great. I hitched a ride in the van, but they're dropping off at a few different stations, so it'd be quicker coming with you."

She jumped down from the wall, grabbing its sturdy copingstone as her boots slid on the grass. "I should warn you I'm in my Corsa, not a pool car."

There was a lengthy pause while Nelson weighed up his travel options.

"Have the chickens been in it recently?" he asked.

She laughed. "Y'know, I leave the bloody window open once, and I never hear the end of it. No, they haven't, and yes, the car is clean."

"See you about seven, then." He disconnected the call, and she clipped her radio back onto her belt. The officers had joined her at the wall and were hovering around a gate that swung on one rusted hinge. She ushered them through and, out of habit, pulled the gate closed behind her.

"Everyone okay?" she asked.

She had no doubt that they were all cold, wet, and miserable, but there were no murmurs of dissent, just nods, yeps, and the occasional "fine."

"You're all bloody brilliant," she said. "Let's see if we can get to the barn in the next hour, and then we'll take a break." A swirling gust of wind blew down her hood and spattered rain in her eyes. Unperturbed, she blinked until her vision cleared. Then she bowed her head and gave the signal to walk on.

❖

"Right, who doesn't need a fag?" Sanne counted five raised hands among the officers huddled beneath the overhanging eaves of the barn. "You lot come inside with me. The rest stay out here until we've cleared it."

Lighters sparked up like eager fireflies, but the smell of cigarette smoke was snuffed out the instant Sanne stepped into the building. She stood just over the threshold and panned her torch around the open space. It looked as if nothing there had been disturbed for a long time. The straw and dust covering the floor showed no signs of footprints or scuffing, and there were thick cobwebs crisscrossing the doorway. Wood that had probably once formed pens had rotted and fallen away, leaving most of the barn visible from her position.

She was fairly confident that Rachel had never been brought here, but she had to make sure. She turned to her non-smokers. "You three start on the far left. We'll head over the other side and meet you in the middle."

The men were taking down their hoods and shaking off their coats, evidently glad to be somewhere dry, and they followed her instructions without question. It was a relief to be out of the wind, but it whistled through gaps in the decaying mortar, as if keen to remind them that it was still out there, waiting for their return. Taking careful steps across the solid stone floor, Sanne smelled damp wool and soiled hay. Rain was dripping through the cracked roof tiles, creating tiny kaleidoscopes when the droplets caught in her torch beam. Something brushed against her cheek. She scratched at it and pulled away a dirty tangle of spider web that clung to her fingers as she shook them. She flicked it to the floor and wiped her hand on her trousers, longing for a hot bath, clean sheets, and an end to this case.

"Nothing here," an officer shouted over to her.

"Nothing here, either." Frustrated, she kicked at a fragment of decaying wood and sent it skidding into the corner. "Get the rest in for a brew if they want one."

Scrunched low in the back of her Corsa, Sanne undid her zip and peeled off her soaked trousers with numb fingers. Rain was battering against the roof, and the torch propped on the seat beside her did little to cut through the darkness. She shivered, wriggling into a dry pair of combats before swapping her sweater and tank top for a thick fleece. The material hugged her damp skin, easing the tremors, and she dragged the sleeves down until they covered her chilled hands. With her feet slowly thawing in clean socks and trainers, she sorted her essentials into the pockets of her trousers, grabbed the lunch she had forgotten to eat, and climbed forward into the driver's seat. Nelson was still chatting to one of the uniforms at the side of the van, so she took the opportunity to stuff half a ham sandwich into her mouth and check the e-mails on her phone.

The first two mails reported the early abandonment of searches in and around the reservoirs and confirmed that nothing of interest had been found. Meanwhile, Meg had written to say that she had called in on Josie for an hour before her twilight shift started, and that Sanne should dismiss any claims that she cheated at cards as scurrilous gossip.

"You bloody well do cheat," Sanne muttered.

She closed Meg's e-mail and clicked on the next: an updated version of Mal Atley's client list. The partial phone numbers now comprised eight digits each, and a new pair of initials—KD and MJ—had been decrypted. Frustrated by a process that was making headway but still couldn't tell them anything useful, Sanne stabbed her finger on her phone to move the message into her work folder.

To compound her sense of another day spent chasing dead ends, a final e-mail from Carlyle took less than ten lines to summarise Ned Moseley's most recent interview: after complaining that no one believed anything he said, Ned had taken the "no comment" route and was now back in a holding cell, pending his transfer to prison.

Sanne put away her phone as Nelson yanked open the passenger door, letting in a blast of wind and rain.

"I think I wrecked it," he said, displaying a crumpled umbrella with spokes sticking out at random angles. He dropped it into the footwell and slammed his door.

"On the bright side, at least your trousers don't need wringing out." Sanne started the engine and tried to clear the mist off her windscreen. Ahead of them, the van began to move off down the farm track, its lights dipping and reappearing as its tyres hit ruts. "I'll give her a few minutes to warm up," she added, pointedly ignoring Nelson's derogatory eye roll.

He pushed back his seat and stretched, in the manner of one settling down for a long wait. "You got any food?" he asked, and ducked to avoid the soggy sandwich that Sanne launched at his head.

The Snake Pass was a challenging road to negotiate at the best of times, and these weren't the best of times. A fierce wind rocked the car as Sanne dropped it into third gear and then second, cursing its lack of power. Its engine whining, it crawled up the steep incline and aquaplaned around the rain-slickened hairpin bend. Once on the descent again, it started to over-rev as its speed increased.

Gripping on to his seatbelt, Nelson didn't utter a word. Sanne suspected he had been struck mute by terror, and she sympathised entirely. The route was so familiar to her that she could describe every one of its twists, but she couldn't allow herself to become complacent. An ever-increasing number of roadside shrines served as a sobering reminder of what happened when people dropped their guard or grew cocky. As she passed Whitelow Farm, she dipped her headlights to avoid dazzling an oncoming lorry. It thundered past in a blur of spray, its weight and speed rattling the Corsa. Nelson lunged for the dashboard, and she gave him a weak smile.

"Bet you wish you'd gone in the van, eh?"

"Not at all. I'm having the time of my life." He peered into the mist curling around the upper reaches of the moors. "I wonder if Abeni knows where I keep the insurance policies."

Sanne smiled and flicked the windscreen wipers up a notch, without taking her eyes off the road. As another lorry approached, she decelerated, preparing for the turbulence in its wake.

"I might have to invest in a four-by-four." She blinked against the lorry's headlights, fighting to keep the tyres on the tarmac and away from the stone-littered verge. "I love this car, but it feels as if it's made out of balsa—"

A muted bang cut her off mid-sentence. The car jolted, then began to fishtail wildly. For a second, she thought she'd hit an animal, but an arc of sparks from the rear told her that a tyre had blown.

"Fuck! Grab on!" Her knuckles blanched on the wheel as she tried to stop the car from flipping over. She turned into the skid, easing off the accelerator and resisting the instinct to brake. Something gave way on the undercarriage, slowing their momentum with a screech of metal. Almost lazily, the car drifted to the verge, clipped a dry-stone wall, and shuddered to a halt with its nose in a ditch.

Sanne stared at the wall, hardly able to believe they were still in one piece. One by one, she unpeeled her fingers from the steering wheel, and then rubbed her neck where the seatbelt had almost throttled her. "Well, that's buggered it," she said. "You okay there?"

The whites of Nelson's eyes seemed huge in the darkness. "I'm fine. What the hell happened?"

"Blow-out, I think." She winced, remembering that her tyres had been on borrowed time for several weeks. "Stay here. I'll see what the damage is and whether we can put the spare on." Without giving him a chance to argue, she shoved open her door and went round to the boot. She had just started to pull on her high-vis jacket when he joined her, torch in hand.

"You're not going to get a spare on that." He circled the beam around the misshapen rim of her tyre.

"It's all fucked." She kicked the exhaust pipe, emphasising the extensive damage to the underside of the car. "We'll have to get a recovery truck out here."

"Yeah. Good job we're not blocking the road."

"There is that. I'll give Red Alert a call."

The car rocked gently as they got back in, but it made no further progress into the ditch. She flicked on the hazard lights and scrolled through her phone's directory until she came to the number for the breakdown company. Upon connection, she was put straight into a queue.

"My queue position is twenty-fourth," she repeated, for Nelson's benefit. "Seems like the weather's playing havoc with a lot of folk. *Twenty-fourth*? Jesus, no wonder these bastards were cheap." The recorded message droned on, concluding with an apologetic estimate of two to three hours for rescue and recovery.

"Balls to that." She ended the call and chose another number. "We might as well cut out the middleman. Red Alert would take the car there anyway."

Nelson nodded, though he clearly had no idea what she was talking about. Sanne watched the fog dance around the wall as she listened to the phone ringing out. She had almost given up, when she heard Joan Cotter's raspy greeting.

"Hi, Joan, it's Sanne Jensen. I'm really sorry to call you so late, but I've just had a blow-out up on the Snake, and I wondered if Geoff or Billy were around."

Nelson's mouth formed an "oh" of understanding as he recognised the names. On the line, Joan coughed, a thick, wet sound that made Sanne hold the phone away from her ear.

"Geoff's still not well, and Billy's out at the Crown. He's probably had a drink by now, love."

"Damn. Okay." The prospect of half an hour on hold, followed by three hours sitting in a draughty, ruined Corsa, made Sanne push her luck. "Can you give me his mobile, just in case? Even if he can't come out, he might know someone else local who could give me a tow."

There was a long pause before Joan relented and reeled off the number. Sanne scrawled it on her hand, thanking her profusely. Wracked by another coughing fit, Joan hung up without saying good-bye.

"Cotter's Garage is only about forty minutes back thattaway," Sanne told Nelson, surprising herself by dialling the first part of Billy's number from memory. "We'd be able to wait there for someone to pick us up. Warm, dry, a nice cup of—oh, hey, Billy, it's Sanne."

"Sanne Jensen." She heard Billy clear his throat and laugh. "To what do I owe the pleasure?"

"A blown tyre and a knackered exhaust. Just shy of the Snake summit. I was hoping you might be a bit quicker than Red Alert." There was no background noise, but even so, she heard him take a few steps and shut a door as if to move somewhere quieter. "Please, Billy, I know it's a crappy night, but I'd really appreciate it."

"Jesus, Sanne, that's a long way to come. Besides, we're so backed up with work, it might be a while before we could fix it anyway." He sounded as if he was pacing now, his tread heavy and measured.

"Oh, I don't care how long it takes to fix." Although she hated the pleading note in her voice, she wasn't above using emotional blackmail. "Did I tell you how tired and hungry I am?"

"You're breaking my heart." He sighed. "I'll be there within the hour."

"Name your price." Standing out in the rain in a display of moral support, Sanne watched Billy hitch her Corsa onto his recovery truck. "Seriously, you can charge me over the odds. I don't care."

He grinned at her from beneath the hood of his coat. "Always had a soft spot for you, Sanne. Go and sit with your mate and get warm. I'll be done in about five minutes."

She flashed him a thumbs-up and went to the front of his truck. Nelson had already taken the passenger seat, so she hauled herself into the rear compartment.

"Nearly done," she said. "Did you speak to Abeni?"

"Yep. The girls are asleep. I told her I might end up crashing at your place, or Meg's."

"Or the Cotters'." She shrugged at Nelson's horrified expression. "Hey, worst case scenario. It'd be better than nothing."

"I don't know about that. 'Nothing' wouldn't come with lung cancer." He kept his voice low, as if Billy had any chance of hearing him over the torrential rain and gusts of wind, and he clamped his mouth shut when the cab door opened a moment later and Billy climbed in.

"Reckon there's anything you can salvage?" Sanne asked, prepared to consign her beloved Corsa to the scrap heap.

Billy fired up the engine and tossed a bag onto the seat beside her. "With a new exhaust bracket, new rim, and three new tyres, she'll be fine." He began to make a cautious turn, the amber lights on top of the truck a warning to other motorists.

"Really? That's great." The bag began to slide toward the floor, and she put a hand on it, catching both the canvas outer and part of its contents.

"I can do the tyres as reconditioned if you want," Billy said. "It'd be a lot cheaper."

"Mm." She nodded, her eyes fixed on the loose end of rope in her hand. "Sounds good."

Without altering her position, she eased the bag open. The rope coiled inside was bright orange, with a synthetic coating. She ran her fingers across it, examining the way it was plaited, its thickness and texture, and remembering how much effort it would take to saw through it using a Swiss Army knife. A nasty grain of suspicion began to form as she lowered the flap of the bag and looked at the mobile number smeared on the back of her hand. In the front of the cab, Nelson and Billy were chatting about football, neither of them paying her any attention. She entered the security code on her phone, anxiety making her fingers clumsy and her chest tight. Forcing herself to take slower breaths, she opened her inbox and then her work folder.

"Sanne, Nelson says you're a Bolton fan. Please tell me he's talking crap." Billy glanced at her in the rear-view mirror.

She plastered a smile on her face and shrugged. "Blame my granddad. He had a season ticket for years. Used to take me to some of the home matches."

Billy's eyes were back on the road before she had finished her explanation. Nelson said something she couldn't hear, and Billy laughed, pulled back into a conversation that didn't include her. She looked down at her phone again and selected the e-mail at the top of the folder. Mal Atley's client list filled the screen. Three lines down, she found the initials "BC" and traced her finger across to the corresponding phone number, tilting her left hand as she did so.

"One of these days, I'll take you to see a real footy team," Billy called to her.

She nodded, her mouth too dry to answer. The number exactly matched the one scribbled on the back of her hand.

For the third time in less than five minutes, Sanne double-checked the number on her e-mail against the one inked on her skin. Nothing had changed. She hadn't been mistaken. The cab was quieter now. Nelson and Billy had run out of the usual conversational topics of strangers, and to cover any awkwardness, Billy had switched on the radio and was humming along to soft rock. Sanne looked out the window. They had dropped below the cloud cover, but the rain was still belting down hard enough to keep them well beneath the speed limit.

Strapped into the cramped back seat, Sanne had had plenty of time to think everything through. It was true that Billy Cotter fitted the profile of the perpetrator. An athletic, single male, he had been raised in the area, and he seemed to have had dealings with Mal Atley. His experience as a mechanic meant that removing the VIN on a Land Rover would be child's play to him. Meanwhile, Sanne was sitting mere inches away from a bag full of rope identical to that used to bind Josie.

She dug her fingers into the seat, aware of how inconclusive her reasoning was. Two minutes on Google would locate any vehicle's VIN, and that particular type of rope was used in many professions. All she had was a series of coincidences amounting to little of any significance, especially compared to the evidence against Ned. A persistent, objective part of her, though—the part not swayed by her friendship with Billy—insisted that it made sense for Ned to have worked in collaboration with someone, that he simply wasn't capable of orchestrating this crime alone. Josie had only ever described one abductor, but her recollection was so poor that she could easily have been mistaken.

Sanne shut her eyes miserably. Her colleagues thought they had closed the case. Their success had been front-page news that morning, and everyone had received a congratulatory e-mail from the brass. Bringing in a second suspect would open a can of worms—and yet she didn't want to be accused of ignoring a lead because it might incriminate a friend of hers.

That alone was enough to make her decision for her. She typed out a text, and covered her bases by writing an e-mail as well. She copied it to every member of EDSOP, hoping that someone would be working late, that Ned would still be in holding and so blindsided by Billy Cotter's being implicated that his reactions would give him away. As she pressed *send*, the truck swerved, knocking her into the doorframe and rattling her teeth.

"Sorry, love," Billy said. "This wind's a devil."

Trying to ignore the sweat trickling down her back, she waved away his apology and wondered how well she knew him after all.

CHAPTER TWENTY

Nelson had an expert poker face. It was a skill he and Sanne often utilised, and it was the reason he regularly trounced her at cards, but she had never appreciated how good it was until the moment he received her text. She had taken a risk including him in the recipients. Cold feet almost made her grab his arm in a panic as he reached for his phone, but his face betrayed nothing. He simply read her message and tucked the phone back into his pocket.

"Just the missus saying good night," he said, in response to Billy's quizzical glance. "She knows the reception out here is dodgy, so she won't be waiting for a reply."

The implicit warning made Sanne's heart sink. She hadn't even considered that. Sure enough, when she checked her signal it was fluctuating between one bar and none.

"Home sweet home," Billy said as the garage came into view. He took the turn wide and edged into the yard. "You two can head in while I get everything put away."

Sanne's legs felt rubbery as she jumped down from the cab. Nelson gripped her arm, steadying her and then pulling her aside. He waited until Billy had driven well beyond them before speaking.

"What the hell is going on, San? Is he a suspect now?"

Behind him, lights flickered on in the reception area. If she and Nelson didn't go inside soon, Billy or Joan would start to wonder why.

"I don't know," Sanne whispered. "Like I said on the text, his number's on the list, and that rope is a match."

"Anyone replied?"

"No." She chewed her lip, at a loss what to do. "I probably didn't even word it right. Did it sound crazy?"

"Yeah, a bit." He gave her arm a reassuring squeeze. "Are you sure about this?"

"No, not at all." But as she peered into the darkened yard, she remembered the small workshops scattered around its perimeter, and a sudden need to find out what was in them began to edge out her uncertainty.

Nelson shook his head, pre-empting her. "We don't have a warrant, San."

"I know, but what if Rachel's—" She stopped speaking as she spotted Joan Cotter's profile in the window. "I'll go in." She raised her voice deliberately. "Why don't you see if Billy needs a hand?"

Nelson glared at her but didn't argue. She watched him hurry around the side of the building until she lost sight of him in the unlit yard. Then she pushed open the reception door.

"Hey, Joan. I really am sorry about this." Heat and smoke hit her full in the face. She tried not to cough, wishing she could turn around and head straight out again.

Joan used her cigarette to wave away the apology, sending ash cascading to the floor. "Where's your partner?"

"Helping Billy." She hadn't mentioned that Nelson was with her, so presumably Billy must have phoned his mum while he was hitching up the truck. The idea made Sanne uneasy, though she couldn't pinpoint why. With no sign of either man returning from the yard, she looked past Joan into the hallway that led to the main garage. She had never been farther than the kitchenette that customers were allowed to use, but she remembered that the corridor connected right through to the Cotters' house. Having forced Nelson into an illicit search, she felt she should do more than stand around and passive smoke, so she played the oldest trick in the book.

"Do you mind if I use your loo? We've been stuck out there for a while." Her voice sounded alien to her. Nervousness made her hop from foot to foot, adding unintentional credence to her request.

Joan took a long drag on her cigarette. Smoke obscured her when she exhaled. "There's one just here. I'll show you where it is."

"Cheers." Sanne followed her down the corridor, furious that she had forgotten about the grubby little cloakroom next to the kitchenette.

Joan stopped in front of it. "Is someone coming to pick you up?"

"Uh, I think so." Sanne didn't have the faintest clue. She knew Meg would still be at work, and she had intended to phone her about a bed for the night but had ended up sidetracked. "I'll double-check with a friend when I'm done."

"Billy can't be taking you to Meg's," Joan said, identifying the "friend" without hesitation. "He's running things on his own at the moment. He needs his rest."

Sanne felt her face redden. The Cotters had done her a huge favour, and yet here she was, snooping around and thinking the worst of Billy. "I'll call a taxi," she said. "We'll be out of your hair in no time, I promise."

Joan gave her a thin smile, showing yellowed teeth clenched around her cigarette. "Use the phone at the desk. You can wait there for your taxi." She left Sanne and went into the house, shutting the door behind her.

Sanne poked her head into the bathroom, grimacing as the odour of urine hit her. The cubicle was probably not somewhere Joan frequented. The seat had been left up, the sliver of soap on the sink was oil-smeared, and there was no toilet paper. Leaning back on the corridor wall, she stared at the carpet. Years of greasy boot prints had left a blackened trail across the red and gold pattern. She longed to follow those prints toward the light still glowing in the reception, to phone Meg, and to radio Nelson and make sure he was okay. They could come here again in daylight, with backup, a search warrant, and Eleanor's blessing.

Instead, she went in the opposite direction, knocked hard on the door Joan had gone through, and pushed it open.

"Joan?" She raised her voice, making sure it carried. "It's only me. Have you got any loo paper?" It was a feeble excuse for going into the house, but she wasn't sneaking around. If Joan came and told her to leave, she would leave. "Joan? Geoff? You there?"

She walked down the narrow hall and stopped when it widened. Remnants of the business gave way to homeliness—a telephone table holding a lamp beside a china bowl of dusty potpourri, a picture of Billy, his arm flung around his dad's shoulders, hanging next to a slightly askew *Bless this Mess* sign. Three doors led off the vestibule. Sanne knocked on the first.

"Joan?" She went through the door as she spoke. "Don't mean to barge in, but there's no loo paper."

A well-worn leather couch took up much of the room's floor space, while used mugs and car magazines surrounded a single armchair pulled close to the television. Something was emitting a slightly rotten scent, although the single visible plate contained only a few crumbs. Joan was nowhere to be seen, but a second door, leading off the living room, had been left ajar. Maintaining her strategy, Sanne knocked again and called out as she ventured onward. She hesitated at the bottom of a flight of stairs. They were in darkness, but she assumed Joan or Geoff must be up there, since they hadn't heard her shouting. Using the handrail as a guide, she began to ascend.

"Joan?" Her voice fell away, and she put her hand over her nose and mouth. "Jesus."

The foul smell she had noticed in the living room was now intense, and it hit her full force. There was no mistaking it: something or someone up there was dead.

"Fuck." She hurtled up the remaining stairs, no longer caring about procedure or how she might explain her actions to her superiors.

To the left of the landing a clock ticked, but not loudly enough to muffle a scrabble of movement in the only room showing a strip of light beneath its door. A harsh, phlegm-rattled cough from behind the door told Sanne she had found Joan. She looked around the landing, struggling to distinguish shapes in the gloom. There was nothing she could use as a weapon, so she pulled her CS gas from the pocket of her combats. Her hands shook as she primed the canister, and she had to take a breath to calm herself. Then she kicked the door open, catching a glimpse of a bloodstained double bed and a pink sheet on the floor in the instant before the light snapped off.

Disorientated, she made a blind grab for the doorjamb. She whipped her head from left to right, trying to gauge where a potential assailant might be, but no one attacked her, and nothing leapt out from the shadows. With her hand still in contact with the wood, she inched forward, willing her eyes to adjust, even as she readied the CS gas.

"Joan, put the light back on," she said.

There was no reply, but she could hear stifled wheezing from the near side of the bed. The vile smell was more distinct, breaking down into its component parts—faeces, blood, and decomposition. She slid her hand over the wall, feeling in vain for a light switch. The squeak and rasp of Joan's breathing stayed constant, a lure just out of reach.

"I'm going to come over to you. I don't want you to move, okay?" She left the relative safety of the door and moved slowly toward the bed, her eyes gradually becoming accustomed to the light, allowing her to make out Joan's profile, black and featureless as she stood waiting.

"I didn't mean to do it!" Joan's frantic hiss made Sanne's skin crawl.

"Didn't mean to do what?" Sanne was close now, not quite within touching distance but close enough to see that Joan's eyes were wide glints of grey-white. "Joan, I can't help you unless you tell me what's going on."

Completely focused on her target, she stumbled as her foot jammed against something solid. She tried to draw back but wavered, off-balance, her trainer snared in the sheet she had forgotten about. She lurched forward, and her hands touched the bed, springs bouncing beneath her fingers and loosening her hold on the gas canister. Sensing movement, she glanced up and saw Joan's raised arm.

"Don't!"

She dropped instinctively, twisting to the side to land in an awkward crouch. She felt the rush of air as a heavy object swung past her ear. Missing her completely, it hit the bed, and she heard Joan grunt with anger and with the effort of lifting it again. Sanne hurled herself forward, colliding with Joan's midriff and then moaning in pain as Joan brought the weapon down across her shoulders. The shock of the blow made her arms and hands numb. She kicked out instead, aiming for Joan's knees and scoring a solid hit on a bone that collapsed beneath her trainer. Joan screeched, flailing for leverage, and Sanne kicked again, hearing the clatter of metal as Joan lost her hold on her weapon.

"It wasn't my fault!" Joan didn't have the energy to scream, but she was trying, her voice rising and falling in a shattered wail. A cough became an uncontrollable bout that racked her thin body.

Folding one of Joan's arms behind her, Sanne shoved her against the bed. Too distracted by coughing, Joan offered no resistance as Sanne found her handcuffs and eventually managed to fasten them around Joan's wrists.

"Where's the fucking light switch?" She hauled Joan closer to her.

Joan spat in her face.

"You're under arrest," Sanne said, wiping her cheek with the back of her hand and retrieving the canister from the bed. "You do not have to say anything, but it may harm your defence if you do not mention when questioned something which you later rely on in court." She recited the Miranda by rote, leaving Joan to curse and rage and demand an ambulance for the hip Sanne had probably broken.

There was a lamp just visible on the bedside table. When Sanne flicked its switch, Joan screamed and buried her face in the mattress. Poised to radio for backup, Sanne froze with her finger on the priority button.

"My God." She looked down at the pink sheet that covered the floor. "What did you do?"

There was a body beneath the sheet. It lay motionless, its distended abdomen an ominous mound. Fluids had seeped into the cotton, creating an obscene Rorschach blotch.

"Is that Rachel?" she whispered, even as she knelt at the head and gently lifted the sheet. She rocked back on her heels as she recognised the face.

"He was going to tell on my boy." Joan's voice, calmer now, cut through the silence with measured precision. "I couldn't let him do that." She held Sanne's gaze, refusing to look at her husband's body. "I couldn't let him do that."

Sanne scrambled to her feet, ignoring the shooting pain across her back and the acrid taste of bile in her mouth. "Where's Rachel? *Where is she?*"

Joan had started to rock back and forth, her eyes glazed. Giving up waiting for a response, Sanne raised her radio instead.

"Nelson?" she shouted over the open channel. "Nelson, please come in. Nelson?" Bypassing priority, she hit the emergency button instead. "I need backup now! Cotters Garage, Lower Bank Road, off the Snake Pass. Officer down. Repeat, officer down!"

Confident that Joan was incapacitated, she sprinted down the stairs. On the radio, a police unit called out an ETA of twenty minutes. She hooked the handset onto her belt as she shoved the living room door open and dodged past the furniture. She slowed as she approached the reception area. It was the most likely place for Billy to launch an attack. She strained to listen for him, her hand tense around the gas canister. All she could hear was her own laboured breathing and panicked heartbeat. The door creaked when she pushed it, the noise grating on her nerves, but the reception was empty. She snatched up a wrench abandoned by the desk, the cool heft of the metal giving her the impetus to go through into the yard.

Keeping to the side of the building, she jogged around to the main garage. Rain and mist obscured the yard, forcing her to dry her eyes every few seconds. Ahead of her, the automated shutters on the garage gaped wide, and a light blinked like a warning beacon as it swayed in the wind. She sobbed quietly when she caught the faint hum of Nelson's radio coming from somewhere beyond the threshold. She could be walking into a trap, she knew, but the thought of Nelson lying injured or worse compelled her to take the quickest route, straight across the yard toward the garage entrance.

She had only covered a fraction of the distance when she was blinded by a sudden flare of light. She stopped dead, unable to pinpoint its source, shielding her eyes and bracing herself for whatever was going to happen. An engine roared, impossibly loud, and tyres spun on the wet gravel, the sound bouncing back off the cavernous building. She had no time to turn. From the corner of her eye, she saw the van bearing down on her, its tyres jumping through potholes and puddles, giving it the appearance of a living thing.

"Oh, fuck—"

Her body responded before her brain could process the danger. Hurtling out of the van's path, she lost her footing almost at once, momentum carrying her forward until she landed sprawled on the gravel. Her forehead thumped against something sharp-edged and unyielding, and for an instant, all light and sound was gone.

When she opened her eyes again, the van was thirty yards away, its rear lights casting a red hue on the mist as it sped past the reception. Gasping, with blood hot on her face, she managed to get to her knees and then stand. The abrupt movement made her retch, and she spat a thin stream of vomit and blood into the dirt. With more caution, she raised her head again. The taillights were still visible, the bumpy track slowing the van to a crawl. She limped after it, determined to see its registration plate and in which direction it would head at the main road, but it gained speed as it approached the junction, the driver not seeming to care about traffic. It swung right without pausing, and a split second later, a tumultuous crunch of metal slamming into metal made Sanne weave precariously. Pulling up short, she watched through the rain as the van folded in on itself, its side buckling under the impact of a ten-wheeler lorry. Smoke poured off the lorry's tyres and its brakes squealed as its momentum took it past the junction, forcing the van ahead of it, its trailer juddering violently, before it finally came to a halt.

Blood trickled from Sanne's forehead, clouding her view of the carnage on the road. The din had set her ears ringing. She set off running toward the crash, rubbing at her eyes, trying not to think about what it might have done to anyone dumped, unrestrained, in the back of the van. As she got closer, she could see the lorry driver in his cab. He was conscious and seemed to be trying to release his seatbelt.

"Are you okay?" she yelled. He nodded, looking dazed. She nodded back and darted round the cab to the van. An anguished cry through its smashed windscreen told her that Billy Cotter had survived the collision. He wasn't her priority, though. The lorry was crushing the driver's side, so she ran around to the far side and wrenched the rear door open. She bent double, her guts aching, when she saw the empty compartment. She took her frustration and relief out on the van, rattling its bodywork as she slammed the door shut.

Billy didn't seem to have noticed her at first. Through the shattered passenger window, she could see that he was trapped, his right leg pinned beneath the steering column. His only other obvious injuries were two deep slashes across his face and neck that were bleeding profusely. He didn't have a weapon. His hands were empty. She opened the passenger door.

"Sanne, help. My leg's stuck." His entreaty came out as a pathetic whine, and she could see teeth gleaming through the laceration on his cheek as he spoke. It wasn't clear what he'd cut himself on, but the wounds were severe.

"I don't give a shit about your leg," she said, and her vehemence made his head jerk. "Where are they?"

"Who? I don't know what you mean. Please, Sanne, get me out of here."

She batted away his hand. "Nelson and Rachel," she said clearly. "Tell me where they are, and I'll radio for an ambulance."

His expression hardened. "I don't know what you're talking about."

He was wasting time. She wanted to grab his neck and smack his face into the steering wheel until he told her the truth. Instead, she yelped, as a hand touched her shoulder.

"Easy, love." The lorry driver stepped back again, out of the line of fire.

She shook her head, splattering crimson on the van's leather seat. "I'm a detective." She pulled her ID from her pocket and angled it to the light so he could see it. "More police are on the way."

There was a coil of rope and a toolbox in the footwell. She grabbed the rope and bound Billy's hands to the steering wheel. She had lost her CS gas and wrench somewhere in the yard, but the toolbox was full of makeshift weapons. She handed the lorry driver a spanner and a hammer, and helped herself to a Maglite.

"If he so much as fucking blinks at you wrong, feel free to clobber him."

"What the hell did he do?" The lorry driver looked from Billy to the hammer.

"Tried to kill me," she said, cutting a long story short. "I need to find my partner. Stay here, okay?"

He shrugged. "You're the boss."

After the shock and turmoil of the crash, the Cotters' yard was eerie in its stillness. Nelson's radio was still chattering, unheeded, as Sanne ran into the garage. She found a panel of switches and tried three before a strip light came on.

"Nelson?"

A deep groan followed by a cough guided her into the second vehicle bay. She spotted his boots first, sticking up out of an inspection pit. He was trying to move, but his efforts were lethargic and uncoordinated. She jumped down beside him and pinched his ear until he opened his eyes. With her other hand, she felt his skull, finding a large swelling at the back of his head.

"Hey, mate," she said, as he licked his lips in confusion. She took off her jacket and tucked it around him. Even though it was soaked, the inner layer would be warm. "You stay still, now. There's an ambulance coming. I'm going to try to find Rachel." Her voice broke as his eyes closed again. She didn't want to leave him, didn't know what to do for the best.

"Third workshop, set back with no windows," he whispered, pushing at her with both hands. "Billy was over there with a van. He saw me watching. Go."

She didn't need telling twice. Following his instructions, it was easy to find the building, even though it was mostly concealed between two larger workshops. Its door was locked but rattled loose in the frame when she shook the handle. Hearing sirens whooping in the distance, she began to pound her foot against the lowest panel. It splintered into pieces, scratching and tearing at her trousers. Holding the Maglite in her teeth, she clawed at the shattered wood, snapping it and throwing it aside until she'd created an opening big enough to crawl through.

Knowing that she was probably too late, she held her breath as she straightened on the other side. The Maglite's thin beam afforded her snapshots of the room's contents: a bucket, a chair lying upended, a bare mattress. She had taken a step, intending to call Rachel's name, when someone barrelled into her with enough force to send her back against the wall. She threw up her hands, catching hold of a bony arm that was trying to shove a shard of crockery into her neck.

"Rachel, stop!" There was no one else it could be.

Rachel gave a weak cry, sagging into Sanne's arms and taking them both onto the cold concrete. The piece of broken plate smashed as she let it drop. Sanne saw thick strings of blood already glistening on the fragments. The wounds she had seen on Billy's face suddenly made more sense.

"It's okay, I'm with the police," she said. "You're safe now, honey. You're safe."

Rachel whimpered, the sound choked and faint and agonised. She clung to Sanne's fleece, wrapping it in her fists. Frayed strands of rope still encircled her swollen wrists, and she was naked apart from an old overcoat. Dried blood and contusions covered the skin left exposed.

"He said he would come back for me." Her voice was so hoarse she couldn't raise it above a whisper. "I couldn't let him touch me again."

She began to cry, her body shaking with the violence of her sobs, but she wore herself out within seconds and leaned limply against Sanne's chest. Somewhere on the road, a howl of sirens reached a crescendo and then stopped. Through the broken wood of the door, Sanne could see far-off flashes of red and blue lights. Rachel cowered as men yelled in the distance, but they seemed to have been distracted by the traffic collision.

"Do you want me to help you out of here?" Sanne asked. The room stank, making the air difficult to bear, and no one beside Nelson knew where they were. She felt Rachel nod, and she guided her to her feet. "Let me just get these sorted." One by one, she fastened the buttons on Rachel's coat.

"Did you find Josie?" Rachel asked, stuttering on the question. She folded her arms as if to protect herself from the answer.

"We found her. She's fine," Sanne said, and the material slipped from her fingers as Rachel's knees buckled. Sanne grabbed her to stop her from collapsing.

"What do you mean?" Rachel was struggling to stand, her eyes fixed on Sanne's in the dull light. "She—she can't be! He said he'd—he told me he'd killed her."

Sanne shook her head, cursing her own lack of forethought. She should have anticipated this. "No, he lied, Rachel. Josie got away from him, so he lied. She's in the hospital, but she's okay."

Rachel's hand flew to her mouth. "Promise me?" she whispered. "Promise me you're telling the truth."

Sanne crossed her heart, the gesture bringing a slight smile to Rachel's face. When she held out a hand, Rachel clasped it in both of hers.

"I promise," Sanne said.

Chapter Twenty-one

There were times when Meg wished she were a smoker, or at least a nail biter. Ordinarily, the prospect of a multi-casualty incident wouldn't faze her, but knowing that one of those casualties was Sanne made it the perfect occasion to start a nasty habit.

"You've already checked that," Emily said, nodding at the IV tray.

Meg gave up fiddling with the tray's contents and chewed the side of her thumb instead.

"Sanne did say that she was all right," Emily reminded her.

"I know." Meg had received a brief text from Sanne minutes after the pre-alert from the ambulance service. Since then, half the police force seemed to have arrived at the hospital, including Eleanor, who had gone upstairs to speak to Josie.

Rachel's a mess, but alive, the text read. *I banged my head, and it's bled a bit. Fine though. See you soon.* Reading between the lines, Meg translated that as, *I am covered in claret. Please don't panic when you see me*, which hadn't exactly filled her with confidence.

"Come on," Emily said. "I can hear sirens."

"Right." Meg dropped her gloves, swore at them, and plucked out another pair.

Stopping in front of her, Emily barred the door. "Breathe, Dr. Fielding."

Meg nodded and took an exaggerated breath.

The first crew passed them halfway down the corridor with a familiar figure strapped to a scoop stretcher. Despite being immobilised, Nelson waved when he spotted Meg.

"Got to stop meeting like this," she said as he was manoeuvred past.

"She's in the next one, by the way," he said.

"Does she look better than you?" Meg called after him. She heard him laugh.

"Always!"

When she turned back, Sanne was the first person she saw. She had prepared herself for the worst, but Sanne was hurrying alongside a stretcher, easily keeping up with its pace, heedless of her bloodied face and the stained dressing wrapped around her head. She tried to smile at Meg, though she couldn't quite manage it.

"Shock room," Meg said, feeling a terrible sense of déjà vu as the unconscious patient—Rachel, she realised—was steered past. She caught hold of Sanne's sleeve, stopping her.

"I need to stay with her," Sanne said, trying to pull away.

"No, you need to get your head looked at."

"I'm okay. I have to—"

"*Sanne.*" Meg tightened her grip. Water was seeping from Sanne's sodden fleece and dripping to the floor. "There's a specially trained officer in there, and a consultant from St. Margaret's. *I* should be in there, and instead I'm arguing with you." She hated herself for using such an underhand tactic, but it worked. The tension left Sanne's muscles, and she stepped back from the door.

"I really am okay," she whispered.

"I know you are." Meg walked her over to a line of wheelchairs and sat her in the first one. "How about a compromise? You stay here, try not to bleed on my floor, and I'll come and get you cleaned up as soon as I can." She rested her hand on Sanne's cold cheek. Sanne closed her eyes and nodded reluctantly.

During her years as a doctor, Meg had had to make some shitty decisions, but abandoning Sanne in the corridor was one of the hardest things she had ever done. She turned her back before she could change her mind, and headed straight into the shock room.

❖

Sanne wasn't sure how she'd avoided being dragged off to provide a statement. So far, it seemed no one milling about the corridor was senior enough to debrief her, and they had all given her a wide berth. She tried to sit up straight for when someone did come, but the movement made her grip the chair until her fingers ached. Her head throbbed, the skin across her shoulders was tense and swollen, and she felt chilled to the bone despite the warmth of the corridor.

The sound of hasty footsteps forced her to lift her head again, and she tried not to groan aloud. A nurse was bustling toward her.

"Mucky bandage and wet-through clothing. You must be Sanne," the nurse said. "I'm Liz." Without giving Sanne a chance to protest, she wrapped a thick blanket around her, draped clean scrubs over the arm of the chair, and handed her a mug of tea. "White, no sugar. Did Meg get it right? Because I never know with her."

"Spot on. Thank you." Sanne cradled the mug, sending needles of heat through her fingers. "How are Rachel and Nelson doing?"

"The policeman? He'll be off to X-ray in a few minutes, but the doc doesn't think his head injury is too serious. They're still assessing Rachel, so I can't tell you much there."

"Is she awake?" The paramedics had given Rachel enough morphine to ensure she was comfortable throughout the journey, and she had slept most of the way in.

"No, she'll be asleep for a while yet." Liz pulled the blanket closed at Sanne's neck, fussing with its edges. "They sedated her so they could examine her properly."

Sanne nodded, but the few sips of tea she had drunk threatened rebellion in her stomach. The elation of finding Rachel alive had swiftly been superseded by the horror of what she had suffered.

"What happened to the bastard who did this?" Liz asked. "He's not coming here, is he?" Twin flares of red coloured her cheeks as she kicked the wheel of the chair behind Sanne.

"No. They took him and his mum to Manchester Central, to keep them away from Rachel and Josie. Their families shouldn't have to—" Sanne realised her voice had risen. Trying to be professional, she tempered it and chose her words carefully. "It wasn't appropriate to bring them here."

Billy's only apparent injuries had been a fracture to his lower leg and the facial wounds Rachel had inflicted, which meant that EDSOP should be able to question him within the next couple of days. As they still had no idea whether anyone else had been involved in the abductions, Ned Moseley remained in custody. Sanne had only just read the messages on her phone informing her that his transfer from the holding cells had made it impossible for anyone to question him about Billy's potential involvement. In any case, events since then had rendered the urgency of her request moot.

"I better get back," Liz said. "You should change out of those wet things."

"I will." Sanne didn't even attempt to sound convincing. She had no intention of moving. Liz made a sceptical noise beneath her breath but left without pushing the point. As her footsteps faded, the sharp tap of heels took their place.

"Is there a reason you're not in a bed?" Eleanor's voice held none of its usual edge, and she crouched so that Sanne didn't have to look up at her.

"I wanted to wait, boss. Meg's going to check me over when she's got a minute." Sanne didn't have the energy to worry about what Eleanor might say. She just sat and waited for the tirade.

Eleanor pulled a chair alongside Sanne's and sighed in relief as she sat down. "Carlyle's over at HMP Nottingham with Ned Moseley. Moseley's admitted to being friends with Cotter. Close as brothers, he reckons, the stupid sod. He agreed to hold on to Cotter's porn stash, after Cotter told him his dad would kick him out if it ever got found at home."

"Christ. Why the hell didn't Ned say something?"

Eleanor opened her hands in exasperation. "Because Cotter was supposed to be his best mate, and in Moseley's words, 'Best mates don't snitch.'"

"Even when facing a jail sentence?"

"I don't think he ever expected things to get to that point. Carlyle said he seemed sure Cotter would come forward and help him out. Instead, it's looking increasingly like Best Mate Billy set the poor sap up. Cotter knew about the garage on Turner Street, and he had his own key to Moseley's house."

Sanne had a hundred questions chasing each other around her aching head, but she couldn't marshal any of them. "Did you tell Josie?" she asked eventually.

"Yes." Eleanor shuddered, the movement so subtle that Sanne almost missed it. "Her family are with her, practically sitting on her to keep her in her bed. I've never seen anyone so happy in one breath and so devastated in the next."

"I can imagine." Sanne put a hand to her forehead, frowning when it came away tacky with blood.

"What took you into the house, Sanne?" Eleanor asked quietly.

"I needed loo paper." Sanne wiped her fingers on the blanket, covering them with fluff. "I shouted for Joan and Geoff, but then there was this smell."

"And you surmised from that that a life was potentially at risk?"

"Yes…" She tried not to make it sound too much like a question.

Eleanor gave a curt nod. "Good enough for me. You broke that bitch's hip, by the way. She's saying nothing, but the ME estimated Geoff had only been dead for around forty-eight hours."

Sanne thought back to the first time Joan had mentioned Geoff being "off sick." It had been at least four days ago. Just when she thought this case couldn't get any more appalling, it took delight in proving her wrong.

"They crippled him and left him to die, didn't they?" she asked.

Eleanor refused to commit. "We'll know more after the post mortem." She stood and smoothed her jacket. "I'm going to need a statement from you, obviously, but I don't want to see you in the office until tomorrow afternoon at the earliest."

Given the gravity of the night's events, that was a generous leave of absence. Sanne nodded her agreement.

"You did well," Eleanor said. "There's still a lot to sort out, but you and Nelson did a great job on this one. I have to get back to the scene. Make sure you wait for Dr. Fielding. That's an order, Sanne."

Sanne watched her go out into the ambulance bay. The corridor was quiet, with only the occasional medic flitting through, paying her no attention. She took hold of the scrubs and pushed up from the chair. The directions on the wall in front of her swam, the letters switching order and their colours merging.

"Shit." Breathing through her nose, she walked slowly to the staff toilet, where a health care assistant entered the code for her. She shut the door, sat on the floor, and threw up into the toilet. Tears blinded her. She wanted to clean her face and rinse her mouth, but she couldn't get to the sink. Resting her head on her knees, she stopped trying.

❖

"Bit shorter than me. Blue fleece and combats. Fucking big bandage on her head. Ring any bells?" Meg didn't mean to shout at the nurses standing around the desk, but they really weren't helping.

"Try the staff loo, Doc."

Meg spun around to face a health care assistant whose name she didn't know.

"I let her in there about ten minutes ago," the man said. "Haven't seen her since."

"Thank you." Meg ran to the toilet and banged on the door, only then realising that its secondary lock wasn't engaged. After three attempts, she managed to punch in the right access code. "Sanne? Sanne, it's me." She opened the door a crack, then swore and opened it fully. On the verge of yelling for help, she changed her mind when she saw Sanne stir. Vomit covered the toilet rim, so she closed the lid and sat on the floor beside her.

"Is Rachel okay?" Sanne sounded drunk, her words blurring together.

"Mostly. She's gone up to HDU. Her injuries were fairly minor, but she's dehydrated, malnourished, and anaemic. They can keep a close eye on her there."

Sanne's head bobbed in a vague semblance of a nod. "Did he rape her?"

"Yes." There was nothing Meg could say to soften it.

Sanne closed her eyes, and a sob rattled her body. "She fought so fucking hard, Meg. Even after everything he did, she stopped him from putting her in that van."

"I know," Meg said, but she couldn't bear to elaborate. Her last task before handing Rachel to the HDU team had been to set Rachel's fractures. She had broken both wrists trying to untie herself. Meg wiped her damp palms against her trousers. It would be a long time before she came to terms with what she had seen in the shock room, if she ever did. She put her arm around Sanne, craving the contact and the reassurance that Sanne was relatively unscathed.

"Still feeling sick?" she asked.

Sanne burrowed into her warmth. "Not really."

"Shall I stitch you up, then we can go home?"

"Can you do it here?"

"That wouldn't be very hygienic."

"Suppose not."

Meg stroked the tufts of hair sticking out from Sanne's bandage. "You've got to stop scaring me like this."

"Sorry," Sanne mumbled. She sounded half-asleep. Hugging her tightly, Meg gave them both a minute to rest.

❖

"All done." Meg smoothed a dressing over the laceration on Sanne's forehead. "Try to keep the stitches dry. I'll snip them out for you in a week or so."

"Thank you." Sanne forced herself to leave the comfort of the pillow and sit on the edge of the bed.

"I'll get my coat. You stay right there, okay?"

"Yep." Staying right there seemed like an excellent idea. She hurt in far more places than she had admitted to, but Meg was fretting enough as it was, and Sanne didn't want to be marched straight home.

Meg was back in the cubicle within minutes, out of breath and already putting on her coat. Her movements became less harried when she saw that Sanne hadn't done anything stupid in her absence.

"Nelson's just gone up to the ward," she said. "Concussion and a hairline fracture. He was asleep when they wheeled him past me, but his wife sends her love."

Relief constricted Sanne's throat. She could only nod and allow Meg to support her as she stood.

Meg regarded her carefully and then tipped her chin with a finger. "You want to go and see Josie, don't you?"

At times Sanne forgot how clearly Meg could read her. She nodded again. Even if Josie was asleep or with her family, Sanne just needed to see for herself that she was all right.

"Come on, then." Meg waggled her finger like a stern schoolmistress. "But the first wobble from you, and you're going in a wheelchair."

"I won't wobble." Sanne focused on putting one foot in front of the other. "I might fall flat on my face, but I won't wobble."

On the Neuro Rehab ward, the nurse recognised Sanne and Meg from their previous visits.

"Ahh…" he said, drawing the word out and looking guilty. It didn't take a genius to fathom what he had done.

"HDU, then?" Sanne asked.

"Yeah. I took her as soon as her mum left. I think she'd have crawled there if I hadn't helped her."

"Can't say I blame you," Meg said.

The creases eased from his brow as his stance relaxed. "I'm guessing you know where it is."

The HDU was a small unit comprising five walled bays. Sanne showed her ID to a doctor, who directed her and Meg to the end of the row where a single light shone and a nurse stood making notes on an observation chart. The nurse put her finger to her lips as they approached. Hesitating in front of the bay, Sanne saw why. She bit hard on the inside of her cheek, but tears still filled her eyes.

Wrapped in each other's arms, Rachel and Josie were asleep, their faces peaceful, their hands clasped together. Although they were unaware of their audience, it seemed too intimate a moment for such a public setting. Sanne longed to pull the curtain closed and give them the privacy they deserved. Instead, she bowed her head and led Meg away without saying a word. They walked in silence past the nurses' station, only stopping once they were back in the corridor.

"Don't cry, love. Here." Meg took out a tissue and dabbed at Sanne's cheeks.

Sanne used the tissue to blow her nose. Exhaustion was making her eyes burn. "This was never going to have a happy ending, was it?"

"No." Meg's voice was hollow and wretched. "I think that's about as happy an ending as you could hope for."

Having parked as close to her front door as she could without hitting the steps, Meg yanked her keys from the ignition and jogged round to Sanne's side of the car. Sanne had become increasingly restless during the journey, and the weak overhead light was enough to show the gleam of sweat on her forehead. Her face went from pale to ashen as she got out of her seat and straightened in agonised increments. She hobbled to the door like a geriatric with widespread arthritis, kicking at her trainers in the hallway to avoid bending.

Crouching in her stead, Meg unfastened the laces. "Sanne Jensen," she said, levering off the first shoe. "What else are you hiding?" She had seen the bruises and scrapes caused by Sanne diving from the path of the van, but nothing that would debilitate her to this extent.

"I'm fine," Sanne whispered. "Can I have a shower?"

Meg didn't argue, merely following Sanne into the bathroom and perching on the side of the bath to watch her fail to get undressed. The scrubs trousers came off without a hitch, but the top defeated her. Suspecting that the problem was muscular, Meg set the bath running and took a pair of scissors from the cabinet. She turned Sanne into the light and pulled the cloth of her top taut.

"Joan hit me," Sanne said, surrendering to the inevitable. "It's just stiffened up, that's all."

"Mmhm." Meg chopped at the cotton, grateful that the NHS budget only ran to cheap, thin material. The shirt fell away, and she gave a low whistle of dismay. The upper third of Sanne's back was one mottled bruise, with a raised purple line stretching between her shoulders. It was little wonder she hadn't wanted to lift her arms. "Bloody hell, San. What did she use, a tyre iron?"

"I'm not sure. I suppose it might've been." Sanne gave a small ironic laugh. "I was too busy trying to stop her from cracking me over the head with it."

"Nasty cow."

Sanne sucked in a breath as Meg touched the inflamed skin. A few inches higher and it could have been worse, so much worse.

"If it's any consolation, I broke her hip," Sanne said, interrupting Meg's morbid train of thought.

"That does make me feel a bit better." Meg kissed Sanne's cheek and led her to the bath, where she eased herself beneath the suds. "Don't duck your head under. I'll wash your hair for you."

The combination of heat, the late hour, and an adrenaline crash made Sanne unusually quiescent. Sighing deeply, she edged onto her side and let Meg tend to her. Once the water began to cool, Meg coaxed her out and wrapped her in a towel.

"Take these. They're paracetamol," Meg said.

Sanne accepted the tablets without complaint.

"And codeine," Meg added, once she was sure Sanne had swallowed them.

Sanne rolled her eyes at the subterfuge, but Meg didn't feel an ounce of remorse. She knew that Sanne needed sleep more than anything, and that she was such a lightweight when it came to drugs that even a low dose of codeine would knock her out. Working quickly, Meg managed to get her dressed and tucked into bed before that happened.

"I'm going to get a shower. I'll be back in five minutes." She stroked Sanne's cheek, urging her to close her eyes. "You have sweet dreams."

The drugs had hit Sanne hard. She mumbled something nonsensical, pressing her lips to Meg's palm.

"I love you too," Meg whispered, and dimmed the light.

Chapter Twenty-two

An undignified roll got Sanne out of bed as the church clock chimed eleven. Neatly folded on the dresser were clothes Meg had set out in readiness: a loose shirt, trousers, and slippers in lieu of socks. Meg must have heard her moving around, because a fresh breakfast of toast and cereal, set alongside a mug of tea and three painkillers, awaited her when she came downstairs.

"Take the white ones now, and the pink one after you've eaten," Meg said, prodding Sanne's stitches with professional efficiency.

"What exactly are they?" Sanne asked, wary of being slipped another Mickey. She needed to be awake enough to go to headquarters and give her statement.

"Paracetamol and Brufen. Nothing stronger, I promise." Meg displayed the packets as proof. "Eleanor phoned an hour ago. Everyone's as well as can be expected, and you're due in at one. Seeing as you have no car and—judging by your buttons—no dexterity, I'll drive you over there."

"You don't need to do that. I can get a taxi." Sanne glanced at her shirt. She'd missed two of the buttons and fastened the rest in an arbitrary order. "Bugger."

Meg knelt by her and began to sort out the mess. "They need to speak to me too, San. I can take a few journals to read while I wait for you to finish. Just humour me, okay?" An unfamiliar pleading note in her voice caught Sanne's attention.

"Hey." Sanne waited until Meg looked up, and for the first time she noticed Meg's barely combed hair and the puffy, blackened skin beneath her eyes. "Did you get any sleep?" she asked quietly.

"A little." Meg seemed to reconsider. "No, not much."

"A lift to work would be lovely," Sanne said, and reached for the paracetamol.

❖

No one in EDSOP stood on ceremony. When Sanne entered the office, there was no applause, no colleagues lining up to hug her and offer their congratulations. Fred and George grinned at her, though, and Jay tipped an imaginary hat, while Mike Hallet lifted his mug in salute. On her desk, she found two Double Decker bars, displaying a Post-it note that read: *Nice one, mate.* Feeling ten feet tall, she stuck the note on her monitor. She was about to switch the computer on when Eleanor summoned her.

"I've asked Jay to take your statement," Eleanor said. "I'm assuming Duncan has already waylaid Dr. Fielding."

"Yes. He met us in the corridor." Meg had given Sanne a parting kiss on the cheek that made Carlyle trip over his feet.

Eleanor ushered Sanne into her office, shutting the door as Sanne sat down.

"First things first. Do you need to speak to a counsellor about what happened last night?" She asked the question in her usual perfunctory manner, but there was genuine concern in her expression, and she paid close attention to Sanne's reaction.

"No, ma'am. Thank you, though."

Eleanor made a note in her file. "How's the head?"

"Sore, but I'd rather get this done."

"I appreciate that. I wanted to bring you up to speed, and then I need to ask you something."

"Okay." Sanne felt remarkably sanguine. She couldn't alter anything that had happened, and she was certain that she would make the same choices again if identical circumstances arose.

"I interviewed Rachel this morning," Eleanor said. "She was able to give a detailed and cogent account. It seems Cotter didn't drug her, so she remembers almost everything." She paused to drink from a mug of coffee that looked hours old. When she continued, her voice had lost its seasoned detachment. "I think it would have been a kindness if he *had* used drugs."

Sanne knew she would have to read the transcript at some point, but with everything still so raw, she tried to focus on the practicalities instead. "Did Rachel say how Billy had come into contact with them? Had they met through the garage?" It was the most obvious explanation, even though he had claimed not to recognise the couple when she and Nelson had initially questioned him.

"Yes. They had a flat battery on their rental car, and Billy went out to the cottage to replace it. Rachel couldn't pinpoint anything unusual about his behaviour, but that day was most likely the catalyst."

Sanne leaned forward, the fog in her head lifting as she began to draw elements of the case together. Her eyes widened as she considered the timeline. "Jesus, Rachel was probably in that workshop when we went to the garage that first time. Billy was so fucking eager to help. He even offered to recheck all their recent jobs for us."

"Easy enough to do that when you know you've purged the one that'd incriminate you. He never billed the car rental agency, so the job wasn't recorded at their end," Eleanor said.

Sanne was on a roll. "What about the Land Rover, and Callum Clark? Was Clark involved in the abductions?"

Eleanor went to take another sip of coffee, and then seemed to have second thoughts and put the mug down. "Yes. Well, no, possibly not in that sense. Rachel identified Billy Cotter as the sole perpetrator. Ned Moseley was released on bail a couple of hours ago, and Clark is down in holding on suspicion of assisting an offender. We got access to Cotter's bank records early this morning, and Scotty's spent the day trawling through them. Four days ago, Cotter purchased an Audi A4. Digging a little deeper, Scotty also found a record of a Land Rover that Cotter bought in February through the same auction centre. No surprise that it matches the vehicle from Turner Street."

"Billy probably bought the Landie as a fixer-upper," Sanne said. "He's always had old wrecks lying around the yard. Most likely he just used it because it was convenient. And Clark bragged about a new car to one of the junior doctors."

Her enthusiastic deduction brought a smile to Eleanor's face. "Clark is the current registered owner of a 2007 Audi A4. According to his preliminary interview, the car was totally worth slicing up his hand for, so that he could feed us information about Moseley's lock-up. He and Cotter were casual drinking buddies, and he didn't ask any questions as to Cotter's motives, because apparently he's a fucking lackwit."

Sanne frowned. "But he didn't tell the police, he told Emily—Ah." She felt herself flush. "He took a roundabout route, didn't he?"

"Exactly. Cotter persuaded him to go to Dr. Fielding. If he'd come directly to us, we might have started to ask why. Throwing in an extra loop made his story more plausible."

"And I took the bait. Hook, line, and sinker. Bloody hell." Sanne hid her face in her hands, mortified that her relationship with Meg had been exploited in such a way. She thought of Ned Moseley, frantic and bewildered during questioning, trying to uphold some misguided code and protect his friend, who in turn had lied and schemed to shift the blame onto him. Greed had motivated Callum Clark's involvement, but Billy had taken advantage of Ned's vulnerability in a particularly insidious way. Had Billy been standing in the workshop with Rachel when he'd answered Sanne's phone call the previous night? The likelihood of that, and the gratitude she had felt when he'd agreed to help her, made her want to punch something hard and keep punching until it smashed.

"Sanne—"

Sanne shook her head to cut off whatever Eleanor might say. She didn't need placating or consoling, she just needed this case to stop fucking around with her. She lowered her hands. "How much did Joan have to do with all this?"

"We're not sure. Plenty, I would guess, but she was in surgery last night, and no one's been able to speak to her yet."

"What about Billy? Has he been interviewed?"

Eleanor made a steeple out of her fingers and leaned forward until her lips rested against them. She appeared to be stalling, which was so out of character that it raised the hairs on Sanne's arms.

"Cotter is on his way over here," she said, choosing her words with care. "Sanne, he's refusing to speak to anyone but you."

❖

Sanne took the paper towel Meg proffered and used it to dry the water she had just splashed on her face. She tossed the towel into the bin, and then held on to the edges of the sink and scrutinised her reflection in the mirror. She looked older somehow, as if the last twelve days had aged her prematurely, adding haggard lines to her brow and draining the colour from her complexion, leaving it a dull grey. The door rattled. She tensed, but the lock held.

"You can still change your mind," Meg said, as the footsteps outside faded to nothing. "I'm sure Eleanor would understand." She smiled when Sanne arched an eyebrow. "What? Were you expecting me to drag you home by your ear?"

"Yeah, something like that."

"San, in the last few days you've thrown yourself over the edge of a rock face, chased down a dark alley after a man twice your size, and beaten up an old lady." She shrugged at Sanne's horrified laugh. "Hey, she tried to knock your head off. Bottom line is, you're a big girl who can make her own decisions, and you're more than capable of taking on a piece of shit like Billy Cotter."

"I'm not that big." Unable to maintain eye contact, Sanne watched the dripping tap instead. "Billy didn't give a reason for demanding to speak to me. What if he's just coming here to play games? I don't want to sit in front of him while he tells me everything he did. Not today. I can't deal with that today."

"So why did you say yes?"

It was a fair question, and one Sanne had been trying to answer for the last hour. "Because I might be able to get a confession, which could save Josie and Rachel from having to testify. He may even tell us what part Joan played, if he thinks there's a chance it would reduce his sentence."

Those were the official reasons, the ones Eleanor had taken to the CPS, who were so sure that witness testimony alone would secure a conviction that they were willing to allow an under-qualified detective to interview their main suspect. Sanne pushed away from the sink and placed her chilled palms against her cheeks, easing the heat from them. Her other reason wasn't officially sanctioned.

"Meg, I think I want to look him in the eye and prove that I'm not scared of him."

"How scared are you?"

Sanne leaned her head onto Meg's shoulder, hiding her face and muffling her answer. "I'm fucking terrified."

❖

Sitting at the table in the interview room, Sanne thought she had prepared herself for Billy's entrance. She imagined him striding through the door, his eyes ablaze with the victory he had won in getting her to agree to this. In all of the scenarios she had envisioned, though, she had forgotten that he'd broken his leg.

A bang on the door only partially opened it, and a flurry of curses preceded a second attempt. Sanne exchanged a puzzled look with Eleanor before a uniformed officer stepped into the room and held the door open fully, allowing his colleague to wheel Billy through. The officer struggled to manoeuvre the wheelchair in the confined space, giving Sanne ample opportunity to study Billy as he was positioned in front of her.

He seemed smaller than she remembered, sallow and unkempt, with a dusting of five o'clock shadow and an ill-fitting prison uniform. The left side of his face was grotesquely swollen and discoloured where Rachel had carved into him. Every time he moved, the cuffs around his wrists clattered against the table, as if he hadn't come to terms with their presence.

Sanne waited until the officers left the room and Billy's lawyer was seated. Then she set the recorder running. The standard opening—stating the time, date, and the names of those present—was reassuring in its familiarity, affording her an immediate sense of control over the proceedings. She didn't react when Billy grinned at her, and his smile quickly faltered. He put a hand to his face as if the effort had pained him, and then looked past her to glare at Eleanor.

"What's she doing here?"

His lack of respect made Sanne bristle. "She's my boss. You can speak to me, that's fine, but DI Stanhope remains in the room."

"Not part of the deal, Sanne." The singsong lilt he wrapped around her name sent acid swirling into her stomach.

"Deal's off, then." She checked her watch. "Interview terminated at—"

"Hey now, come on, play nice." He had the audacity to look offended. "I wanted to apologise for last night."

She couldn't help but do a double take. "You what?"

Billy shook off the warning hand of his lawyer. "Oh, like keeping quiet will make a fucking difference," he snapped at him. He turned back to Sanne. "I never meant for you to get hurt. We're mates, aren't we?"

"You drove your van at me! You almost killed me and my partner."

He opened his hands wide, straining the cuffs to their limit. The overhead strip light glinted off the metal. "Your mate poked his nose where it didn't belong. You were collateral damage."

"Is that what Josie Albright was?" Sanne asked, sensing a way to get the interview on track. "Was she just collateral damage to you? It was Rachel you wanted really, but you took them both so you could use one to control the other, didn't you?"

A smile spread slowly across Billy's face, and for the first time Sanne glimpsed the man she had spent almost two weeks hunting down. He used his index finger to wipe a slick trail of saliva from his bottom lip.

"It worked well, for a while." He spoke in a hushed voice, as if divulging a secret. "After a little persuasion, Rachel did everything I asked, and the other one didn't have a fucking clue what was going on. I blame Mal, y'know. Fucker cuts his stuff with a right load of shit. Probably sold me a weak batch. I get back there, and that bitch has scarpered."

"Mal—that would be Malcolm Atley," Sanne said.

Billy tried to appear nonchalant at the mention of Atley's name, but an involuntary twitch at the corner of his jaw gave him away. "You've been doing your homework. Is that how you knew it was me? Because I've been wondering. I thought Ned might finally have cracked, but I don't think he did, did he?"

"No, you had Ned right where you wanted him. He never gave you up."

Billy beamed, obviously proud. "I was so close, *so* close to pulling this off. I just held on to her for too long. Couldn't let her go, you see? My mum nagged me, even offered to do it herself, but I begged, *begged* for another week, and look where it got me." He rattled the handcuffs.

Sanne could practically feel Eleanor's eyes burning into her back, urging her not to fuck this up. Billy, still full of bravado, didn't seem to recognise the significance of what he had said.

"What did your mum offer to do, Billy? Did she have a plan to get rid of Rachel?" She kept her voice level and conversational, as if the questions weren't a big deal.

Billy nodded, unthinking. "Yeah, we were going to weigh her down at one of Ned's lakes, once the fuss died down a bit. My mum knew you'd been searching out there."

Eleanor let out a breath as Billy's lawyer shook his head in dismay. Sanne ignored them both. "Your mum knew about the pornography as well, didn't she?"

Billy's face reddened slightly, giving the impression he was more ashamed of that than of anything else he had done. "She told me to hide it. She said my dad would leather me if he found it."

"So you asked Ned to keep hold of it, and voilà, he's your perfect fall guy."

Billy smirked. "Had you all chasing your fucking tails for a while, didn't I? You and your mate standing there in my garage, asking your questions. You know what I'd been doing half an hour earlier?"

Sanne didn't want to know. She couldn't even bear for him to keep looking at her, so she shut him down. "When did your mum kill your dad, Billy?"

He gaped at her and then closed his mouth so viciously that his teeth slammed together. A faint pink spot on one of his dressings began to spread and darken. "I'm not talking about that," he muttered.

She didn't care that he was bleeding. She wanted to push him until he snapped. She wanted this to be over. "Did he find Rachel? Was he going to come and tell us?"

"I fucking mean it, Sanne. I'm not—"

She slammed her palms on the table, cutting him off. "How long did he live for after she hit him? Days? Was he conscious, Billy? Did he understand what was happening to him?"

"Shut the fuck up!" Billy tried to stand, but his fractured leg collapsed beneath him. "Shut the fuck up, you bitch. I mean it."

Sanne didn't even blink. "Would you like to take a break?"

"No." He was sweating, the sharp smell filling the room.

"Okay." She couldn't remember the bullet points Eleanor had suggested, and the notes in front of her seemed nonsensical. She stopped trying to decipher her handwriting. There was only one more thing she needed to know. "Why Josie and Rachel? Why did you choose them?"

He closed his eyes, twining his fingers around the length of chain between his wrists and stroking it gently. "I asked Rachel out for a drink," he said, still working the metal. "The day I went to the cottage to fix their car. The other one laughed at me. I didn't get it at first, didn't realise what the joke was." He dropped the chain and looked directly at Sanne. "I knew where Ned kept the keys to the cottage. I found a route they'd planned, and I followed them up onto Corvenden. They couldn't have made it easier for me. It was the perfect place to teach them a lesson."

He lunged suddenly, his hands sliding across the table to brush against Sanne's. Her chair scraped the floor as she shoved herself beyond his reach.

"I wanted you to know." He was panting, his nostrils flaring. "That's why I came here, Sanne. I wanted you to know how fucking lucky you are."

Eleanor stepped forward and slammed her hand onto the recorder to stop it. She shouted for the officers, who came and hauled Billy back into his wheelchair, but he never took his eyes off Sanne. Blood soaked into his bandages as he laughed at her.

"Get him out of my sight," Eleanor told the officers. She waited until his lawyer followed him out. When the door had closed, she turned back to Sanne. "Are you okay?"

"No." Sanne couldn't move from the chair; her legs were shaking.

"Do you know what he meant by that?"

Sanne nodded silently.

Eleanor ejected the disc from the machine. "Off the record, Sanne."

The room felt as if it were collapsing in on Sanne, Eleanor's question barely making it through the ringing in her ears.

"About three years ago, Billy asked me out," she whispered. "I laughed at first. I thought he was mucking about. I had to tell him I was gay."

"Jesus Christ."

Sanne wrapped her arms around herself, shivering uncontrollably. "Can you find Meg? I want to go home."

The late evening sun still felt warm on Meg's face. Above her, the treetops caught the lingering rays, their leaves bright and lush after all the rain. The stream was high, rushing over her bare feet and splashing her ankles. Keeping her toes in the water, she leaned back on the rug spread across the bank.

"I think I need a holiday," Sanne said, shifting a little to give her more room. They were the first words she'd spoken since Meg had brought her down into the garden. She sounded shattered.

"Where do you fancy?" Meg kept her tone light, trying to engage Sanne's interest.

"I have no idea." Sanne turned toward her. "Somewhere with perfect blue sea, sandy beaches, and wall-to-wall sunshine."

Meg looked at her in mock-horror. "Sanne Jensen, are you actually planning to leave the country?"

The ghost of a smile touched Sanne's lips. "I might well be. Not till after the trial, but yeah, a break would be good."

"Do you think it will go to trial?"

"I'm not sure." She sighed, and her shoulders dropped in defeat. "The weight of evidence against Billy is enormous, but some people like him get a thrill out of forcing their victims to testify. He didn't even mention that today. He just…well, you know what he did."

"I know, love." Meg had coaxed most of the details from her before they left headquarters. She still felt livid, but she tried to keep her expression neutral. Sanne was upset enough and didn't need Meg's reaction to contend with. Instead, Meg returned to a less emotive subject. "So, what about one of the Greek Islands? They're supposed to be beautiful."

"Mm." Sanne yawned and scratched her nose absently. "Do you want to come with me?"

"I'd love to, but I'd cramp your style something rotten."

"That's not true." Already half-asleep, Sanne didn't seem to be processing much of the conversation.

Meg took hold of her hands and pulled them until she sat up. "Bedtime, San."

"I'm comfy here. Can't we camp out?"

"No." She saw Sanne's frown and ticked off the reasons on her fingers. "We'll get midged to death, it's already getting chilly, and we're not twelve years old. Our bones are too brittle to spend a night on the ground." She hauled Sanne to her feet. "Oh, and did I forget to mention your head injury and the bruise covering most of your back?"

"Okay, okay, point taken." Sanne stumbled up the bank and walked zombie-like toward the patio doors.

"Go and get ready for bed," Meg said. "I'll be with you in a minute."

"Can I have a cup of tea?"

"I reckon I can manage that for you."

Sanne stopped in the kitchen doorway. "And a couple of biccies?"

"Don't push your bloody luck."

Sanne laughed as she carried on up the hallway, the sound so heartening that Meg found a brand new packet of biscuits for her, and then added cake.

Epilogue

Ireally appreciate this," Sanne said. The traffic jam ahead of them crept forward as people lugged suitcases from car boots and ran through the rain into the departure lounge.

"Not a problem." Nelson pulled on his handbrake and let the engine idle. "We bring the girls here sometimes to watch the planes. I might park up, grab a bacon butty, and wave at you taking off. Who are you flying with, again?"

"QuickJet." Dread made Sanne's mouth dry. A plane roared overhead. She craned her neck to watch it go over, trying to convince herself that thousands of people did this every day and hardly anything bad ever happened.

Following her sightline, Nelson could guess what she was thinking. "Come on, you'll love it. It's no different from being in the chopper, really." A smile lit up his face, all the strain of the last two months vanishing.

"You're going to text me and let me know about the sentencing, aren't you?" she asked.

"As soon as I hear anything, I promise." He gestured to the newspaper on her lap. "What does that have to say?"

Unfolding the paper and holding up the front page so he could see the headline, she paraphrased the lead article. "Last-minute change to a guilty plea by mother and son. CPS delighted for the victims and the victim's families. Sentencing to be determined in the next ten days, and both defendants can expect lengthy prison terms. DI Stanhope is very proud of everyone involved in the investigation, and wishes Sanne Jensen all the best on her first holiday abroad."

Nelson laughed. "You made that bit up, you bugger."

"I might have embellished a little." She refolded the paper, leaving the back page uppermost. "Let's see the local forecast. Rain, rain, rain and wind, oh, and more rain."

"I hate you." He pulled into a drop-off slot. "Need a hand with your bag?"

"I'll manage, thanks." She leaned over and kissed his cheek. "Don't get into any trouble while I'm gone."

"Wouldn't dream of it, partner." He shooed her away. "Go on, before I start blubbing."

She dragged her holdall from the backseat and set it on its wheels as cars farther back in the queue beeped their horns impatiently. She blew Nelson a kiss and waved until he rounded the corner. The rain began again with renewed vigour. She touched her pocket to check her passport was still there and joined the crowd heading into the departure lounge.

Jetting off to a private villa on a Greek island had sounded dynamic and adventurous, but thus far it had involved a mauling from a woman on security, followed by a lot of sitting around. Sanne played her finger over the shutdown option on her phone before deciding to leave it on for another five minutes. Although her flight had been called, nothing seemed to be happening at the gate. The screen of the phone had gone blank, and it stayed blank. It was only eight a.m.; Meg was probably still in bed after her late shift.

Hugging her rucksack to her chest, Sanne rested her chin on it and tried to look on the bright side—two weeks of sea and sunshine, with a list of gay-friendly bars and restaurants that Meg had downloaded for her. As the people in the priority boarding group began to form an orderly line, she buried her face in her bag and wondered what the hell she had been thinking when she'd booked this holiday. She had never been on a plane before, she'd never even left the country before, and she didn't speak a word of Greek.

On the verge of turning around and fleeing back through Duty Free, she remembered the twenty Euro note tucked into her wallet, and the panicky sensation eased a little. Her mum had given her the money yesterday afternoon, a gift she must have rushed out to arrange the instant she heard about Sanne's last-minute deal. All she'd wanted in return was a postcard and plenty of photographs.

A woman with a fake tan to match the airline's bright orange uniform announced the second boarding group. Sanne checked her ticket, even though she knew she should be joining the queue. The budget airline allocated its seats on a first come, first served basis. If she didn't move soon, she'd end up squashed in the middle of a row. She inched to the edge of her seat but got no farther.

"Are you going to sit here all day, or are you getting on the bloody plane?"

The familiar voice made Sanne snap her head up. At first she thought she'd been mistaken. All she saw was a wide-brimmed straw hat and a pair of legs sticking out of rain-dampened shorts, but then Meg laughed and plonked down in the seat beside her.

"What on earth are you doing here?" Sanne said. It came out more abrupt than she intended, but the last she'd heard, Meg's request for leave had been denied.

Meg proudly displayed her boarding pass. "Well, after I did all that research for you, I got to thinking that two weeks wearing my skimpies and drinking cocktails in the sunshine sounded like a lot of fun. I did a few swaps, called in a bunch of favours, and just finished"—she paused to do the calculation—"fifty or so hours of shifts. I'm quite tired. Could do with a holiday." The toothy grin fell from her face as Sanne continued to gape at her. "Fucking shit. You'd rather go on your own, wouldn't you? I'm going to be a complete cramper of your style. Bollocks."

Sanne shook her head so vigorously that her hair slapped in her eyes. "*No!* I just..." She paused and smiled. "I'm really glad you're here."

"Yeah?"

"Yes." She looked at the dwindling number of passengers in the line. "Shall we continue this conversation on the plane?"

The flight was almost full, but they found a row at the back with two spare seats, one of which came with a window. Sanne cinched her seatbelt, unconvinced that it would do her any good in a catastrophe, but bound by the rules regardless. She squeaked as the plane began to taxi. "Shit, shit, shit."

Meg grabbed her hand. "Squeeze tight if you want to."

"I might." Rain sluiced down Sanne's tiny window. On the tarmac, she saw a man wearing headphones, guiding the plane toward the runway. "I phoned Josie yesterday," she said, attempting to distract herself. "After the news broke."

"How was she?"

Sanne hesitated, as a smiling flight attendant stopped to check their bags were correctly stowed. "Relieved," she said, once the attendant had moved on down the aisle and they were assured of privacy. "I didn't stay on long, but they're doing better now they're back in Edinburgh. We have an open invitation to visit."

Meg nodded. "Maybe give them a while, eh?"

"I can't imagine I'll ever go. I'd only remind them of what happened." Sanne rubbed her neck, trying to relax her muscles. The case felt like a constant weight, pressing down on her, no matter what. She didn't want to keep thinking about it, but it always seemed to lurk in the background, and she'd been suffering nightmares for weeks.

"San?"

"Mmhm?"

Meg waited until Sanne looked at her. "We're on holiday. Leave it behind, okay?"

"Okay."

The plane came to a sudden stop, and Sanne could see the runway stretching ahead of them. She clamped down on Meg's hand and shut her eyes as the engines roared and the force of the plane's acceleration pushed her back in her seat. Seconds later, a weird, floating thump in her chest told her they were airborne.

"San, look."

Sanne shook her head, willing the plane to keep climbing.

"You're missing it all!"

Steeling herself, Sanne peeked out of the window. Below them, the redbrick sprawl of Manchester's suburbs and the plains of Cheshire spread almost to the horizon, the hills of the Peak District and Saddleworth rising gracefully beyond. The plane began to shudder as it rose into the thick cloud blanketing the region, and a grey shroud distorted and then obliterated the view.

Meg interlaced their fingers, holding on to Sanne through the turbulence. "There you go," she said softly, nudging Sanne toward the window again.

"Oh." Sanne caught her breath. Brilliant blue sky now surrounded them, and the clouds formed a pristine carpet of white.

"Didn't you know, San? It's always sunny up here."

Sanne smiled, tracing her fingertips across the ice crystals forming on the glass. "No one ever told me that."

"It's pretty, but it's not as pretty as me in my new bikini." Meg waggled her eyebrows.

Sanne elbowed her in the ribs. "Do you mind? I'm trying to have a moment here."

"It's red and black, and *very* flattering." Meg shaped curves with her hands, making the man across the aisle cough and turn scarlet.

Feigning a sudden interest in the inflight magazine, Sanne used it to hide her face. "I can't take you anywhere."

"Apparently, you're taking me to your Grecian villa."

The magazine pages rustled as Sanne started to laugh. "I might just leave you at the airport. You'd get into far less trouble there."

"You don't mean that. You'd miss me."

"Maybe," Sanne conceded. "A little."

The flight attendant paused at their row, and Meg ordered two teas and a KitKat. She broke the chocolate bar in half and raised her plastic cup. "Here's to getting away from it all."

Sanne tapped her cup against Meg's. "That sounds bloody lovely."

The End

About the Author

Cari Hunter lives in the northwest of England with her wife, two cats, and a pond full of frogs. She works full-time as a paramedic and dreams up stories in her spare time.

Cari enjoys long, windswept, muddy walks in her beloved Peak District and forces herself to go jogging regularly. In the summer she can usually be found sitting in the garden with her feet up, scribbling in her writing pad. Although she doesn't like to boast, she will admit that she makes a very fine Bakewell Tart.

Her first novel, *Snowbound*, received an Alice B. Lavender Certificate for outstanding début. Her second novel, *Desolation Point*, was shortlisted for a Goldie award and a runner-up in the 2013 Rainbow Awards, and its sequel, *Tumbledown*, was a runner-up in the 2014 Rainbow Awards.

Cari can be contacted at: carihunter@rocketmail.com.

Books Available from Bold Strokes Books

Hardwired by C.P. Rowlands. Award-winning teacher Clary Stone, and Leefe Ellis, manager of the homeless shelter for small children, stand together in a part of Clary's hometown that she never knew existed. (978-1-62639-351-6)

No Good Reason by Cari Hunter. A violent kidnapping in a Peak District village pushes Detective Sanne Jensen and lifelong friend Dr. Meg Fielding closer, just as it threatens to tear everything apart. (978-1-62639-352-3)

Romance by the Book by Jo Victor. If Cam didn't keep disrupting her life, maybe Alex could uncover the secret of a century-old love story, and solve the greatest mystery of all—her own heart. (978-1-62639-353-0)

Death's Doorway by Crin Claxton. Helping the dead can be deadly: Tony may be listening to the dead, but she needs to learn to listen to the living. (978-1-62639-354-7)

Searching for Celia by Elizabeth Ridley. As American spy novelist Dayle Salvesen investigates the mysterious disappearance of her ex-lover, Celia, in London, she begins questioning how well she knew Celia—and how well she knows herself. (978-1-62639-356-1)

The 45th Parallel by Lisa Girolami. Burying her mother isn't the worst thing that can happen to Val Montague when she returns to the woodsy but peculiar town of Hemlock, Oregon. (978-1-62639-342-4)

A Royal Romance by Jenny Frame. In a country where class still divides, can love topple the last social taboo and allow Queen Georgina and Beatrice Elliot, a working class girl, their happy ever after? (978-1-62639-360-8)

Bouncing by Jaime Maddox. Basketball Coach Alex Dalton has been bouncing from woman to woman, because no one ever held her interest, until she meets her new assistant, Britain Dodge. (978-1-62639-344-8)

Same Time Next Week by Emily Smith. A chance encounter between Alex Harris and the beautiful Michelle Masters leads to a whirlwind friendship, and causes Alex to question everything she's ever known—including her own marriage. (978-1-62639-345-5)

All Things Rise by Missouri Vaun. Cole rescues a striking pilot who crash-lands near her family's farm, setting in motion a chain of events that will forever alter the course of her life. (978-1-62639-346-2)

Riding Passion by D. Jackson Leigh. Mount up for the ride through a sizzling anthology of chance encounters, buried desires, romantic surprises, and blazing passion. (978-1-62639-349-3)

Love's Bounty by Yolanda Wallace. Lobster boat captain Jake Myers stopped living the day she cheated death, but meeting greenhorn Shy Silva stirs her back to life. (978-1-62639-334-9)

Just Three Words by Melissa Brayden. Sometimes the one you want is the one you least suspect. Accountant Samantha Ennis has her ordered life disrupted when heartbreaker Hunter Blair moves into her trendy Soho loft. (978-1-62639-335-6)

Lay Down the Law by Carsen Taite. Attorney Peyton Davis returns to her Texas roots to take on big oil and the Mexican Mafia, but will her investigation thwart her chance at true love? (978-1-62639-336-3)

Playing in Shadow by Lesley Davis. Survivor's guilt threatens to keep Bryce trapped in her nightmare world unless Scarlet's love can pull her out of the darkness back into the light. (978-1-62639-337-0)

Soul Selecta by Gill McKnight. Soul mates are hell to work with. (978-1-62639-338-7)

The Revelation of Beatrice Darby by Jean Copeland. Adolescence is complicated, but Beatrice Darby is about to discover how impossible it can seem to a lesbian coming of age in conservative 1950s New England. (978-1-62639-339-4)

Twice Lucky by Mardi Alexander. For firefighter Mackenzie James and Dr. Sarah Macarthur, there's suddenly a whole lot more in life to understand, to consider, to risk…someone will need to fight for her life. (978-1-62639-325-7)

Shadow Hunt by L.L. Raand. With young to raise and her Pack under attack, Sylvan, Alpha of the wolf Weres, takes on her greatest challenge when she determines to uncover the faceless enemies known as the Shadow Lords. A Midnight Hunters novel. (978-1-62639-326-4)

Heart of the Game by Rachel Spangler. A baseball writer falls for a single mom, but can she ever love anything as much as she loves the game? (978-1-62639-327-1)

Getting Lost by Michelle Grubb. Twenty-eight days, thirteen European countries, a tour manager fighting attraction, and an accused murderer: Stella and Phoebe's journey of a lifetime begins here. (978-1-62639-328-8)

Prayer of the Handmaiden by Merry Shannon. Celibate priestess Kadrian must defend the kingdom of Ithyria from a dangerous enemy and ultimately choose between her duty to the Goddess and the love of her childhood sweetheart, Erinda. (978-1-62639-329-5)

The Witch of Stalingrad by Justine Saracen. A Soviet "night witch" pilot and American journalist meet on the Eastern Front in WW II and struggle through carnage, conflicting politics, and the deadly Russian winter. (978-1-62639-330-1)

Pedal to the Metal by Jesse J. Thoma. When unreformed thief Dubs Williams is released from prison to help Max Winters bust a car theft ring, Max learns that to catch a thief, get in bed with one. (978-1-62639-239-7)

Dragon Horse War by D. Jackson Leigh. A priestess of peace and a fiery warrior must defeat a vicious uprising that entwines their destinies and ultimately their hearts. (978-1-62639-240-3)

For the Love of Cake by Erin Dutton. When everything is on the line, and one taste can break a heart, will pastry chefs Maya and Shannon take a chance on reality? (978-1-62639-241-0)

Betting on Love by Alyssa Linn Palmer. A quiet country-girl-at-heart and a live-life-to-the-fullest biker take a risk at offering each other their hearts. (978-1-62639-242-7)

The Deadening by Yvonne Heidt. The lines between good and evil, right and wrong, have always been blurry for Shade. When Raven's actions force her to choose, which side will she come out on? (978-1-62639-243-4)

Ordinary Mayhem by Victoria A. Brownworth. Faye Blakemore has been taking photographs since she was ten, but those same photographs threaten to destroy everything she knows and everything she loves. (978-1-62639-315-8)

One Last Thing by Kim Baldwin & Xenia Alexiou. Blood is thicker than pride. The final book in the Elite Operative Series brings together foes, family, and friends to start a new order. (978-1-62639-230-4)

Songs Unfinished by Holly Stratimore. Two aspiring rock stars learn that falling in love while pursuing their dreams can be harmonious—if they can only keep their pasts from throwing them out of tune. (978-1-62639-231-1)

Beyond the Ridge by L.T. Marie. Will a contractor and a horse rancher overcome their family differences and find common ground to build a life together? (978-1-62639-232-8)

Swordfish by Andrea Bramhall. Four women battle the demons from their pasts. Will they learn to let go, or will happiness be forever beyond their grasp? (978-1-62639-233-5)

The Fiend Queen by Barbara Ann Wright. Princess Katya and her consort Starbride must turn evil against evil in order to banish Fiendish power from their kingdom, and only love will pull them back from the brink. (978-1-62639-234-2)

Up the Ante by PJ Trebelhorn. When Jordan Stryker and Ashley Noble meet again fifteen years after a short-lived affair, are either of them prepared to gamble on a chance at love? (978-1-62639-237-3)

Speakeasy by MJ Williamz. When mob leader Helen Byrne sets her sights on the girlfriend of Al Capone's right-hand man, passion and tempers flare on the streets of Chicago. (978-1-62639-238-0)

Venus in Love by Tina Michele. Morgan Blake can't afford any distractions and Ainsley Dencourt can't afford to lose control—but the beauty of life and art usually lies in the unpredictable strokes of the artist's brush. (978-1-62639-220-5)

Rules of Revenge by AJ Quinn. When a lethal operative on a collision course with her past agrees to help a CIA analyst on a critical assignment, the encounter proves explosive in ways neither woman anticipated. (978-1-62639-221-2)

The Romance Vote by Ali Vali. Chili Alexander is a sought-after campaign consultant who isn't prepared when her boss's daughter, Samantha Pellegrin, comes to work at the firm and shakes up Chili's life from the first day. (978-1-62639-222-9)

Advance: Exodus Book One by Gun Brooke. Admiral Dael Caydoc's mission to find a new homeworld for the Oconodian people is hazardous, but working with the infuriating Commander Aniwyn "Spinner" Seclan endangers her heart and soul. (978-1-62639-224-3)

UnCatholic Conduct by Stevie Mikayne. Jil Kidd goes undercover to investigate fraud at St. Marguerite's Catholic School, but life gets complicated when her student is killed—and she begins to fall for her prime target. (978-1-62639-304-2)

Season's Meetings by Amy Dunne. Catherine Birch reluctantly ventures on the festive road trip from hell with beautiful stranger Holly Daniels only to discover the road to true love has its own obstacles to maneuver. (978-1-62639-227-4)

Myth and Magic: Queer Fairy Tales edited by Radclyffe and Stacia Seaman. Myth, magic, and monsters—the stuff of childhood dreams (or nightmares) and adult fantasies. (978-1-62639-225-0)

Nine Nights on the Windy Tree by Martha Miller. Recovering drug addict, Bertha Brannon, is an attorney who is trying to stay clean when a murder sends her back to the bad end of town. (978-1-62639-179-6)

Driving Lessons by Annameekee Hesik. Dive into Abbey Brooks's sophomore year as she attempts to figure out the amazing, but sometimes complicated, life of a you-know-who girl at Gila High School. (978-1-62639-228-1)

Asher's Shot by Elizabeth Wheeler. Asher Price's candid photographs capture the truth, but when his success requires exposing an enemy, Asher discovers his only shot at happiness involves revealing secrets of his own. (978-1-62639-229-8)

Courtship by Carsen Taite. Love and justice—a lethal mix or a perfect match? (978-1-62639-210-6)

Against Doctor's Orders by Radclyffe. Corporate financier Presley Worth wants to shut down Argyle Community Hospital, but Dr. Harper Rivers will fight her every step of the way, if she can also fight their growing attraction. (978-1-62639-211-3)

Lightning Source UK Ltd.
Milton Keynes UK
UKHW010834190819
348184UK00001B/24/P

9 781626 393523